Tales from the
Italian and Spanish

Three complete novels, one Italian and two Spanish

Manzoni's "Betrothed Lovers"
Cervantes' "Don Quixote" and
Valdés' "Marta y Maria"

Four other famous stories:

Valera's "Pepita Jiménez"
Aleman's "Guzman of Alfarache"
Mendoza's "Lazarillo of Tormes"
and Quevedo's "Paul of Segovia"

159 Short Stories
118 Italian
41 Spanish Tales of To-day
49 Translated for the first time for this set
26 Stories of L o v e and Revenge
34 Stories of Heroism and Romance
58 Stories of Humor and Adventure

Originals of famous literary w o r k s: "Patient Griselda," "Romeo and J u l i e t," and "Merry Wives of Windsor" (Shakespeare), the stories of "Gil Blas," and some of the comedies of Moliére, and of the grand opera, "Cavalleria Rusticana."

32 Illustrations, chiefly f r o m f a m o u s paintings

Full explanatory introductions to each volume, with descriptive historical notes to many of the stories.

Stories of Humor   Stories of Revenge
Stories of Adventure   Stories of Romance
Stories of Love   Stories of Local Color

Authors Represented

Italian

Manzoni, Boccaccio, Machiavelli, Masuccio, Fogazzaro, D'Annunzio, Verga, Deledda, De Roberto, Da Porto, De Marchi, Firenzuola, Capuana, Bandello, Neera, Manni, Fiorentino, Boito, Giacosa, Sabbadino, Ojetti, Pirandello, Rovetta, Palmarini, Gozzi, Da Ceno, Bottari, Doni, Sacchetti, Sanvitale, Parabosco, Cinthio, Soave, Sozzini, Lando, Grazzini, Colombo, Fucini, Malespini, Serao, Brevio, Straparola, Da Lodi, De Amicis, Erizzo, Granucci, Fortini, Martini, Sansovino, Castelnuovo, Bisaccioni, Illicini.

Spanish

Cervantes Velera, Valdés, Galdos, Calderon, Aleman, Mendoza, Quevedo, Ibañez, Picón, De Truba, Pardo-Bazan, Caballero, De Alarçón, Selgas, Nieto, Antor, Blasco, Solano, De Anellano, Calson, Ruiz, Becquer, Hartzenbusch.

Mexico:
López-Portillo y Rojas
De Zayas

Chile:
Gana y Gana
Varas

Cuba:
Castellanos

Venezuela:
Blanco-Fombona

Costa Rica:
Guardia

Peru:
Palma

Colombia:
Isaacs

Argentine:
Ugarte

Philippines:
Rizal

"I MIGHT HAVE BEEN. PERFECTLY HAPPY HAD I RESISTED THE
OPPORTUNITY OF GAMING"

(From the etching by R. de Los Rios)

TALES
FROM THE
ITALIAN
AND
SPANISH

A NEW SORT OF FICTION

REALISM AND ROMANCE,
ADVENTURE AND HUMOR,
REVEALING THE SOUL
OF THE LATIN LANDS

IN EIGHT VOLUMES
ILLUSTRATED

WILDSIDE PRESS

TALES FROM THE SPANISH

———

THE SPANISH ROGUE

Including

LAZARILLO OF TORMES

BY

DIEGO HURTADO de MENDOZA

GUZMAN OF ALFARACHE

BY

MATEO ALEMAN

AND

PAUL OF SEGOVIA

BY

FRANCISCO QUEVEDO Y VILLEGAS

With Four Illustrations

Contents

THE SPANISH ROGUE

LAZARILLO OF TORMES

GUZMAN OF ALFARACHE

BOOK THE FIRST

BOOK THE SECOND

iii

THE SPANISH ROGUE

THE SPANISH ROGUE

THE SPANISH ROGUE

THE SPANISH ROGUE

Book the Second

Illustrations

THE SPANISH ROGUE

TALES FROM THE SPANISH

LAZARILLO OF TORMES

BY

DIEGO HURTADO de MENDOZA

INTRODUCTION

IF asked to name the chief contribution of each nation to the literature of the world, most cultured people would probably select at once epics and tragedies from Greece, satire from Rome, the essay from France, the novel of manners and character from England, and from America the short story conveying a single impression. It would be equally true to say that the picaresque story, or the romance of roguery, is the peculiar gift of Spain. For, in the early seventeenth century, there developed in Spain a kind of fiction in which the hero of romance, clad in flashing mail and exhibiting the loftiest virtues of chivalry in his impossible quests, was replaced by the ragamuffin rascal practicing the most knavish trickery in a world that was all too real.

Probably the chief reason for this development was that Spain was actually full of such rogues during the latter half of the sixteenth century. The age of golden adventure in America passed away. The dreams of wealth without toil which lured thousands from the honest work of the farm and the bench now faded into the shadowy realm of romance. Those no longer bound for El Dorado had to pick up a precarious living by their wits in the purlieus of Seville or Madrid. Beggars and bullies thronged the alleys and wandered about from one haunt to another in search of fresh victims of their cunning. Laws were powerless. Poverty and roguery advanced steadily hand in hand.

INTRODUCTION

At length literary men turned aside from the fantastic adventures of knighthood, which are satirized so deliciously in *Don Quixote,* filling the fifth volume of this series. These venturesome authors took the rogue to be met at every turn of the street, followed him into every nook and cranny of contemporary life, and thereby set in a glaring light the evils of the age.

Because of its novelty, this faithful, fearless, and mocking reflection of contemporary society was attended with remarkable success. Even the first of the species enjoyed popularity. *Lazarillo of Tormes,* published at Burgos early in 1554, saw the next month another edition brought out at Alcalá. The next year it was reprinted at Antwerp, where a good many Spanish books were published, soon to be followed by a second edition. The Antwerp publisher then offered the public a continuation, or second part, which likewise saw a second edition within the year. Yet fifty years intervened before the second romance of roguery, *Guzman of Alfarache,* was given to this eager public.

The founder of this type of fiction is one of the unsolved mysteries of Spanish literature. No one has ever been able to establish who was the author of *Lazarillo.* More than half a century after its publication, to be precise, in 1605, a certain Juan de Ortega, a general in the Catholic order of San Géronimo, was said to have written it, for on his death a manuscript of the story was supposed to have been found in his cell. To explain how so holy a man wrote a book whose irreverent treatment of church dignitaries had kept the real author silent for a half century, it was declared that Ortega had composed it while a student at Salamanca. Two years later, however, a German catalogue asserted that *Lazarillo* was the work of the very famous poet and historian, Don Diego Hurtado de Mendoza. It was later added that *he* had written it while a student at Salamanca. But, famous as the story was, it was not included in Mendoza's collected works nor mentioned in his first biography. Many vigorous essays have been written for and against his claims, but we are no nearer the secret than were the people of three hundred years ago.

Lazarillo is one of the great works of Spanish fiction. The simple narrative pictures to us most vividly two or three of the typical figures of the age. The blind beggar who teaches little Lazarus the necessity of trickery was at once recognized as so true that his actions passed into proverbs. Indeed, thereafter, *lazarillo* became a synonym for " leader of the blind." In roguishness none have ever surpassed him. The finest figure in the book and the most typical of Spanish character is the *hidalgo* or gentleman whom Lazaro met walking in the streets of Toledo, fairly well dressed and groomed. This hungry esquire displays all the unbending pride of the Castilian noble at the period when the victorious Emperor Charles the Fifth entered the famous city of Toledo and when the glorious Spanish empire was outwardly most flourishing. His desperate clinging to the appearance of gentility goes to the heart of sixteenth century Spain, which preferred to seem rather than to be. The type lives because of the masterly way in which it is drawn. The stately dignity which dared not admit its misery or beg for relief is depicted with a sympathy that makes the poor *hidalgo* one of the truest and most memorable specimens of Spanish humor.

Thus the main, the absorbing interest in this great exemplar of the picaresque story is the social conditions of Spain in the sixteenth century. The little rogue merely furnishes the eyes with which we look upon that society, eyes that penetrate to the realities behind the glamor. In *Guzman of Alfarache,* the second great rogue story, the personal interest emerges distinctly from the stream of satirical incident, and in the third specimen of the type in this volume, it has developed into the dominant motive for the story. The reader, though absorbed in the manifold adventures of these ingenious rascals, is thus enabled to watch the change that came over this unique type of fiction which mirrored the life of Spain three hundred years ago.

Lazarillo de Tormes

CHAPTER I

YOU must know then, in the first place, that my name
is Lazaro de Tormes, and that I am the son of
Thomas Gonzales and Antonia Perez, natives of Tejares,
a village of Salamanca. My surname was acquired by
the singular circumstance of my birth, which happened
in the river Tormes, and in the following manner. My
father (to whom God be merciful) was employed to superintend the operations of a water-mill, which was worked
by the course of the above river (a situation that he held
above fifteen years), and my mother at that time being
enceinte with me, while staying one night at the mill was
suddenly seized with the pains of labor, which terminating
happily, it may with truth be said, that my surname, borrowed from the river, was not inaptly bestowed.

I had only reached my ninth years, when my unfortunate father was charged with administering certain copious but injudicious bleedings to the sacks of customers
to the mill—a lowering system which was voted by them
to be neither salutary nor profitable. He was forthwith
taken into custody; when, not being able to deny the indiscreet application of his professional ability, he experienced
the usual penalty of the law. It is, however, to be hoped
that he is now reaping the reward which has been faithfully promised by the evangelist to all those who have
suffered persecution for justice's sake; for they are declared to be in the highest degree fortunate in such their

tribulations. By this disaster, my poor father, being thrown out of employment, joined an armament then preparing against the Moors, in the quality of mule-driver to a gentleman; and in that expedition, like a loyal servant, he, along with his master, finished his life and services together.

My widowed mother, thus bereft of husband and of home, determined, in order to acquire a reputation, to associate herself with people of character; she therefore hired a small place in the city, and opened an eating-house for the accommodation of the students, adding likewise to her gains by washing linen for the servants of his Excellency the *Comendador* of the order of Magdalena. It was in the exercise of the duties of this latter branch of industry that she became acquainted with a groom of the stables, a man of color rather than of character or fortune. Under the pretense of buying eggs he would continually come to our house, and at last obtained an intimate footing therein. At first, in consequence of his color and the roughness of his manners, I was frightened at him; but when I found that our scanty fare was changed by his visits into abundance, for he always brought bread and meat, and in winter wood for our fire, I not only conquered my repugnance, but even hailed his approach with pleasure. One unpleasantness attended this intimacy, which was that my mother presented me with a little brother, very pretty, though of a darkish complexion, and whom I was obliged to assist in nursing and bringing up.

Matters were not carried on so secretly, however, but that some intelligence of Zayde's gallantry reached the ears of the *comendador's* majordomo, who, on inquiry, found a terrible deficiency in the barley, to say nothing of currycombs, brushes, and such like movables, which had been unaccountably lost; and it was found, also, that when nothing better offered itself, even the horses were unshod for the sake of the iron, and all was unluckily traced to my mother for the support of my little brother.

One can hardly wonder at a priest or a friar, the one robbing the poor, the other his convent, for the sake of their fair and devout believers, when love can stimulate a poor slave to do the like. All this was fully proved; for when they came to me, like a child as I was, and fearful of the threats of punishment, I discovered to them all I knew of the matter, even to the very horseshoes which my mother had directed me to sell to the farrier. My poor father-in-law was soundly flogged, and his flesh tickled with drops of scalding fat; while my mother was forbidden the house of the *comendador,* and was commanded, under the severest penalties, never to receive Zayde into her presence again. Not to make matters worse, my mother fulfilled the obligation of the sentence, and to avoid danger, as well as to escape further scandal, she engaged herself to serve the guests at the inn of the Solana, where, notwithstanding she suffered a thousand inconveniences, she managed to rear my little brother. As to myself, I went on errands, and endeavored to make myself as useful as possible.

About this time a blind man came to lodge at the house, and thinking that I should do very well to lead him about, asked my mother to part with me for that purpose. My mother recomemnded me strongly, stating that I was the son of an excellent man who died in battle against the enemies of our faith.

"I trust in God," added she, "that he will never make a worse man than was his father."

She confided me to his care as an orphan boy, and entreated him to use me with kindness. The old man promised to receive me, not as a servant, but as a son; and thus I commenced service with my new though blind and aged master. We remained in Salamanca some few days, but my master finding his gains in that city to be very inconsiderable, determined to seek greater profits elsewhere. When we were ready to depart, I went to take leave of my mother, who, with an abundance of tears, from which I, too, could not refrain, gave me her blessing and said:

"My son, this may probably be the last time I shall

ever see you; endeavor then for my sake to be good, and may the Almighty assist you. I have reared you from childhood, and now provide you with a kind master; look to yourself for the future, and farewell."

I then went to rejoin my master, who was waiting for me at a short distance.

We left Salamánca, and having arrived at the bridge, my master directed my attention to an animal carved in stone in the form of a bull, and desired me to take him near it. When I had placed him close to it, he said:

"Lazaro, if you put your ear close to this bull, you will hear an extraordinary noise within."

In the simplicity of my heart, believing it to be as he said, I put my ear to the stone, when the old man gave my head such a violent thump against it, that I was almost bereft of sense, and for three days after I did not lose the pain I suffered from the blow. My old master laughed heartily at the joke.

"You rogue," said he, "you ought to know that a blind man's boy should have more cunning than the very devil himself."

It seemed to me as though that moment had awakened me from the simplicity of childhood, and I said to myself:

"The old man says truly. I am now alone, and if I do not keep a sharp lookout for myself, I shall find none to assist me."

We commenced our journey, and in a very few days I began to reap the benefit of my master's instruction. As he found me an apt scholar, he was much pleased, and would say:

"I have no silver or gold to give you; but, what is far better, I can impart to you the result of my experience, which will always enable you to live; for though God has created me blind, yet He has endowed me with faculties which have served me well in the course of my life."

And I verily believe that, since God created the world, He never formed a human being with intellect more acute than that of my blind old master. He was as keen as an eagle in his own calling. He knew upwards of a hundred prayers by heart. His tone of voice was pleasing, and, though low, was distinct enough to be heard all over the church where he usually recited them. His countenance was humble and devout; and his deportment, when he recited his prayers, was free from affectation and distortion of visage, which so many are apt to practice.

Besides this, he had a thousand other ways of making money. He could repeat prayers which were available for all occasions; for women who had no children; for those who had expectancy; for those likewise who were unhappily married, and sought to increase the affection of their husbands. He could also prognosticate truly to ladies whether the result of their travail would be a boy or a girl; and with respect to the medicinal art, he would tell you that Galen himself was an ignoramus compared with himself. Indeed, he acted as though he really thought so; for no one ever came to consult him that he did not say without the slightest hesitation, " Take this, do that;" and in such a manner, that he had all the world after him, especially the women, who had the utmost confidence in everything he told them. By these means his profits were very considerable. He gained more in one month than a hundred other blind men would in a year.

With all this, however, I am sorry to say that I never met with so avaricious and so wicked an old curmudgeon; he allowed me almost to die daily of hunger, without troubling himself about my necessities; and, to say the truth, if I had not helped myself by means of a ready wit and nimble fingers, I should have closed my account from sheer starvation.

Notwithstanding all my master's astuteness and cunning, I contrived so to outwit him that generally the best half came to my share. But to accomplish this, I was obliged to tax my powers of invention to the uttermost. Of this I will recount a few specimens, although perhaps they may not tell much to my credit. The old man was accustomed to carry his bread, meat, and other things in a sort of

5

linen knapsack, which was closed at the mouth with an iron ring, and secured also by a padlock; but in adding to his store, or taking from it, he used such vigilance that it was almost an impossibility to cheat him of a single morsel. However, when he had given me my pittance, which I found no difficulty in dispatching at about two mouthfuls, and closed his budget, thinking himself perfectly secure from depredation, I began my tactics, and by means of a small rent, which I slyly effected in one of the seams of the bag, I used to help myself to the choicest pieces of meat, bacon, and sausage, taking care to close the seam according as opportunity occurred. But in addition to this, all that I could collect together, either by fraud or otherwise, I carried about me in half-farthings; so that when the old man was sent for to pray, and they gave him farthings (all which passed through my hands, he being blind), I contrived to slip them into my mouth, by which process so quick an alteration was effected, that when they reached his hand they were invariably reduced to half the original value.

The cunning old fellow, however, suspected me, for he used to say,

"How the deuce is this? ever since you have been with me they give me nothing but half-farthings; whereas before, it was not an unusual thing to be paid with halfpence, but never less than farthings. I must be sharp with *you*, I find."

Whenever we ate, the old man took care to keep a small jar of wine near him, which was reserved for his own special service; but I very soon adopted the practice of bestowing on this favorite jar sundry loving though stolen embraces. Such pleasures were short-lived, for the fervency of my attachment was soon discovered in the deficiency of the wine; and the old man afterwards, to secure his draught, never let the jar go without tying it to him by the handle. But I was a match for him even there; for I procured a large straw, and dipping it into the mouth of the jar, renewed my intimacy with such effect, that but a small share was his who came after me. The old traitor was not long in finding me out; I think he must have heard me drink, for he quickly changed his plan, and placed the jar between his knees, keeping the mouth closed with his hand, and in this manner considered himself secure from my depredations.

Being thus deprived of my customary allowance from the jar, I was ready to die with longing; and finding my plan of the straw no longer available, I took an opportunity of boring a very small hole in the bottom of the jar, which I closed very delicately with wax. At dinnertime, when the poor old man sat over the fire, with the jar between his knees, the heat, slight as it was, melted the little piece of wax with which I closed the hole, and I, feigning to be cold, drew close to the fire, and placed my mouth under the little fountain in such a manner that the whole contents of the jar came to my share. When the old boy had finished his meal, and thought to regale himself with his draught of wine, the deuce a drop did he find, which so enraged and surprised him, that he thought the devil himself had been at work; nor could he conceive how it could be.

" Now, uncle," said I, " don't say that I drank your wine, seeing that you have had your hand on it the whole time."

But he was not satisfied with my declaration of innocence, so turning and twisting the jar about in every direction, he at last discovered the hole, which at once let him into the secret of my ingenious contrivance. He concealed his discovery so well, that I had not the slightest suspicion that my ruse was detected; so the next day, having prepared my jar as before, little foreseeing the consequences, nor dreaming of the wicked thoughts which were passing in the old man's mind, I placed myself under the jar, which presently began to distil its delicious contents, my face turned towards heaven, and my eyes partly closed, the better to enjoy the delightful draught.

The evil-minded old man, judging this to be the time to take his vengeance, raised with both hands the sweet,

though alas, to me, bitter jar, and let it fall directly on
my mouth, adding to its weight by giving all the impetus
in his power. The poor unhappy Lazaro, who little
reckoned on such a disaster, but had quietly resigned himself to the delicious enjoyment of the moment, verily believed in the crash which succeeded, that the heavens,
with all they contained, had fallen upon him. The blow
was so tremendous that my senses fairly left me, and the
jar breaking, cut my face in many places, several pieces
remaining in the wounds, "besides breaking nearly all my
teeth, the loss of which I feel to this very day.

From that hour I bore an inveterate grudge against my
old rogue of a master, for though he attended to me, and
cured me of my wounds, I could plainly see that he enjoyed my cruel chastisement. He washed the wounds
with wine which the broken jar had made in my face;
and would say smiling, "Lazaro, my boy, what is that
which makes you ill, cures you, and gives you strength?"
with other little witticisms, which he would repeat, not by
any means to my taste.

When I was nearly cured of my wounds and bruises,
considering that by a few more such pleasantries the old
man would effectually get rid of me, I began to think how
I might in the best manner get rid of him; however, I
resolved to wait until an opportunity should offer of effect-
ing my purpose with safety to myself, and more to my satisfaction with regard to the past proceedings of my master.

Although I might in time have pardoned the jar adventure, yet the continual ill-treatment to which I was hence-
forward subjected, kept alive the vindictive feeling which
it originally occasioned; for now, upon the slightest occasion, and even without cause, he would beat and flog me
without any mercy. If any humane person interfered, he
immediately recounted the history of the jar, prefacing
it with some such expression as,

"Don't believe the young rogue is quite so innocent as
he looks; just listen, and then say whether the devil himself would ever have had the cunning to do the like."

Those who listened would reply, "Who could have thought that so much wickedness could be packed in such a small compass?" and they would laugh heartily at my exploit, and say, "Thrash him well, good man; thrash him well; he deserves it richly!"

With such encouraging advice he persevered to the very letter, and I can say to my cost that in his leisure hours he did little else; in return, I took him over the worst roads I could find, and led him wherever there was the slightest chance of his hurting himself. If stones were near, over the very sharpest; if mud, through the deepest; and although this mode of traveling was not the pleasantest, yet if I inconvenienced myself, I annoyed the old man still more, which was all I desired to do. It is true that my head and shoulders were subjected in consequence to the angry visitations of his staff; and though I continually assured him that his uneasy traveling was not the result of my ill-will, but for want of better roads, yet the the old traitor had too much cunning to believe a word I said.

That I may not be tiresome, I shall omit many curious anecdotes of this my first service, and will only relate the following, and then say how I at last took my leave of my blind master. We were in Escalona, a place belonging to the duke of that name, when one day he gave me a piece of a large sausage to cook. While the sausage was in the roaster before the fire, he regaled himself with the dripping; and then taking out his purse, gave me a halfpenny to fetch him some wine. I don't know how it was, unless the devil placed the means before my eyes, but I was tempted to play the thief; for on looking round I saw a turnip, not unlike the shape of the sausage, which had been thrown away as unfit for use. There was nobody near us, and I, with a raging appetite, still further stimulated by the savory smell of the sausage, which I knew full well was all the old man intended for my share, without a thought for the consequences, snatched the sausage from the roaster while the old man was fumbling for his money, and in a twinkling supplied its place with the turnip.

As I started for the wine, my master began to blow up the fire, thinking the more speedily to cook what his miserable parsimony and my urgent appetite had caused to vanish. On my road for the wine, I was not long in despatching the sausage; and when I returned, I found the miserable old sinner with the turnip stuck between two slices of bread, preparing, as he thought, to make a most delicious repast. As he bit through the bread, however, thinking to take part of the sausage, his teeth encountered the cold hard turnip, when the truth flashing on his mind, he exclaimed in an altered tone,

"Lazarillo, how is this?"

"Mercy on me," said I, "do you suspect me? Have I not this instant returned with your wine? Somebody has been here and played this trick upon you."

"No, no," said he, "my hand has been on the roaster all the time, that is impossible."

I turned to swear and forswear myself as being innocent of this fraud, but little did the old man credit me. He arose, and seizing me by the head, as he possessed as keen a scent as a spaniel, determined to satisfy himself of the truth; so opening my mouth by main force, he thrust therein his ugly nose, which was long and pointed, and at that time had increased considerably in length from spite and anger. With this, and the excessive fear which came over me, added to the shortness of time allowed for my stomach to settle, and more than all, the tickling of that immense proboscis, so unpleasant a feeling began to manifest itself, that hardly had the old man withdrawn his trunk, than the whole contents of my stomach followed, and with such force as entirely to cover his face. Had he not been blind before, his eyesight could hardly have escaped such an explosion. O heavens! what were my feelings at that unhappy moment! never shall I forget it! Such was the rage of that diabolical old man, that had not my screams attracted some people, I verily believe I should never have escaped with my life.

I escaped from his hands in the best way I could, leaving the few hairs that remained to me in his grasp, my face, neck, and throat bearing the marks of his vindictive talons. Lest the bystanders should compassionate me, the old man recounted my exploits to them, which set them into such a roar of laughter, that the place soon became thronged like a fair. And with such humor did the old rogue varnish my misdeeds, that, weeping and wounded as I was, I could easily forgive their mirth.

While this was going on, the remembrance of a singular want of wit and keenness occurred to me, which not only betrayed my incapacity, but a cowardly and groveling fear, for which I could not easily forgive myself. It was that, when I had the opportunity, I did not bite off the old fellow's nose, seeing at one time it was so completely in my power, and by that means save myself all the unpleasantness I now endured by not being able to turn the laugh against my tormentor.

The innkeeper's wife, and some others who were there, now washed my face and neck with the wine I had brought, and this afforded the old man another opportunity for a joke, saying, " Of a truth, this boy costs me more wine for one washing of his wounds than I drink in two days." And then he told how many times he had sacrificed me and cured me with wine; " If ever man in the world," he said, " is fortunate by wine, it will be you." Those who were bathing my face could not help laughing at the old fellow's humor, though I was wincing with teh smart, not only of his jibes but of his blows. This prophecy of the old man did not turn out false; and oftentimes have I since thought of him, and what he made me suffer, though in the end I paid him well for it, little dreaming that what he then rapped out in jest would so turn out.

Considering the injuries I had sustained, in addition to the ridicule to which I was continually exposed, I determined at all hazards to leave the old tyrant to his fate, and chose the following opportunity of doing so. The next day we went about the town to ask alms; but as the weather turned out ver ywet, we did not stir from beneath the arcades, with which this place is provided. As the night approached, and the rain had not ceased, the old man said,

"Lazaro, this wet weather is very unwholesome, and as night comes on it will be still more so, let us therefore get home in good time."

On our return we had to pass a small stream of water, which with the day's rain had considerably increased. I therefore said,

"Uncle, the brook is very much swollen; but I see a place a little higher, where, by giving a little jump, we may pass almost dry shod."

"Thou art a good lad," said the old man; "I like you for your carefulness. Take me to the narrowest part, for at this time of the year to get one's feet wet would be dangerous."

Delighted that my plot seemed to succeed so well, I led him from beneath the arcades, and took him directly opposite to a pillar, or rather a large stone post, which I observed in the square.

"Now, uncle," said I, "this is the place where the brook is the narrowest."

The rain was pouring down, and the old man was getting very wet; and whether it was by the haste he made to avoid it, or, what was more probable, Providence had at that moment beguiled him of his usual cunning, that he might the more readily fall into the snare and give me my revenge; so it was, that for once he believed me, and said:

"Now place me directly opposite the spot, and then jump yourself."

I placed him exactly opposite the pillar, so that he could not miss it, and leaping myself, I took my position immediately behind it, crying out:

"Now, master, jump with all your force, and you will clear the water."

I had hardly said the words, when the poor old rogue jumped up as nimbly as a goat, giving all his strength to the leap, and taking a step or two backwards by way of impetus, which lent him such force, that instead of alighting on soft ground as he supposed, he gave his poor bald pate such a smash against the pillar, that he fell on the pavement without sense or motion.

"Take that, you unhappy old thief," said I, "and remember the sausage;" then leaving him to the care of the people who began to gather around, I took to my heels as swiftly as possible through the town gates, and before night reached Torrijos. What became of the old man afterwards I don't know, and neither did I ever give myself any pains to inquire.

CHAPTER II

HOW LAZARO ENTERED INTO THE SERVICE OF A PRIEST, AND WHAT ENSUED

THE next day, not considering myself quite safe where I was, I went to a place called Maqueda, where, as it were in punishment of my evil deeds, I fell in with a certain priest. I accosted him for alms, when he inquired whether I knew how to assist at mass. I answered that I did, which was true, for the old man, notwithstanding his ill treatment, taught me many useful things,—and this was one of them. The priest, therefore, engaged me on the spot.

There is an old proverb which speaks of getting out of the frying-pan into the fire, which was indeed my unhappy case in this change of masters. The old blind man, selfish as he was, seemed an Alexander the Great, in point of munificence, on comparison with this priest, who

13

was, without exception, the most niggardly of all miserable devils I have ever met with. It seemed as though the meanness of the whole world was gathered together in his wretched person. It would be hard to say whether he inherited this disposition, or whether he had adopted it with his cassock and gown. He had a large old chest, well secured by a lock, the key of which he always carried about him, tied to a part of his clothing. When the charity bread came from the church, he would with his own hands deposit it in the chest, and then carefully turn the key.

Throughout the whole house there was nothing to eat. Even the sight of such things as we see in other houses, such as smoked bacon, cheese, or bread, would have done my heart good, although I might have been forbidden to taste them. The only eatable we had was a string of onions, and these were locked up in a garret. Every fourth day I was allowed *one;* and when I asked for the key to take it, if anyone chanced to be present, he would make a serious matter of it, saying, as he gave me the key, " Take it, and return quickly; for when you go to that tempting room, you never know when to come out of it;"—speaking as though all the sweets of Valencia were there, when I declare to you, as I said before, the devil a bit of anything was there but this string of onions hung on a nail, and of these he kept such an account, that if my unlucky stars had tempted me to take more than my allowance, it would have cost me very dear.

In the end I should in fact have died of hunger, with so little feeling did this reverend gentleman treat me, although with himself he was rather more liberal. Five farthings' worth of meat was his allowance for dinner and supper. It is true that he divided the broth with me; but my share of the meat I might have put in my eye instead of my mouth, and have been none the worse for it; but sometimes, by good luck, I got a little morsel of bread. In this part of the country it is the custom on Sundays to eat sheep's heads, and he sent me for one

that was not to come to more than three farthings.
When it was cooked, he ate all the tit bits, and never left
it while a morsel of the meat remained; but the dry bones
he turned over to me, saying:

"There, you rogue, eat that; you are in rare luck; the
Pope himself has not such fare as you."

"God give him as good!" said I to myself.

At the end of the three weeks that I remained with
him, I arrived at such an extreme degree of exhaustion,
from sheer hunger, that it was with difficulty I stood on
my legs. I saw clearly that I was in the direct road to
the grave, unless God and my own wit should help me out
of it. For the dextrous application of my fingers there
was no opportunity afforded me, seeing there was nothing
to practice on; and if there were, I should never have
been able to have cheated the priest as I did the old man,
whom God absolve, if by my means it went ill with him
after his leap. The old man, though cunning, yet wanting sight, gave me now and then a chance; but as to the
priest, never had any so keen a sight as he.

When we were at mass, no money came to the plate
at the offering that he did not observe: he had one eye
on the people and the other on my fingers. His eyes
danced about the money-box as though they were quick-
silver. When offerings were given, he kept an account,
and when it was finished, that instant he would take the
plate from my hands, and put it on the altar. I was not
able to rob him of a single *maravedi* in all the time I
lived with him, or rather all the time I starved with him.
I never fetched him any wine from the tavern, but the
little that was left at church he locked up in his chest,
and he would make that serve all the week. In order to
excuse all this covetousness, he said to me:

"You see, my boy, that priests ought to be very abstemious in their food. For my part, I think it a great
scandal to indulge in viands and wine as many do."

But the curmudgeon lied most grossly, for at convents
or at funerals, when we went to pray, he would eat like

a wolf, and drink like a mountebank; and now I speak of funerals—God forgive me, I was never an enemy to the human race but at that unhappy period of my life, and the reason was solely that on those occasions I obtained a meal of victuals.

Every day did I hope, and even pray, that God would be pleased to take His own. Whenever we were sent for to administer the sacrament to the sick, the priest would of course desire all present to join in prayer. You may be certain I was not the last in these devout exercises, and I prayed with all my heart that the Lord would compassionate the afflicted, not by restoring him to the vanities of life, but by relieving him from the sins of the world; and when any of these unfortunates recovered— the Lord forgive me—in the anguish of my heart I wished him a thousand times in perdition; but if he died, no one was more sincere in his blessings than myself.

During all the time I was in this service, which was nearly six months, only twenty persons paid the debt of nature, and these I verily believe that I killed, or rather that they died, by the incessant importunity of my particular prayers. Such was my extreme suffering, as to make me think that the Lord, compassionating my unhappy and languishing condition, visited some with death to give me life. But for my present necessity there was no remedy; if on the days of funerals I lived well, the return to my old allowance of an onion every fourth day seemed doubly hard; so that I may truly say, I took delight in nothing but death, and oftentimes I have invoked it for myself as well as for others. To me, however, it did not arrive, although continually hovering about me in the ugly shape of famine and short commons. I thought many times of leaving my brute of a master, but two reflections disconcerted me; the first was, the doubt whether I could make my way by reason of the extreme weakness to which hunger had reduced me; and the second suggested, that my first master, having done his best to starve me, and my next having succeeded so far in the same humane object as to bring me to the brink of the grave, whether the third might not, by pursuing the same course, actually thrust me into it.

These considerations made me now pause, lest, by venturing a step farther, it would be my certain fate to be a point lower in fortune, and then the world might truly say, "Farewell Lazaro."

It was during this trying and afflicting time, when, seeing things going from bad to worse, without anyone to advise with, I was praying with all Christian humility that I might be released from such misery, that one day, when my wretched, miserable, covetous thief of a master had gone out, an angel, in the likeness of a tinker, knocked at the door—for I verily believe he was directed by Providence to assume that habit and employment—and inquired whether I had anything to mend? Suddenly a light flashed upon me, as though imparted by an invisible and unknown power:

"Uncle," said I, "I have unfortunately lost the key of this great chest, and I'm sadly afraid my master will beat me; for God's sake try if you can fit it, and I will reward you."

The angelic tinker drew forth a large bunch of keys, and began to try them, while I assisted his endeavors with my feeble prayers; when lo! and behold! when least I thought it, the lid of the chest arose, and I almost fancied I beheld the divine essence therein in the shape of loaves of bread.

"I have no money," said I to my preserver, "but give me the key and help yourself."

He took some of the whitest and best bread he could find, and went away well pleased, though not half so well as myself. I refrained from taking any for the present, lest the deficiency might be noticed; and contented myself with the hope that, on seeing so much in my power, hunger would hardly dare to approach me.

My wretched master returned, and it pleased God that the offering my angel had been pleased to accept, remained undiscovered by him. The next day, when he went out, I went to my farinaceous paradise, and taking a loaf between my hands and teeth, in a twinkling it became invisible; then, not forgetting to lock the treasure, I capered about the house for joy to think that my miserable life was about to change, and for some days following I was as happy as a king. But it was not predestined for me that such good luck should continue long; on the third day symptoms of my old complaint began to show themselves, for I beheld my murderer in the act of examining our chest, turning and counting the loaves over and over again. Of course I dissimulated my terror, but it was not for want of my prayers and invocations that he was not struck stone-blind like my old master—but he retained his eyesight.

After he had been some time considering and counting, he said:

"If I were not well assured of the security of this chest, I should say that somebody had stolen my bread; but, however, to remove all suspicion, from this day I shall count the loaves; there remain now exactly nine and a piece."

"May nine curses light upon you, you miserable beggar," said I to myself—for his words went like an arrow to my heart, and hunger already began to attack me, seeing a return to my former scanty fare now inevitable.

No sooner did the priest go out, than I opened the chest to console myself even with the sight of food, and as I gazed on the nice white loaves, a sort of adoration rose within me, which the sight of such tempting morsels could alone inspire. I counted them carefully to see, if perchance, the curmudgeon had mistaken the number; but, alas! I found he was a much better reckoner than I could have desired. The utmost I dared do, was to bestow on these objects of my affection a thousand kisses, and, in the most delicate manner possible, to nibble here and there a morsel of the crust. With this I passed the day, and not quite so jovially as the former, you may suppose.

But as hunger increased, and more so in proportion as I had fared better the few days previously, I was reduced to the last extremity. Yet all I could do was to open and shut the chest, and contemplate the divine image within. Providence, however, who does not neglect mortals in such an extreme crisis, suggested to me a slight palliation of my present distress. After some consideration, I said within myself:

"This chest is very large and old, and in some parts, though very slightly, is broken. It is not impossible to suppose that rats may have made an entrance, and gnawed the bread. To take a whole loaf would not be wise, seeing that it would be missed by my most liberal master; but the other plan he shall certainly have the benefit of."

Then I began to pick the loaves on some table-cloths which were there, not of the most costly sort, taking one loaf and leaving another, so that in the end, I made up a tolerable supply of crumbs, which I ate like so many sugar-plums; and with that I in some measure consoled myself and contrived to live.

The priest, when he came home to dinner and opened the chest, beheld with dismay the havoc made in his store; but he immediately supposed it to have been occasioned by rats, so well had I imitated the style of those depredators. He examined the chest narrowly, and discovered the little holes through which the rats might have entered; and calling me, he said:

"Lazaro, look what havoc has been made in our bread during the night."

I seemed very much astonished, and asked what it could possibly be?

"What has done it?" quoth he, "why, rats; confound 'em, there is no keeping anything from them."

I fared well at dinner, and had no reason to repent of the trick I played, for he pared off all the places which he supposed the rats had nibbled at, and, giving them to me, he said:

"There, eat that, rats are very clean animals."

In this manner, adding what I thus gained to that acquired by the labor of my hands, or rather my nails, I managed tolerably well, though I little expected it. I was destined to receive another shock, when I beheld my miserable tormentor carefully stopping up all the holes in the chest with small pieces of wood, which he nailed over them, and which bade defiance to further depradations.

"O Lord!" I cried involuntarily, "to what distress and misfortunes are we unhappy mortals reduced; and how short-lived are the pleasures of this our transitory existence! No sooner did I draw some little relief from the measure which kind fortune suggested, than it is snatched away; and this last act is like closing the door of consolation against me, and opening that of my misfortunes."

It was thus I gave vent to my distress, while the careful workman, with abundance of wood and nails, was finishing his cruel job, saying with great glee:

"Now, you rascals of rats, we will change sides, if you please, for your future reception in this house will be right little welcome."

The moment he left the house, I went to examine his work, and found he had not left a single hole unstopped by which even a mosquito could enter. I opened the chest, though without deriving the smallest benefit from its contents; my key was now utterly useless; but as I gazed with longing eyes on the two or three loaves which my master believed to be bitten by the rats, I could not resist the temptation of nibbling a morsel more, though touching them in the lightest possible manner, like an experienced swordsman in a friendly assault.

Necessity is a great master, and being in this strait, I passed night and day in devising means to get out of it. All the rascally plans that could enter the mind of man, did hunger suggest to me; for it is a saying, and a true one, as I can testify, that hunger makes rogues, and abundance fools. One night, when my master slept, of which disposition he always gave sonorous testimony, as

I was revolving in my mind the best mode of renewing my intimacy with the contents of the chest, a thought struck me, which I forthwith put in execution. I arose very quietly, and taking an old knife, which, having some little glimmering of the same idea the day previous, I had left for an occasion of this nature, I repaired to the chest, and at the part which I considered least guarded, I began to bore a hole. The antiquity of the chest seconded my endeavors, for the wood had become rotten from age, and easily yielded to the knife, so that in a short time I managed to display a hole of very respectable dimensions. I then opened the chest very gently, and taking out the bread, I treated it much in the same manner as heretofore, and then returned safe to my mattress.

The next day my worthy master soon spied my handiwork, as well as the deficiency in his bread, and began by wishing the rats at the devil.

"What can it mean?" said he; "during all the time I have been here, there have never been rats in the house before."

And he might say so with truth; if ever a house in the kingdom deserved to be free from rats, it was his, as they are seldom known to visit where there is nothing to eat. He began again with nails and wood; but when night came, and he slept, I resumed my operations, and rendered nugatory all his ingenuity.

In this manner we went on; the moment he shut one door, I opened another: like the web of Penelope, what he spun by day, I unraveled by night; and in the course of a few nights the old chest was so maltreated, that little remained of the original that was not covered with pieces and nailing. When the unhappy priest found his mechanical ability of no avail, he said:

"Really this chest is in such a state, and the wood is so old and rotten, that the rats make nothing of it. The best plan I can think of, since what we have done is of no use, is to arm ourselves within, against these cursed rats."

He then borrowed a rat-trap, and baiting it with bits

of cheese which he begged from the neighbors, set it under the chest. This was a piece of singular good fortune for me, for although my hunger needed no sauce, yet I did not nibble the bread at night with less relish because I added thereto the bait from the rat-trap. When in the morning he found not only the bread gone as usual, but the bait likewise vanished, and the trap without a tenant, he grew almost beside himself. He ran to the neighbors, and asked them what animal it could possibly be that could positively eat the very cheese out of the trap, and yet escape untouched. The neighbors agreed that it could be no rat that could thus eat the bait, and not remain within the trap, and one more cunning than the rest observed:

"I remember once seeing a snake about your premises, and depend on it that is the animal which has done you this mischief, for it could easily pick the bait from the trap without entering entirely, and thus too it might easily escape."

The rest all agreed that such must be the fact, which alarmed my master a good deal.

He now slept not near so soundly as before, and at every little noise, thinking it was the snake biting the chest, he would get up, and taking a cudgel which he kept at his bed's head for the purpose, began to belabor the poor chest with all his might, so that the noise might frighten the reptile from his unthrifty proceedings. He even awoke the neighbors with such prodigious clamor, and I could not get a single minute's rest. He turned me out of bed, and looked amongst the straw, and about the blanket, to see if the creature was concealed anywhere; for, as he observed, at night they seek warm places, and not unfrequently injure people by biting them in bed. When he came, I always pretended to be very heavy with sleep, and he would say to me in the morning:

"Did you hear nothing last night, boy? The snake was about, and I think I heard him at your bed, for they are very cold creatures, and love warmth."

22

"I hope to God he will not bite me," returned I, "for I am very much afraid."

He was so watchful at night that, by my faith, the snake could not continue his operations as usual, but in the morning when the priest was at church, he resumed them pretty steadily as usual.

Looking with dismay at the damage done to his store, and the little redress he was likely to have for it, the poor priest became quite uneasy from fretting, and wandered about all night like a hobgoblin. I began very much to fear that, during one of these fits of watchfulness, he might discover my key, which I placed for security under the straw of my bed. I therefore, with a caution peculiar to my nature, determined in future to keep this treasure by night safe in my mouth; and this was an ancient custom of mine, for during the time I lived with the blind man, my mouth was my purse, in which I could retain ten or twelve *maravedis* in farthings, without the slightest inconvenience in any way. Indeed, had I not possessed this faculty, I should never have had a single farthing of my own, for I had neither pocket nor bag that the old man did not continually search. Every night I slept with the key in my mouth without fear of discovery; but, alas! when misfortune is our lot, ingenuity can be of little avail.

It was decreed, by my evil destiny, or rather, I ought to say, as a punishment for my evil doings, that one night when I was fast asleep, my mouth being somewhat open, the key became placed in such a position therein, that my breath came in contact with the hollow of the key, and caused—the worse luck for me—a loud whistling noise. On this my watchful master pricked up his ears, and thought it must be the hissing of the snake which had done him all the damage, and certainly he was not altogether wrong in his conjectures.

He arose very quietly, with his club in his hand, and stealing towards the place whence the hissing sound proceeded, thinking at once to put an end to his enemy, he

23

lifted his club, and with all his force discharged such a blow on my unfortunate head, that it needed not another to deprive me of all sense and motion. The moment the blow was delivered, he felt it was no snake that had received it; and guessing what he had done, called out to me in a loud voice, endeavoring to recall me to my senses. Then touching me with his hands, he felt the blood, which was by this time in great profusion about my face, and ran quickly to procure a light. On his return he found me moaning, yet still holding the key in my mouth, and partly visible, being in the same situation which caused the whistling noise he had mistaken for the snake. Without thinking much of me, the attention of the slayer of snakes was attracted by the appearance of the key, and drawing it from my mouth, he soon discovered what it was, for, of course, the wards were precisely similar to his own. He ran to prove it, and with that at once found out the extent of my ingenuity.

"Thank God," exclaimed the cruel snake-hunter, "that the rats and the snakes which have so long made war upon me, and devoured my substance, are both at last discovered."

Of what passed for three days afterwards, I can give no account; but that which I have related, I heard my master recount to those who came there to see me. At the end, however, of the third day, I began to have some consciousness of what was passing around me, and found myself extended on my straw, my head bound up, and covered with ointment and plasters.

"What is the meaning of all this?" I cried, in extreme alarm.

The heartless priest replied, "I have only been hunting the rats and the snakes, which have almost ruined me."

Seeing the condition in which I was, I then guessed what had happened to me. At this time an old nurse entered, with some of the neighbors, who dressed the wounds on my head, which had assumed a favorable appearance; and as they found my senses were restored to me, they anticipated but little danger, and began to amuse themselves with my exploits, while I, unhappy sinner, should only deplore their effects.

With all this, however, they gave me something to eat, for I was almost dying with hunger; and at the end of fourteen or fifteen days I was able to rise from my bed without danger, though not even then without hunger, and only half cured. The day after I got up, my worthy and truly respectable master took my hand, and opening the door, put me into the street, saying:

"Lazaro, from this day look out for yourself, seek another master, and fare you well. No one will ever doubt that you have served a blind man; but for me, I do not require so diligent nor so clever a servant."

Then shaking me off, as though I was in league with the evil one, he went back into his house and shut the door.

CHAPTER III

HOW LAZARO BECAME THE SERVANT OF AN ESQUIRE, AND WHAT HAPPENED TO HIM IN THAT SERVICE

NOTWITHSTANDING the weak state to which I was reduced, I was obliged to take heart, and with the assistance of some kind people, I gradually made my way to the famous city of Toledo, where, by the mercy of God, I was shortly cured of my wounds.

While I labored under sickness there were always some well-disposed persons who were willing to give me alms; but no sooner was I recovered, than they said:

"Why do you stay idling here? why don't you seek a master?"

On which the reply would rise to my lips, "It is very easy to talk, but it is hard to find one."

In this manner I went on seeking my living from door

to door, and a mighty poor living it was, for Charity has left us mortals here to take a flight to heaven long since. But one day I accidentally encountered a certain esquire in the street; he was of a good appearance, well dressed, and walked with an air of ease and consequence. As I cast my eyes upon him, he fortunately took notice of me, and said:

"Are you seeking a master, my boy?"

I replied that I was.

"Then follow me," said he; "you have reason to thank your stars for this meeting:—doubtless you have said your prayers with a better grace than usual this morning."

I followed him, returning thanks to Providence for this singular good turn of fortune, for, if one might judge from appearances, here was exactly the situation which I had so long desired. It was early in the morning when I was engaged by this kind master, and I continued to follow him, as he desired, till we made the tour of a great part of the city. As we passed the market, I hoped that he would give me a load to carry home, as it was then about the hour that people usually made their purchases of that nature; but he passed by without taking the slightest notice.

"Peradventure," quoth I to myself, "these commodities are not exactly to his taste; we shall be more fortunate in some other quarter."

It was now eleven o'clock, and my master went into the cathedral to hear prayers, where I likewise followed him. Here we stayed until the whole service was finished and the congregation were departed; and then my master left, and proceeded towards one of the back streets of the city. Never was anybody more delighted than I, to find my master had not condescended to trouble himself about supplying his table, concluding, of course, that he was a gentleman whose means enabled him to consign to others such inferior domestic cares, and that on our arrival at home we should find everything in order—an anticipation of great delight to me, and, in fact, by this time almost a matter of necessity. The clock had struck one, when we arrived at a house before which my master stopped, and throwing his cloak open, he drew from his sleeve a key with which he opened the door.

I followed my master into the house, the entrance of which was extremely dark and dismal, so much so as to create a sensation of fear in the mind of a stranger; and when within found it contained a small court-yard and tolerably sized chambers. The moment he entered, he took off his cloak, and inquiring whether I had clean hands, assisted me to fold it, and then, carefully wiping the dust from a seat, laid it thereon. He next very composedly seated himself, and began to ask me a variety of questions, as to who I was, where I came from, and how I came to that city; to all which I gave a more particular account than exactly suited me at that time, for I thought it would have been much more to the purpose had he desired me to place the table and serve up the soup, than ask me the questions he then did.

With all this, however, I contrived to give him a very satisfactory account of myself, dwelling on my good qualities, and concealing those which were not suitable to my present auditory. But I began now to grow very uneasy, for two o'clock arrived, and still no signs of dinner appeared, and I began to recollect that ever since we had been in the house I had not heard the foot of a human being, either above or below. All I had seen were bare walls, without even a chair or a table—not so much as an old chest like that I had such good occasion to remember. In fact, it seemed to me like a house laboring under the influence of enchantment.

"Boy, hast thou eaten anything today?" asked my master at last.

"No, sir," I replied, "seeing that it was scarcely eight o'clock when I had the good fortune to meet your honor."

"Early as it was," returned my master, "I had already breakfasted, and it is never my custom to eat again till the evening; manage as you can till then; you will have the better appetite for supper."

It may be easily supposed that, on hearing this, my newly raised hopes vanished as rapidly as they had risen; it was not hunger alone that caused me to despond, but the certainty that fortune had not yet exhausted her full store of malice against me. Already I saw in perspective my troubles renewed, and I turned to weep over my unhappy anticipation. The consideration which prevented my taking an abrupt departure from the priest arose to my remembrance—that of falling from bad to worse—and I beheld it, as I feared, realized. I could not but weep over the incidents of my past unfortunate career, and anticipate its rapidly approaching close; yet withal, concealing my emotion as well as possible, I said:

"Thank God! sir, I am not a boy that troubles himself much about eating and drinking; and for this quality I have been praised even to this very day by all the masters whom I have ever served."

"Abstinence is a great virtue," returned my master, "and for this I shall esteem thee still more; gormandising is only for swine, men of understanding require little to allay their appetite."

"I can understand that sentiment right well," quoth I to myself; "my masters have all advised the same course; though the devil a bit do *they* find the virtues of starvation so very pleasant, by all that I have seen."

Seating myself near the door, I now began to eat some crusts of bread which I had about me; they were part of some scraps I had collected in my career of charity.

"Come here, boy," said my master; "what are you eating?"

I went to him and showed him the bread. He selected from the three pieces which I had, the best and largest, and said:

"Upon my life, but this seems exceedingly nice bread."

"Yes, sir," I replied, "it is very good."

"It really is," he continued; "where did you get it? was it made with clean hands. I wonder?"

"That I can't answer for," I replied, "but the flavor of it does not come amiss to me."

"Nor to me either, please God!' said my poor devil of a master; and, having finished his scrutiny, he raised the bread to his mouth, and commenced as fierce an attack on it as I quickly did on the other.

"By heavens! but this bread is beautiful!" exclaimed he; and I, beginning to see how matters stood with him, redoubled my haste with the remainder, being well assured that if he finished first, he would have little hesitation in assisting me: but luckily we finished together. He then carefully picked up the crumbs which had fallen, and entering a small chamber adjoining, brought out an old jar with a broken mouth. Having drank therefrom he handed it to me, but to support my character of abstemiousness, I excused myself, saying:

"No, sir, I thank you; I never drink wine."

"The contents of the jar will not hurt you," he said; "it is only water!"

I took the jar, but a very small draught satisfied me, for thirst was one of the few things from which I suffered no inconvenience.

Thus we remained till night, I anticipating my supper, and my master asking me many questions, to all of which I answered in the best manner I was able. Then he took me into the chamber whence he had brought the jar of water, and said:

"Stay here, my boy, and see how to make this bed, as from henceforth you will have this duty."

We then placed ourselves on each side of this bed, if such it can be called, to make it; though little enough there was to make. On some benches was extended a sort of platform of reeds, on which were placed the clothes, which, from want of washing, were not the whitest in the world. The deuce of anything was there in the shape of feather-bed or mattress, but the canes showed like the ribs of a lean hog through an old covering which served to lie upon, and the color of which one could not exactly praise. It was night when the bed was made, and my master said:

"Lazaro, it is rather late now, and the market is distant; likewise the city abounds with rogues; we had better therefore pass the night as we can, and tomorrow morning we will fare better. Being a single man, you see, I don't care much for these things, but we will arrange better in future."

"Sir, as to myself," I replied, "I beg you will on no account distress yourself. I can pass a night without food with no inconvenience, or even more indeed, if it were necessary."

"Your health will be all the better for it," he said, "for take my word for it, as I said today, nothing in the world will insure length of life so much as eating little."

"If life is to be purchased on such terms," said I to myself, "I shall never die, for hitherto I have been obliged to keep this rule, whether I will or no; and, God help me, I fear I shall keep it all my long life."

My master then went to bed, putting his clothes under his head instead of a pillow, and ordered me to seek my rest at his feet; which I accordingly did, though the situation precluded all hope of sleep. The canes of which the bedstead was composed, and my bones, which were equally prominent, were, throughout the night, engaged in a continual and most unpleasant intimacy; for considering my illness and the privations which I had endured, to say nothing of my present starving condition, I do not believe I had a single pound of flesh on my whole body. Throughout that day I had eaten nothing but a crust of bread, and was actually mad with hunger, which is in itself a bitter enemy to repose. A thousand times did I curse myself and my unhappy fortunes—the Lord forgive my impiety; and what was a sore addition to my misery, I dared not to move, nor vent my grief in audible expressions, for fear of waking my master. Many times during this night did I pray to God to finish my existence!

As the morning appeared, we arose, and I set about cleaning my master's clothes, and putting them in order; and helped him to dress, very much to his satisfaction. As he placed his sword in his belt, he said:

"Do you know the value of this weapon, my boy? The gold was never coined that should buy this treasure of me. Of all the blades Antonio ever forged, he never yet made its fellow."

And then drawing it from the scabbard and trying the edge with his fingers, he added, "With this blade I would engage to sever a bale of wool."

"And I would do more than that with my teeth," said I to myself; "for though they are not made of steel, I would engage to sever a four-pound loaf, and devour it afterwards."

He then sheathed his sword and girded it round him, and with an easy, gentlemanlike carriage, bearing himself erect, and throwing the corner of his cloak over his shoulder, or over his arm, placing his right hand on his side, he sallied forth, saying:

"Lazaro, see to the house while I go to hear mass, and make the bed during my absence; the vessel for water wants filling, which you can do at the river which runs close by; though take care to lock the door when you go, lest we should be robbed, and put the key on this hinge, in case I return before you, that I may let myself in."

He then walked up the street with such an air of gentility, that a stranger would have taken him for a near relation of the Count of Arcos, or at least for his *valet de chambre*.

"Blessed be the Lord!" said I, "who, if He inflicts misfortunes, gives us the means of bearing them. Now who, on meeting my master, would dream but that he had supped well and slept well; and, although early in the morning, but that he had also breakfasted well? There are many secrets, my good master, that you know, and that all the world is ignorant of. Who would not be deceived by that smiling face and that fine cloak? and who would believe that such a fine gentleman had passed the whole of yesterday without any other food than a morsel of bread, that his boy had carried in his breast for a day and a night? Today washing his hands and face, and, for want of a towel, obliged to dry them with the lining of his garments—no one would ever suspect such things from the appearance before them. Alas! how many are there in this world who voluntarily suffer more for their false idea of honor, than they would undergo for their hopes of an hereafter!"

Thus I moralized at the door of our house, while my master paced slowly up the street; and then, returning within, I lost no time in making the tour of the house, which I did, though without making any fresh discovery whatever, or finding anything of a more consolatory nature than my own gloomy thoughts.

I quickly made our bed, such as it was, and taking the water-jar, went with it to the river. There I saw my gay master in one of the gardens by the river side, in close conversation with two ladies, closely veiled, for there were many who were in the habit of resorting thus early in the morning to enjoy the fresh air, and to take breakfast with some of the gentlemen of the city, who likewise frequented the spot. There he stood between them, saying softer things than Ovid ever did; while they, seeing him apparently so enamored, made no scruple of hinting their wish to breakfast. Unfortunately his purse was as empty as his heart was full, therefore this attack on his weaker position threw him somewhat suddenly into disorder, which became evident from his confusion of language and the lame excuses of which he was obliged to avail himself. The ladies were too well experienced not to perceive, and that quickly, how matters stood; it was not long, therefore, before they exchanged him for a more entertaining gallant.

I was all this time slyly munching some cabbage-stalks, for want of a better breakfast, which I despatched with considerable alacrity, and then returned home, without being seen by my master, to await his orders respecting breakfast on his return.

I began to think seriously what I should do, still hoping, however, that as the day advanced my master might return with the means to provide at least for our dinner, but in vain. Two o'clock came, but no master; and, as my hunger now became insupportable, without further consideration I locked the door, and, placing the key where I was told, sallied out in search of food. With a humble subdued voice, my hands crossed upon my breast, and the name of the Lord upon my tongue, I went from house to house begging bread. The practice of this art, I may say, I imbibed with my mother's milk; or rather that, having studied it under the greatest master in all Spain, it is no wonder that I was so great an adept in all its various branches.

Suffice it to say, that although in this city there is no more charity than would save a saint from starvation, yet such was my superiority in talent, that before four o'clock I had stowed away nearly four pounds of bread in my empty stomach, and two pounds more in my sleeves and in the inside of my jacket. Passing then by the tripe market, I begged of one of the women that keep the stalls, who gave me a good-sized piece of cow-heel, with some other pieces of boiled tripe. When I got home, I found my good gentleman already arrived, and having folded and brushed his cloak, he was walking about the court-yard. As I entered he came up to me, as I thought, to chide me for my absence, but, thank God, it was far otherwise. He inquired where I had been, to which I replied:

" Sir, I remained at home till two o'clock; but when I found that your honor did not return, I went out, and recommended myself so well to the notice of the good people of this city, that they have given me what you see."

" I then showed him the bread and the tripe which I had collected. At the sight of these delicacies his countenance brightened up.

" Ah! " said he, " I waited dinner for you some time; but as it grew late I finished. You have nevertheless acted very properly in this matter; for it is much better to ask, for the love of God, than to steal. I only charge you on no account to say you live with me, as such proceedings would not exactly redound to my honor, although

I hardly think there is any danger, seeing that I am known so little in this city."

"Do not alarm yourself, sir, on that head," said I, " for people thought as little of asking who was my master as I of telling them."

"Eat away, then, you young rogue," said he, "and with the blessing of God, we shall not long have need of such assistance, though I must say since I have been in this house good fortune has never visited me. There are houses, from some reason or other, so unlucky that every one who occupies them becomes infected with their ill-fortune, and this is without doubt one of them; but I promise you that directly the month is up I will leave, even if they should offer it to me for nothing."

I seated myself on the end of the bench, and commenced my supper with the tripe and bread. My poor unhappy master all the time eyed me askance, and never once took his eyes from my skirts, which at that time served me instead of a dinner-service. Providence had that day so favored me, that I resolved my master should partake of my abundance, for I could well understand his feelings, having experienced them of old, and to that very day, indeed, I was no stranger to them. I began to think whether it would exactly become me to invite him to my repast, but as he had unfortunately said he had dined, I feared lest he might take it amiss. However, I very much wished that the poor sinner might have the benefit of my labor, and break his fast as he had done the day before, particularly as the food was better and my hunger less. My good wishes towards him were speedily gratified, as they happened to jump with his own humor, for directly I commenced my meal he began walking up and down the room, and approaching me rather closely.

"Lazaro," said he, "I really cannot help remarking the extreme grace with which you make your meal. I don't think I ever saw anyone eat with more natural elegance; certain it is, that an observer might benefit by your example."

".Doubtless, my good sir," thought I, "it can only be to your extreme amiability that I am indebted for this compliment." Then, in order to give him the opportunity which I knew he longed for, I said, "Good materials, sir, require good workmen. This bread is most delicious, and this cow-heel is so well cooked and seasoned that the smell alone is sufficient to tempt anyone.''

"Cow-heel, is it?" said he.

"It is, sir," I replied.

"Ah!" said he, "cow's heel is one of the most delicate morsels in the world, there is nothing I am so fond of."

"Then taste it, sir," said I, "and try whether this is as good as you have eaten."

He seated himself on the bench beside me, and laying hands on the cow-heel, with three or four pieces of the whitest bread, commenced in such good earnest that one might easily see his rations were not disagreeable to him—grinding every bone as ravenously as a greyhound.

"With a nice sauce of garlic," said he, "this would be capital eating."

"You eat it with a better sauce than that, my good sir," thought I.

"By heavens," said he, "anybody would think, to see me eat, that I had not touched a morsel today."

"I wish I was as sure of good luck as I'm sure of that," said I to myself.

He asked me for the water-jug, and I gave it to him, which, by the way, was a sure proof he had eaten nothing, for it was as full as when I brought it from the river. After drinking we went to bed in the same manner as on the night before, though it must be confessed in a much more contented mood.

Not to dwell too much on this part of my story, I shall only say that in this manner we passed eight or ten days, my worthy master taking the air every day, in the most frequented parts, with the most perfect ease of a man of fashion, and returning home to feast on the contributions of the charitable, levied by poor Lazaro.

Many times did the reflection suggest itself, that, when with former masters I prayed so heartily to be released from such miserable service, my desire was certainly gratified, though with this difference, that not only did my present one decline feeding me, but expected that I should maintain him.

With all this, however, I liked him very much, seeing he had not the ability to do more—in fact, I was much more sorry for his unfortunate condition than angry at the situation in which his deficiencies placed me; and many times I have been reduced to short commons myself, that I might bring home a certain share for my unlucky master. But he was poor, and nobody can give what he has not got—an excuse which I cannot make for the old scoundrels I served before—though, as God is my witness, to this very day I never see a gentleman, like my master, strutting along as though the street was hardly wide enough for him, without marking the singular way in which Fortune apportions her favors. I pitied him from my heart, to think, that with all his apparent greatness he might at that moment suffer privations equally hard to endure. But with all his poverty I found greater satisfaction in serving him than either of the others, for the reason I have stated. All that I blamed him for was the extravagance of his pride, which, I thought, might have been somewhat abated towards one who, like myself, knew his circumstances so intimately. It seems to me, however, that the poorest gentlefolk are always the most proud; but there is consolation in the thought that death knows no distinction, but at length most generally places the commoner in higher ground than it does the peer. I lived for some time in the manner I have related, when it pleased my miserable fortune, which seemed never tired with persecuting me, to envy me even my present precarious and unhappy condition.

It appeared that the season in that country had been unfavorable to corn, therefore it was ordained by the magistracy that all strangers who subsisted by alms should quit the city, or risk the punishment of the whip. This law was enforced so rigidly that, only four days after its promulgation, I beheld a procession of miserable wretches who were suffering the penalty through the streets of the city; a sight which so alarmed me that I did not dare for the future to avail myself of my accustomed means of subsistence. It can hardly be possible to imagine the extreme necessity to which our house was reduced, or the mournful silence of those who were expiring within; for two or three days we neither spoke a word nor had we a mouthful to eat. With regard to myself, there were some young women, who earned their living by cotton-spinning and making caps, and with whom, being near neighbors of ours, I had made some slight acquaintance-ship—out of their pittance these poor girls gave me a morsel, which just served to keep life within me.

I did not, however, feel my own situation so keenly as I did that of my poor master, who, during the space of eight days, to the best of my knowledge, never touched a mouthful; at least, I can say, the deuce a morsel ever entered our door. Whether he ever got anything to eat when he went out I cannot determine; but I know well that he sallied out every day with a waist as fine as a greyhound of the best breed; and the better, as he thought, to evade suspicion, he would take a straw from the mattress, which could even ill spare the loss, and go swaggering out of the house, sticking it in his mouth for a toothpick! He continued to attribute all his ill-fortune to the unlucky house in which we were lodged.

"The evils we have to bear," he would say, "are all owing to this unfortunate dwelling—as you see, it is indeed sad, dark, and dismal: nevertheless, here we are, and, I fear, must continue a while to suffer; I only wish the month was past, that we might well be quit of it."

It happened one day, suffering, as I have described, this afflicting persecution of hunger, that, by some extraordinary chance, I know not what, nor did I think it dutiful to inquire, there fell into my poor master's poverty-stricken possession the large sum of one *real*, with which he came home as consequentially as though he had brought the treasure of Venice, saying to me, with an air of extreme satisfaction and contentment:

"Here, Lazaro, my boy, take this—Providence is at last beginning to smile on us—go to the market and purchase bread, meat, and wine; we will no longer take things as we have done. I have other good news likewise. I have taken another lodging, so that there will be no occasion to remain in this wretched place longer than the end of the month. Curse the place and he who laid the first brick; by the Lord, since I've been here not a drop of wine have I drunk, nor have I tasted a morsel of meat, neither have I enjoyed the smallest comfort whatsoever; but everything has been, as you see, miserable and dismal to the last degree. However, go, and quickly, for today we will feast like lords."

I took my *real* and jar, and without another word set out on my errand with the utmost speed, making towards the market-place in the most joyous and light-hearted mood imaginable. But alas! what enjoyment could I expect, when my adverse fortune so preponderated that the slightest gleam of sunshine in my career was sure to be overtaken by a storm? I was making my way, as I said, in extremely good spirits, revolving in my mind in what manner I should lay out my money to the best advantage, and returning heartfelt thanks to Providence for favoring my master with this unexpected stroke of fortune, when I saw a great crowd at the other end of the street, among whom were many priests; and I soon found to my horror that they were accompanying a corpse. I stood up against the wall to give them room, and as the body passed I beheld one, who, as I supposed, from the mourning she wore, was the widow of the deceased, surrounded by friends. She was weeping bitterly, and uttering in a loud voice the most piteous exclamations.

"Alas!" she cried, "my dear husband and lord! whither are they taking you? To that miserable and unhappy dwelling; to that dark and dismal habitation; to the house where there is neither eating nor drinking!"

Good heavens! never shall I forget the moment when I heard those words; it seemed in my fright as though heaven and earth were coming together. "Miserable and unhappy wretch that I am," I exclaimed in an agony of mind, "it is to our house then that they are bearing this body!"

I rushed from the place where I stood, through the crowd, forgetting in my fright the object of my errand, and made with all speed towards home. The instant I arrived, I closed the door, barred and bolted it, and cried out to my master with the utmost earnestness of manner to help me to defend the entrance. He, greatly alarmed, and with the impression that it was something else, called to me:

"What is the matter, boy? Why do you slam the door with such fury?"

"O master," said I, "come here and assist me, for they are bringing a dead body here! I met them in the street above, and I heard the widow of the dead man crying out, 'Alas! husband and master, whither do they take you? To the dark and dismal house; to the house of misery and misfortune; to the house where they neither eat nor drink.' To what other house, then, can they be bringing him than this?"

Directly my master heard these words, albeit in no merry humor, he burst out into such a fit of laughing that it was some time before he could utter a word.

During this time I was holding fast the door, placing my shoulder against it for better security. The crowd passed with the body, though still I could not persuade myself but that they intended to bring it in. When my master was more satiated with mirth than with food, he said to me, in a good-tempered manner:

"It is very just, Lazaro; according to what the widow said, you were right in thinking as you did; but as they have thought better of it and passed on, open the door and go on your errand."

39

" Stop a little longer, sir," said I, " let them pass the end of the street, that we may be sure."

But he would not wait, and coming to the street door, he opened it and forced me away, for I hardly knew what I did with fright, and so he despatched me again to the market.

We dined well that day, though my appetite was but indifferent; and it was some time before I recovered from the effect of that misadventure, though it was an excellent source of mirth to my master whenever it was brought to his recollection.

In this manner I lived some little time with my third and poorest master the esquire, having great curiosity to know what could possibly have induced him to come to that part of the world, for I knew he was a stranger on the first day I lived with him, from the fact of his not knowing a single soul in the city. At last my wish was gratified; for one day, when we had feasted pretty well, and were consequently in good humor, he told me a little of his history. He was a native of Old Castile, and had quitted his country because he had refused to salute a neighboring gentleman of consequence by taking off his hat first, which, according to *punctilio,* was construed into an insulting mark of disrespect. My honorable master wished to convince me that, being a gentleman, the other, though superior, had an equal right to doff his bonnet to him.

" For," said he, " though I am, as you see, but an esquire, I vow to God, if the count himself were to meet me in the street, and did not take off his hat to me, ay, and entirely off, the next time we met I would turn into some shop, pretending business, rather than pay him the least mark of respect. And though you see me here but poorly off, yet in my own country I have an estate in houses in good condition and well rented, only sixteen leagues from the place where I was born, worth at least two hundred thousand *maravedis;* so you see that they must be of good size and in good repair. I have likewise a dovecot, which if

it were taken care of, which it is not, would furnish upwards of two hundred young birds annually; and many
other things I possess, which I have relinquished solely
because I would not have the slightest imputation cast
upon my honor, by yielding precedence to one who was
in fact no better than myself; and I came to this city
hoping to obtain some honorable employment, though I
have not succeeded so well as I could have wished."

In this manner my master was going on with his narrative, giving me an account of the honorable proceedings
by which he had suffered, when he was interrupted by
the appearance of an old man and woman; the former
came to demand the rent of the house, and the latter that
of the bed. They brought the account, and claimed for
two months more than he could raise in a year; I think it
was about twelve or thirteen *reals*. He answered them
very courteously, that he was then going out to change
a piece of gold and should return in the evening. But
he made his exit this time for good; and when the good
people came for their money, I was obliged to tell them
that he had not yet returned. The night came, but without my master, and, being fearful of remaining in the
house by myself, I went to our neighbors, to whom I
related the circumstance, and they allowed me to remain
with them.

Early in the morning the creditors returned and inquired
of the neighbors. The woman replied that his boy was
there, and the key of the door ready for them. They then
asked me about my master, and I told them that I knew
not where he was, and that I had not seen him since he
went out to change the piece of gold; but that I thought
it was most likely he was gone off with the change.

On hearing this news they sent for a lawyer and a constable, and called on me and others to witness their taking
possession of my master's effects in payment of their demands. They went all over the house, and found just as
much furniture as I have recounted before, when they
demanded of me:

"What has become of your master's property? where are his trunks? and where is his household furniture?"

"I am sure I don't know," I replied.

"Doubtless," said they, "the property has been removed during the night. Señor Alguazil, take that boy into custody; he knows whither it has been taken."

On this up came the *alguazil*, and, seizing me by the collar, said, "Boy, thou art my prisoner, if thou reveal not where thy master hath hid his effects."

I, as if quite new to this sort of thing, expressed the utmost surprise and terror, and promised to state everything I knew, which seemed a little to disarm his anger.

"That is right," exclaimed all, "tell all you know, and fear nothing."

The man of law seated himself at a desk, and desired me to begin.

"Gentlemen," I continued, "my master is in possession of a good stock of houses and an old dovecot."

"So far well," was the reply; "however little worth, it will meet the debt he owes us. In what part of the city do they lie?"

"On his own estate, to be sure," was my answer.

"That is all the better," they exclaimed; "and where is his estate?"

"In Old Castile," I replied, "as he told me."

Both *alguazil* and notary laughed out at hearing this, exclaiming, "Quite enough—quite enough to cover your claim, though it were even greater."

The neighbors who had gathered round us now said, "Gentlemen, this here is a very honest boy; he has not been long in the 'squire's service, and knows no more of him than does your worship; the poor little sinner came knocking at our doors, and for charity's sake we gave him something to eat, after which he has gone to sleep at his master's."

Seeing that I was innocent, they let me go free; but the notary and the *alguazil* now came on the owners for the taxes, which gave rise to no very friendly discussion and a most hideous din; the man and woman maintained very stoutly that they had neither the will nor the means to pay them. The others declared they had other business in view of more importance; but I left them without stopping to see the issue of the affair, though I believe the unfortunate owner had to pay all; and he well deserved to do it, for when he ought to have taken his ease and pleasure, after a life of labor, he still went on hiring out houses to increase his gains.

It was in this way that my third and poorest master took leave of me, by which it seems I put the seal to my bad fortune, which, while exercising its utmost rigor against me, had this singularity in it that, though most domestics are known to run away from their masters, it was not thus in my case, inasmuch as my master had fairly run away from me. . . .

TALES FROM THE SPANISH

———

GUZMAN OF ALFARACHE

BY

MATEO ALEMAN

INTRODUCTION

The most popular of all picaresque stories was published first in Madrid in 1599. Within a year it appeared in other parts of Spain, in Portugal, France, and Flanders, and was translated into French at Paris. But this immediate and immense success added little to Mateo Aleman's income. A hard-working government official, he conducted himself so scrupulously that his ambition of dying a poor philosopher rather than a rich flatterer was completely satisfied. In fact, in 1602 he was imprisoned for debt. Probably on this account he went to Mexico, there to continue his voluminous literary labors. With right good will had he written, in *Guzman of Alfarache*, his satiric review of society from bottom to top. The merry Guzman soon learns from his experiences in inns the golden rule of roguery: "Do unto others as they will do unto you, and do it first." On becoming a servant he begins the energetic practice of roguery in Spain. Next he seeks out Italy as a field for his talents, rising from a successful member of the fraternity of beggars to a most wily page in the establishment of the Spanish ambassador.

These diverting escapades and the frank satire contained therein were to be followed by a second part. In the preface Aleman divulged the fact that Guzman was writing from the galleys after a most irreverent period of study for the church. The extraordinary success of the book led a lawyer of Valencia, Juan Marti, to bring out in 1602 a second part. To deceive the public, he signed his name Mateo Luxan de Sayavedra, native of Seville.

47

The audacious compliment stimulated Aleman to bring out the true second part in 1605, heaping coals of fire on Marti's head in this fashion: " I must acknowledge in this my competitor . . . his great learning, his nimble wit, his deep judgment, his pleasant conceits, and his general knowledge in all humane and divine letters, and that his discourses throughout are of that quality and condition that I do much envy them, and should be proud that they were mine."

But on the title-page he warned the reader that the second part which had previously appeared was not his, that this was the only genuine continuation. Besides, you will find that he gets even in the story itself by introducing a rascal named Sayavedra, who tries to fleece Guzman, steals his baggage, is punished therefor, and at length has the humiliation of entering Guzman's service as a lackey. The point is made still more clear by giving Sayavedra a brother named Juan Marti. On the way back to Spain Sayavedra goes mad, calls himself Guzman, and leaps overboard in a storm. Thus did Aleman deal out justice to the literary pirate.

The second part, beginning with Book the Fourth, as the reader will observe, differs from the first. The author is not so much interested in castigating society as he is in the rascally hero. The story is not so much a beacon-tower of human life, as Aleman called it, as it is a moving picture film about a vagabond most entertaining in his knavery. His unfailing shrewdness and ingenuity throughout the book gained him a welcome everywhere. France and Germany received him with open arms. England adopted him as a son. Indeed, he marched through Europe as a popular hero. The highest praise that could be given any notorious criminal whose life might be hawked about the streets was to call him a Guzman. As one preface put it, " Our English Guzman is as famous in these times as ever the Spanish in his time."

Here, then, is a romance of the underworld with an international reputation, in which you will follow through adventure after adventure a knave who has captivated the popular imagination for centuries, and in which for a few brief hours you are absorbed in the pictures of a bygone society as vivid as the scenes in a photo-play.

The present edition of this most celebrated and influential of picaresque stories omits all the monotonous moralizings which burdened the original. It also leaves out the romantic or tragic stories taken by Aleman chiefly from the Italian story-tellers, for they are exactly like the stories from Boccaccio and Masuccio presented in the first three volumes of this set. The narrative now stands as an unbroken succession of diverting episodes typical of Spanish life at the opening of the seventeenth century.

Guzman of Alfarache

BOOK THE FIRST

CHAPTER I

OF THE PARENTS OF GUZMAN, BUT MORE PARTICULARLY OF
HIS FATHER

M Y ancestors, as well as my father, were originally
from the Levant; but having settled in Genoa, and
been ingrafted with the noblesse there, I shall call them
Genoese.

They employed themselves in the traffic of exchanges,
which was much practiced among the gentry of that city.
It is true that they acted in such a manner in their commerce, that their credit was soon publicly cried down, and
they were accused of usury; it was moreover said of them
that they lent money at an exorbitant interest, upon plate
and other good security, for a limited time, at the expiration of which the pledges, if not redeemed, remained at
their disposal; sometimes they even denied themselves,
and evaded persons who came for the purpose of re-
claiming their property at the stipulated time, and very
frequently restitution could only be obtained by an appeal
to justice.

My parents well knew that they were reproached with
these and the like villanies, but as they were prudent,
peaceful people, they always went on their own way, and
cared not what detractors said of them. In fact, when
one behaves with decorum, why pay any regard to such
slander? My father was a constant attendant at church,
and always carried about with him a rosary of fifteen

complete sections, each bead of which was larger than a hazelnut. He never failed at mass; humbly kneeling before the altar, with his hands folded together and his eyes turned up towards heaven, he uttered such ejaculations, and sighed with so much fervency, that he inspired all around him with devotion. Can it be believed, then, without injustice, that with so truly religious an outward appearance, he was capable of the infamous transactions of which he was accused? God only is able to form a correct judgment of the heart of man. I confess, that if I saw a religious man enter a house in the night-time, armed with a sword, I might suspect his intentions; but that such a man as my father, who was constantly seen to act in this Christian-like manner, should be taxed with hypocrisy, is a piece of malignity which I cannot pass over.

Thus, though he had determined to treat all these unpleasant reports respecting him with contempt, he found that he had not always resolution sufficient to bear them with *patience*. That he might hear no more of them, therefore, he determined upon leaving the city. Another reason for his taking this resolution was, that he had received information that his correspondent at Seville, with whom he was engaged for a considerable sum, had become a bankrupt. At this distressing intelligence he embarked immediately for Spain, in the hope of meeting with that person. But the vessel in which he sailed being taken by the corsairs, he was made a slave and carried to Algiers.

My father was now not only afflicted at the loss of his liberty, but he was obliged to give up all hope of regaining his money. In his despair he took the turban; and having, by his insinuating manner, been happy enough to be well received by a rich widow at Algiers, he shortly afterwards married her.

In the meantime it was known at Genoa that he had been taken prisoner by the pirates, and this news soon came to the ears of his correspondent at Seville, who was the more rejoiced at it, as he fancied he had got rid of his principal creditor, whom he considered a slave for life. Finding, therefore, that one way or other he had sufficient remain-

"WELL RECEIVED BY A RICH WIDOW AT ALGIERS, HE SHORTLY AFTER-
WARDS MARRIED HER"

(From a sketch by John Lewis)

ing to satisfy the others, he arranged his affairs with them immediately. So that, having discharged all his debts, according to the mode prescribed for bankrupts, he found himself able to commence business again in a better condition than ever.

On the other hand, my father's thoughts were still completely occupied with the remembrance of his correspondent's bankruptcy, and he never failed to make inquiries respecting him in all his letters to Spain. He learned by this means that his debtor had adjusted his affairs, and was in a better condition than ever. This afforded some consolation to our captive, who began to hope from that moment that he should recover some part of his debt. As to his having taken upon him the Turkish habit, and married in Algiers, nothing appeared easier to him than to clear himself from any difficulty on that score. The first thing he did was to persuade his wife to turn all her property into ready money, telling her that he was desirous to trade again. In respect to what jewels she had, he made not the slightest scruple to possess himself of them before she had the least suspicion of his intention.

When he had thus got everything in readiness, his next business was to find out some Christian captain who, out of *compassion* for him *and for a reasonable remuneration,* would undertake to transport him to the Spanish coast, and he was fortunate enough to meet with one who was an Englishman, with a feeling heart and a proper sense of religion, which the majority of his nation generally possess. Everything was so well ordered that they had got a considerable way out to sea with my father and his treasure before his wife had any knowledge of his departure. To add to his good luck, the vessel was bound for Malaga, whence it is but three short days' journey to Seville. No sooner had my father landed, than the idea of soon securing his rascally debtor seemed to complete his joy. The first thing he did was to get reconciled to the Church; more, perhaps, from the fear of penance in this world, than from dread of punishment in the world to come.

Having got rid of an affair of so great importance, he thought of nothing but Seville, whither he hastened immediately. The news of my father's having embraced Mahometanism had got to Seville long before him, and his correspondent felt so well assured of it, that he was enjoying his money without entertaining the slightest apprehension of ever being compelled to make any account of it; judge, therefore, of his surprise upon seeing the Genoese strut into his house one fine morning, with an imperious air, and dressed in a manner bearing but little resemblance to a slave. He could not but believe him for some moments to be some spirit in the form of his principal creditor; but recollecting, in spite of himself, that it was my father, in his own flesh and blood, he was obliged at length to come to some explanation. With the utmost effrontery, therefore, he agreed that *it was but right to settle accounts;* but that they had so many and long dealings together, that their business required a long discussion. It may be boldly asserted, that during their commerce there had been a thousand rogueries on both sides, known to themselves only; and as these slights of hand, or mutual juggles, are never entered on tradesmen's books, this roguish correspondent had the audacity to deny three-fourths of them, unmindful of the good faith and honor which thieves are said so religiously to observe towards each other.

What more have I to tell you? After the perusal and reperusal of many papers *pro* and *con;* after an infinity of demands and replies, accompanied by reproaches and reciprocal hard words, an accommodation was made, by which my father was content to lose the greater part of his demand. Of water spilt we must recover what we can, and certainly my father acted wisely in ridding himself at Malaga of *the itch of Algiers.* If he had not taken this precaution, he would have obtained no redress, nor would he have touched a farthing of his debt. A man of his correspondent's character might easily have taken advantage of the circumstances at Seville, perhaps by giving the half of his debt to the Brothers of the Holy Inquisition to undertake the cause for him. You may judge of the feeling he entertained towards him by the reports that he spread to his disadvantage throughout Seville. What absurdities did he not relate to all the merchants upon 'Changè, of two former petty bankruptcies of the Genoese, which, in fact, were not without fraud; but do other merchants act differently? Is it not hard, then, thus to cry down one unfortunate speculator who, to repair and patch up his deranged affairs, has recourse to a little bankruptcy? This is nothing among merchants; they easily make amends to each other by a compliment of the like nature. If it were so very great a crime, would not justice take care to remedy it? Undoubtedly; for so severe is she, that we see many a poor devil well whipped and sent to the galleys for less than five or six *reals*.

This rascal of a correspondent was not content with having destroyed my father's reputation by divulging his two bankruptcies; his malignity went so far that he endeavored to make him appear ridiculous in the world, by giving out that he took more pains with his person than an antiquated coquette, and that his face was always covered with red and white paint. I grant you that my father curled his hair and perfumed himself, and took a vast deal of pains with his teeth and hands. But what of this? he loved himself, and not hating women, he neglected nothing that he thought would make his person agreeable to them. This afforded fine sport for our correspondent, who at first did some harm; but as soon as my father became somewhat better known at Seville, he contrived to efface all the bad impressions that slander had made, for he conducted himself in so plausible a manner, and made a show of so much uprightness and sincerity in all his actions, that he gained the esteem and friendship of the first merchants in that city.

With the sum of money that he had brought with him from Algiers, added to what he had recovered from his correspondent, my father now found himself worth about

55

40,000 *livres,* which was not an inconsiderable sum for him, who knew well how to conduct his business as a wholesale trader. Nobody made greater noise than he on the Exchange: so well did he get on, that after some years he purchased a house in town and another in the country; he furnished them both in a magnificent manner, especially his house of pleasure at St. Juan d'Alfarache, whence I derive my title. But as he loved pleasure, this house was the cause of his ruin, by the very frequent expenses he was led into; so that he insensibly neglected his affairs and trusted to his clerks; and to keep up appearances he was obliged to have recourse to play with rich merchants whom he invited and entertained for that purpose, and of whom he generally won.

CHAPTER II

GUZMAN RELATES HOW HIS FATHER MAKES AN ACQUAINTANCE WITH A LADY, WITH THE CONSEQUENCES THEREOF

SUCH was the life my father led, when being one day on 'Change among other merchants, he discovered afar off a christening which seemed to belong to persons of distinction; everybody hastened to see it pass, especially as it was whispered that it was the child of some person of quality, whose baptism was wished to be as private as possible.

My father followed with the rest to the church, and stationed himself at the font; not so much out of a desire to see the ceremony, as the face of a lady whom an old knight led, and who, as it appeared, was to stand for the infant, with this superannuated cavalier. Both the face and figure of this lady were so admirable, that my father was much struck with her appearance. Although in an undress, he could not but admire her graceful deportment, and, as she chanced to raise her veil for an instant, he beheld a face which completely charmed him: there certainly was not a more lovely woman in Seville. He kept his eye immovably fixed upon this charmer, who was far from being displeased at observing it; for beautiful women are never vexed at a man's looking at them with admiration, although he be of the very dregs of the people. She, in her turn, took a very minute survey of the merchant, and not considering him unworthy of a tender look, she bestowed one on him, which had the desired effect so completely that he scarcely recollected where he was. He was not, however, so entirely lost as to forget to follow his mistress, after the ceremony, to ascertain where she resided and who she was. He found that she lived with this old knight, and was kept by him in a very expensive style, out of an income that he derived from two or three rich benefices in his possession.

My father was not displeased at this discovery, for he felt sure that such a woman could not live very contentedly with her old companion. With this thought, he contrived all the ways he could to see her again and to speak to her, but in vain; he never met her without her old gallant, who never lost sight of her. But these difficulties only added fuel to his flame, and served but to make him sharper and more eager. At length he was fortunate enough, by dint of presents and promises, to gain over to him a duenna, without whose aid he could never have succeeded; this was apparently a good, religious old woman, who (dissembler as she was) had free admittance into the knight's house, and was not in the least mistrusted. This hypocrite, a true agent of Satan, at length introduced the old knight and his lady into my father's house. . . . Compliments passed on both sides, but more particularly on that of my father, whose fine speeches and polished manners, though they cost him nothing, entirely won the old man's heart, insomuch that he himself conducted him to his lady.

It not being yet the proper time to walk, the party entered a small arbor in the garden, which was the more refreshing as it was situated on the bank of the river. They began to play at *primero* and the lady won, my father being too gallant a man not to allow himself to lose in such a case. After the game they took a turn round the walks, which was followed by a good supper, which lasted so long that they no sooner rose from table than they were obliged to return to Seville by water, in a small barge which my father had caused to be set off with green boughs and flowers for that purpose. To complete their entertainment, they heard concerts of music performed by some persons that sung and played on several instruments in a small boat, which immediately followed theirs down the river Guadalquivir. At last, the lady and her old gallant, after having been most agreeably entertained, returned hearty thanks to my father for his handsome reception of them, which had such an effect on the old knight that he thought he never could make sufficient acknowledgments for it; and so great was the friendship he conceived for my father, that I do not think he could have made up his mind to leave him so soon without the promise of seeing him again the next day.

This friendship was so well managed by the lady and my father that it lasted during the life of the old knight, who in truth did not live much longer. He was a worn-out rake, an old sinner, who had given himself up entirely to pleasure, without the least fear of the other world, or regard to what might be said of him in this. I was already four years old when he died, but was not his only heir. The good man had several other children by other mistresses, and we lived in his house like tithe-loaves, every one of a different oven. Perhaps, if the truth was known, he was no more their father than he was mine; but however that might be, as I was the youngest, and from the tenderness of my age not so well able to help myself as my brothers, I should have come but badly off among them had I not in my mother a person well able to take my part. In short, she was a woman of Andalusia.

She did not wait till the old man was dead to feather her nest; for no sooner was he given over by his physicians than, having all the keys, and being mistress of the house, she took possession of everything worth carrying away, leaving nothing but rags for his next of kin. Even the very day that he died his house was laid waste in a deplorable manner; while he was gasping for life he lost even the sheets from his bed; and everything of value was spirited away before the breath was out of his body. Nothing but the four walls were left standing when his kindred came about him, big with expectation. In vain they examined everything; it was very evident that some-one had been there before them, and they found themselves obliged to be at the expense of his funeral for the honor of the family. They behaved, however, as well as they could without shedding many tears on the occasion; but who ever mourns much for a person that leaves nothing? It is for heirs only who are well paid for it to appear to be afflicted.

My mother was now mistress of at least ten thousand ducats, which sum was the means of saving my father from another stoppage he was on the point of making, and enabled him to make as good a figure as ever among the merchants. He was, unfortunately, passionately fond of company, splendor, and show; but as he could not long satisfy this ruling passion without plunging himself into the same difficulties again, from which my mother's money had but just extricated him, he found himself, a few years after his marriage, obliged to become bankrupt again for the last time; I say the last time, because, finding himself without resource, and utterly unable to keep up his former equipage and appearance, he chose rather to die with chagrin than to survive the date of his prosperity.

Life had more charms for my mother, who bore my father's loss with considerable fortitude, though she was much afflicted at his death. Our houses were obliged to be given up to his creditors. We had now only a few jewels left, besides the furniture, which my mother turned into money, and retired to a small house where she determined to live in a private manner as well as she could. She did not take this step on account of her inability to maintain us by fresh intrigues; for, although she was already in her fortieth year, she had always taken such good care of herself, that even at this time of life she was not a conquest to be despised; but as she could not make up her mind to make the first advances to men who had formerly sought her favors with ardor, this noble feeling of pride so ill accorded with the situation of our domestic affairs, that they daily grew worse and worse.

When I had entered my fourteenth year, I resolved to leave my mother and my country and to seek my fortune elsewhere. My wish to travel was for the purpose of seeing and knowing a little of the world, and I always had a particular desire to visit my father's relations at Genoa. So that, not being able any longer to defer the execution of my design, I left Seville on a beautiful day, with my purse almost as destitute of money as my head was crammed with idle fancies and chimeras.

CHAPTER III

GUZMAN SETS OUT FROM SEVILLE. HIS FIRST ADVENTURE AT AN INN

AS I remembered to have heard said that it was usual with such as have to seek their fortunes to give themselves names of consequence, without which they would pass for nobody in strange countries, I took my mother's name, which was Guzman, and added to it d'Alfarache. This appeared to me so well imagined, that I felt fully persuaded in my own imagination that I was already nothing less than the illustrious Don Guzman d'Alfarache.

This newly-created signor, not having set out until late

in the afternoon, went but a short distance the first day, though he made what haste he could for fear of being pursued. In fact I went no farther than the chapel of St. Lazarus, which is but a short way from the city. Being already fatigued I sat down on the steps rather sorrowfully, beginning to feel some anxiety as to what would become of me. After having sat there thinking for some time, a religious idea came across my mind, which I immediately gratified by entering the chapel, where I addressed myself to God, beseeching Him to inspire me with His counsels. My prayer was fervent, but short, the time not allowing me to make it longer, for it was just the hour for closing the chapel, which I was therefore obliged to quit, and I was left on the steps again, where I remained not without fear of what might happen to me.

Represent to yourself at the door of this chapel a child who had been accustomed to every indulgence and maintained in plenty. Consider that I knew not where to go, nor what to decide on. There was no inn near to the place, though my appetite informed me that it was quite supper-time. There was certainly plenty of clear water running within a few paces of me, but this was a cheerless prospect. I began now to find the difference between a hungry man and one who has his belly full; between a man who is accustomed to a table covered with good victuals, and one who has not a morsel of bread to eat. Not knowing what to do with myself, nor at what door to venture to rap, I made up my mind to pass the night where I was. I laid myself down therefore at full length, covering my face with my cloak as well as I was able, not without fear of being devoured by wolves, which I sometimes fancied I heard not far from me.

Sleep, however, at last suspended my uneasiness, and took so fast possession of my senses that the sun had been up two hours before I awoke, and which perhaps I had not done then but for the noise of tambours, made by a number of country wenches who passed me singing and dancing along the road on their way to some festival. I

61

rose quickly, and perceiving several ways equally unknown to me, I chose the pleasantest, saying:

"May this road, which I take by chance, conduct me in a straight line to the temple of fortune."

I was like that ignorant quack of la Mancha, who generally carried about with him a bag full of prescriptions, and when he visited any sick person put his hand in at random, giving the first that came uppermost, saying, "God grant it may do thee good!" My feet performed the office of my head, and I followed them without knowing whither they led me.

I walked two leagues that morning, which was not a short distance for a lad to do who had never traveled so far in his life before. I believed myself already arrived at the Antipodes, and that I had discovered another world, like the famous Christopher Columbus. This new world, however, was nothing but a miserable tavern, which I entered all in a perspiration, covered with dust, and dying with fatigue and hunger. I asked for dinner, and was informed that there was nothing but fresh eggs in the house.

"Fresh eggs!" cried I; "well, I must be content; make haste, then, and prepare me an omelet of about half a dozen."

The hostess, who was a frightful old woman, began to examine me with attention, and seeing that I was a raw, herring-gutted looking lad, and very hungry, she thought she might safely venture to pass upon me for fresh some eggs which were about half hatched. With this opinion she came up to me, and laughing in my face with as pleasant an air as she could affect, she asked me whence I came. I told her from Seville, and entreated her afresh to let me have the eggs; but before she did what I desired she thrust her nasty hand under my chin, saying, "And where is my little wag of Seville going?" At the same time she wished to kiss me; but I turned quickly round to avoid this felicity. I was not, however, so quick as entirely to escape her stinking breath, the fumes of which made me fear it would have communicated her age and distempers to me; fortunately, I had nothing but wind on my stomach, or I should certainly have vomited over her, as the only return I could make her for such a compliment.

I told her I was going to Court, and entreated her again to let me have something to eat. She then made me sit down on a broken stool, before a stone table, on which she laid a napkin, which looked as if it had but newly cleaned the oven. On this she placed for a salt-cellar the bottom of a broken earthen pot, and some water in a vessel of the same ware, out of which her fowls generally drank, together with a coarse piece of cake, as black as the before-mentioned table-cloth. After making me wait about a quarter of an hour longer, she served up, on a filthy platter, an omelet, or what might more properly have been termed an egg poultice. The omelet, plate, bread, drinking-pot, salt-cellar, salt, napkin, and hostess appeared to be precisely of the same color.

My stomach ought to have revolted against such disgusting appearances; but, independent of my being a young traveler, I had fasted so long that my bowels reproached me most violently with their unkind usage; so that, notwithstanding the uncleanly arrangements on the table and the bad seasoning of the eggs, I attacked the omelet as hogs do acorns. I felt indeed something grate between my teeth, which ought to have made me suspect that all was not right, but I took no notice of it; but when I had got to the few last mouthfuls, I could not help thinking that this omelet had not exactly the same taste as those I had eaten at my mother's house; but this I good-naturedly attributed to the difference of the country, imagining that eggs were not in all places equally good, as if I had been five hundred leagues from home. After I had demolished this excellent dish, I felt myself so much better than I was before. that I was more than usually happy in having got so good a meal, so true is it that "hunger is the best sauce."

I did not so soon get through the bread, it being so bad that I was obliged to eat slowly, or I should certainly have choked myself with it. I began with the crust and ended with the crumb, which indeed was so little baked that it was little better than dough; notwithstanding which, however, I played my part very creditably, but not without the assistance of the wine, which was delicious. I rose from table as soon as I had finished my dinner, paid my hostess, and set forward on my journey again in good spirits. My feet, which before were scarce able to bear me, seemed now to have completely regained their former activity.

I had already got about a league from the inn, when what I had eaten beginning to digest, seemed to create such a combustion in my belly, accompanied by such a rising in my stomach, that I began to suspect something. I had not forgotten the resistance that my teeth had met with in getting through the eggs, and after reflecting what it could be for some time, I doubted no longer that my omelet had been amphibious, and must have had something in it that should not have been there.

CHAPTER IV

GUZMAN MEETS WITH A MULETEER AND TWO FRIARS; OF THEIR CONVERSATION; AND IN WHAT MANNER THE MULETEER AND HE WERE REGALED AT AN INN AT CANTILLANA

I REMAINED for some time leaning against the wall of a vineyard, very pale and much weakened by the retchings that I was making. A muleteer passed by with some unladen mules; he stopped to look at me, and seeing me in such a condition, asked what ailed me. I told him what had happened to me, but no sooner had I said that I imputed my illness to the omelet that I had eaten at the inn, than he began to laugh so violently that, if he had not held himself fast on his mule with both hands, he must infallibly have fallen to the ground.

THE SPANISH ROGUE

When one is afflicted it is by no means agreeable to be laughed at. My face, which just before was as pale as death, became as red as fire in an instant, and I looked with so ill an eye upon this rascal as sufficiently gave him to understand that I was far from being pleased at his behavior; but this only made him laugh the more, so that, perceiving that the more I vexed myself the more he laughed, I allowed him to go on until he was completely exhausted; besides, I had neither sword nor stick, and at fisticuffs I should have fared but badly; I was, therefore, prudent enough to speak him fair. A wise man, however much he may be offended, never sets up for a bravo when the party is too strong against him; besides, I did not think fit to disoblige my man for the sake of his mules. I could not, however, entirely refrain from mentioning it to him. "Well, my friend," said I, "and why all this violent mirth? does my nose stand awry?" But the only answer I could obtain to these questions was a renewal of his immoderate laughter.

It pleased God, however, that he at length gave over; and recovering himself by degrees, he said to me, gasping for breath all the while:

"It is not at your adventure, my little gentleman, that I laugh, for it is certainly very unfortunate for you; but your relating it reminded me of another which has just happened to that same old hag that treated you so ill. Two soldiers whom she regaled in the same manner have sufficiently revenged you all three. As we are going the same way," added he, "jump up on one of my mules, and I will tell you the story as we ride along."

Without waiting to be twice asked I mounted one of his beasts, and was ready to hear what he had to tell me respecting these two soldiers, whom I recollected to have met entering the inn just as I left it.

"These two wags," said he, "asked the hostess what she had to give them. She told them in the same manner as she did you that she had nothing but eggs; they bade her make ready an omelet, which the old woman soon brought them, but in cutting it their knives found resistance from something which they proceeded to examine with attention, and discovered three small lumps, much resembling the heads of unformed chickens, whose beaks were already so hard as plainly to show what they were. The soldiers, after having made so rare a discovery, without taking any notice of it, covered the omelet with a plate and asked the hostess if she had nothing else she could give them; she promised to broil them two or three slices of shadfish, which they accepted and soon despatched with the assistance of white sauce; after which one of these rogues going up to the old woman, as if for the purpose of paying the reckoning, with the omelet concealed in his hand, clapped it full in her face, and so completely rubbed it all over her eyes and nose that she bawled out for help most lustily, whereupon the other soldier, seeming to blame his comrade and pity the poor old woman, ran up to her under the pretense of consoling her, and stroked her over the face with his hands all bedaubed with soot. This done they both left the house, still continuing to abuse your old acquaintance, who got no other payment for her entertainment. I assure you," said the muleteer, "it was a high treat to see mine hostess in this delicate condition, with the agreeable distortions of countenance that she made, crying and laughing at the some moment."

The recital of this ridiculous story somewhat consoled me for my own adventure, and inclined me to forgive the laughter of the muleteer, who did not fail to set to again as soon as he had ended his narration. All this while we were trotting onwards; we overtook two friars who, having seen us from afar off, had waited till me came up, that they might have the benefit of the mules. They quickly agreed with the muleteer to carry them to Cazalla, whither he also was going, and having mounted their mules we continued our journey.

The muleteer was still too much taken up with the recollection of his pleasure at the inn to give up speaking of it so soon. He could not resist telling us that there was sufficient in that adventure to serve him for laughter for the remainder of his days.

"And I," cried I, interrupting him abruptly, "shall have cause to repent all my life that I did not serve that poisonous old hag even worse than the soldiers did; but she is not yet dead," added I, "and I may have my revenge still."

The friars, remarking with what eagerness I uttered these words, were curious to know what had been the occasion of it. The muleteer, who desired no better sport, that he might have another excuse for a good hearty laugh, related the story anew to these gentlemen, and in the course of it introduced my misfortune also, which was no small mortification to me.

The friars condemned exceedingly the conduct of the old hostess, and blamed my resentment no less.

"My son," said the elder of the two to me, "you are but young; hot blood carries you away and deprives you of the use of your reason; know that you have sinned as much in having regretted that you have lost the opportunity of committing a crime as if you had really committed one."

The holy man did not finish his remonstrance here, but held a long discourse upon anger and the desire of revenge. It appeared to me so like a sermon that I was persuaded he had preached it more than once, and that he was glad to have the opportunity of refreshing his memory by repeating it. Certain it is that the most part of what he addressed to me was far above my comprehension, as well as that of our muleteer, who, thinking of nothing but the old woman, was laughing in his sleeve all the time that the preacher was throwing away his time upon us. At length we arrived at Cantillana, where the two friars took leave of us until the next morning, and went to take up their night's lodging at a friend's house.

For my part I did not leave the muleteer, who told me that he would undertake to carry me to one of the best inns in the town, where the host was an excellent cook, and where I need not be afraid of having hatched eggs passed upon me. This assurance pleased me exceedingly, for I required a good meal to set me to rights; and we proceeded to the door of a house of tolerable good appearance, the master of which received us with great civility. This was perhaps the completest knave in that part of the country, and I only got out of the frying-pan into the fire, as the saying is. The muleteer led his beasts to the stable, where he remained for some time to provide for their wants, and as I was much fatigued, the soles of my feet being much swollen, and my thighs feeling as if they were broken from riding three or four hours without stirrups, I laid myself down and rested until the muleteer returned, who asked me whether I was not ready for my supper, for that he had resolved to set out next morning at break of day that he might reach Cazalla before night, and should therefore be glad to get to bed early. I answered that there was nothing would give me greater satisfaction than to sit down to table, provided he would assist me to rise, and even to walk, as I could scarcely support my own weight. He did me this service so readily that I felt much obliged to him.

We then called the landlord and told him that we wished for a good supper.

"Gentlemen," answered he, "I have such excellent provisions in the house that you will have yourselves only to blame if you do not fare well, for you have only to say what you would like."

This answer pleased me exceedingly, but I was afraid that he exaggerated, for I fancied that he had the looks of a rogue; no matter, said I to myself, let him be as much a rogue as he pleases so he use us but well; he was a pleasant sort of fellow, and a man of some humor.

"Will you allow me," said he, "to dress you a part of the pluck of a calf that I killed yesterday? I will make you a ragout of it fit for the gods; it was the prettiest little calf," added he, taking me kindly by the hand, "that you perhaps ever saw. I was extremely mortified that I was obliged to kill it, but the drought of the season would not allow me to keep it."

We begged that if our supper was ready he would let us have it quickly.

"It is not only ready dressed," said he, "but well seasoned also;" upon which he skipped into the kitchen, and returned in a few minutes with two plates, in one of which was a salad, and in the other a part of the pluck of this much-lamented calf.

My companion seemed to fancy the salad, for which I cared but little, but fell on the pluck, which looked tolerably good. All that I complained of was, that there was but very little of it for two such hungry fellows; for no sooner had I touched a bit than I bolted it down, and I was so hungry that I had no time to judge of what I was eating. The muleteer, observing from the manner in which I set to that I should soon empty the plate, quitted his salad that he might at all events dispute the last mouthfuls with me, which were demolished in a moment. We called for another plate, but our provoking host brought us less than before to sharpen our appetites, so that we might still wish for more; this second plate therefore amused us but a very short time, and was followed by a third.

Being by this time, however, about half satisfied, I found myself obliged to slacken my pace; neither did I think it so good as before. I desired our host therefore to let me have anything else that he might have in the house; he answered that if we pleased he would make an exquisite ragout of the calf's brains in an instant; in the meantime he sent us up an *andouille* made of the tripe and caul of the same beast, which he told us we should find most delicious eating; but I could not entertain so favorable an opinion of it when I had tasted it, for it savored so strongly of rotten straw that I was fain to leave it to my companion, who still went on at the same rate, and demolished the whole of the *andouille* in the twinkling of an eye.

At length the ragout of brains was served up, which I

hoped would have revived my appetite; it was dressed with eggs, so that it was a kind of omelet, which the impudent muleteer had no sooner noticed than he set up another of his hearty laughs; this offended me, for I thought that he wished to disgust me with this omelet by putting me in mind of the one I had dined off. I gave him to understand as much, at which he only laughed the more, which produced a pleasant scene enough; for our host, who neither knew why he laughed nor why I was so angry, listened to us attentively, thinking himself concerned in the affair. Not feeling his conscience quite at rest respecting either the brains, the *andouille,* or the other dish with which he had regaled us, he was under as much apprehension as a criminal who is afraid of everything he hears; and his fears redoubled when he heard me threaten the muleteer if he continued laughing at me to throw the brains against the wall. Our host turned pale at these words, thinking that we meant to accuse him; but wishing to appear firm and resolute, he came up to us, cocking his bonnet with a most furious look, and said:

"Before God, gentlemen, I will not submit to so much laughter; I do maintain, and ever will maintain, it to be good calf's brains. If you will not believe me I can produce evidence to prove the fact of more than a hundred persons who saw me kill the calf."

My companion and I were not a little surprised at the passion of a man whom we had not so much as thought of. The muleteer redoubled his laughter; and I could not refrain from following his example on the occasion, though from another cause I felt no great inclination for it at that time. This put our host completely out of countenance, who doubting no longer that we had detected his villany became more furious, and snatching the plate rudely from the table,

"You may go laugh and eat elsewhere," said he, "for I will no longer entertain people who make a jest of me to my face; you have only to pay me therefore and leave my house; after which you have my permission to laugh as long as you please."

My comrade, who was still hungry, and did not see the plate handed off without regret, finding it no joke, said to the host in a voice not the most agreeable:

"What ails you, friend? has anyone been asking your age? has anyone been calling you chucklehead?"

"Chucklehead or not," replied our host, "I affirm it is a most excellent calf's head."

He pronounced these words as if he intended to thrash us both; but the muleteer, who knew him better than I, and who was a good match for him, rose from the table, and taking upon himself the braggadocio in his turn, "S'death!" cried he, "is there any law that prescribes how much a man may laugh in this inn? or is there any tax laid upon laughing?"

"I never said that there was," replied the host, apparently somewhat more mild. "I only say that I will not be turned into ridicule in my own house, nor be made to pass for one who treats his guests ill."

"Who says anything of ill-treatment?" replied the muleteer; "who thinks of turning you into ridicule? Be quick and replace the ragout of brains on the table, and you shall soon see that it was not that we laughed at. I cannot see, however, what objection you can have to allow persons to laugh or cry as much as they please in your house as well as elsewhere."

The muleteer's speech had its effect; the delicious ragout which had been thus torn from us was returned, and we were all very friendly again. My companion resumed his seat, and continuing to address himself to the host.

"Be assured," said he, "that had I been laughing at you, my character is such that I should not have concealed the cause from you: we were not laughing at you; but the sort of omelet you have dressed us reminded me of an adventure my little comrade here had today in an inn where he dined."

If the muleteer had been content to stop there, I should have got well off; but I was obliged to listen patiently for the third time to his relation of the history of the two soldiers, together with my adventure, which he recited to our host with such glee that he seemed never to be in his element but when telling that story.

Our host had time enough to recover his temper before this long story was finished; and judging that he had been alarmed without cause, he thought proper to commence playing another character, and interrupted the muleteer every moment while his story was telling, by—"Holy Virgin! Great God of Heaven!" and other such exclamations, which made the house to ring again, and which were accompanied by the most hypocritical grimaces.

"May God punish," said he, when the muleteer had done speaking, "all who do not perform their duty!"

As his duty was to thieve, and he could not be accused of neglecting it, he did not appear to consider himself at all concerned in this imprecation. After this he continued silent for some time, walking up and down the room; but suddenly breaking forth with a thundering voice.

"How is it possible," cried he, "that the earth hath not yet opened itself to swallow up that house and the wretched woman that keeps it? I have never met with any traveler yet but complained both of her and her provisions: not a passenger goes out of her doors but curses her, and makes oath never to stop at her inn again. If the officers of justice, whose duty it is to put a stop to her practices, suffer her to go on without notice, they know very well what they are about. Good God! in what times we do live!"

Here this honest man sighed deeply and kept silent, to give us to understand that he thought more than he chose to say, and I was in hopes that he would not have annoyed us any longer in this manner; but I was much mistaken. He went on again more violently than before upon the old woman's knavery, in a harangue which occupied a long half hour; after which he finished by saying:

"I return a thousand thanks to Heaven, that I bear no resemblance to that cursed old hag, and that I am a man of probity and honor, that I may hold up my head in any part of the world without fearing the least reproach from any man. Poor as I am, nothing of that sort goes on in my house; everything, thank God, is here sold for what it really is, and not a cat for a hare, nor a sheep for a lamb. Let no one give up his mind to cheating others, for he only cheats himself in the end. He who deals ill must expect ill treatment in return."

Happily for the muleteer and myself our host was obliged to stop here from want of breath. I took advantage of this opportunity to ask if he had any fruit? He answered that he had got some very fine olives. During the time that he was gone to fetch them my comrade made an end of the dish of calf's brains, which I could not much relish, thinking it too much like the *andouille;* but this did not prevent its being entirely demolished. No hungry wolf ever fed more greedily than the muleteer, whose appetite seemed never to be appeased: we had been at least an hour at table, and his appetite seemed to continue as sharp as when we first sat down. For my part I relished the olives extremely, which, as well as the wine, were excellent; as to the bread, though bad enough, it was much better than what I had met with at dinner.

Such was our supper, and as we intended to set out early the next morning we desired our host to get our breakfast ready in time; we then laid ourselves down on some straw, after having spread thereon some of our mule furniture to serve to cover us and keep us warm. The fatigue of our journey and the quantity of wine I had drank made me sleep so soundly that, although I was bit by the fleas that fed on me all night, they were not able to rouse me, and I verily believe I should have slept till the next evening if the muleteer had not awaked me at break of day, giving me notice that it was time to think of our departure. I was soon ready, having only to shake off the bits of straw that were sticking about my hair; but the fleas had left me in such a condition that I looked like a young monster, having so disfigured my face that I might well have been taken for one who had just recovered from the small-pox. If I had been transported to the market-place of Seville, I doubt whether any of my friends would have recognized me.

It being Sunday we began the day by going to mass, after which we returned to the inn, where my hungry companion had not forgotten to order breakfast; it was the first thing he thought of after he was up.

"Gentlemen," said our landlord, "I have stewed you a piece of the same veal that you supped off last night, and I have taken great pains to cook it to your satisfaction."

The muleteer, whose mouth watered at this speech, placed himself at table in a trice and commenced an attack upon the ragout, which appeared to him as delicate as peacock's flesh. For my part, either because I had no appetite so early in the morning, or that I had eaten too much supper the preceding night, I did nothing for some time but look at him, without feeling the least inclination to follow his example; but finding that he enjoyed it as if it were the finest dish in the world, and fearing that I might possibly have reason to repent at dinner of not having partaken of so good a breakfast, I made an effort to swallow a few mouthfuls; but instead of finding them so savory as my companion seemed to fancy them, there was something in them extremely disagreeable to my palate; as for the seasoning, as our host had good reasons for being prodigal of his pepper and salt, it seized hold of the throat, so that I was obliged to give over as soon as I had tasted it; in addition to which the flesh was so hard that I could not help remarking that I thought the meat as tough as leather, adding that I did not consider that it had altogether the taste of veal.

"Don't you see," said our host, who heard what I said, and who, in spite of his impudence, could not refrain from blushing a little—"don't you see," said he, "that it has not been kept long enough to be tender?"

The muleteer, who believed what the landlord advanced,

or at least thought that I was too delicate, answered in a jeering tone of voice:

"That is not the reason; but our young gentleman of Seville has always been accustomed to be fed with new-laid eggs and cracknels, so that he finds fault with everything else."

I contented myself by shrugging up my shoulders at this bantering of my comrade's, and said not a word, not knowing whether I was not actually too dainty, or, what is more probable, beginning to feel so queer that I almost fancied myself in the other world. I could not make up my mind to touch this meat again, but was occupied with numerous thoughts far above my age. I recollected the passionate behavior of our host at our laughter at supper the evening before, the unnecessary oaths that he made on the occasion; and as a man undoubtedly renders himself suspected who is anxious to justify himself before he is accused, I considered that there must be some knavery in the business. When my imagination was once thus prepossessed against him, the very sight and smell of his veal ragout quite turned my stomach, so that, not being able to remain much longer, I rose from table and waited patiently until the muleteer did the same, which was very shortly afterwards. Although the piece of veal was such as required a most determined assailant to get through it, my companion appeared to have made but a slight repast of it, after which I requested him to get the reckoning of our host to ascertain what each had to pay, but he answered me in an obliging manner that it was such a trifle that I was not to think of it, for that he would take care to see it settled.

This generous behavior from a man of his rank in life surprised me extremely, or rather charmed me. Had I been in different circumstances I could not in honor have allowed this man to pay for me, but my purse was so low that it did not either become or suit me to refuse his generosity. I allowed him therefore, without ceremony, to discharge the reckoning, and by way of return I assisted him in every way in my power in getting his mules ready for our journey. I would have done almost anything for him, so much was I affected by his noble behavior towards me.

CHAPTER V

THE LANDLORD STEALS GUZMAN'S CLOAK. A GREAT UPROAR AT THE INN

To enable myself the better to assist my friend the muleteer in getting his mules ready for our journey, I threw my cloak off, which I folded up, and placed on a bench; but, about a quarter of an hour afterwards, happening to look that way, I perceived that my cloak was no longer there. This alarmed me at first; but I did not vex myself extremely about it, thinking that either our host or the muleteer had concealed it from me for the purpose of amusing themselves by observing the anxiety it would occasion me.

I could not suspect anyone else of having played me this trick, for no other person had entered the stable whence my cloak had been taken. I inquired first of the muleteer, who told me that he never amused himself in that way. I then addressed myself to our host, who instantly had recourse to oaths to persuade me that he had no hand in the theft I complained of. Upon that I determined to search the house for it, and went over it from top to bottom, without forgetting the least corner in which it might be secreted, feeling firmly convinced in my own mind that our host was the one guilty of the theft, whose physiognomy alone sufficiently justified my presumption.

I came at last by chance to a backyard, the door of which I found some difficulty in opening, and the objects that I perceived there were sufficient to turn my mind for some minutes from thinking of my cloak. I observed upon the pavement a large pool of blood that had been but newly spilt, at the side of which lay the skin of a young mule, spread out, with the four feet still hanging to it, as well as the ears and head, which had been opened to take out the brains and the tongue. I beheld this sight not without horror, and said to myself:

"There, there lie the remains of our excellent veal; it is but proper that my companion should witness this sight with his own eyes, being at least as much interested in it as myself."

I ran to the stables where he was, and whispered to him that if he would accompany me I would show him something that would be well worth his trouble. He followed me to the back court, where I pointed out to him the remains of the two fine repasts that we had made.

"Well, my friend," said I, "and what do you say to all this? Do you still think that I feed upon nothing but fresh eggs and cracknels? Contemplate with voluptuousness this delicate calf, of which our host made for us those ragouts which you found so savory. You now see how that skillful cook of yours has regaled us."

The good muleteer was so ashamed that he had not a word to answer.

"This is, then," continued I, "the man of probity, who never sells cats for hares, sheep for lambs; but who at the same time makes no scruple of giving us a mule instead of a calf."

My companion, sad and pensive, returned to the stable, and I went to look for our host, to speak to him more stoutly, thinking that, to oblige him to restore my cloak, I had only to apprise him that I had discovered all his villainy, and to threaten to give notice to the magistrates; for it was prohibited by an express law, and under heavy penalties, for any person to have a mule in his possession, the breeding of that animal being unlawful in Andalusia. Our host had cared but little about observing this law; for having about eight days before had a young mule out of an ass and a little Gallatian mare, whom he had trusted in the same stable together, he thought he might safely venture to pass it off upon travelers, who are generally very hungry, for veal.

I met him at the well in the yard, washing another piece

of this supposed veal, which he endeavored to hide as soon as he perceived me. I came up to him with a resolute air, and desired him in a determined tone to return me my cloak, or that I should immediately make my complaint elsewhere; but at these words, which did not frighten him in the least, he looked at me disdainfully, called me a little jackanapes, and threatened to whip me.

The loss of my cloak had not provoked me so much as this behavior of his; so that, giving myself up to my resentment, without considering the inequality of our strength, I answered that he was nothing but a thief and a knave, and that I dared him to touch me. He appeared stung by my answer, and made up to me as if to put his threat in execution; but without waiting for this giant (for he was one in comparison with myself), I took up a large stone and threw it at his head, but fortunately for him it only just grazed one of his ears. Instead, however, of closing with me and crushing me with the weight of his body, he ran to his chamber, whence he returned in an instant with a long naked sword in his hand. Far from flying before this bravo I began to reproach him in the most abusive terms, upbraiding him as a coward and poltroon, for not being ashamed to make use of a sword against a young boy who had no other weapon than a stone to defend himself with.

All the servants ran out to see what was the matter, and were not a little frightened to see their master with a drawn sword in his hand. My comrade, who bore a spite against the scoundrel for the abominable ragout that he had been made to eat, came up to my assistance with a pitchfork, so that (the muleteer and I of the one part, the host, his wife, children, and servants of the other), we made such an uproar between us that anyone passing must have thought there was some desperate work going forward in the inn. All the neighbors were alarmed and came to the house, where they knocked at the door, but not waiting for its being opened from within they broke it open, that they might the sooner ascertain the cause of the horrid tumult they heard, then entered a troop of the police with numerous armed attendants and the *alcaids,* for on account of the wickedness of the inhabitants there were two *alcaids* in this town of Cantillana.

These two *alcaids* had no sooner got into the house with their followers than each of them pretended that the cognizance of this affair belonged to him alone, which formed two parties. The armed attendants were also divided according to their different interests, and their division excited a furious dispute amongst them. As the quarrel grew worse the noise grew louder, till at last no one could hear himself speak; the two parties grew so warm that they no longer scrupled to betray each other's feelings, but allowed the most unpleasant truths to escape them. From these revilings they would probably have proceeded to blows if some honest inhabitants of the town, who had entered the inn at the same time with them, had not interfered and reconciled them; which being accomplished, God knows how, nothing remained but to ascertain the cause of our quarrel, and as a cord always breaks first where it is weakest they began by seizing hold of me. I was a stranger, without favor and without acquaintance—Justice therefore could not fail to begin with me.

Let me, however, give these *alcaids* their due, for they certainly did not send me to prison without a hearing. I related to them in a simple manner the subject of my dispute with our host respecting my cloak; then, taking them apart, I added the story of the mule, informing them that they would still find that animal's skin in the back court, and some pieces stewing in the kitchen. Upon this last article of my deposition, my judges forgot all about my cloak, and repaired to the back court, after having, by way of precaution, seized our host, who did nothing but laugh, thinking that it was all about the cloak, which no one had seen him take; but when the mule's hide and other appurtenances were brought forward in judgment against him, he became in an instant as pale as a condemned criminal, and during his examination confessed even more than he was accused of; unluckily for me, however, my

79

cloak was the only subject on which he remained firm: the rascal, from a spirit of revenge, would not confess he had stolen it.

The *alcaids* sent this rogue to prison, which gave me some pleasure in the midst of my troubles; I say in the midst, for I had not yet got over them. The *alcaids'* clerks, a sort of people quite as humane as they are disinterested, thinking that I was of a good family and might have a rich father, recommended the *alcaids* in the most Christian manner to detain me also at all chances. This advice, which was much approved of by my judges, would certainly have been followed, had not the citizens who were present opposed so great an injustice by saying aloud that, if that were done, I should be punished merely for having done my duty. The murmurs of these honest men prevailed for this once over the good will of the officers of justice, who pardoned me through policy.

The muleteer, who had been witness to all that had passed, and was not a little apprehensive that they would seize his mules and him, whispered me to leave as quickly as I was able this blessed part of the country, where a man need not think himself badly off if he escaped with the loss of his cloak only. I approved of his advice; we mounted our beasts in haste and rode out of the inn-yard. . . .

BOOK THE SECOND

CHAPTER I

GUZMAN BECOMES AN INNKEEPER'S BOY

BEHOLD me now, friendly reader, in the best inn at Cazalla, twelve leagues from Seville, where the money I had left was sufficient to pay for a good supper and a good bed to lie down on. Instead, however, of enjoying a profound sleep, which such excellent fare was calculated to procure me, the state of my affairs presented itself to my imagination in a thousand distressing forms, and prevented me from sleeping a wink the whole of the night.

"Hitherto," said I to myself, "I have always had plenty to eat and drink. But this will now soon be over. When a man has bread to eat he may support himself under any affliction. 'Tis well to have a father; 'tis well to have a mother; but nothing is to be compared to a good bellyfull."

Necessity with her heretic visages now stared me full in the face, and occasioned the most terrible apprehensions in my mind; and I would gladly have returned to Seville, had I not considered that money was quite as necessary to repair my folly as to pursue my fortune. I could compare myself to nothing but some half-starved cur, who, having lost his way, finds himself surrounded by a number of larger dogs barking and growling at him on all sides. In addition to this, how could I without shame return to my mother's house after having left it with so much resolution. The loss of my cloak also recurred to my remembrance,

81

which I imagined would be a fine subject for ridicule on my return. This last consideration was sufficient to determine me not to return to Seville; in addition to which I was not less concerned that I must stop when I was in so fair a way.

A point of honor then seized me, and I resolved to continue my journey, abandoning myself to Providence. I took the direct road to Madrid, the ordinary residence of our kings, hoping to see something of the Court, which I had been told was most brilliant from the great number of noblemen that composed it, and above all from the presence of a young king newly married. All this excited my curiosity, and I encouraged the most flattering ideas, building castles in the air without number. I fancied that a lad of my air and figure would soon be noticed in such a country, where I should soon make friends, and could not fail of making my fortune. Full of these deceitful visions I had little inclination to sleep, and lay expecting the day with impatience. But no sooner had it arrived, and I had set out for Madrid, than all these chimeras vanished, leaving nothing before my eyes but a long and tedious journey.

"Courage, Signor Guzman," said I to myself; "consider that you cannot now retreat. Keep up your spirits, therefore, my friend, and do your best whatever may happen. Instead of having a cloak upon your shoulders, which would only incommode you at this time of the year, be content that you have a good stick which will assist you in walking."

I passed the whole day without eating, and at night laid myself down on the grass at the foot of a large tree, where I fell asleep from fatigue, and did not wake until the sun had risen the next morning, when I began to feel that I could have made a very hearty breakfast if I had had any provisions; but not having even a morsel of the coarsest bread, I found myself obliged to set forward again upon an empty stomach, and with an appetite increasing every moment. Towards night, my hunger became such, that I could scarcely walk from weakness. In vain did my stomach plead its emptiness; my legs seemed unwilling to support my weight any farther.

Just at this moment two gentlemen who by their looks seemed to be rich merchants, trotted briskly past me upon mules.

"Thank God!" thought I, "here are two gentlemen who will in all probability defray my charges today."

The hope of obtaining a good meal at their expense inspired me with fresh strength, and I resolved not to lose sight of them. A meal was now of the most serious consideration for me. With this impression I followed them so closely that we arrived together at the inn where they stopped. I looked more dead than alive when I came up with them; yet, tired as I was, I showed myself disposed to make myself useful by holding the bridles of their mules while they alighted, and offering my services to carry their portmanteau with a bag containing their provisions into their apartments. But, whether my officiousness rendered me suspected by them, or that they were naturally rough and distrustful, no sooner had I laid my hands on the bag than one of them called out to me in a voice which made me tremble from head to foot:

"Out of the way, boy! stand off!"

I obeyed without making any answer to this disagreeable reception, and formed but a bad presage in favor of the gratification of my appetite; but determined not to be so easily got rid of. I therefore walked behind them to their room in a very humble manner, with my hat in my hand. They had brought good provisions with them, as is customary in Spain. I saw a roast shoulder of mutton drawn from their bags, with part of a ham, some bread and wine. This only increased my extreme desire to serve them. To obtain their favor, therefore, I advanced towards the table and took up a glass, intending to rinse it for their use, but the other merchant, who had not yet spoken, snatched it from me, saying in a rougher manner than his friend:

"No, no, leave that glass alone. We have no occasion for your services."

"O traitors!" thought I, "enemies to God and man!

hearts of flint! I find that I have exhausted my breath and strength to little purpose in following you hither."

I resolved, however, not to leave them, in the hope that they might feel more charitably disposed when their bellies were full, and throw me a bone to pick, or even a bit of bread, out of compassion. I was again mistaken; they continued eating without deigning to cast a look towards me. I devoured their provisions with my eyes all this time; but this would not satisfy my craving appetite. To complete my mortification, I saw these monsters put up the remains of their dinner in their wallet, even to the smallest bit of bread, with which they left the inn. What barbarity! what a sight for a lad starving with hunger! I was ready to run distracted with grief and inanition when a friar of the order of St. Francis entered the room in which I stood.

I conceived but little hope of relief from this quarter. What assistance could I expect from a poor monk who traveled on foot, from a begging friar who seemed himself to stand in need of assistance? He perspired freely, and appeared much fatigued. He brought a wallet with him, which he placed on the table, and upon which I fixed the most attentive and eager looks. I could have stolen it even from the altar; it made my mouth water before I knew its contents. When his reverence took out his provisions, which consisted of a large loaf of white bread, and a piece of salt beef, which I would have longed for even at my mother's table, I fixed my eyes upon them, and stood in an ecstacy with my mouth wide open. How did I wish that I had been his little brother! I fancied that I felt in my own throat every morsel that he swallowed.

He happened to look at me by chance in the course of his meal, and perceiving what I wanted, for my looks spoke, " Good God! " cried he, animated by a holy zeal, " approach, my child; I will not allow thee to languish from want; though I had but this bit of bread, it should be thine. Here, my son," added he, giving me half his bread and meat, " take a little nourishment. I were unworthy to exist did I not share with thee."

84

THE SPANISH ROGUE

O Providence! who makest many of Thy creatures to subsist even in stone, Thy Divine goodness never forsakes us! I implored blessings on the head of the reverend father for this act of chartiy towards me, and began to show him that he was not deceived in my half-starved appearance; and being now pretty well replenished, I returned thanks to Heaven for this fortunate rencounter. How pleased should I have been had I been doomed to travel any distance with this friar! My fate would have been enviable; but, as chance would have it, he was going to Seville, so that we parted immediately after dinner. Before we separted he put his hand into his wallet and gave me half of another small loaf, saying, that I should have my full share of all he had. I put up this last half-loaf in my pocket, and after having eaten the first with the beef, and drank some good, fresh water, for the good friar had nothing better to offer me, I set out again in good spirits towards Madrid.

I traveled about three leagues farther during the day, and in the evening reached Campanis, a large village in New Castile, where I entered an inn, and supped upon the half-loaf I brought with me, having nothing better to eat. This inn was where the muleteers of Tuxillo lodged, for whom all the beds were engaged, and who came in towards night. The landlord allotted me a lodging in the hay-loft. whither I mounted very contentedly, not being in a situation to make any difficulties. I stretched myself on the straw, and slept soundly until daybreak, when I rose with a light stomach, which, as you will recollect, was by no means overloaded the preceding night, and had already got out of the inn, when the rascally landlord was uncivil enough to stop me, demanding payment for my night's lodging, for which he charged four *maravedis*. As I had not even one in the world, I struggled to escape from his grasp, but he held me fast, and perceiving that my coat was made of good cloth, he was on the point of taking it off, by way of settling the dispute, had not a muleteer who was standing by taken pity on me.

"Leave the lad alone," said he to the host, "I will pay for him. I see how the matter stands; this young man has run away either from his father's or his master's house."

At these words the landlord looked at me, and asked me if I was disposed to serve him, having occasion for the assistance of a boy like me in his inn.

At any other time such a proposal would have appeared ridiculous to me, and I should have been offended at it; but misery relieves one from such scruples, and reconciles the greatest hardships. After having considered for a few moments, the prospect of starvation made me accept his offer.

"Enter my house, then," said he; "there are but two things I shall require of you: to give out the oats and straw to the passengers, and to be sure to render me a good and faithful account."

I promised to acquit myself in this noble post to the utmost of my abilities, after which I was engaged beyond the power of retracting.

However hard service was to me, who had hitherto been accustomed to be waited upon myself, I was at first tolerably well content with my situation. Very few gentlemen passed that way in the course of the day, so that, generally, I had nothing to do but to eat and drink until night, when the muleteers arrived. I soon learnt all the manœuvres of inns; how to swell the corn to three times its quantity with boiling water, and how to measure it out afterwards to the best advantage. There was no occasion to point out to me more than once the peculiar construction of the mangers, for after one attempt I well knew how to watch my opportunity to deprive the passengers of at least a third part of the corn they paid for, and even the muleteers did not always escape; but when by chance any young cavaliers distinguished by their insignia and the nice cut of their whiskers, happened to stop at our house without servants, we were particularly assiduous in our attentions. No sooner did we perceive them than we ran out to assist them to alight.

These young gentlemen, for the most part, affecting to be persons of great importance, would not condescend to enter the stable, but were content to recommend their horses or mules to our care, which recommendation had so powerful an effect that we never failed to lead the poor beasts where there was neither hay nor a single grain of corn. We tied them to the rack and left them to their meditations. Occasionally, however, out of pity, we gave them a handful of corn, just by way of a *bon-bouche*, before their departure, though of this scanty pittance the poultry in the yard caught up half, and sometimes even the jackass got his share of it.

In this manner were all those cavaliers served who relied upon our honesty; and if we made them pay well for what their beasts had never eaten, judge in what manner we charged them for their own expenses. I was overjoyed when it fell to my lot to reckon with them. "Your bill amounts to so many *reals,*" said I, "and so many *maravedis,*" adding in a graceful manner: *"Y haga les luen provecho "*—" Much good may it do you "—a compliment which always procured for me something for myself. You will very easily believe that we always charged this sort of customers twice as much as they owed, in spite of all the regulations of the police, to which my master paid little attention, though they were fixed up all over his house. He was satisfied with having them in his possession, and so long as he was able to pay the officers their dues, he cared but little about observing their ordinances.

The more experienced travelers always paid without hesitation whatever was demanded, knowing that it was useless to contend; but others who thought themselves more cunning would frequently have the landlord called that they might reckon with him. On these occasions, our master, for fear of doing himself wrong, always increased the price of every article; and when he had once taxed the bill at a ceratin amount his sentence was without appeal, and they were obliged to draw their purse-strings. Woe to that traveler who presumes to complain of his treatment, and to threaten an innkeeper in Spain for having cheated him. As they are almost all of them members of the Holy Brotherhood, he will be sure to cause him to be arrested at the first village through which he passes, accusing him either of a design to burn his house to the ground, of having assaulted him, or of having violated his wife or his daughter, so that the poor traveler may esteem himself more than ordinarily happy if he got off by paying double what was before demanded of him, after having begged pardon of his landlord into the bargain.

There were several pretty servant-maids in our inn, but it was, dangerous to have anything to say to them. It was well for those who had their wits about them when they left the house; for whatever happened by chance to be forgotten and left behind was sure never to be heard of again. What roguery! what infamous tricks what wickedness is constantly going on at these inns! God is not feared, and justice is compounded with. One would think that when a man becomes an innkeeper he is at liberty to do what he pleases, and has an absolute power over the property as well as the persons of such as are obliged to stop at his house.

CHAPTER II

GUZMAN BECOMES DISGUSTED WITH HIS SITUATION, LEAVES THE INN, AND REPAIRS TO MADRID, WHERE HE ASSOCIATES WITH SOME BEGGARS

BESIDES that I was of too flighty a disposition to be long contented in the same way of life, I could not consider the one that I now led by any means suitable to a spirited lad who had left his mother's house for the sole purpose of seeing the world. In addition to this, the servant of an innkeeper ranked lower in my opinion than that of a blind beggar. I saw every day boys of about my own age and size pass our door, who, after having asked alms, went gaily along the road again. This sight roused my feelings.

"What," said I to myself, "does the dread of hunger hold me here, while these young fellows, who have no more resolution than I ought to be master of, expose themselves courageously to hunger and thirst! I am in all probability as well deserving as they, and ought not, therefore, to be less courageous."

These reflections inspired me with resolution, and defying fortune, I again set out for Madrid, after having demanded my dismissal of my master, who gave me three *reals* for my services during the time I had been with him.

With this money, and the little I had saved from the liberality of our customers,. I was able to advance as far as the celebrated bridge of Arcolis upon Zagus, whence I pursued my route as the others had done, by holding out my hand in every village through which I passed, and to every gentleman I met; but the harvest had been so extremely bad that year that people in general were but little disposed to be charitable. I was therefore soon obliged to sell my clothes, so that I cut a most elegant figure when I reached that celebrated capital of Spain. I was reduced to a tattered pair of breeches, with a shirt black and torn, a pair of stockings with a thousand holes in them, and shoes which had no other soles than those of my feet. I looked more like a fellow just escaped from the galleys, than a gentleman's son of good family, and could not possibly. hope to be employed in any gentleman's service, which was now the height of my ambition.

My miserable appearance was not calculated to prepossess any one in my favor, and he must have been a bold man indeed who could have made up his mind to admit me into his house. No one could look at me attentively without saying in his own mind, There is a young chap who only wants the opportunity to perform some desperate trick. At length, finding that my appearance was such that no one would receive me either as page, footman, or even as a turnspit, I turned my eyes towards a company of beggars

whom I perceived at a church door. I considered them
with attention, and they seemed so healthy and void of care
that I thought I could not do better than enroll myself in
their company. I joined them accordingly, and was received by them as a member whose mien and equipage were
not unworthy of their fraternity.

Before I reached Madrid I had taken good care to leave
all my modesty on the road, as a load too heavy for a foot-
passenger to carry about with him. If I had not ere this
got rid of this cruel enemy to hunger, I should soon have
lost every speck of it in the company of these good folks,
who were severally and collectively the most complete birds
of prey. I followed them everywhere, acting as a sort of
assistant to them, until I should become sufficiently experienced to contribute my share towards making the pot
boil, in which there never failed to be plenty. Twice a day
we had a fine dish of soup, of which I was sure to partake,
provided I attended punctually to the hours of dinner and
supper, otherwise, being only on underling, I should have
found nothing but the empty tureen for my share.

After supper we generally sat down to play; I soon
learned the games of quince, one and thirty, quinola and
primera, with a thousand tricks on the cards. I had so
happy a knack, and my disposition was so well suited to
this science, that I made visible progress under these excellent masters. Little as I was, I felt desirous to imitate
some of my companions, who, lest they should be punished
as vagrants, posted themselves with baskets in the different
markets, offering the citizens to carry home for them the
provisions they might purchase. This employment appeared
rather laborious to me at first, but I soon got so well accustomed to it that I thought no man's lot preferable to my
own.

"How charming," thought I, "to live thus in plenty,
without being obliged to use either needle or thread, the
hammer or the thimble; nothing but a basket and a little
industry being necessary for subsistence! The life of a
beggar is a delicacy without bone, and uninterrupted stream

of pleasure, an employment exempt from trouble and vexation. How void of sense must my ancestors have been to
have taken so much pains to live in wretchedness! In
how many perplexities have they been involved for the sake
of supporting their commerce and reputation! O absurd
honor of this world, thou art but a millstone to sink such
fools as consent to be burdened with thee!"

One day as I was carrying home a quarter of mutton
in my basket for an honest shoemaker who walked before
me, I picked up a paper which I perceived lying in the
street, containing some verses of an old ballad, which I
began to read and sing to myself. The shoemaker, surprised to hear me, said with a smile:

"What, you ill-looking little dog, can you read?"

"And write, too," answered I.

"Is it possible?" cried he, much astonished. "If you
will teach me merely to sign my name, I will pay you well
for your trouble."

I asked of what possible use the knowing how to sign
his name only could be to him, and he told me that having
obtained a good situation through the influence of a certain
person, whom he named, whose family he had supplied with
shoes *gratis,* he should be glad to be able to sign his name
when necessary, that he might not be obliged to confess
that he could not write.

As soon as we entered his house he caused pen, ink, and
paper to be brought, and I commenced my occupation of
writing-master, showing my scholar how to hold his pen,
and guiding his hand. I then made him form the letters
that composed his name so many times over, that he fancied
he had already acquired the elements of the art of writing.
After having scribbled over and blotted five or six sheets
of paper, he was so well satisfied, that he made me try on
a pair of new shoes, which fitted as if they had been made
for me, and which he presented me with. I then took leave
of him, assuring him that whenever I wanted a new pair
of shoes, I would call and give some further lessons to
make him quite perfect in his writing.

CHAPTER III

GUZMAN IS ENGAGED BY A COOK

I WAS well content in this new way of life, in which I enjoyed that liberty so eagerly desired by all the world, so boasted of by philosophers, and so often sung of by poets; I possessed that precious treasure which is preferable to gold and silver; but unfortunately I did not long retain it, for a cursed cook soon deprived me of it. This cook was one of my most constant employers.

"My friend," said he one day, "I am well pleased with you, and am willing to put you in the way of making your fortune; quit your idle companions, and come and fill the place of scullion at my master's, which is now vacant; I will myself teach you the duties of the kitchen out of friendship, and qualify you to become cook to the king himself. Happen what may, the very least advantage you can derive from a knowledge of this fine art is to enable you to return to your own country a rich man."

In short, he so completely cajoled me, that I willingly accepted his proposal.

He then conducted me to the hotel of the nobleman whom he served, where I took my post and my scullion's cap, that is, a nightcap, with a white apron. The first thing that was given me was some parsley to shred, which is always considered like the alphabet to those who aspire to the higher degrees in the kitchen. The cook, my master, was a married man; he had a house in the neighborhood where his wife lived, and where we both went home to sleep every night; but I passed the principal part of the day at the hotel, where I was always ready to oblige everybody. My activity and good-nature soon gained me the esteem of my fellow-servants of both sexes. I performed their commissions with punctuality, secrecy, and fidelity, and was rewarded by many small gratifications in return. In the kitchen I performed my duty to admiration, and my master was so well satisfied with me, that he often said I was born to tread in his footsteps.

I grant that all this cost me no small trouble, but then I was amply recompensed by the many advantages that my exertions procured me. Next to the profession of begging, which is undoubtedly the most charming condition of civilized society, I could not possibly fare better than I did in this kitchen; having been bred to good cheer, I felt myself completely in my element. No plate came in or went out of the kitchen but I had a lick at it, no sauce but what I tasted, and I can assure you my master made most exquisite ragouts. The cooks of St. Giles's, of St. Dominick, of the Gate of Sun, the great Market Place and Toledo Street, must excuse me if I rank him far above them in this art, notwithstanding the high reputation they have established.

I might have been perfectly happy had I resisted the opportunity of gaming; but I could not long withstand the temptation of joining the lackeys and pages, who were at cards almost the whole of the day. At first I spent only now and then a quarter of an hour with them, or half an hour at the utmost; but when I found that my natural inclination for this cursed habit was not sufficiently satisfied by day, I was induced to steal from my master's house in the night-time, as soon as I believed him to be asleep, for the purpose of joining my companions at the hotel, with whom I generally remained until sunrise the next morning. If my master had been informed of my conduct he would undoubtedly have horse-whipped me handsomely; but no one apprised him of it, for fear of getting me into trouble.

Meantime I lost all the money that I had earned in the execution of commissions, without losing my taste for gaming—on the contrary, my desire for play increased daily, and I was induced to steal to supply me with means; this I had never yet been guilty of, although I well knew that, from my master downwards, all the servants in the hotel were in the habit of appropriating to their own use everything they could lay their hands on. Every one took good care of himself and what is more surprising, though they were all well aware of each other's practices, no one ever impeached the rest, but kept the secret which equally affected them all.

Though I had not been a gamester from inclination, and though I had not been from nature eagerly disposed to possess myself of the property of another, these examples alone would have been more than sufficient to corrupt me. I soon began, therefore, to follow the fashion. I cast my eyes with eagerness all over the house, and whatever I could pilfer without being observed was soon converted into money; but, unfortunately for me, I had no sooner acquired it than I lost it again at play.

In addition to the opportunities which presented themselves to me to exercise my sleight-of-hand at the hotel, which might be compared to a sea open to all sorts of fisherman, I had my master's private house, which, though indeed but a small river, in which it was not likely to take fish of any considerable size, yet afforded me one day tolerable good sport. My master regaled some of his friends, all good bottle-companions and fond of good cheer like himself, with a collation one afternoon, treating them with *andouilles* and hams, which caused them to drink three times as much as usual. During this entertainment I was at the hotel, and when I had finished my work, returned home to see if I was wanted. The visitors were already gone, and I found the parlor intolerably hot and full of dust, the cloth still on the table, and the floor strewed with empty bottles, most of them broken. My master, whom I did not see, but whom I heard plain enough, was snoring on his bed so loud as to make the whole house ring with the noise; and my mistress, who was about as sober as her husband, lay by him sleeping as sound as a top.

I contemplated for some moments the remains of this debauch, when I happened to cast my eyes on a silver goblet which stood on the table, and resolved to steal it. I was certain that nobody had seen me come in, and I could leave the house again equally unobserved. This reflection was sufficient to determine me: "With your leave, Mr. Goblet," whispered I, putting it into my pocket, "you shall pay me for these broken bottles;" then closing the door softly after me, I placed my booty in a safe place, and returned to the hotel as though nothing had happened. Towards evening my master came into the kitchen, somewhat recovered of his debauch, but in so peevish a humor that he complained of the merest trifles, and immediately began to quarrel with me for having a fagot too much on the fire. I made no answer, but accompanied him home after supper, where he immediately went to bed. As to his wife, she had so comfortable a nap that she was now as composed as usual, except that she appeared dull and vexed about something. I inquired the cause with as much effrontery as if I had been entirely ignorant of it. She informed me that she could not find the goblet, telling me at the same time that it was not the value of the thing that she regretted, but the passion that her husband would be in when he missed it, from whom she should never hear the last of it.

I endeavored to console her—not to the utmost of my power, for nobody was so well able as myself had I been disposed—but by representing to her that this goblet was not of so singular a manufacture but that a fellow to it might be found in Madrid; that she had nothing therefore to do but to purchase another of the same make and fashion, telling her husband that it was the same which she had had fresh-washed, or that it was a new one she had bought by giving the other and a few *reals* in exchange.

She approved of my advice, and requested me to endeavor to procure one for her; and so next day I carried the stolen goblet itself to a goldsmith's a good way off from our house, desiring him to have it washed, which he promised to get done in such a manner for me that it should appear as good as new. I communicated this good news to my mistress.

"Madam," said I, "I have been fortunate enough to find a goblet at a jeweler's shop exactly resembling the one you have lost, but the quality and fashion of it are so excellent that the very lowest price at which it can be procured is fifty-six *reals*."

Anxious to avert the storm that threatened her, she counted me out that sum without hesitation, and gave me half a *real* for my trouble. I accordingly carried the aforesaid goblet to her in the evening, which she thought so exactly like the other that she said she was convinced her husband would never know to the contrary.

The fruits of this worthy exploit enabled me to game afresh. It was, indeed, a considerable sum for a scullion to apply to such a purpose; but, alas! all these *reals* soon fell into the gulf which had already swallowed up the produce of my former knaveries. Those with whom I played were more experienced in the art than I was, although I had learnt among the beggars how to shift the cards, to make false cuts, and many other villainous tricks of the like nature.

About this time my master was desired to prepare an elegant dinner for a foreign prince who had newly arrived at Madrid. Early in the morning of the day preceding that on which this entertainment was to be given, the cook took me with him into the kitchen, where the purveyor had just sent provisions of every description necessary for the fête. We immediately began, before the others joined us, to set apart whatever we considered our dues of office, and soon filled a large sack with loins of veal, hams, tongues, and all kinds of fowls, which we concealed until night, when I was desired to convey it home as privately as possible. This I could not do without great fatigue, so heavily was I laden. I afterwards returned to the kitchen, where I found employment until midnight in preparing fowls for dressing on the next day, and after I had finished my work, my master charged me with the care of a second sack, contaning hares, pheasants, and partridges, saying:

"Here, Guzman, carry this home safely, and go to rest, my little friend; you will tell my wife that I know not how long it may be before I come home."

The liar! he knew well enough he should be obliged to remain all night at the hotel, where his presence was absolutely necessary to superintend the other cooks, who were actively engaged under his directions. But he was rather inclined to be jealous, although his wife was no beauty; and he only sent her this message to deceive her, that she might regulate her conduct accordingly.

The bustle and confusion in which our kitchen now was, in preparing to entertain the prince who was expected, would have formed a fine subject for a painter. Every one was in action, not only those employed in the kitchen, but also those who were constantly passing to and fro. We needed only to ask to have anything, which every one took care to do pretty freely. The provisions seemed to vanish as quickly as they appeared; one said, "Bring me sugar for the tarts," and another cried, "Bring me more tarts to be sugared." This it was with all the rest; nothing was necessary but to vary the manner of asking a little, to obtain anything twice or thrice over. We call these grand entertainments, jubilees, as though we thought to obtain indulgences by robbing the master whose bread we were eating. It is certain that the river overflowed on these occasions on all sides, and the fish swam in deep water. For my own part, being but a small sparrow-hawk, I waited patiently until the kites and other larger birds of prey had their talons full; in the meantime, however, my hands itched so immoderately, that I could not refrain from dipping into a basket of eggs, and slipped half a dozen of them into my pocket.

Ill luck still pursued me; my master saw me, and wishing to establish the reputation of an honest man and zealous servant at my expense, in the presence of so many of the house servants, he came up to me with a savage countenance, and gave me such a kick that he laid me sprawling on the ground, and as I happened to fall on that side where I had the pocketful of eggs, they all broke, and made an omelet which ran down my thighs, to the great amusement of the company present, with the exception of my master, who still looked very serious, and adding menaces and reproaches to insult, told me, that " he would teach me to steal in so great a lord's house."

I was so enraged at the behavior of this rascally cook towards me, that it was with great difficulty I refrained from answering, that nobody, indeed, could teach me better than himself; and that those eggs for which he had chastised me were laid by the fowls he had ordered me to carry home to his house the night before; but I held my tongue, and thereby escaped any further kicking, with which so laconic an answer would certainly have been rewarded. Take lesson from my behavior on this occasion, reader, if you happen to be so fortunate as to recollect it, when you feel desirious to show your wit by some satirical speech which may be of ill consequence to you in your future welfare.

Notwithstanding this unlucky accident, I managed afterwards to pocket unobserved two partridges, four quails, and half of a roast pheasant, with some sweetbreads of veal, which I secured less from interest than to try my dexterity; not being willing to have it said of me, that I had been at Court without seeing the king, or at a wedding without kissing the bride. The banquet being over, as my master and I were returning home together in the evening, he said to me:

" Guzman, my friend, think no more of what passed between us in the kitchen this morning; forget the kick I was obliged to give you; it behoved me more than you can imagine to treat you in this manner; it was a piece of policy for which I was sorry in the main. But think of it no longer, my lad, and to make you amends for this little accident I will make you a present of a new pair of shoes tomorrow."

This was an article I was so much in need of, that I was delighted with the promise, and my resentment against him instantly subsided. He did not, however, keep his word, being prevented by what happened the next day.

I went to bed, resolved to sell the game and veal sweetbreads I had stolen the next day. I rose so early in the morning, that I left my master in bed, and ran to the market, quite sure that I should have abundance of time to dispose of my merchandise, and still to get to the hotel before him. I soon found a purchaser in an old cook, whom I never fail to curse whenever I happen to think of him, who professed himself ready to buy whatever I had. I was so pressed for time that the bargain was soon struck; and I agreed to let him have my provisions for six *reals,* and was only waiting for my money to start off as swift as a roebuck; but this old dotard was as punctilious and slow as I was hasty and impatient. He must first put a register which he held in his hand under his arm, then take off his ragged gloves, and hang them to his girdle; after which he pulled out his spectacles and spent about half an hour in cleaning them to examine the money he was going to pay me.

In vain did I entreat him to make more haste, telling him I had an affair of consequence which called me elsewhere; he was deaf to my prayer. How long a time did he consume in untying his purse, and how many pieces of money did he amuse himself with looking at, one after another, before he began counting the money into my hands, by quarters and half quarters of *reals,* and even *maravedis;* all this almost drove me mad.

"What, old fumbler," muttered I between my teeth; "can such a trifling old cur wish to enrage me, or to amuse me here, until my master, who is already suspicious of me, and who, perhaps is at this moment looking everywhere for me come up and surprise me?"

This, it appears, I had more reason to apprehend than I imagined; the cook had heard me leave the house, and was much surprised at such extraordinary diligence; and suspecting that I had some new scheme in my head, he got up and dressed himself hastily that he might be at my heels; so that he stood immediately behind me at the very moment the old man had at last got over the ceremony of paying me.

"Ho! ho! my boy," cried my master, seizing me by the hand and taking the money, "what fine bargain is this you are making?"

At these words I stood more confounded than a smuggler who is caught in the fact. I made no reply, and was even patient enough to submit to another good kick, accompanied by a thousand reproaches. He did not leave me until he had forbidden me ever to enter his house again, and threatened to thrash me soundly if I was ever insolent enough to pass the door of the hotel. My friend the merchant, unluckily for him, remained on the spot until the close of this scene, which was in consequence little better for him than for me; for, attributing my present misfortune to this old sorcerer, I fell on him in my passion, and snatched my partridges and pheasants, telling him I was determined to have my own goods, and that he might get his money if he could from the knave who had run off with it. Thus saying I disappeared like a flash of lightning, to sell my game in some other market, leaving this phlegmatic old gentleman to his own thoughts upon the adventure, which he most probably considered a plan concerted between the cook and me to cheat him out of his money.

CHAPTER IV

FROM THE SERVICE OF THE COOK, GUZMAN RETURNS TO THE BEGGING TRADE, AND ROBS AN APOTHECARY

WISDOM is better than riches, since Fortune is but a fickle goddess, who bereaves us one day of what she has bestowed on us the preceding. During the course of our lives she makes us resemble comedians, who have every day new parts to study, and must appear in different characters. Who could have thought that after having served the cook so faithfully he would have turned me out of doors for so trifling an offence? It is true that thus the world wags, and that persons of much greater consequences than myself are constantly treated in the same manner by the great upon the most trivial occasion, after having rendered them a thousand services.

Stop, Guzman, cry you, or you will lose yourself in moral reflections. Whither will this learned discourse lead you? To my basket again, reply I; yes, my friend, to my basket, which, having now become to me as useful as eloquence was to Demosthenes, or stratagems to Ulysses, consoled me under by present misfortune. Long may the basket trade flourish, which a man having once tried will never fail to resume. I must candidly confess that when I returned to it I was much in the same condition as when I was fool enough to leave it; for all the produce of my former knaveries during the time I had been scullion had gone as lightly as it came, and, with the exception of a finer suit of clothes, I was no better off than before.

That my returning to my old employment, however, might not be attributed to my indolent and discontented disposition, I determined, before I purchased a new basket, to offer my services to some cooks of my master's acquaintance who knew me. If they had received me, it was my intention to have rendered myself thoroughly knowing in kitchen affairs, in which I had already made so good a beginning, and for which I might boast a most happy disposition; but they had heard of my inclination for gaming, and that nothing was safe within my reach when I wanted money, and thus, finding there was no chance of obtaining another situation of this description, I was compelled to resume my former occupation. I therefore took up my basket again; and though I did not fare so well among my comrades as at the hotel from which I had been dismissed, yet I was once more independent and completely master of my own actions. Being naturally sober, this sort of life was more adapted to my inclinations than the other, so that I had but little reason to regret leaving a house in which I was led into a thousand intemperances.

We basket-bearers had a small row of houses, or rather hovels, near the market, which we had bought at our own expense. Here it was that we usually regaled ourselves and held our merry meetings. I always got up with the sun, and was ready at everybody's call, by which means I never failed to secure a profitable day's work from such of the citizens as kept no servants, who employed me to carry home the provisions they purchased; and the faithful manner in which I performed their commissions soon established my credit in the several markets.

About this time commissions were issued to the different regiments to raise new levies. When anything of this nature happens the report soon gets abroad, the people assemble in every direction to discuss the subject, and a council of state is held in almost every house. In ours, as you may imagine, we canvassed the designs of the Court as freely as the best of them, and had some politicians among us whose conjectures were not very far from the truth.

Good sense is to be found in every condition. When we were all assembled at night each reported what he had heard or seen during the day in the principal families in the city, and we formed our opinions accordingly; and I can assure you that, though some among us reasoned absurdly, yet there were others, the solidity and good sense of whose arguments were fully justified by the occurrence of events which they predicted. I well remember that, among others, our fraternity could boast of a certain beggar with wooden legs, who never left his post on a bridge, where he begged the whole of the day, whose acquaintance with state affairs would have astonished a prime minister.

We concluded then that these new levies that were making, the destination of which was concealed, must be intended for Italy; and this, you will see, proved to be true. The first time I heard these troops mentioned they brought into my mind my intended journey to Genoa, and made such an impression on my spirits that I did not sleep a wink the whole night. I felt more anxious than ever to see my relations, from whom I did not doubt I should obtain a brilliant fortune, everybody telling me that they were exceedingly rich, and many of them without children, which latter I considered would be charmed to have an heir of so great merit as myself. To these flattering expectations, however, unpleasant ideas soon succeeded.

"How," thought I, "can I have the insolence to appear before these noble Genoese in this miserable dress? and though I tell them I am their kinsman, are they likely to credit my assertions? I hope they may be simple enough to believe me; but I fear they cannot fail to treat me like a rogue and an imposter, if only to support the honor of the family. Perhaps I may not escape even so well as this, for my father, who was thoroughly acquainted with the disposition of his countrymen, has often said that a Genoese is not to be trusted in any case where his interest or reputation is concerned.

"Still," thought I, "they may be honest like my father; and I am persuaded that they will entertain too great a respect for the memory of their deceased relative to refuse to assist me in my present distressing situation. They are too prudent to venture to treat me as an impostor before they have interrogated me as to our family affairs; and in this respect I shall be well able to answer, for I can tell them such particulars as none but my father's son could possibly be acquainted with, and which, being not proper to be made public, they will undoubtedly be obliged to do something for me that I may not divulge them."

Thus I wavered betwixt hope and fear. Sometimes I thought that I flattered myself too much, and at other times that I desponded without reason. I paused at the latter reflection, which was the more consolatory of the two, and, hoping to fulfil the proverb which says, "He that wishes to be Pope, need only fancy himself one," I resolved to avail myself of the favorable opportunity which now presented itself of getting into Italy, by joining the levies that were raising. One day as I was sitting at my usual post reflecting on the pleasures I should enjoy at Genoa, my agreeable reverie was disturbed by some one who called me two or three times. I turned round to see who it could be that was so well acquainted with my name, and perceived that it was an old apothecary who had often employed me before. He beckoned me to come to him, and I ran immediately; but two of my companions, who were nearer to him, got before me and proffered their services before I came up. He, however, repulsed them sharply, saying:

" No, no; get you gone, birds of prey; this is not a morsel for you, but for my faithful Guzman."

He little thought he spoke so truly. Then addressing himself to me, who had just come up, "Open thy basket," added he, and he threw into it three bags of money, which he had with him wrapped in the corner of his cloak.

" To what brazier must I carry all this copper?" quoth I with a smile.

" This copper!" answered the apothecary, laughing out-right; "here's a pretty rogue of a beggar that takes silver for copper. Come, march on," continued he, "for I am in haste; I have engaged to pay a foreign merchant this money today, who has sold me some drugs."

This might have been his intention, but I had formed another to defeat it the instant I heard those charming words, "open thy basket." The news of the birth of an only son causes less joy to a tender parent than I felt at those sweet words, which engraved themselves on my heart, if I may so express it, in letters of gold. I looked on these three bags as a present sent me from Heaven to enable me to support the part I had to perform at Genoa, and concluded them already my own. As my man had not the slightest suspicion of me, being already well convinced, as he conceived, of my honesty, he walked before, and I followed him, pretending now and then that I was obliged to rest myself a little, as if my burden were too great, although, in truth, I could have wished it much heavier.

I never was so anxious to meet a crowd of people as on this occasion, or even a sly turning by which I could suddenly disappear from my unsuspecting friend, the apothecary. We chanced, however, shortly to pass a house with which I was well acquainted, the front and back doors of which stood most invitingly open. I could not allow this opportunity to escape me, but entered instantly, and passed through the house without meeting with any interruption, and in less than two minutes had got through two or three streets as though I had wings on my feet. I then resumed my usual pace to avoid suspicion, being far enough from my apothecary, and walked on as demurely as though nothing had happened.

In this manner I soon arrived at the gate De la Vega, that is to say, the open country, whence with the same grave countenance I gained the bank of the Mancanares; then, crossing over to Casa del Campo, I traveled a good league through woods and thickets, and, as night approached, stopped among some poplars very near to the river, where I began to consider how I should proceed.

"It is not enough," said I, "to have begun so well, I must continue in the same manner. Of what use will this prize be to me if I cannot take care of it now that I have got it? If I should happen to be nabbed, I shall not only be obliged to refund, but may lose both my ears to boot; let me therefore look out for some place where I may deposit my money in safety."

After having looked about for some time I made a hole about two feet deep at the bottom of the river, and let down my basket and bags of money into it. Then covering them with large stones to prevent them from floating, I set up a stake in the sand near the spot, that I might be sure of recollecting where my darling treasure lay concealed. After this grand operation I went to sleep at the foot of a tree hard by, where I passed the night, not altogether free from anxiety, though perfectly well satisfied with the reflection that I was now so well off. When daylight appeared I hid myself in a thicket until it was dark again, when hunger, which drives the wolf from the wood, obliged me to leave my haunts to go and purchase some provisions, not at either of the villages in the environs, where in all probability the apothecary would have sent the *alguazils* after me, but at Madrid itself, where I could best be concealed. Having a little money in my pocket, independent of my hoard, I ventured into the town, whence I returned in about three hours with a hamper containing provisions sufficient for eight days, and spent the greater part of the night in cramming myself with this good cheer.

When I awoke the next morning, I felt most curious to examine the contents of the three bags. In vain did I reflect that it must be the devil that tempted me, and that I could not satisfy my curiosity without running the risk of being observed. I could not help yielding to this gratification, which was certainly the sincerest I had ever felt in my life. I advanced to the side of the river, and after having looked on all sides to see if anybody was near, I drew my basket out of the water and carried it, dripping with wet as it was, into my place of retreat. Here I opened my bags, and found about two thousand five hundred *reals* in them, all in silver, with the exception of thirty *pistoles* in gold, which I discovered carefully wrapped up in one of the bags. I spent the whole of this day with the sincerest pleasure in counting my pieces over and over again; and when night came on, I put the whole into the basket again, and secured them in their former hiding-place.

As it is not my intention, however, to pretend to entertain my reader with a journal, I need only add that, after having concealed myself in this manner in the wood for a full fortnight, I considered that I had no longer anything to fear, and that all the hounds of justice had by this time so completely lost scent of me as to have given over their pursuit. I fished up my treasure again, which I deposited at the bottom of my hamper, under some fresh provisions which I had been again to Madrid to procure. As to my basket, I left that in the water with the stones upon it. I then cut me two good sticks, one to carry by burthen on my back, and the other I made into a sort of pilgrim's staff; after which, like a new pilgrim, I took my route towards Toledo across the fields, thinking it more prudent to avoid the highroads.

CHAPTER V

GUZMÁN ON HIS WAY TO TOLEDO MEETS WITH A YOUNG MAN: WHAT PASSED BETWEEN THEM

I TRIPPED along so briskly that after two nights' trudge I found myself in the midst of the Sagra, near a wood called Acuqueyca, within about two leagues of Toledo. I entered this wood, intending to rest there the whole of the day, that I might not enter the city till night. I sat down under a shady tree, and began to think in what manner I should spend my money. I soon determined on so many fine purchases that four times what I possessed would have been insufficient to have procured them. It were impossible to enumerate the variety of visions and fancies that possessed my mind. I was no longer afraid of appearing before my relations like a beggar, but now looked forward with pleasure to my arrival in Genoa, and all the purchases that I made in my mind were with a view to cut a most brilliant figure among them.

A stream of clear spring water ran at my feet, with which I found myself much refreshed, and, beginning to feel hungry, I spread my provisions on the grass for breakfast. Scarcely had I eaten a mouthful when I heard a noise, and, turning round hastily, I was much alarmed at perceiving a man close behind me, seated also on the grass, with his head reclining against a tree. But when I considered him with attention I soon found that I had nothing to fear. He appeared to be about my own age, but seemed as raw and inexperienced as if he had not been long weaned from his mother's breast. Although he was well dressed and had a large bundle lying at his side, through which I could discern some clothes and linen, he looked so unhappy that I judged his purse could not be very full, and set him down for some knight-errant like myself, who had been fool enough to forsake his family to wander about the world.

We stared at each other for some moments without saying a word; but when I observed that he looked with a longing eye on my provisions, I could not help pitying him. His eager looks reminded me of my own feelings when I stood before the kind-hearted monk at the inn, and I determined not to be less generous than his reverence. I therefore immediately invited this young man in the most polite manner to breakfast with me. Shame prevented him at first from accepting my offer; but when I repeated it he laid aside his modesty, and confessed to me that he had not tasted anything for the last four and twenty hours. This I found no difficulty in believing when I saw in what style he demolished the meat and the bread and cheese I gave him.

During the repast we inquired of each other concerning our travels. He told me that he had come from Toledo

and was going to Madrid; and I acquainted him that I had
just come from Burgos and was on my way to Cordova.
He then related a most romantic story about the occasion
of his pilgrimage, and I was not more sincere with him;
considering that he was but a novice, he lied with a very
good grace, and by no means disgraced his countrymen,
who have the reputation for wit and smart answers on
every occasion. I asked him how he came to set out on
his journey without providing himself with victuals. He
replied that he had not had time to procure any, having
been forced to leave the place with precipitation, and that
he was more laden with clothes than money.

"So much the worse," said I, "so much the worse;
money is the most necessary commodity for a traveler
nowadays; for even though you were going on a pilgrimage to St. Jago in Galicia, I would not advise you to reckon
much upon charity, which has grown very cold of late;
you will find something more than your staff necessary to
support you by the way."

"I perfectly agree with you," replied the Toledan, "and
am well aware of my imprudence in setting out without
provisions; but as it cannot now be remedied, it is useless
to regret it."

"It is in your own power," answered I, "to repair your
neglect by disposing of a part of the clothes contained in
that large bundle, which you must find extremely burden-
some. Money is more portable."

"Granted," said he, "and I need not inform you that
it is my intention to sell at least half of them as soon as
I can find a purchaser."

"Perhaps," replied I, "without going any farther, you
have a man before you who is willing to relieve you of the
greater part of your load, and give you as much for them
as they are worth. Show me the contents of your bundle,
and I will select such as I am inclined to purchase."

My little gentleman turned pale at these words; he considered me a knave who intended to repay myself for the
breakfast by robbing him of a part of his property, or at

least that I was willing to amuse myself at his expense; for when he surveyed my elegant attire, which was not worth four *maravedis,* he could not for a moment think that I was in earnest. Every one is apt to judge in this manner, forming opinions of strangers from the difference of dress and outward appearances. " Such as I see you, such I take you to be."

I observed his confusion, or, rather, saw plainly that he suspected my intentions; and as he made no answer, I drew out one of my bags, very deliberately untied it, and exhibited a handful of *reals* to his astonished eyes.

" I believe, my little hero," said I, " that here is enough to pay for what I wish to buy of you."

The color was soon restored to his cheeks at this sight; he immediately left off eating, and ran to fetch his bundle, saying that all he had was at my service. At the same time he was proceeding to show me his best suits, but this I would not permit until we had finished our meal. His hopes seemed to serve as a fresh sauce to his appetite, and he fell to again as though he could not do sufficient honor to my breakfast; he could scarcely contain the joy that he felt.

That he might not form an ill opinion of me on account of my appearance, and to prevent his suspecting that the money which he had just seen was ill got, I addressed him to this effect:

" Whatever you may take me for," said I, " be assured that I am in reality as well born as yourself. This I have thought fit to inform you, that you may learn not always to judge of people by their looks. When I left Burgos I had as good clothes as you, but I sold them in the first village I passed through, to relieve myself of so inconvenient a burden, and contented myself with these tattered garments, which would excite the pity, or at the worst the compassion, of thieves, whom a better dress would probably have tempted. If I had not taken this precaution I should have been robbed a hundred times ere this, and be at this moment without a single *maravedi* in my pocket. As, however, it is my intention to stop at Toledo for some time on my way to Cordova, I have now immediate occasion for a good suit of clothes; and if you have any that will fit me, I am ready to be a purchaser."

The Toledan, burning with impatience to commence business, with his mouth still full, began to spread out on the grass a complete suit, the cloak of which was of most excellent cloth of a light gray color, together with two fine shirts, and a pair of silk stockings. I tried them all on, and they fitted me exactly. This the young man did not fail to tell me, to make me have the better opinion of them. He seemed apprehensive that my money would slip through his fingers, or that I should change my mind. He need have been under no such fear, for I was as anxious to buy as he was to sell, so that our bargain was soon struck. He asked me a hundred *reals,* and I agreed to give him this price upon condition that he would truck his clothes-bag with me for my hamper.

This he consented to, and I put my money into it, with the two shirts and silk stockings. My new clothes I still wore; and I hung up the old suit and the rest of my rags on a tree, as a trophy of my success in beggary. The Toledan, on his side, filled the hamper with his goods and the victuals that were left. During all this time the sun was insensibly going down, and the hour of parting having arrived, we embraced each other with a thousand professions of friendship; after which we each pursued our particular route, both well satisfied with our bargain.

CHAPTER VI

GUZMAN ARRIVES AT TOLEDO, AND ACTS THE MAN OF FOR-
TUNE THERE

IT was past nine o'clock when I entered the famous city
of Toledo. I combed my hair and put myself in order,
taking particular pains to rub the dust off my shoes that I
might with the greater assurance be able to assert that I
came in a coach. I requested to be directed to the best
inn, whither I repaired, requiring my supper and lodging
like a young man of fortune, who troubled himself but little
about expense. As these are the sort of customers who are
sure to be well treated at inns, I was immediately shown
into an excellent chamber with a good bed in it, and waited
upon like any prince. I supped perfectly to my satisfaction, and slept better than I supped.

The next morning, after having taken my chocolate,
which I called for in order to impress them with an opinion
of my quality, I desired them to send for a hatter, a shoemaker, and a swordmaker, for it was indispensable for me
to have a new hat, sword, and shoes, to correspond with
the rest of my equipage. But the most essential thing
of all was to procure a tailor to disguise the suit I had
bought as much as possible, lest when I went abroad I
might happen to meet some of the relations of the young
man of whom I had purchased it, which might have raised
suspicions dangerous to me in my present situation. I
might very reasonably have supposed that they would know

it again, and perhaps accuse me of having stolen it and assassinated the young man. Justice would then have interfered, and this I had more reasons than one to dread. I sent therefore for a tailor, who in a few hours so completely disguised the suit, by covering the sleeves with taffeta, changing the buttons, and putting a velvet collar on the cloak, that the devil himself could scarcely have known it again.

I paid my tailor handsomely; and well pleased that I could now venture out without the dread of getting into difficulty on account of my dress, I took a walk towards the evening in the Zocodover, where the fashionables usually promenade. Metamorphosed as I was, I was not altogether free from apprehension of meeting some one who might recognise me. This fear, however, did not prevent my feeling gratified in observing that I was particularly noticed by the prettiest women of slender virtue, who, looking upon me as a handsome well-shaped young fellow who had never yet been to Cythera, appeared most anxious to have the honor of setting me in the right road; but I had resolution enough to resist all their seducing glances.

What most surprised me was the extreme neatness of all the gentlemen. My dress, notwithstanding all the tailor's endeavors to adjust and beautify it, appeared so shabby in comparison with those around me that I resolved on having another. Just at this moment a gentleman mounted on a beautiful mule crossed the Zocodover in so handsome and stylish a dress that I determined to get one exactly similar made for myself. I could scarcely refrain from sending for my tailor that very night. I managed, however, to wait till morning, though I never closed my eyes the whole of the night, so completely was I amused and delighted in considering how handsome I should look in these new trappings. But when I reflected on the probable expense of them, I began to hesitate, notwithstanding the eager desire I felt to appear in them.

"Well, Signor Guzman," said I to myself, "you presume

then to dress magnificently, and to supplant all the gallants at Toledo! well done, courage, by friend. Spend your *reals* without reflecting on the deep game you have played to possess yourself of them. That is not worthy of your consideration; all you seem to wish is to get rid of your money, and you will find it go quick enough. Let a suit be made agreeable to your fancy, and begin courting the ladies, and you will soon come to your basket again. Rely upon this; but do not think that you can every day meet with apothecaries who will allow themselves to be purged like your friend at Madrid."

All these wise reflections presented themselves, but without effect; for no sooner was it daylight than I sent for my tailor, to whom I gave the order, after having given him an exact description of the dress I had seen. He promised to make me one exactly similar, undertaking to go himself and purchase the materials, and assuring me that I should have it as soon as possible; for I required him to be as expeditious and punctual as though I were going to be married and only waited for my wedding clothes. He accordingly sent it home two days later, and I had never seen anything more stylish and elegant, the gold glittered all over it. When I put it on I was in raptures at my handsome appearance and the beauty of my figure, which was already perfectly well formed, though scarcely fifteen years of age. I thought that I was the very image of my father when he was young, having a delicate white and red complexion like him, with light-brown hair. I should never have been tired of looking in the glass, though I felt most anxious to go abroad again to be admired in the city. No one who was not so eminently pleased with his own figure as I was could have been fool enough to have satisfied my tailor without disputing his bill, which I might most conscientiously have reduced two-thirds; but I did not then think that I could possibly pay too much for so tasteful an equipage. Mine hostess, seeing me superbly dressed, told me I ought at least to have a lackey. I immediately engaged one therefore that looked like a page, for whom

I was obliged to find new clothes, to be worthy of a master of my importance.

The first Sunday I failed not to attend the great church, followed by my lackey, to whom I had given proper instructions that he might do me honor. The congregation was of the first quality in the city; I thrust myself in the midst of them with a vast deal of assurance, and visited all the chapels one after another, which caused many to think that I had some design in my head; it was, however, only to show myself off.

I placed myself between the two choirs, having observed that the principal ladies were always in this part of the church. It was here that I displayed all the fine airs I had seen practiced by other young fools at Madrid, and which I had performed at least twenty times over in the morning at my glass. The first thing I did was to choose a spot where I could be seen from head to foot. Then I thrust out my breast, and stood firm upon one leg, while I extended the other in so stiff a position that it scarcely touched the ground, showing by this means my fine stockings, and that I wore garters of the German fashion which were then in vogue. As this posture cramped me extremely I was obliged to vary it every minute, making divers grimaces at the ladies who looked at me. I smiled upon one, looked coldly upon another, with languishing eyes upon a third, and with sparkling eyes upon a fourth. In short, I so far over-acted my part that all the ladies and gentlemen who observed my manœuvres began to titter at my expense. This I took no kind of notice of, for I had too good an opinion of myself to imagine they could find anything ridiculous in my behavior. . . . When I arrived at my inn I met an *alguazil* there, who, I was informed, had just arrived from Madrid and had been making very particular inquiries of the landlord for a certain quidam of whom he was in search. I did not hear this without uneasiness; nevertheless, alarmed as I was, I managed to put a bold face on the matter, but I was so agitated the whole of the night that I could not get a wink of sleep. I rose early the next morning, still thinking of this cursed *alguazil,* and went out to walk in the Zocodover. I had not gone once round the square before I heard a man crying:

"Two mules returning to Almagra."

I determined to avail myself of this opportunity, and resolved in a moment to hire these two mules, as though I had foreseen that I should find a company of soldiers at Almagro on the point of departure for Italy. I spoke to the crier and we soon agreed, after which I sent my lackey to pay my landlord and to fetch my baggage, which consisted of a portmanteau in which was my fashionable dress, some fine linen, and what remained of my money. As soon as he rejoined me I gave him one of the mules, mounted myself on the other, and, rejoiced at having found so favorable an opportunity of leaving Toledo, where I could no longer remain in peace, I took the route towards Orgas, where I slept that night. . . .

A few moments before daylight the muleteer entered my chamber to give me notice that breakfast was ready, and that if I wished to reach Malagon at any reasonable hour that day I had no time to lose. I was soon up and dressed, and after having eaten a good breakfast of what the host chose to provide for me, I was just going to mount my mule when she directed a violent kick at me, which would certainly have crippled me for the remainder of my days had I been at a greater distance, but I was luckily so close to the plaguy beast that she could not do me much harm.

We arrived at Malagon at night, whence I set out again the next day, without any other scurvy trick of fortune except having lost one bottle of wine, which I missed when we had got about three or four leagues from the town. . . .

Just as the muleteer was stopping his beast another muleteer of his acquaintance came up to us, of whom I asked what was going on at Almagro, whence he had just come, and he informed me that there was a company of soldiers there newly raised, and destined, he believed, for Italy. I was enraptured at this news, and felt disposed to forgive Fortune, now that she presented me with so favorable an opportunity of gratifying my violent desire to go to Genoa, for all the hardships that she had hitherto made me endure.

CHAPTER VII

GUZMAN OFFERS HIMSELF TO SERVE IN THE COMPANY NEWLY RAISED. HIS RECEPTION BY THE CAPTAIN, AND HOW THEY AFTERWARDS LIVED TOGETHER

ALL my fear was that the muleteer had been misinformed, but on entering Almagro I was soon convinced that he had told the truth. I perceived a flag suspended from a window of one of the houses, where I supposed the captain had taken up his residence.

I proceeded therefore to an inn in the neighborhood, where I took up my lodging for that night, and in the morning I dressed myself in my best suit of clothes and finest linen and went to church, where I heard mass, and from thence to wait upon the captain, whom I saluted with an air calculated to make him believe me a young man of quality, telling him that I had come express to Almagro to have the honor of serving the king by joining his company. My behavior and appearance had the desired effect of casting a mist before the eyes of this officer, who was an extremely well-bred man. He received me therefore in the most polite manner, testifying his joy at finding me disposed to enter so early in the career of glory. He then thanked me for the preference I gave his company, which would be proud to receive among them a cavalier of noble race, which he could easily perceive I was.

"All I regret," added he, "is that all the posts are filled up; but though I cannot therefore offer you a commission, you shall at least share mine with me, and we will live together as though you were captain as well as myself."

To convince me that these excessive civilities were not mere compliments, he insisted on my staying to dinner, and regaled me in good style. He did not, however, forget to charge one of his servants in private to inquire of mine who I was. My page, who had frequently heard me style myself Don Juan de Guzman of the house of Toral, answered this question by saying that this was the name I bore, and that was all he knew of me. This was reported to the captain, who most firmly believed that I was certainly one of the younger branches of that illustrious house.

The next day I invited him in my turn to dine with me at my inn, and spared no expense to render the entertainment as complete as if I had been in reality the cavalier my valet had represented me to be. I did not stop here, but gave so many other dinners to the captain and the principal officers of the company, that it is no wonder they all esteemed me and considered me an honor to their corps. The captain in particular was so extremely attentive to me that I was frequently quite confused at his kind professions of regard. It is true that, to secure a continuance of his friendship, I sent him almost every day some little present by my page, which he was so kind as to accept of as a mark of my affection.

In the meantime my purse, having no flux and reflux like the sea, began to empty itself visibly, without any prospect of being filled again. What with my clothes, my gallantries, and my traveling expenses, in addition to these entertainments and presents, I had already squandered away more than half of my *reals*, without reckoning what I had lost at play with the officers, the majority of whom knew better than myself how to take advantage in gaming of every turn of fortune in their favor. I had still, however, a sufficient sum remaining to support my assumed character for some time longer, when orders were given for marching, and I followed the company, in quality of a volunteer, to the coast, where we had orders to wait until the galleys which were to transport us into Italy with other troops arrived at Barcelona, where we were to embark. But it was God's pleasure that this embarkment should not take place till three months afterwards. This completed my ruin; for being willing to continue to live with the captain and other officers as I had begun, I was soon compelled to make use of my *corps de reserve,* I mean my thirty *pistoles,* which were yet untouched, and which I soon ran through with as little frugality as my *reals.* When I found my resources thus at an end I was obliged to sell my fine clothes and linen, and to get rid of my valet, who went back to seek his fortune elsewhere, and, having no money to game with, I ceased to associate with the officers, who guessed but too rightly the reasons that obliged me thus to alter my conduct towards them.

Reflections now came thick upon the prodigal child; and though I had not given way to them while my money lasted, now that it was gone at least a million presented themselves to my imagination. I recalled to mind all my past follies, and reproached myself as severely as a professed pedagogue could have done, resolving to manage better for the future, as though I had still several bags of *reals* in my portmanteau. I chiefly repented of having given such fine entertainments to the captain, who no longer invited me to dinner as usual, now that my money was gone. The other officers, thinking that I had nothing more to lose, turned their backs upon me. The sergeants, who had before been in the habit of visiting me as a second captain, and who had considered themselves honored by my condescending to converse with them, no longer came near me. There was not a single soldier but avoided me, and I question if even the blackguards that followed them would have deigned to associate with me had I been inclined to have been their comrade.

But it was but just, after such useless extravagance, that I was punished as I deserved. If there was anything that could console me in my unfortunate situation, it was that during the whole course of my prosperity I had not committed the least knavery. This gave my captain a good

opinion of me, who, believing as firmly as ever that I was
a young man of high birth, still retained some esteem for
me in my misery. He had himself too well profited by
my foolish conduct not to forgive me from the bottom
of his soul; and when I called upon him one evening he
received me much as usual, without taking any notice of the
situation of my affairs, though he was in reality much affected, and he could not avoid saying to me one day that
I was more melancholy than usual.

"My dear Guzman, I should indeed be hard-hearted and
ungrateful were I insensible to your troubles, after the
many proofs you have given me of your friendship. But
you have yet to learn that my fortune is but little better
than your own, and I am sincerely afflicted that I am utterly incapable of convincing you of my good wishes by my
actions. All I can pretend to offer you in your present distress is a lodging in my house and the table of my servants;
for myself, I am obliged to dine out, from my utter incapacity to receive my friends at home."

This proposal, which he did not make without a blush,
was tendered in so obliging a manner that I accepted it.
Pride becomes nobody, but still less a man who has no
money and knows not where to lay his head; it is a chame-
leon, which lives only on the wind. From his companion
I was now become his servant. But I owe him this piece
of justice: instead of treating me like a common servant,
he behaved in the most considerate manner towards me.
When he wished me to do anything for him he requested
instead of commanding it, and, on my side, I was always
more anxious than the other domestics to make myself useful to him, that I might preserve his friendship, and not eat
the bread of idleness; and I so completely succeeded in my
desire to please him, by anticipating his every wish, that,
believing me to be faithful, and even prudent, though I had
sufficiently proved myself the reverse by my former dissipa-
tions, he resolved to make me acquainted with the present
state of his affairs, to convince me that he placed entire
confidence in me.

He confessed to me then that he was so much reduced that a few jewels which he possessed were his only resource.

"Can you guess," added he, "what has reduced me to this extremity?—the time that was consumed in soliciting my employment and the great presents I was obliged to make to obtain it. Yes, were I to begin life afresh, I would renounce such a profession, notwithstanding the desire that every Spanish gentleman naturally has to acquire glory in the army. I cannot reflect on what I have submitted to without blushing, for besides the money that I have expended, how many whole days have I passed with my hat in my hand, soliciting, flattering, bowing to the ground, kicking my heels at levees, sometimes to speak to one person, sometimes to meet with another, cringing, acting a servant's part, and a thousand other meannesses of which I am ashamed!

"But the most provoking treatment that I met with, and which I felt most sensibly, was on the day preceding that on which I had been promised my commission. After having consumed more than eight months in solicitations in the manner I have just described to you, I accompanied my patron as he came out of the palace, and conducted him, with the most profound respect, to the steps of his carriage, which was in waiting for him, but unfortunately put my hat on a moment before the carriage drove off. The minister noticed this, darted a haughty look at me, and soon convinced me that this accident had offended him, for my commission was not delivered to me for above four months after. I even ran the risk of losing both my trouble and my money by not obtaining it at all.

"God deliver every honest man," continued he, raising his eyes towards heaven, "from persons who possess power and bad dispositions united! How blind are these idols of the Court, who expect to be adorned like deities! They must surely have forgotten that they are but miserable comedians, appointed to play principal characters, and that at the end of the piece, that is to say, of their lives, they must leave the stage like ourselves, and be thought of no more."

I was so affected by this relation that I felt more interested in my captain's misfortunes than my own, and assured him, in the most impressive terms, my heart could dictate that there was nothing I would not undertake for him, and that I would willingly expose my life to be of service to him. He thanked me for my good wishes.

"But what assistance," added he, smiling, "can I expect from you in your present condition?"

"That we shall see," answered I; "for though I am young, necessity inspires wit, and may supply my deficiency of experience. Leave it to me to find you the means of living at east until we embark."

The captain smiled again at these words, and, without making reply, shook his head, to show me that he placed but little reliance on professions dictated by my inconsiderate zeal to serve him. Had he known my talents he would have formed a different opinion, but I soon obliged him to do me justice.

As the galleys were a long while ere they arrived, we were obliged to be billeted, upon short allowance, in the different villages, and frequently moved our quarters. At every house I left a dozen billets, which brought us in at least twelve *reals* each, and from some of the more opulent inhabitants fifty. For my own part, I gained admittance into every house at free cost, without quartering myself on any one in particular; and I never failed to leave proofs at each that I had the perfect use of my hands. I really think that I would even have carried off water from their wells rather than have gone away empty-handed. By these means I so completely re-established my captain's finances, that he was enabled to keep open table again as before, and the dexerity of my hands supplied him abundantly with good cheer at a cheap rate: fowls, capons, geese, pullets, and pigeons fell as thick as hail into the kitchen, and hams were not wanting to complete the larder.

If by chance the master of a house happened to catch

me in the fact, in case it were but a small theft I made a
jest of it, and though a greater, the worst that could happen to me was to be carried before my captain, who repri-
manded me in a severe manner, and sometimes caused me
to be imprisoned in a chamber, where I received by his
orders a hundred lashes which I never felt at all; but I
always made the room ring with cries as if I were being
torn in pieces, though I was never so much as touched all
the while. This satisfied the injured parties and saved the·
honor of the officer. Sometimes the complainants themselves would intercede with the captain on my behalf, con-
juring him out of pity to forgive me.

Jests like these, however, generally grow serious. After
these petty thefts, I was not content until I ventured upon
greater. For this purpose I selected five or six of the most
resolute fellows in our company; we all disguised ourselves
and went on the highway, where we stopped several travelers, who, by immediately surrendering their money, prevented the crimes which their resistance might have caused
us to commit.

Our captain was no sooner informed of these dangerous
proceedings than, dreading the consequences both to himself and me, he positively forbade my carrying on this game
any longer, desiring me to confine myself to more innocent
amusement for the future, such as finding false musters, to
which science I was a perfect adept. By a false beard, or
a patch on the eye, I could easily make the same soldier
receive pay three times over, without detection. In short,
I became so useful to the captain that he confessed to me
that my industry alone was worth much more to him than
the whole income that he derived from his company.

CHAPTER VIII

GUZMAN PROCEEDS WITH THE COMPANY TO BARCELONA, WHERE HE PLAYS A TRICK UPON A JEWELER, AND EMBARKS FOR ITALY.

THE galleys at length arrived at Barcelona. As soon as we received this intelligence, we marched thither to embark, but as the wind was not favorable we were obliged to remain a considerable time in that city, where something more than my usual address was necessary to enable us to live in plenty at so cheap a rate as before. I soon remarked that my captain was relapsing into his former despondency, and I easily guessed the cause. Well might I know the nature of his complaint, since I was the physician who had already cured him of it.

For this once, however, I felt at a loss how to prescribe, being entirely unacquainted with the map of Barcelona and the disposition of its inhabitants. I did not, however, forget to tender my exertions as a specific to my patient, who replied, in a serious manner, that we had no longer peasants to deal with, and that I must be very cautious what I did. Difficulties tended only to quicken my apprehension, and an idea occurred to me which I resolved to follow. I have already told you that the captain had some jewels which he reserved for a rainy day. Amongst these jewels was a gold reliquary, set round with diamonds, which he intended to dispose of for subsistence until we embarked. I requested him to show it me, and asked if he could place so much confidence in me as to entrust it to me for a day or two, adding that I would return it to him with usury.

"Oh! oh! my little Guzman," answered he with a smile, "what piece of roguery have you now in contemplation?"

"You have only," replied I, "to let me have the reliquary, and keep up your spirits. If, notwithstanding all the precautions that I can take to perform safely the trick I have in my head, I should be so unfortunate as to meet with any check from justice, I can at least pledge myself to save your honor, and to bear all the ill consequences of it myself."

My captain could hold out no longer, but gave me the reliquary, saying that he wished me success in my enterprise whatever it might be. Nobody, indeed, had more interest in it than himself, to whom all the profit would accrue. I put the jewel into a purse which I hid in my bosom, the string of which I tied to the buttons of my doublet; after which I went to the first jeweler's I could meet, who, fortunately for me, was well known in the city as a noted usurer. I asked him if he was inclined to purchase a fine reliquary. I showed it him, and could easily perceive that he liked it very well, although he pretended not to think much of it. I did not wait until he asked me the usual questions, but told him that I was a soldier in a company newly raised, and that was destined for Italy; that I had spent all my money, and having no other resource, found myself reduced to dispose of this jewel, that I might not be entirely destitute.

"You are at liberty," added I, "to go and ascertain from my captain, from the other officers, and even soldiers, who I am; they will inform you that I am styled Don Juan de Guzman; upon their report of me you can make up your mind whether you will buy the reliquary or not. While you are making these inquiries I will go and wait for you on the quay, where I have a little business to settle."

The jeweler, who was not willing to allow this jewel to escape him, took his cloak immediately, and hastened to the place where I told him we lodged, and did not fail to question several of the officers and soldiers as to the character of a certain Don Juan de Guzman, who described himself as belonging to their company. Every man of them (for I was generally beloved) assured him I was a young man of quality, who intended to pass over to Italy with them, and that they had known me make a most brilliant figure. In short, they spoke so well of me that he soon returned to look for me on the quay, where he had no great difficulty in finding me, for I had no other business there but to wait for and entrap him. He requested me, as soon as he came up, to allow him to see the reliquary again, which he was come to treat for.

"Willingly," replied I; "but let us retire a little, as I have no wish to have a crowd assembled about us."

I then drew the jewel out of my purse and handed it to him; he looked at it on all sides, and, after having examined it minutely, asked me what I would have for it. I told him two hundred crowns; and though that was not half its value, the old usurer pretended to be quite astonished at such a price, and began to tell me that the gold was by no means of the finest quality, besides which he found great fault with the workmanship, as well as with the diamonds; nevertheless, he offered me one half, and I was surprised in my turn.

"That will not do," cried I; "you take advantage of my situation; but, distressed as I am for money, I declare you shall not have it for less than a hundred and fifty crowns."

He still continued to make so many objections that I was at last contented to conclude the bargain at a hundred and twenty, and he requested me to accompany him to his shop to receive the money. This I refused, telling him that I expected a person to meet me on the quay, and, therefore, could not leave it; that if he would return home and procure the sum agreed on, he would find me again in the same place. The jeweler, finding that I could not be prevailed on to accompany him, and being apprehensive that the person whom I expected might be another jeweler, whom I had appointed to meet on the same subject, ran home with great haste, lest he should be deprived of his bargain before his return.

The old rogue soon returned to me again, quite out of breath, bringing with him in a small bag the hundred and twenty crowns, which he counted into my hand. I requested the bag of him in which I put the money, and offered him in exchange the purse that the reliquary was kept in; but affectng to find great difficulty in untying the strings, which I had purposely well fastened, I snatched, as though from impatience, a knife which I observed in a sheath at his girdle and cut them asunder. Although this action seemed to surprise him a little, he was so far from guessing the cause that he departed and walked towards home, well satisfied with his purchase, and very far from suspecting the snare that I had laid for him.

After having allowed him to proceed a few steps, I beckoned to one of my comrades, as great a rogue as myself, whom I had stationed near at hand so as to be ready when called for, and desired him to carry the crowns to our captain. Then I ran as fast as I could after my jeweler, for I had not lost sight of him, and overtook him at a part where the roads met, where there happened to be some soldiers assambled, to whom I pointed him out, crying aloud:

" Stop thief, fellow soldiers, stop thief! for God's sake, stop that old rascal there, who has just robbed me; let him not escape! "

The soldiers, some of whom belonged to our own company, stopped the poor jeweler, immediately, asking him how he had given me cause to complain thus of him. He was at first so bewildered with fear and astonishment, that he had not the power of uttering a word. Had he spoken, however, it would not have availed him, for his voice would have been drowned by that of his accuser; nobody was to be heard but myself, who kept up a continued roar; and, to make more impression on the soldiers, I fell down on my knees before them and, forcing some tears into my eyes, implored their assistance.

127

"Gentlemen," said I, "you see before you in that old rogue one of the greatest hypocrites in Spain. I chanced just now to be standing by him on the quay, where he remarked that I had a purse in my bosom, and asked me what was in it? 'A reliquary,' answered I, 'which my master the captain accidentally left at the bed's-head this morning, and that I have taken care of to give it to him again,' upon this the old rascal whom you have secured requested me in a civil manner to show it to him, telling me that he was a goldsmith and was curious in jewels. I satisfied his curiosity, and he asked me if I would dispose of this reliquary. 'That cannot be,' said I, 'for it is my master's;' at the same time I replaced it in my purse which was tied to my button; whereupon my thief, while he amused me with words, drew forth a knife which he had in a sheath at his gridle, and suddenly cut the strings, the ends of which are still to be seen. Take the trouble, gentlemen, of searching him, I beg of you," added I, "and you will find the purse containing the jewel somewhere about his person, for I have followed him so closely that he has not had an opportunity of otherwise disposing of it."

The soldiers instantly began to search him, they drew forth the purse containing the reliquary from his bosom where he had placed it, and, perceiving that the strings had really been cut, they no longer doubted the goldsmith's guilt; in vain did he protest and swear that I had sold it him, they would not believe him, it being so extremely improbable that an old and experienced jeweler could consent to purchase so rich a reliquary of a young soldier, without suspecting that it must have been stolen.

"Once more," cried the accused, "I assure you that I paid this young man for the reliquary a hundred and twenty crowns in gold, which I reckoned into his hand, and which he must now have about him; you have only to search him also to find these gold coins, which I paid him only a few minutes since."

The soldiers, to satisfy him, rummaged my pockets out; and, finding no money about me, they began to revile him

most unmercifully and even to beat him. Nevertheless, as
he insisted on being conducted to a judge, they carried us
both before one.

Here I related my case in the same manner as I had reported it to the soldiers, who, upon being interrogated by
the judge, said more than was sufficient to convince him
that the jeweler had really seized this reliquary from me
by force, in addition to which, this citizen being so well
known as a covetous man, who would not scruple at a trifle,
they were the more disposed to think him guilty. The
magistrate, however, out of consideration for his family,
which consisted of some of the first persons in the city,
was content to reprimand him severely, and delivered the
jewel into my hands again, desiring me to carry it to my
master, which I did immediately.

When I related this adventure to the captain he returned
thanks to Heaven that it had ended so well; he had feared,
and with some reason, that I should have come but scurvily
off in so slippery an affair, and my boldness made him
tremble. Although he was the only person that profited by
my rogueries, yet he resolved to get rid of the rogue, fearing that I should at last ruin him as well as myself by some
unlucky adventure. He was impatient for the day when
we should embark, which at length arrived. The galleys
left the harbor of Barcelona, and transported us in safety
to Genoa, where we were no sooner landed than my captain said to me in private:

"My dear Guzman, we are now in the country whither
you have been so extremely anxious to come" (for I had
communicated to him my intentions of visiting my kindred); "we must now, with your leave, begin to think of
parting, for I am not more afraid of all the devils together
than of the consequences of these legerdemain tricks of
yours; farewell, my fried," added he, putting a *pistole*
into my hand, "I much regret that I am not in a situation
to make you a better acknowledgment for your services."

Thus saying, he departed, leaving me so thunderstruck
with his compliment that I could not utter a word. But

what could I have said to him? was it necessary to represent to him all the dangers I had faced on his account? he was well aware of them, for what else was it that caused my dismissal. I could not be surprised at his behavior. I had only the common fate of rogues, who, like vipers and scorpions, are made use of while anything useful can be extracted from them, and afterwards thrown to the dogs.

BOOK THE THIRD

CHAPTER I

A S soon as I had quitted the captain, or rather when I found myself abandoned by him, my only thought was how to console myself under this misfortune, and I soon forgot it when I reflected that I was now at Genoa, where I had so long desired to be. I inquired in the city about my relations, and was informed that they were the most rich and powerful persons in that republic. I was overjoyed at this news, for I did not doubt that I should receive the greatest assistance from them when they knew that I was a branch of their noble family.

I looked about for another inn where I could live thriftily, until I should be rather a more decent figure to visit my relations. My *pistole* could not do much for me, part of which I was obliged to expend in procuring a pair of shoes, which I was sadly in want of; my clothes were also much worn, as well as my stockings and hat, so that my whole dress was in a ruinous condition.

" So much the better," said I; " my relations can never suffer me to remain long in such a state to be a disgrace to them. Let me quickly, therefore, make myself known to them, that I may the sooner be relieved from my misery."

I then immediately set forward with this intention, and asked the way to their house, boasting to every one I spoke to that I had the honor to be of their family, which was soon reported to them by some of their enemies, who, thinkink that the sight of a lad so wretchedly equipped would afford them no great pleasure, were the more anxious to communicate to them the agreeable news. My generous relations were almost desperate. They looked upon my poverty as an infamous disgrace to them; and I verily believe that could they, without danger to themselves, have caused me to be poniarded they would not have hesitated a moment, for such practices were but too common in that country. But as I was already talked of all over the city, where my father had been so well known, if I had disappeared all of a sudden the cause would have been easily guessed.

Do not be surprised, reader, at my ill opinion of my relations; had you been in their place I do not think that you would have behaved much better towards me. Suppose yourself for a moment as rich as they were, and tell me candidly how you would have received a beggar, who comes up to you as suddenly as if he had just fallen from the clouds, and salutes you in the middle of the street, saying, "Good morning, uncle, or brother, I am a son of your brother, or of your mother;" would you not be extremely mortified? and yet I was so imprudent as to address them in this public manner; thus I never saluted one of them that did not treat me with the titles of rascal and impostor, accompanying these epithets with threats:

"Take our advice," said they, "and do not remain much longer at Genoa, lest you pass but an unpleasant time here."

In vain did I name my father, protesting that he ranked among the noble Genoese; they seemed all to have forgotten that there had ever been such a person in existence.

One evening I met a venerable looking old man, who accosted me in a polite and insinuating manner.

"My son," said he, "is it not you who have reason to complain of certain titled personages who have not chosen to acknowledge you for one of their noble blood?"

I answered in the affirmative, and told him who was my father.

"I recollect him well," replied the old man, "and there are certainly in this city several of the principal nobles who are his relations. I can even introduce you to a banker who must have been a most intimate friend of your father's, and who tomorrow, for it is too late today, will, I doubt not, be happy to satisfy you in every particular concerning your family. In the meantime," continued he, "come and take up your lodging at my house; I feel quite indignant at the behavior of your cousins towards you, who ought rather to have received you with the greatest affection; but follow me, and be assured that the banker will put it in your power to be fully avenged of them for their hard-heartedness."

I accepted the old man's offer of a lodging in his house by returning thanks to Heaven for so fortunate a rencounter. His appearance was such that I did not in the least mistrust him. He had a good-natured, serious air, his bald head and white beard rendering his appearance truly venerable; he walked with a staff, and wore a long robe; in fact, I looked upon him as another St. Paul. When we arrived at his house, which appeared to me like a magnificent hotel, a servant came to meet him to take off his long robe; but the old gentleman, from an excess of politeness, would not part with it, but sent the servant away, after having communicated something to him in Italian, which was so much Hebrew to me.

He then conducted me into a large parlor, where we conversed concerning the affairs of Spain for above an hour, and from them proceeded insensibly to those of our own family, respecting which he seemed extremely curious, questioning me more particularly concerning my mother, and I answered him in the most cautious manner. This discourse was beginning to grow tedious, when the servant returned; they had another short conversation together in Italian, which I understood no better than the former. But immediately afterwards the good old man addressed himself to me in Spanish.

"I suppose," said he, "you have of course supped, you must be weary, and it is time to be abed. We shall meet again in the morning."

Then turning to his servant, "Antonio," continued he, "show this gentleman to the finest chamber in the house."

I had much more inclination to eat than to sleep, for I was literally half dying with hunger, having unfortunately dined very sparingly at my inn that day, for my *pistole* was just at an end. That I might not, however, presume upon the goodness of an host who seemed so disposed to be of service to me, I followed his servant as if I had had a good bellyful, and was carried through an enfilade of seven or eight rooms paved with alabaster, each vying with the others in magnificence. From thence we entered a gallery which led into a fine chamber, in which there was a very rich bed with superb tapestry.

"You see your chamber," said Antonio, "and the bed that is destined for you; none are allowed to sleep there but princes and some few of my master's nearest relatives."

After having allowed me to admire the richness of the furniture for a while, this servant offered to undress me, but I declined his assistance for very good reasons; my ragged shirt was by no means in a state to be exhibited, and, in addition to this, the rest of my clothes were now of so very fine a texture that they required a hand more interested in their welfare than his was to take them off delicately. Either through malice, however, or that he thought I declined his good-natured offer merely from politeness, he returned to the charge, and, seeming determined to assist me in spite of my teeth, he caught hold of me and drew off one of my sleeves so suddenly that, had I not prevented him with my other hand, he would undoubtedly have torn it to pieces. I then entreated him in a peevish tone to leave me to my rest, and he prevented my further anger by desisting as I desired. I retired to the side of the bed, threw off my rags, which were held together only by a few laces, and jumped into bed, the sheets of which were clean and completely perfumed. This done, I told the servant he might take away the candle.

"I am not so inconsiderate," replied he, "it would be the means of causing you to pass a very uneasy night; for it is very common for large bats, which are very numerous in this country, to conceal themselves in chambers with so lofty a ceiling, and you will be much disturbed by them if you remain without light. Added to this," continued he, "there are certain evil spirits that frequent the principal houses in this city, by whom you will infallibly be tormented if you neglect to keep lighted candles in the room, the brightness of which, it is said, they are afraid off."

He told me all this tale with an ingenuous air, and I listened to him with all the credulity of an infant, instead of mistrusting this Antonio, whose knavish countenance ought to have been sufficient to have excited my suspicions.

No sooner had he left the chamber than I got out of bed and bolted the door, less from fear of being robbed than in the hope of thus securing myself from the persecution of the aforesaid spirits. Considering myself then in perfect safety, I lay down again, and reflected on the benevolence of my venerable landlord. So far from suspecting him of any bad design, which, had I possessed a little more experience, I should not have failed to have done, I represented myself that he could be no other than one of my nearest relatives, who had not chosen to make himself known to me overnight that he might surprise me the more agreeably in the morning.

"I would lay a good wager," said I to myself, "that when I wake tomorrow morning, I shall find a tailor in waiting to take measure of me for a fine suit of clothes. I may rest assured that in future I shall never want for anything, and that I have not lost my labor in coming to Italy."

Flattered by these agreeable thoughts, my senses were beguiled by degrees into a most profound sleep.

Although Antonio had told me that the evil spirits were so averse to light, my candles did not secure me from the persecution of four figures in the shape of so many devils who entered my chamber. It was some time before I heard the noise created by these demons; but as it was very far from their intention to respect my repose, they advanced towards the bed, drew the curtains, two of them seized me by the arms, and the other two by the legs, and dragged me out of bed. At length I awoke; and finding myself thus dangling in the air in the clutches of four devils, I was so terribly frightened that I was more dead than alive. They were each habited exactly as the devil is represented; with huge long tails, frightful vizards, and horns on their heads.

I had just sufficient sense remaining in me to invoke the assistance of some saint whose name occurred to me at that moment. But had I offered up prayers they would have been equally unavailing. These apparitions were not to be driven from their purpose; exorcisms even would have been useless, for the devils that I had to deal with had been baptized. They placed me in one of my blankets, and, each taking a corner, began to toss me in the air with such violence that they threw me to the ceiling at every toss, against which I expected every moment that either my head or one of my arms would be broken. But they contented themselves with only bruising me, though they did not cease to make me vault in this manner until they were completely fatigued, or, rather, until their noses informed them that my fear grew laxative. They then placed me in bed again, covered me over as they found me, extinguished the light, and vanished the same way as they had entered.

In this pitiable condition I remained until daybreak; and with the most dreadful sensation of fear still on my mind, I made an effort to get up, with the intention of hastening as quickly as possible out of a house where the duties of hospitality had been so scurvily fulfilled. But I could not rise or dress myself without the greatest difficulty and pain, the cause of which I could not remember without bestowing a thousand curses on the old rascal who had caused me to be thus cruelly treated. He no longer seemed to me that personage so worthy of veneration, no longer that benevolent character the meeting with whom had so much delighted me, but an old sorcerer, destined to be damned from the creation of the world.

Before I quitted the chamber I was curious to know how these malignant spirits could have entered it. I first examined the door, and, finding it still bolted as I had left it before I fell asleep, I could not reasonably imagine that they had found their way to me by that means. But having lifted up the hangings, I perceived a large window covered by them, which opened into the gallery. This was still open, the apparitions not having taken the trouble to close it after them. I made not the least noise, lest there should be something still in reserve for me, and thought of nothing but how to extricate myself from this cursed place. I had already left the room with this view, when I met Antonio in the gallery, who informed me that his master was waiting for me at the nearest church. All the answer I made was to request him to show me to the street-door, which he did with as much *sang-froid* as if he had not been one of the goblins who had amused themselves so much at my expense. I no sooner got out of doors than I scampered off as if I had not a bruise about me. What wonderful strength is imparted by fear! I ran as fast as my legs would carry me.

As soon as I considered myself in perfect safety, my hunger, which had been suspended for a while by fear, became such that I was obliged to satisfy it by buying some baked meat and a slice of bread, which I amused myself with eating as I walked along. I did not stop till I had got quite out of the city, and then, seeing a tavern before me, I went in and drank a glass of good wine. This so completely reanimated my courage that, after a slight repast, I was able to set out again, taking the road towards

Rome, reflecting on the affectionate reception I had met with from my relations, and especially from my old friend, I made a solemn oath never to forget the detestable night that this gray-bearded old wolf had allured me under his roof, for which I resolved to be fully avenged on him at the very first opportunity.

CHAPTER II

WHAT BECOMES OF GUZMAN AFTER HAVING LEFT GENOA

I TRAVELED some distance from Genoa, without so much as turning my head once towards that city, as though I feared that the sight of it would have petrified me. I resembled one of those who escaped from the battle of Roncesvalles; I walked on without having any determined route, though it was my wish to go to Rome. At length I reached a town about ten miles from Genoa, where I stopped some hours to rest myself, and spent what remained of my *pistole*. Then, resigning myself entirely into the hands of Providence, I resumed my journey.

It was well for me that I had been accustomed to misfortunes, and that I had already made some progress in the art of begging. What would have become of me without this resource? I should have been much to be pitied. Anyone that possesses the talent of exciting his neighbor's charity may travel all over Italy without money. I must render this justice to Italy, that no nation in the world has more charity in it—in proof of which assertion I reached Rome without spending a single *sou* of all the money that I was able to collect on the road, and which I carefully reserved. In the different villages through which I passed I had more meat and bread given me than I could possibly consume. Mendicity in that country is a fine resource for persons of spirit in bad circumstances who cannot make up their minds to be industrious. For my own part, I

was so naturally inclined to that trade that I wished for
no better. I must confess that when I found myself in the
capital of the Catholic World, with money enough in my
pocket to buy a new suit of clothes, I was at first somewhat tempted to employ it in that way, with a design to
offer my services to some nobleman; but I had courage
enough to resist this desire, which I considered in no other
light than as a temptation of the devil.

"Oh! oh! Guzman," said I to myself, "do you wish to
give yourself the same airs here as at Toledo? Suppose,
when you have expended all your little hoard in dress, you
should be so unlucky as to find no one willing to employ
you, who do you think will feed you, my friend? Do you
imagine that a fine new coat is likely to excite charity?
Undeceive yourself. You will be more likely to fare better
in your present dress. Be wise and rather endeavor to
profit by your old follies than to seek after new ones.
Be contented as you are, and do not resume your former
vanities."

Reasoning with myself in this manner, I tied up my
purse with a double knot, and addressing myself to the
money within it, "Remain thus secure," said I, "until I
find a better opportunity of making thee useful."

I began then to traverse the streets of Rome in my rags,
soliciting alms like one who believed himself a master in
the art, but who was in reality a mere apprentice in comparison with the professors of that country. Among these
was a young fellow, who, remarking the manner of begging that I adopted, found that I required a few lessons,
which he was kind enough to give me. We associated together; and, to render me useful to the society, he taught
me the different manners and the several tones in which
alms should be asked of different people, and that the same
speech would not always do.

"Men," said he, "are not in the least affected by the
plaintive and lamentable tones adopted by most beggars.
They will be much more likely to put their hands in their
pockets when you implore their assistance boldly for God's

sake. As for women," continued he, "as some pay their devotions to the Holy Virgin, and others to our Lady of the Rosary, it is by one of these that we wheedle them. It has frequently a good effect also to pray that they may be preserved from all mortal sin, from false witnesses, the power of traitors, and from slanderous tongues; such wishes as these, pronounced in energetic terms, and in an impressive tone of voice, will almost always make their purses fly open to assist you."

He taught me, moreover, how to excite the compassion of the rich, and, what is still more difficult, of professed devotees. In a word, he gave me such good instructions, and I made so good a use of them that I soon received more money than I could spend. I was already perfectly acquainted with Rome, from the Pope down to the very lowest scullion in the city. For fear of troubling my customers too often, I divided the city into seven parts, allotting one for every day in the week. I never failed to present myself at the several churches on holidays, where I was sure to pick up something. As to the pieces of bread that were usually given at doors of private houses, I sold what I did not want to distressed objects who were ashamed to beg, but who, by being relieved in private by the faithful, were well able to pay for what they bought of me. Country people and others, who made it their business to fatten fowls and hogs, were also frequent purchasers; but the spicecake makers were my best customers. I likewise made something considerable by the old rags which were given me by charitable persons, who could not without pity see a lad of my age almost naked, especially in winter.

Having by this time become acquainted with the first professors in the art of begging, I was now perfect master of the trade by following their directions and example. It happened one day that about thirty of our fraternity were collected before the door of the ambassador of France, when I heard one of my comrades behind me cry:

"Look at that Spanish glutton there, he'll certainly spoil

our trade. When once he is well filled with the soup or meat that is given him, he declines taking any more; this it is that ruins our business. By these means people will be apt to think that poor people like us have too much given them."

One of our veterans, who knew me, overhearing this, said to the beggar who uttered this complaint:

"Peace, comrade, do you not see that this novice is a stranger who is not yet acquainted with our regulations? Leave him to me and I will undertake to instruct him. He is a pretty apt scholar, I assure you, and will in a very short time be a match for any of us."

After having thus taken my part, he called me aside in a low voice and asked me several questions, as, in what part of Spain I was born? what was my name? and how long I had been at Rome? When I had answered all these queries in a very laconic style, he proceeded to represent to me, but in a very mild manner, the mutual feeling that beggars were bound to observe towards each other, that a proper decorum might be supported among them; that they ought to be so united as to play into each other's hands like brother pickpockets in a fair. From thence entering into a long detail, he revealed so many secrets to me as soon convinced me how inferior I was to these great men. Amongst other things which I had never yet heard of, he taught me how to enlarge my stomach, so as to be able to eat four times as much as usual without incommoding myself, not forgetting to recommend me never to eat before people without affecting extreme greediness, for he assured me it was most essential to persuade them that beggars are dying with hunger. He concluded by informing me at what hours I should be sure to be at such and such places; that in some houses I might venture to enter the kitchen, and even as far as the parlor; but that in others I must not dare to enter the door.

I now thought that he had completely exhausted the subject, but all these things were nothing in comparison with the begging-laws, which he made me read at his own house, whither he led me as soon as the alms of the French ambassador were distributed. He did not content himself by allowing me merely to read these admirable regulations, but insisted on my taking a copy of them, that by being well acquainted with them I might never again infringe them in so shaemful a manner. . . .

CHAPTER III

HOW GUZMAN EXCITED THE COMPASSION OF A CARDINAL, AND WHAT FOLLOWED

HAVING risen one fine morning betimes, as was usual with me, I seated myself at the gate of a cardinal who passed for one of the most charitable men in Rome, having first taken great pains to swell and dress up one of my legs into an ulcer, which might have deceived the most skillful surgeons. I had not forgotten to make my face as pale as possible, for I should have been inexcusable indeed had I committed such a fault. I began begging in the most dolorous tone tha tmy voice was capable of, and several of the servants who were passing in and out were much affected by my plaintive moans; but this was merely practicing for the game I had in view. It was the pity of their master that I hoped to excite, who no sooner made his appearance than I redoubled my cries and complaints, addressing him in these words:

"O noble Christian! friend of Jesus Christ! take pity on a poor afflicted sinner, diseased and crippled in the flower of his age; be pleased, your eminence, to take compassion on my misery, and praised be the passion of our Redeemer."

The cardinal, who was a holy man, stopped to listen to me, and, hoping to please the Lord in extending his charity towards me, he turned to his domestics, saying:

"Take this poor wretch in your arms, and convey him into my chamber; there let these rags be taken from off him, furnish him with clean linen, lay him in my own bed, and have another prepared for me in the next apartment."

These orders were instantly obeyed. O charity! which may serve for an example to other prelates, who in general consider Heaven as indebted to them when they pay the slightest attention to the misery of the poor! The cardinal did not stop here, but sent for two of the most celebrated surgeons in Rome, desiring them to examine my leg, and do everything in their power to cure it; and, after having promised to reward them well for their trouble, he left them to their own proceedings.

On the faith of this promise the surgeons immediately began to inspect my ulcer, which at first seemed to them incurable. Mortification seemed already to have taken place. This was occasioned, however, by nothing but the herbs I had applied, and could only last for a certain time, after which, by omitting the application, my leg would have been restored to its natural healthy state. They then threw off their cloaks, drew out their cases, and ordered some fire to be brought them in a chafing dish, some fine white linen, and some eggs and milk. While all these things were preparing, they began to question me concerning my disorder, how long I had been afflicted with it, and if I knew how I first came by it? if I drank any wine? what I was accustomed to eat? In short, they asked me all the questions usual with persons of their profession on such occasions, to which I was not able to answer a word, so dreadfully frightened was I at the terrible preparations that were making before my eyes. I knew not what saint I could presume to implore, for I could not flatter myself that there was one to be found in heaven willing to intercede for such a knave as myself.

The surgeons, after having turned my leg in all directions twenty times over, retired into another chamber to discourse together, and communicate their observations to each other more privately. I was terribly alarmed as to what would be the result of this consultation, not knowing but they might decide on cutting my leg off. I leaped straightway

143

out of bed, therefore, to follow and listen to them, fully resolving to confess the truth if I should find they had determined upon amputation. I approached the door, and while I listened most attentively to their conversation, heard one of these sages say to the other:

"We may make a good job of this, brother, if we can understand each other; the leg is dreadfully inflamed, and must take a long time to cure."

"You certainly must be jesting," answered the other; "there is no more inflammation on that leg than on my hand; it is a kind of disorder which I am sure I can convince you may be removed in less than two days."

"Do not believe it," replied he who had first spoken; "by St. Comas, I flatter myself I have some knowledge in ulcers, and I do maintain that this is a decided mortification."

"No, no," retorted the other; "believe me, our patient is an arrant rogue, and has no real disorder whatever to complain of; I know well enough how a sham ulcer may be raised, for I have often met with similar cases, and can even tell you the herbs this impostor has made use of to reduce his leg into its present apparently diseased state."

The surgeon who had been my dupe was quite abashed at these words; but, thinking that it concerned his reputation to persist in his first assertion, he would not yield to his comrade's opinion. The dispute would have grown very hot between them, had not the second surgeon been politic enough to terminate it by entreating his brother to examine the leg afresh.

"Just inspect it again," said he, "and you will no longer doubt the deception."

"Willingly," replied the other; "and if I find the ulcer such as you have affirmed, I will readily yield to your judgment."

"That is not enough," replied the former; "in acknowledging your error, you must also agree that I deserve to have a greater share of the profits than you."

"By no means," cried his companion; "do not take so

much merit to yourself for such a discovery, which I might have made without your assistance. I insist that we share equally whatever fees his eminence may give us."

They disputed afresh on this point, and their quarrel grew so high that they came at length to the resolution of laying the full particulars of the case before the cardinal.

When I found how things were likely to end, I hesitated no longer, but entered the room suddenly, threw myself at their feet, and with tears in my eyes (for I had a peculiar talent in being able to cry when I would), addressed them in these words:

"Take compassion, my dear gentlemen, on one who is but a man like yourselves. You well know that the rich are so hard-hearted nowadays that it is impossible for the poor to excite their pity, otherwise than by covering themselves with wounds and sores, and that it is but seldom that we can obtain anything but the most miserable pittance even by these means. What can you gain by discovering my knavery? You will lose the reward which has been promised you, which cannot escape you if you can consent that we all three concert matters together. You may safely venture to place confidence in me, for the fear of punishment will insure my discretion."

The surgeons, after a little reflection, made up their minds to profit by this opportunity of touching the cardinal's money. This was no sooner agreed to than we returned to his eminence's chamber, where they seated me on a chair, and began to re-examine my leg, which they plastered up with the drugs they considered most likely to make the sore last as it was. They then bound it up, and wrapped a napkin round it, and, observing the cardinal enter the room at that very instant, took me up in their arms to keep up appearances, and placed me on the bed again. His eminence, who was extremely uneasy on account of my ulcer, inquired about it immediately.

"My lord," said one of the surgeons with a grave countenance, "this poor lad's situation is truly pitiable; his leg is already mortified; we trust, however, that, with God's assistance, we may be able to do something for him, but his cure must be the work of time."

" It is most fortunate for him," said the other surgeon, "that he has this day fallen into our hands; one day more must have proved fatal; and Heaven had certainly ordained that his life should be saved by sending him to the door of your eminence."

The cardinal was extremely pleased at this report, and told them that they might take as much time as they pleased, provided they cured me in the end. He besought them afresh to neglect nothing that might contribute to my recovery, promising that he would see that I should be well treated in his house. They assured him that his confidence should not be misplaced, and that they would not fail, one or other of them, to call and see me twice a day; for that it would be necessary for them to consult together upon the slightest change that might take place in my disorder. After this they withdrew, and left me more at ease in my mind; for to this moment I had been very suspicious of these two treacherous rascals, lest they should expose my knavery, while they pretended to be accomplices. These unconscionable dogs obliged me to keep my chamber for three months, which appeared three ages to me, so difficult is it to lose the desire for gaming and begging. In vain did I lie in a fine bed; in vain did I fare like his eminence himself; nothing could recompense me for such confinement.

At length I pressed, I tormented my surgeons so eternally to bring this comedy to an end, that they were obliged at last to yield to my importunities. They left my ulcer, therefore, to take its course, and when they found that my leg was restored to its natural state, acquainted the good cardinal with it, who was quite astonished at so wonderful a cure, and dismissed these quacks, after having paid them much more than they deserved. His eminence had been so kind as to pay me several visits during the course of my pretended illness. I had frequent conversations with this holy prelate, who, having discovered in me a sort of wit which pleased him, had taken a great fancy to me! as a proof of which he proposed and seemed to wish to take me into his service, among the number of his pages, an honor which was too gratifying to me to think of refusing.

CHAPTER IV

GUZMAN BECOMES PAGE TO THE CARDINAL, AND COMMITS A THOUSAND MISCHIEVOUS TRICKS IN HIS SERVICE

THUS did I all of a sudden become a page. This was, in truth, a fine leap for me, although between knave and page there is no difference but their dress, for their propensities are precisely the same; it served, however, to amuse me, and prevented my growing idle, though I felt like a fish out of water in my new employment. As a beggar I was in my element; accustomed to the soups of Egypt, I felt myself at home nowhere but in the tavern. I was therefore by no means pleased by the life I led in this house, where everything was regulated by rule and compass; where at one time I was employed with a flambeau in my hand running up or down stairs, to light our visitors as they entered or left the house, and at another was obliged to dance attendance in the ante-chamber, kicking my heels there for about two hours, until I received my orders. Always in readiness to follow carriages by night as well as by day, or to wait at table and devour with my eyes only all the dishes that were served up; in a word, it was necessary for me to be at hand on all occasions, and that not for a few days only, but from the first day of January to the last of December.

Ah! miserable slave, you will naturally say, what profit could you possibly derive during a year of so much trouble? Alas! I must answer, I was servant to everybody; a fine coat was certainly given me, but that not so much for my own use as my lord's honor. I got nothing in this service but the itch and severe colds, except some ends of flambeaux which I stole and sold to the cobblers; and it was necessary to be very cautious to commit even these little thefts with impunity. Woe to us pages if we were ever caught in the fact! we were sure to get well lashed. Besides the pieces of wax that we cut off the flambeaux, we sometimes laid our hands upon some tit-bits that were served up at table, which we ate in private.

But such tricks as these required more dexterity than was possessed by any of my comrades, and a pretty accident befell one of these silly fellows. As he was clearing away the dishes after having waited at table, he thought proper to steal some honey fritters, which he wrapped up hastily in his handkerchief, and crammed into his pocket. The fritters being very hot, and pent up in so close a place, began to discharge their honey, which ran all down the poor page's leg. Ill-luck directed the cardinal's eyes that way, who, guessing at first sight what it was, began to laugh most heartily.

"Page," said he, addressing himself to this simpleton, "I perceive blood trickling down your legs; are you anywhere wounded?"

At this question all the company, which was very numerous, and even the servants, turned about to look at the culprit's leg, and the poor devil of a page stood confused and mortified, knowing that his crime was discovered. Happy for him had he been let off for the shame of enduring the extreme laughter which he excited, but he paid much more dearly the next day for his fritters, the honey of which was but sour to him.

Most of my other comrades were as green as this one when I was first received among them, and as I could not refrain from following my old habits, I employed myself in robbing them of whatever they had worth stealing, in spite of all the pains they took to secure themselves from my clutches. This soon taught them to be rather more vigilant. Our master kept in a closet adjoining his own bed-chamber a large chest, filled with all sorts of dried sweetmeats, which he was extremely fond of. In this chest, among other things, were prunes from Genoa, bergamot-pears from Aranjuez, melons from Grenada, citrons from Seville, oranges from Placentia, lemons from Murcia, cucumbers from Valencia, love-apples from Toledo, peaches from Arragon, and raisins from Malaga. In short, the most delicious sweetmeats and dried fruits of every description were to be found in this enviable chest, which never failed to make my mouth water whenever his eminence gave me the key to get some out for him.

On such occasions, however, he always took good care to be present himself, distrusting, as I supposed, my thieving disposition. I was much mortified at this suspicion, which only served to excite my desire, which was already strong enough to have a taste of these fine preserves, and, not being able any longer to resist the temptation, I thought of nothing but the means of gratifying my inclination. The chest was about a yard wide, and two yards and a half long, and had only one lock in the middle. Seeing this, I procured a wooden wedge and raised a corner of the lid, by which means I made an opening large enough to admit my arm; but as I could then only choose such sweetmeats as lay within my reach, I fastened a hook to the end of a long stick, with the assistance of which I had the pleasure of picking and choosing where I pleased. Thus I made myself complete master of the chest without having the key of it.

Notwithstanding the great quantity of fruits in the chest, my stick was so frequently at work that they began to diminish apace. The cardinal observed large holes here and there, which did not much please him; but one day, being desirous to taste a very fine citron which he had taken particular notice of the preceding evening, what was his astonishment when he found it flown? He summoned his principal officers before him, and told them he was determined to know which of his domestics had been so insolent as to open his chest and touch the fruits he so much prized, charging his major-domo, a sour, ill-natured priest, to leave no stone unturned to find out the thief. Suspicion fell upon the pages, and we were ordered to assemble in the hall, where we were searched one after another; but to no purpose were our pockets ransacked, in vain were we threatened, for I had long ere this not only eaten the citron, but digested it.

This affair soon blew over, and no more was said of it. The cardinal, however, had not forgotten it, and I was obliged to be so much on my guard that I did not venture to pay another visit to my favorite chest, even to look at it, for several days. This vexed me exceedingly; for I had acquired a particular relish for his eminence's sweetmeats, and, so far from thinking of giving them up, was waiting anxiously for the first opportunity of having another touch at them. One day, therefore, while the cardinal was engaged at play with some other cardinals ofter dinner, I doubted not that I should have abundance of leisure to resort to my old sport again.

Quite confident of this, I ran for my tools, which I had hid in a snug place, and glided into the closet without being perceived by anyone. Scarcely had I raised the lid and thrust in my arm, when his eminence entered the chamber, and finding neither of his pages there, assisted himself to what he wanted. I heard him, and endeavored to release my arm with so much haste and fear that I struck the wedge out with my elbow, and the lid fell on my arm, so that I was caught like a bird in a trap. The cardinal, hearing the noise, began to be alarmed for his sweetmeats, and entered the closet immediately, where he found me in this ludicrous situation.

"Ah! ah! friend Guzman," cried he, "is it then you who rob me of my sweetmeats?"

The grimaces that I made at finding myself so fairly caught were so ridiculous that he could not restrain his laughter. He even called the other cardinals that they might enjoy my confusion, who left off playing and ran up immediately; and after they had diverted themselves for some time at my expense, they entreatd him to forgive me this time, saying that they were convinced I should not again transgress. But my master was inexorable; all that their prayers could obtain for me was that I should receive only a dozen lashes instead of four-and-twenty, which I had so richly deserved. This chastisement could not bé remitted; and the major-domo, Signor Nicola, my mortal enemy, was charged to inflict it in his own apartment, which duty he acquitted himself of with such hearty good will that I was scarcely able to stir for above a fortnight after.

It was not many days, however, before I was avenged on him for this hard usage. You must know that this chanced to be just the season for mosquitoes, with which Rome was more than usually swarmed that year. Signor Nicola, who loved his ease, was complaining one day in my presence how much he was annoyed in his bed by these troublesome companions.

"Signor," said I, "you will have only yourself to blame if you are not quickly rid of them forever. In Spain we have an infallible secret to secure ourselves from being plagued by these insects, which, if you please, I shall be happy to communicate to you."

"You will oblige me beyond measure," answered Nicola.

"You have only," replied I, with a serious countenance, "to lay at your bed's-head a good bunch of parsley well steeped in vinegar, of which these vermin are extremely fond, and which is sure to kill them."

He believed me, and tried the experiment that very night, but it had a very different effect, for he found himself assailed more cruelly than ever, and was even fearful that they would have eaten his nose off or torn out his eyes, and had given himself a thousand violent thumps on the face during the night to get rid of them. Thus had he fought with them until daylight, when he found that he had not come very victoriously off, for that even of such of his enemies as he thought he had crushed, very many had escaped. I did not fail to go into his chamber to see, him the first thing in the morning, and his swollen eyes quickly assured me of the success of my plan. He told me how he had been tormented, saying that my secret was not worth a farthing. I affected great astonishment.

"You cannot then," said I, "have left the parsley long enough in the vinegar, or the vinegar you were supplied with must have been very weak and bad; for I assure you, that by carrying a bunch of parsley prepared in the same manner into my own chamber, I have entirely cleared it of these troublesome guests, who were there in swarms before I used this remedy."

The major-domo was fool enough to believe me again, and left a whole bundle of parsley to soak for above six hours in the strongest vinegar he could procure, and then not only put it into his bed, but scattered it all over his chamber. God knows what furious attacks he was therefore exposed to; I verily believe that all the mosquitoes in the neighborhood poured down in legions upon him to devour him, and made so furious an assault that they left him like a leper all over his body. What a thrashing would he have given me had he met me on the following day; but his eminence, to prevent accident, called us both into his presence, desiring him not to treat me harshly on the occasion, and at the same time gave me a slight reprimand, though he could scarcely restrain his laughter at the success of my scheme.

"For what reason," said the good prelate, "have you played such a scurvy trick upon Signor Nicola?"

"My lord," replied I, "for no other reason than that when he had orders to give me a dozen lashes for my exploit among the sweetmeats, he accommodated me with more than twenty on his own account. I have only therefore avenged my scars by those I have inflicted on him."

Thus ended this notable affair. Ever since my unlucky adventure of the sweetmeat chest, I had been discharged from the chamber of the pages. The flogging I got was not the only way in which I was punished, for I had been passed into the chamberlain's department, to serve among the foot-boys until I had sufficiently atoned for my offense to be reinstated in my former post. The chamberlain was a man of honor and sincerity, but rather too scrupulous, and even inclined to be visionary. He had several relations in the neighborhood, who were very virtuous girls, but so poor that he would send every day two-thirds of his own meals to enable them to subsist. He went occasionally to dine or sup with them. This afforded an opportunity to the officers of the family, and especially our major-domo, to rally him before his eminence, who was greatly diverted by it.

One night when the chamberlain came home, after having dined with his relations, finding himself rather indisposed, he retired into his own chamber and went to bed. The cardinal, not seeing him at supper, inquired after him.

"My lord," said one of the servants, "he is not very well."

The cardinal, who was anxious to know what could ail him, sent one of his gentlemen to see, who returned with a report that the chamberlain only required a good night's rest. and that he doubted not he would be perfectly well again by the morning. This passed off well enough; but the secretary Nicola, who was always ready to pick a hole in the chamberlain's coat, having learned the next morning that he was much better, caused one of the pages to be dressed up in a young woman's clothes, who, with the assistance of a bribe to one of the foot-boys, introduced himself into the bedroom while the chamberlain was fast asleep, and glided to the side of the bed where he was concealed by the curtains. Immediately after this the secretary went to wait on the cardinal, who inquired after the invalid the first thing.

"He has passed but an indifferent night, I understand," answered Nicola, "but is much better this morning."

The cardinal, who loved all his domestics as a father loveth his children, resolved, upon hearing this, to go and see the chamberlain himself, who was disturbed from his slumbers to be apprised of the honor intended him.

His eminence then entered the sick man's chamber, and sat down on a chair at the side of the bed, but scarcely was he seated when he saw the metamorphosed page slip suddenly from the bedside, who, counterfeiting most naturally the embarrassed female anxious to escape, got off at length, crying:

"Oh! good God, I am ruined forever! What must his eminence think of me?"

The cardinal, who had not been prepared for this scene, and who believed his chamberlain to be a religious, steady man, appeared to be extremely surprised at this sight; but great as his astonishment was, it amounted to nothing in comparison with that of our visionary chamberlain, who, as if just roused from a most horrible dream, cried aloud that it was assuredly the devil himself come to tempt him in the shape of a woman. This idea caused so excessive an agitation of his spirits that he could scarcely be restrained from leaping out of bed in his shirt before his eminence, and taking to his heels. As all the servants who were present were privy to the secretary's design, they could not avoid laughing, from which the cardinal soon perceived that it was only a trick upon his chamberlain, and had the goodness to relieve his distress by undeceiving him himself. After which he retired.

All this was just over when I reached home, having been out on different commissions the whole of the morning. Finding the worthy chamberlain very low-spirited on my return, I inquired the cause, and he related the whole affair to me, saying he had no doubt that Nicola was at the bottom of it.

"I would willingly, my dear Guzman," added he, "most willingly, sacrifice one of my eyes to be amply avenged on him for this plot, and with your assistance I doubt not I may be able to return him a 'roland for his oliver.' A knowing shaver like you will soon devise some good trick to play him."

"I must confess," answered I, "that were I in your place, the secretary should have no occasion to go to the pope for absolution; I would make him do sufficient penance for his trick. Remember, however, that he is my superior, and it is not for me to interfere with officers who are above me. If I was excused for the trick I played Master Nicola on my own account, it was only because what I did was to revenge myself for his former cruel conduct towards me."

In vain did I represent to the enraged chamberlain that I dared not take up his cudgels lest I should repent it; he would admit of no excuse. His prayers, my great friendship for him, the mortal hatred I had for the secretary, and, above all, my natural propensity to mischief, determined me at length to espouse his cause.

" Well, then," said I, " leave it to me; I will undertake to make my talents useful to you. All I require of you is to behave towards the secretary as though you had the most distant thought that he was the author of the late plot."

The chamberlain, simple as he was, played his part so well that all the servants thought he had forgiven all that had passed.

In the meantime I was on the alert in preparing everything to keep my promise. I bought some rosin, mastic, and frankincense, reduced the whole into a powder, and mixed them well together in a paper packet which I kept in my pocket until an opportunity presented itself of making use of it. This offered itself very opportunely a few days after. It was the Spanish post-day, and Mr. Secretary being very much engaged, I went to his apartment in the morning, and entered his wardrobe where his servant was.

" James," said I, " my dear fellow, I have a loaf and a fine slice of fried ham below. I want but a bottle of wine to make a good breakfast. If you can supply this, you shall share with me; otherwise, I must look for someone else."

" Mr. Guzman," answered James, his eyes sparkling with joy, " I am your man; I can easily get you a bottle of the very best wine, and if you will but wait here, I shall be with you again in an instant."

155

Thus saying, he disappeared, leaving me master of the wardrobe. Then, looking about for his master's breeches (for I knew the secretary did not put them on in the morning, having slipped on his dressing gown over his shirt that he might write more at his ease), I perceived them on the back of a chair. I took them up and turned them inside out, and after having strewed my powders all over the inside of them, I replaced them exactly as I found them. James soon returned with the wine, but scarcely had we begun breakfast when his master called him to assist in dressing, and detained him in his room so long that I was obliged to find another to share my bottle with me, waiting most anxiously for the time when I should have the pleasure of seeing my composition operate.

It had its full effect at the cardinal's dinner, where there were a number of visitors that day. As we were in the middle of the dog-days, the extreme heat of the weather was very favorable to my trick. Mr. Nicola was in waiting in the parlor with the other officers. I soon remarked by his distortions that he felt a great itching in a part of his body where, through respect, he dared not put his hand. He knew not how to keep his countenance, and, unfortunately the more he shrugged himself about the more he increased the pain. As he was naturally as hairy as a bear, the powder stuck in his hair and flesh, and twitched him like the points of a thousand needles. This was not all, for the cardinal, having some orders to give him, called him, and whilst in the act of whispering to him his eminence was obliged to stop his nose all at once, saying:

"What on earth have you about you, that you smell so strong as rosin and frankincense?"

The secretary colored at these words, and stood farther off from his master, who, perceiving that almost all my comrades, whom the chamberlain had let into the secret, were whispering and laughing among themselves, began to suspect that I had been at my tricks again. I stood very near to him looking very demurely all the while.

"Guzman," said he, "what is the fun now that seems to cause so much tittering?"

"I know not, indeed," answered I, "unless it be on account of our secretary's having taken a laxative draught composed of turpentine this morning."

The cardinal laughed most heartily, and the whole table followed this example. Nicola now began to see through the business, and, not being any longer able to endure the jeers and laughters with which the dining parlor resounded at his expense, took to his heels with a precipitation which redoubled the pleasure of the company. After he had left the room, the cardinal, impatient to know what was really the matter, addressed himself to the chamberlain, who concealed nothing from him. This adventure established my reputation in the palace as a most formidable character.

After having been banished two months from the chamber of the pages, I was at length recalled and re-established in my former post, the duties of which I resumed with as much effrontery as if nothing had happened. This brought to my mind a fable which you have doubtless heard, of the Air, the Water, and Shame, who having kept company together for some time, and being at length obliged to part, were desirous to know where they should see each other again. Quoth the Air:

"You will always find me on the top of mountains."

"And I, without fail," said the Water, "may always be found in the bowels of the earth."

"As for me," said Shame, sighing, "if I am once parted with, it is impossible to meet with me again."

Nothing can be more true; in my own case I felt it, for I was now no longer susceptible of shame at the commission of a bad action: the only shame I felt was in being detected. In short, I was so naturally disposed to knavery, that I really believe I would have thrown myself headlong from the top of the Castle of St. Angelo if I saw anything at the bottom worth stealing.

As the good cardinal was a great lover of sweetmeats, especially of those that came from the Canaries in barrels, he would always send for more when his stock was out; and when the barrels were empty they became the property of the first servant who took possession. One fell to my share in this manner, in which I kept my handkerchiefs, cards, dice, and other effects of a poor page. One day a man called to inform his eminence that a merchant had just received twelve barrels of fruits of this description. The cardinal ordered them for himself. I heard this order given, and said within myself, " It shall go hard but I have one of them."

I retired to my chamber to consider how I could make myself master of one, and resolved on this plan: I instantly emptied my barrel of my old rags, and having filled it with earth and straw, I closed it down, and put on the hoops again so neatly that it looked as if it had never been opened. This done, I went down into the court-yard to wait the arrival of those that were full of sweetmeats. I had not waited long before I perceived them coming with the major-domo at their head, who ordered us to carry them immediately into the closet where his eminence usually kept them. Each of my comrades carried up a barrel. I took good care to be the last with mine, having my reasons for wishing to walk after all the rest. We had necessarily to pass by my chamber, so that, seeing myself followed by no one, I slipped in unperceived, and, changing the barrels in the twinkling of an eye, carried the one I had so well filled with earth and straw and laid it boldly among the rest in the cardinal's closet. His eminence was himself there to see them, and when they all were all arranged in order he turned towards me, with a smile on his countenance, and said:

" Well, Guzman, what think you of these barrels? it will not be so easy a matter to thrust an arm into these, or to use wedges, as with the former ones."

" If wedges will not do," replied I coolly, " I may be tempted to employ my nails, for the hand sometimes does the office of the arm."

" Ah!" replied his eminence, " but I defy thee to pilfer

these barrels, which have no corners to be lifted up as the chest had."

"True," replied I, "but I beseech your eminence not to defy me in anything; for the devil may in such a case furnish me with the means of deceiving you."

"Be that as it may," cried the cardinal, "I give you leave with all my heart to steal these sweetmeats if you can, and I give you eight days to do it in. Should you be dexterous enough to succeed, you shall not only be allowed to keep what you steal, but I promise you as much more; on condition, however, that should your genius be obliged to yield, you will without murmuring submit to whatever penalty I may choose to inflict."

"That is but just, my lord," said I, "and I agree to the alternative. Yes," continued I, "I do not perform my task in four and twenty hours, for I ask not eight days for so trifling an affair, I will submit to any punishment Signor Nicola may be pleased to sentence me to, who, after the affair of the mosquitoes and that of the turpentine, is not likely, you will allow, to be too lenient a judge."

The cardinal laughed at these last words, and it was finally agreed that I should be punished or rewarded on the following day.

What precautions did not his eminence take to secure his barrels from my cluthes! besides keeping the key of the closet in his own possession, he set some of his most confidential domestics to be most constantly on the watch. The next day at dinner the good prelate, fancying me a little thoughtful, said, with a smile:

"Guzman, I see plainly what makes you so dull; you are reflecting on the luxury of receiving a hundred lashes from the vigorous arm of Signor Nicola."

"Indeed, my lord," replied I "nothing was farther from my thoughts, for the sweetmeats are already in my possession."

The cardinal, fully persuaded that no one could possibly have gained access to his closet or touched his sweetmeats, seemed surprised at my effrontery, and rallied me all dinner-time on the strapping that was justly my due. I allowed him to divert himself as long as he pleased, but when the dessert was about to be served up, I stole privately out of the dining-room up to my own chamber, and drew out of my barrel some of the sweetmeats, with which I filled a basin I had taken off the sideboard for that purpose, and carried them to his eminence's table. He was so strangely surprised at the sight of them that he could scarcely believe his own eyes.

"Here," said he to the chamberlain, giving him the key of the closet, "go and count the barrels attentively; there must be one short.

The chamberlain returned with an assurance that they were all safe.

"Ah, ah!" said the cardinal, "I now see through your *finesse*, my poor Guzman. You have purchased some of the same merchant who sold me these fruits, and now hope to make me believe that you have stolen them; but it will not do, Mr. Guzman; your undertaking was to open and pilfer one of my barrels and take out some of the sweetmeats; this was our wager as you will be pleased to recollect—you cannot, therefore, escape the punishment. Come, Signor Nicola," continued he, "seize this rash youth, and inflict on him such chastisement as he may appear to you to deserve."

"Softly," my lord,' said I at these last words, "I confess that I amply deserve all this if the sweetmeats that I have just laid before you are not some of those your eminence bought yesterday; but you must allow also that I have won if I prove the contrary by convincing you that I have at this moment in my own chamber one of the twelve barrels that were yesterday brought into your palace."

"Be cautious what you affirm, page," interrupted the chamberlain; "there are twelve barrels in my master's cabinet, which I have counted over and over again."

"That may be," said I to the chamberlain, "but recollect that 'the wolf often eats the counted sheep.'"

The cardinal, anxious to know the truth of the matter,

hastened his dinner over, that he might examine his closet, whither he repaired accompanied by all the guests that dined with him that day, who for the most part felt convinced, by the bold face I assumed, that the affair would not end to my disadvantage.

His eminence counted the barrels himself, and finding twelve, " Guzman," said he, " here are the twelve barrels that I bought."

" My lord," answered I, " there are certainly twelve, but they are not all of sweetmeats."

The cardinal, losing patience, wished to have them opened.

" No, no," cried I, " I will save you that trouble." Saying which, I pointed out to him the barrel I had filled with earth and straw, and while they were opening it I ran to my chamber, whence I returned with the other, which was still half full of fruit, and related in what manner I had gained possession of it.

All the company present applauded me for my dexterity, and laughed most heartily at the adventure. His eminence, agreeably to promise, presented me with a second barrel, which I resigned to my comrades, to show that what I had done was but to amuse my worthy master. Diverted, however, as he was by my sleights-or-hand, he dismissed me from his service, for example's sake. . . .

CHAPTER V

GUZMAN ENTERS INTO THE SERVICE OF THF SPANISH AM-
BASSADOR.

M Y ridiculous pride long prevented me from perceiving the extreme folly of my behavior. At first I amused myself by strolling about the streets of Rome, and eating at the houses of my acquaintance, but I found that my civil reception among them did not last long; scanty fare and gloomy looks saluted me everywhere, and I was soon at a loss for a dinner. This verifies the Spanish proverb, " Live a week with your uncle or cousin, a month with your brother, a year with your friend; but in the house of your father you may live for life."

I soon perceived that sponging was a villainous trade, and began to regret that I was exiled from the table of the cardinal's pages; but the fault was then irreparable, since at that time his eminence fell sick and died. He left to all his servants, by his will, money enough to support them comfortably for the remainder of their lives. This circumstance drove me to despair, as I could not forgive myself for having, by my deplorable folly, excluded myself from the provision which would otherwise have been made for me. I saw no other resource but to offer my services to the Spanish ambassador, who had been one of the most intimate friends of my deceased master, and knew me very well. He had also in more than one instance given me tokens of his good will.

I had no sooner expressed my desire of entering into his service, than he testified the utmost willingness to receive me. He had often condescended to honor with a smile the jests and stories he had heard from me at the palace of the cardinal. He considered me as a dexterous young fellow, and very well adapted for his buffoon and pimp. This last honorable employment was what he chiefly designed for me, as you will soon perceive. But first I must depict the character of this minister.

He was chosen to conduct an embassy to Rome at a very critical period; this situation required a penetrating genius and a man of great address. His excellency perfectly justified the confidence which the king reposed in him. But he had a foible—a little too common amongst men of rank—that of being too much addicted to women. But for this circumstance, he would have been more esteemed than any other ambassador at that court. Having then judged me worthy to have the management of his intrigues, he began to inform me of his virtuous intentions.

Then, that I might give him a specimen of my abilities, he employed me in some trifling messages of gallantry, in which I had the good fortune to acquit myself to his entire satisfaction.

This *coup d'essai* was followed by two or three commissions of the same nature, though somewhat more difficult, which were conducted with equal success. Nothing more was necessary to establish me perfectly in his good graces, and he conceived such a friendship for me that I soon became his favorite page. From this moment Signor Guzman was all in all in his master's house. I did as I pleased, and everything that I did was well done. The other domestics did not see my growing greatness without envy, especially those of longest standing; some called me my master's buffoon, and some his pimp in ordinary. Nevertheless, I did not presume upon the favor of the ambassador, and was so far from doing these spiteful gentry any ill offices with his excellency that I gladly seized every opportunity of serving them, in consequence of which they forebore to show me any particular mark of their ill will, and we lived together on pretty tolerable terms.

While I was with the ambassador I did not disgrace the reputation I had acquired on account of my frolics at the palace of the cardinal, and I was not very sparing of my tricks, as there could not be any place in the world that could open a wider field for them than the house of my new master. Parasites often came in at dinner time. My fellow-pages and I were not at a loss to distinguish them from respectable people whom my master was really happy to see at his table. We took care to be very attentive to the latter, but as for the spongers, who were most of them mere adventurers, they had but scurvy commons, which diverted the ambassador exceedingly. One was suffered to ask in vain for drink during the whole meal; it was of no use to make signs, we pretended not to understand them. Another had his glass handed to him half full, and the glass shaped in such a fashion that half the liquor would remain in the glass, which only tantalized his thirst. Another was served with water prepared of a red color. If a dainty morsel was carved for any one of these gentry, we changed his plate so quickly that the poor devil had scarcely time to taste it. In a word, we did everything in our power to drive them all from his excellency's table, and were sometimes lucky enough to succeed.

Among the adventurers who were drawn together by the savory fumes which proceeded from our kitchen, there was a foreigner who surpassed all the others in impudence. He affirmed himself to be a relation of the ambassador, though his manners were as opposite as possible to those of a man of quality. His brazen impudence was his only introduction, and, in spite of the frozen reception he met with from his excellency, he assiduously pestered him with his company at dinner. He did nothing but boast of himself and of his country; the politeness of his countrymen—their civilities to strangers and their honesty were topics of which he was never tired. As for the women, the wives were all Lucretias, and the daughters Vestal Virgins. I should never have done if I were to repeat all the praises which he heaped upon the people of his own country; at last he wearied all the company with his foolish discourse. but especially my master, who, being quite out of patience, said to me one day in Castilian, which his blade did not understand:

"You know not, Guzman, how weary I am of this fellow's rhodomontade."

It may be supposed that this hint was not lost upon a page who was neither deaf nor a fool. I understood well enough that this troublesome presonage must absolutely be got rid of. To accomplish this end, I posted myself behind his chair at dinner, and whenever he asked for a drink, which happened almost every minute, I took a very large glass, which I filled to the brim with so strong a sort of wine that it could not fail to intoxicate him speedily; when I saw that this was effected, I tied one of his legs to his own chair with a piece of silk twist, without any of the guests perceiving what I did. When dinner was ended, the ambas-

sador rose, and the company followed his example, but
when my gentleman would have done the same, he and the
chair had such a heavy fall together that I am much mistaken if his nose and jaws did not rue the circumstance for
a long time afterwards. I pretended to help him up and
gently untied the string. Nevertheless, in spite of all the
wine that he had drank, he perceived that everybody
laughed at his expense, and, suspecting the cause of his
disaster, he went away in a rage and never came again,
which pleased his excellency beyond measure that he had
so easily got rid of such a troublesome guest.

Having thus driven this sponger from the field, my companions and I next undertook the discomfiture of the
others, but we found some who were not to be so easily
disposed of. Amongst others, there was a Spanish bully,
who called himself a gentleman of Cordova. He came
one day about dinner time, and saluted his excellency the
ambassador very ceremoniously, informing him that he was
in pecuniary distress, and that his pressing necessity obliged him to disclose his situation.

My master, who easily understood the drift of all this
harangue, took out a purse of *pistoles,* which he gave him
unopened, and, bowing politely, turned away from him;
but the Cordovan, far from retiring upon this hint, followed
him closely, and began talking of the dangers he had gone
through, and at last had the effrontery to take a seat next
to his excellency at the table.

"I hope," said he, "your excellency will not be offended
at the liberty I am taking, but even if I was not a gentleman
of family, my having served in his Majesty's army is sufficient to entitle me to the honor of eating with princes.
Besides," added he, "the table of a nobleman of your reputation should always be open to officers whose services have
not met with merited recompense."

After this fine speech he fell on the dish nearest him
with the greatest avidity. He ate like a half-starved glutton, as he was. Then looking at me, who was nearest to
him, he beckoned to me five or six times to bring him some

wine; but, unluckily for my gentleman, instead of paying any attention to his signs, I pretended that I did not observe them.

If he thought at first this neglect arose from carelessness or stupidity, he was soon undeceived, and perceived my roguish malice plain enough.

"Page," said he to me in a loud voice, "have you been ordered to let me die with thirst?"

Upon this, my master, who had no small inclination to laugh at this scene, nodded to me to serve this adventurer; but I took good care to give him one of the smallest glasses, and was even spiteful enough to hand it to him half empty.

Just as this happened, and when I was carrying back the salver to the sideboard, there entered two other parasites whom I knew by having frequently seen them at the ambassador's table. Not being able to find any vacant seats, they began to examine the guests, and particularly the pretended noble of Cordova, and as they seemed to me to regard him with an air of contempt my curiosity was excited. I approached the newcomers, and asked them if the gentleman whom they examined so attentively was one of their acquaintance.

"Gentleman, indeed!" cried one of the two, "surely you are jesting, my friend; learn that this fellow who is now filling at that table the seat which is only for respectable men, and whom you think to be of noble blood, is the son of a man who has often made boots for me, and who keeps a shop near the cathedral church of Cordova."

"If he comes in my way," said the other, "I shall tell him something more than he will like to hear."

Speaking thus, these braggadocios looked very big, twisted their mustachios, and retreated together into the courtyard to consider what steps they should next take.

When they had been there a short time, I went out and joined them.

"Gentlemen," said I, "this man whom you despise so much affirms that you are a couple of despicable fellows, and says he is surprised at your impudence in daring to intrude yourselves here. If you will wait till he has dined, he will come and tell you more himself."

"Let him come, let him come!" cried they both together; "we will let him know whom he has to deal with."

Having thus enraged them against the officer of Cordova, I returned to the latter, and in a whisper loud enough to be heard by the whole company, informed him that there were two gentlemen below who wanted a moment's conversation with him.

"Let them have patience," answered he; "I shall not quit his excellency while he is at table."

"They affirm," added I, "that you have announced yourself falsely as a cavalier of noble birth, and that you are but the son of a cobbler."

"Heaven and earth!" cried he, with a furious aspect; "can there be anyone so tired of his life as to dare to scoundrels?" continued he, rising from the table, "where talk in this manner of a man like me? Where are these are they? Their ears, at least, shall pay for their temerity."

"You have but to follow me," said I, "and I will bring you to them instantly."

At these words I took him by the arm and led him out of the room, though he seemed to have but little desire to quit it.

Immediately the ambassador and the company hastened to the windows which looked into the courtyard, to see the termination of the quarrel which I had contrived to stir up between these three bullies.

"Gentlemen," said I to the two wo where walking in the court, "here is the person whose father, if you are to be believed, is a Cordovan shoemaker."

"Let him thank his stars," cried they, "that our hands are tied by the respect we owe to this place, which we consider as belonging to the king of Spain."

Seeing the officer in such a panic that he could not utter a single syllable, I took up his cause. "Gentlemen," said I, "this cavalier will go out directly if you wish it, and is ready to terminate his dispute with you in the street."

" No, no," answered they, retreating with the utmost pre-cipitation, " we shall take another opportunity to meet him."

Their retreat brought back the courage of our gallant, who pretended to treat them as cowards. He himself there-fore went out a moment after them, but took care to choose a different road. The ambassador and his guests were infi-nitely diverted with this ridiculous adventure, and a thou-sand witty things were said at their return to table at the expense of our three adventurers. After dinner everyone retired, whilst his excellency withdrew to his chamber to enjoy his afternoon's nap. . . .

BOOK THE FOURTH

CHAPTER I

GUZMAN RESOLVES TO LEAVE ROME ON A TOUR THROUGH
ITALY, WITH THE INTENTION OF VISITING EVERYTHING
WORTHY OF NOTICE IN THAT COUNTRY

I SPENT nearly all my time now in my own room, where
every day was passed in reading and in receiving a few
visitors. One day a young Spaniard chanced to call in.
No sooner had he informed me he was my countryman,
than I asked him in what part of Spain he was born?

"I am," said he, "a native of Seville, and Sayavedra
is my name."

Upon hearing this I redoubled my civilities, as I knew
it to be one of the most illustrious families in our city.
His accent was certainly Andalusian, and I was not myself
better acquainted with Seville; though, in fact, he was a
native of Valencia, which he had his reasons for concealing. I offered him my own services, and the credit of my
master upon any occasion he might require them. He
thanked me for my good wishes, and told me that he had
a suit in the ecclesiastical court, which he hoped would
terminate favorably; but that if the persons whose interest
he relied on should not be successful in their exertions,
he would certainly avail himself of my proffered mediation in his favor. In the course of conversation I happened to mention that I might generally be found at home,

as I very rarely left the house. He very much approved
of this, and offered to accompany me himself with his
friends. I felt truly grateful for so obliging an offer, and
embraced him with every token of friendship, and overwhelmed him with acknowledgments. He was not behindhand with me in politeness, and though he very much approved of my confining myself at home, he seemed to think
that I must lead a very tiresome life, and recommended me
to travel; he mentioned Venice, Bologna, Pisa, and Florence, assuring me that I should find each of those places
well worthy of my inspection and concluded by remarking
that I could return to Rome, whenever I thought proper.

I gave Sayavedra to understand that nothing could be
more to my taste than what he proposed, and that I should
not hesitate to follow his advice, provided I could gain
the consent of my master, as I wished to be ruled by him
in everything. Then this imp of Satan, who was both
Andalusian and Valencian, and who had, I daresay (according to his own account afterwards), been a native of
half the cities of Europe, gave me such an engaging description of all the places he mentioned that my inclination to visit them increased vehemently. My thoughts
were so occupied with this scheme that the ensuing day,
as I was dressing the ambassador, I spoke to him in these
words:

"I do not know, my lord, if you will approve of a design
which I intend to execute if I obtain your permission. I
wish to make a tour of Italy, and indeed I think it would
not be amiss if I were to absent myself from Rome for a
short period."

"Guzman," cried he, "I am charmed with the scheme
beyond measure; yes, my friend, you will act wisely. I
have often wished to tell you so, but could never resolve
to undertake so disagreeable a task. Depend upon it, Guzman," continued this excellent master, "you shall find
yourself in a situation to travel in affluence to any country you may wish to visit: you will be treated as a servant
whom I esteem, and I part with you with sincere regret."

When the ambassador had concluded, I returned him a thousand thanks for his favorable opinion of me, and for his kind intentions towards me; and I had no sooner left his apartment than I despatched one of the scullions for the carrier of Siena. I had already begun to pack up my clothes in three trunks which had served for my wardrobe, when Sayavedra, whom I already reckoned among the number of my friends, paid me a visit. He affected some surprise at the sight of my clothes and effects, all spread out in my chamber, and my trunks open before me.

" Ah, Signor Guzman ! " cried he, " do you then intend to follow my advice ? "

" You have guessed right," answered I. " I have mentioned my intention to my master, who has given it his hearty concurrence. Everything is decidedly fixed upon. I purpose in two days time to quit Rome for Siena, where I shall make some stay at the house of a friend of mine, a merchant of the name of Pompey. I am not personally acquainted with him, but he has in his letters testified so much gratitude for some services I have had it in my power to render him in this city, that I have no doubt that he will be delighted with an opportunity of repeating his acknowledgments to me at his own house. So that I expect much pleasure in my stay at Siena, whither I am going to send forward my baggage today, addressed to the care of Pompey, that I may not be encumbered with it during my journey."

If Sayavedra paid all possible attention to this informatoin, he certainly paid no less to me, for while I was packing up my clothes in the trunks, he took exact notice where I placed those of the greatest value, and that he should see that I was possessed of such pleased my foolish vanity and love of parade. A gold chain, some valuable jewels, and three hundred good *pistoles,* which I had hoarded up during my stay at the ambassador's, did not escape his observation. I had wholly quitted the gaming table, and I had saved up with the utmost frugality every present that had been made me.

Would to Heaven that I had been destined to reap the fruits of my improved behavior; but, alas! that happiness was reserved for thieves, and not for me. I filled the other two boxes with what was of less value, and having carefully locked them, left the bunch of keys upon a table that stood by. We then continued our conversation, until a lackey came to inform me that I was wanted by a person below. My room not appearing to be in a fit state for receiving company, I begged my new friend to excuse me for a few minutes while I waited on the person who wanted to speak to me. It was the carrier, whom in the bustle I had almost forgotten having sent for. I told him on what day I should set out, and that we might agree on the sum he was to charge for the carriage of my baggage, I took him upstairs to show him of what it consisted.

Meantime Sayavedra had done the deed. This rascal, seeing the coast clear, took the impression of my keys on some wax, which I suppose was part of the ammunition he always carried about with him, and seeing a letter lying by, which he knew I had just received from Pompey, he impressed that also into his service. I showed my trunks to the carrier, who lifted them up, that he might judge of their weight. I gave him what he asked for their conveyance to Siena, and he withdrew, saying that he would return immediately with his people to help him away with the boxes, and would set out with them in three hours' time. He had no sooner quitted the house than this friendly Spaniard offered to take leave of me under a pretense that his visit retarded the preparations I was making for my journey. It was to no purpose to assure him that he by no means incommoded me, nor even to press him to stay and take breakfast with me; nothing could prevail upon him to stay, as he was upon the rack of impatience to go and order the false keys.

"At least then, my dear friend," said I, "acquaint me with your place of abode. I can by no means think of quitting Rome without returning your visit."

He replied that he would rather dispense with that ceremony, and gave me to understand, with a very mysterious air, that he lived privately with a lady, and for reasons, which as a man of honor he must conceal, he was under the necessity of debarring himself the pleasure of receiving the visits of his friends. As after hearing this I could urge him no longer, I suffered this favorite of the ladies to depart, who, no doubt, hastened with all speed to his companions, to consult on the measures they should adopt to get possessions of my trunks. He was in league with four rogues, who had for their leader a famous and notorious thief, called Alexander Bentivoglio. He generally conducted their enterprises, and assigned to each the part he was to play, sustaining the chief character himself. But on this occasion he yielded that honor to Sayavedra, who, being a Spaniard, appeared to him the most proper person to represent a Castilian. As they were well provided with disguises of all kinds, they dressed themselves in character, and set off the next morning for Siena, which they reached on the following day.

Sayavedra, followed by two of the others dressed in livery, put up at the best hotel in the town, and gave himself out as the gentleman in waiting to the Spanish ambassador. As for Alexander, who was well known for a rogue throughout Italy, he did not dare to play the part of a third lackey, but thought proper to lodge elsewhere with the fourth cavalier of his company. Sayavedra, putting on a lofty air, desired to be conducted to the best apartment in the hotel, and having taken possession of it, sent one of the people to inform Signor Pompey that his friend Don Guzman had just arrived post from Rome, but was so fatigued with his journey that he begged to be excused waiting on him at present. Pompey, delighted at the arrival of Don Guzman, hastened to pay his *devoirs* to a man to whom he was under so much obligation. He flies to the hotel, and is shown into a fine chamber, where he sees a cavalier reposing himself upon a couch, who, seeing him approach, runs to meet him with open arms.

"Ah, Signor Pompey," cries he, "I flatter myself that

173

you will pardon the liberty I took in sending my baggage to your house."

"I can readily excuse that," replied Pompey, with a smile, " but I shall not so soon forgive your coming to this place in preference to my house."

"You are extremely polite," replied the false Don Guzman, " but, upon my honor, riding post has fatigued me so much that I could not think of being so troublesome."

"For that very reason," replied the merchant, "you would have been more comfortable at my house."

"Another reason, too," continued Sayavedra, "opposed to the desire I had to alight at your door; I am merely passing through Siena. Tomorrow I set out for Florence by the order of my dear master, who has given me some commissions to execute in that place, wherefore I thought it best not to give you the trouble of receiving me for so short a visit; but, to make amends," added he, with a gracious smile, "I will return in a few days, and promise myself the pleasure of making some stay with you."

Pompey did not let slip this opportunity of pressing him to take a supper and bed at his house, though but for a single night, but he declined it with so much earnestness that the merchant, fearful of offending him, dropped the subject, after which he prepared to take his leave, assuring him that he would not fail to return in the morning to see him again before his departure, and wish him a pleasant journey. Upon this, Sayavedra cried aloud to one of his valets—

"Here, Gradelin, take these keys; they belong to my trunks. Signor Pompey will have the goodness to allow me to send to his house for the clothes and linen which I shall want during the next eight days. Don't forget," added he, "to bring the dressing-gown, which you will find in the largest box."

"Would it not be better," interrupted Pompey, running inconsiderately into the snare, "to let the trunks be brought here to you, when you can take out what you want at your leisure?"

"You are quite right," said the false Guzman; "I will make up a parcel of those things I shall absolutely want, and put them into the smallest trunk, which I can carry with me to Florence, and I will send back the other two, which I shall be much obliged by your taking care of till my return."

The merchant then quitted the hotel, and half an hour after my dear trunks were carried thither by the companions of Sayavedra and one of the grooms, accompanied by a person who presented to the false Guzman a present from Pompey, consisting of a basket of fine fruit, and half a dozen bottles of excellent wine. Sayavedra received this present with all the politeness imaginable, and dismissed the bearer with a small gratuity for himself and a thousand thanks for his master.

No sooner were the trunks conveyed to the hotel than Alexander Bentivoglio, who had already learned the success of the scheme, hastened to the spot. The false keys they had obtained opened two of them, and they picked the lock of the third, which contained my money and jewels, which they divided among them, or, to speak more correctly, which Signor Alexander appropriated to himself; for he was a bully who awed the rest of the gang, so that he gave them just such a share of the plunder as he chose to part with. All that they received was thirty *pistoles* each and the least valuable clothes. After which he filled the smallest trunk with what remained for his share, and had the other two crammed with straw and stones. Then, that no time might be lost, he despatched one of the band to hire post horses to start by break of day for Florence. This accommodation was easily procured by these worthy gentlemen, who, when they paid the innkeeper, ordered him to send back to Signor Pompey the two trunks which they left at the hotel.

While this fine game was playing at Siena, I was employed very busily at Rome in bidding farewell to my real friends, without the slightest suspicion of this trick. Nothing now remaining but to bid adieu to my master, I entered the room with a sorrowful countenance, and, after having assured him that I should never forget his kindness towards me, I threw myself at his feet and kissed his hand, which I bathed with my tears. He was as much affected as I was, and testified extreme regret at parting with me.

This excellent nobleman exhorted me to a virtuous course of life in as earnest and paternal a manner as if he had been speaking to his own child. He even embraced me, and throwing round my neck a gold chain which he usually wore, he told me that he gave it to me as a memorial of his affection. He added to this proof of his friendship a purse of fifty *pistoles,* and one of the best horses in his stables. All the servants followed his example in expressing their unwillingness to part with me: in truth, I had never done them any ill offices with my master, but had often rendered them services, so that there was not one of them who had just reason to complain of me.

CHAPTER II

GUZMAN LEAVES ROME, AND ARRIVES AT HIS FRIEND POM-
PEY'S HOUSE AT SIENA, WHERE HE HEARS BAD NEWS

I TOOK my leave of Rome, well mounted, but poorer, alas! than I imagined. Assuming a consequential air, and anticipating much pleasure, I proceeded towards Siena, where I imagined my friend Pompey would be most eagerly expecting me. Having arrived there, I repaired straightway to his house.

He was at home, and received me in a civil manner, though not without evident embarrassment.

" Signor Pompey," said I, embracing him, " your friend Guzman can scarcely express his extreme joy at being at length introduced to your personal acquaintance."

My very name seemed to astonish him.

" How," answered he with surprise, " can you be that

Guzman to whom I am under so many and such great obligations?"

I was almost frozen by these words, for I knew they could portend no good.

"For what possible reason," cried I with emotion, "can you be so much astonished at seeing me?"

"You will soon know that to your cost," replied the merchant. "I see plainly that I have been duped, and that you are in reality that Guzman d'Alfarache whom I expected."

These words were like a thunderbolt to me, and I instantly foresaw that some accident had happened to my property. Impatient to discover the truth, I entreated Pompey to explain himself more clearly.

"Well, then," said he, "you must know that there has passed through Siena a cavalier calling himself gentleman to the Spanish ambassador, who came hither from Rome, followed by two servants, on his road to Florence with despatches from his master. This spark introduced himself to me as the Guzman d'Alfarache who had been of so much service to me in my late lawsuit, and he had in his possession the keys of your trunks."

I thought I should have fallen into convulsions even at these words, but a more circumstantial detail of the whole adventure drove me almost to madness. I requested to be allowed to inspect my trunks. He conducted me immediately to the chamber prepared for my reception, and, pointing out two large ones—

"There are the two that are left behind," said he, "but even these have been in their power as well as the third."

I sighed bitterly when I recollected that my gold and jewels were in the one that was missing. I failed not, however, to open the others, and should have been somewhat appeased if the thieves, satisfied with having my money, had not meddled with my clothes; but no such consolation was in store for me.

In justice to Pompey, I must acknowledge that he was not less afflicted than myself when I informed him that I had been robbed of two thousand crowns. After all, however, his affliction may have been principally caused by the fear that I should hold him accountable for the loss of my property, whatever he might be able to urge in his own justification. So far from thinking of making him uneasy on this point, however, I tried all in my power to conceal the grief which consumed me. It appeared to me that a man who wished to assume the carriage of a gentleman ought not to show much vexation at the loss of his clothes. Nevertheless, I was really half distracted, and Heaven knows I had reason enough, not being in posesssion of another coat except the one I had on, nor any linen but two shirts in my portmanteau.

In vain did I rack my brain with conjectures as to who could be the person who had taken the impression of my keys. I knew not whom to suspect. As for Sayavedra, I esteemed him too sincerely to entertain the slightest mistrust of him. It was not Pompey's fault, however, if I was so long in discovering the thief; for as, in his relation of this affair, he described the person of the false Guzman, he gave me an exact portrait of Sayavedra: the figure, the hair, the voice, and the manners were all his. So prejudiced was I in his favor that I should have thought it quite a crime to have suspected him on occount of the resemblance. I will say more: though I remembered that I had left him alone in my chamber when the carrier of Siena came to look at my boxes, my respect for Sayavedra was proof against the recollection of even this circumstance.

While my host and I were making very useless reflections upon my loss, a servant came to tell us that supper was ready. We accordingly went down into the parlor, and sat down to table with gloomy faces, and without much inclination to eat. Pompey, perceiving that this vexatious affair had completely taken away my appetite, said to me—

"Signor Guzman, your property is not so entirely lost as to render its recovery quite hopeless. I have not been idle. The *bargello,* who is a friend of mine, has undertaken the pursuit of the thieves, and I assure you I place

great reliance on his exertions. He will return this evening or tomorrow, and I trust he will be the bearer of good
news."

"I hope so too," answered I; "but, between ourselves,
I don't think that much confidence ought to be placed in
persons of that kind, especially in an affair where restitution is to be made."

Though the table was covered with well-dressed dishes
and excellent wine, we were so little inclined to eat or
drink that supper was soon over. I pretended to be
very much fatigued, my host conducted me to my chamber,
and soon withdrew, to my great satisfaction, for I found
his conversation very tiresome. I spent part of the night
in pacing my chamber absorbed in meditation, and did not
retire to rest till near daybreak, when my mind was so
overwhelmed and fatigued with the different thoughts that
agitated it by turns that at last I fell asleep. My slumbers
were soon disturbed, a loud noise on the staircase awoke
me suddenly, and I heard several persons vociferating at
the same time—

"The thief is taken! the thief is taken!"

I drew back the bed-curtains, being scarcely able to believe my ears, and I was going to rise, that I might know
what to think of it, when in rushed the merchant's whole
family, wife, children, and servants, all speaking together,
and repeating what I had heard before. I requested the
wife to explain the meaning of all this.

"It means," said she, "that the *bargello* is expected in
the course of an hour with one of the thieves in his custody; he sent one of his attendants forward to give Pompey notice of it, who is dressing himself that he may wait
upon you."

My host was not slow in bringing this man before me,
to whom I put some questions, and he informed me that
the thief who was taken was he who had sustained the
character of Guzman.

This news revived me a little, and I began to flatter myself that I should recover at least a part of my effects, since

we had apprehended the thief. Pompey also indulged the same hopes, and the whole family evinced the greatest joy at this fortunae event. I gave a *pistole* to the man who had ridden all the way at full gallop to bring me the news, and hastened to dress myself, that I might recognize the scoundrel who had personated me. Pompey also prepared to accompany me, that he might speak to the magistrates in my favor.

While we were conversing on the subject a servant came to inform us that the *bargello* was at the door on horseback, and that his myrmidons were conveying the thief to prison. The merchant sent a request to the provost that he would alight and favor us with his company upstairs.

The *bargello,* as great a scoundrel as ever was born, marched in with an air of triumph. First of all he related to us the intrepid manner in which he had secured the thief, and made me quite impatient by long digressions which did little honor to his modesty. I interrupted his heroic recital to inquire what was of most importance to me to know, namely, whether he could give me any information respecting my money.

"As for the money," said he, with an air of great nonchalance, "he had about him but five-and-twenty *pistoles,* which is not much to be wondered at. Though he played the chief character in the piece, he is not at the head of the gang. That honor belongs to a certain Alexander Bentivoglio, of whom I have heard but too often, and who may yet some day fall into my clutches; however," continued he, "console yourself, the scoundrel who is the cause of your mismortune is in our power, and I promise you that he shall be hanged."

I could scarcely repress my rage at this impertinent discourse. I fairly wished them all at the devil together— the provost who talked to me in that manner, his man who had cost me a *pistole,* and the merchant who, by his imprudence, had placed me in this embarrassing situation. I began to be angry in good earnest. The *bargello,* perceiv-

ing that so far from thinking of rewarding him as he expected, I was highly dissatisfied, took his leave very much
displeased with my lordship, and telling Pompey that if he
had known that I should have received his services so un-
gratefully, he should not have taken much trouble about
the affair.

As soon as he was gone Pompey called for his cloak,
and expressed an intimation of going to solicit the judges.
As for me, I had a great curiosity to see the thief who
was in prison, and, having repaired thither, it was with no
small astonishment that recognized Sayavedra, though he
had been accurately described to me. He threw himself
at my feet the moment he saw me. He was pale as death,
and earnestly begged me to pardon him.

"My dear Signor Guzman," cried he, drowned in tears,
"have pity on a wretch who sincerely repents having betrayed you."

He was going on in this strain, for he had prepared a
long harangue to excite my pity, but I did not allow him
time to say more. I loaded him with reproaches, but even
while I thus reviled him I felt my anger growing weaker
every moment. All the feelings of indignation which agitated me gave way insensibly to emotions of pity, which I
should have been weak enough to have suffered him to
perceive, had I not hastened from the presence of a traitor
who would at least have been condemned to the galleys,
if the administrators of justice in Siena had acted with a
little wholesome severity.

The judges of that period, however, as you will soon perceive, acted as a thousand others have done before them,
and ten thousand since. The next day they sent to me one
of their clerks to propose that I should bind myself to
prosecute the prisoner. I answered that I should be very
ready to do it, provided that they would engage that my
lost property should be restored to me; but that otherwise
I would not; that I did not wish for the death of the offender, and that hanging him would not at all replenish my
money and my clothes, and that I had given up all hopes

of them, since they were in too good hands for me to have
any chance of regaining them.

The clerk had no sooner reported to the judges what I
said, than, considering that there was no more spoil to
be gleaned from this affair, except the *pistoles* which they
had taken from the thief they had secured, they satisfied
themselves with condemning him to the pillory for two or
three hours, and perpetual banishment from Siena. These
upright magistrates urged in defence of so mild a punishment that, as the culprit had no marks of branding on his
shoulders, it was a proof that he had never been guilty before, and that consequently he deserved some indulgence.
A pretty reason this for suffering a professed thief to
escape! And is it not a most judicious arrangement to
banish him from the country where he had robbed? It
was as if they had said to him, " Go, friend, and rob elsewhere."

I did not yet know what punishment the judges intended
to impose on Sayavedra, and I was at dinner with Pompey,
when one of his servants, who had heard the sentence pronounced, rushed into the room quite out of breath, and
cried out, with as much apparent satisfaction as if he had
announced the restoration of my property—

" Huzza! Signor Don Guzman, the thief who has robbed
you is condemned to the pillory and the iron collar, and he
is just now going to be fastened into it. It will be your
own fault if you do not witness his punishment."

I regretted at this moment that this fool was not my own
servant, and that I was not at liberty to knock his teeth
down his throat for it; for if ever I was tempted to strike
a man, it was upon this occasion. I was obliged, however,
to endure this mortification, as well as the cold treatment
which I experienced from that time from my host. He
changed all at once from one extreme to the other, and
looked upon me only as a stranger who incommoded him,
and whom he wished to get rid of.

Is it possible? you will say. What! the Pompey to whom
you had been so serviceable, and who in his letters pro-

fessed himself so sincerely obliged,—could this very Pompoy repay you with ingratitude? Alas! it was but too true. He assumed all at once a cool and distant air, and gave me to understand by his behavior that he desired my absence. This conduct was owing in a great measure to my telling him that I should not return to Rome for some time. He concluded from this that I should not have it in my power to render him any further service, and in all probability, as we should have no continued connection between us, he was quite indifferent as to whether I was dissatisfied with him or not.

He even went so far as to ask me without ceremony when I intended to proceed on my journey. I answered him that I should set out the next day; upon which he replied, with a distant air, that he was sorry to part with me so soon, though he never made the slightest motion to press me to stay any longer. I was not a little vexed to think of having taken so much pains to oblige a man who felt so little gratitude, that far from offering me any assistance to make me some amends for what he had caused me to lose, he was so unfeeling as to count the minutes with impatience until I was out of his house. So that the first thing I did the next morning was to take leave of Signor Pompey, and I took care by my manner towards him to let him see the opinion I entertained of his conduct.

CHAPTER III

SOON AFTER HIS DEPARTURE FROM SIENA GUZMAN MEETS WITH SAYAVEDRA, WHOM HE TAKES INTO HIS SERVICE AND CARRIES WITH HIM TO FLORENCE

I WAS so anxious to escape from Siena that, clapping spurs to my horse, I disappeared like lightning from the eyes of the ungrateful Pompey. After proceeding some miles I perceived at a distance a man on foot, who appeared exactly to resemble my thief Sayavedra. In fact it was he, who, in pursuance of his sentence of banishment, was hastening to quit the territory of Siena to exercise his talents in some other place.

I could not help feeling an emotion of pity at the sight of this miserable wretch, and thinking less of his treachery than of the infinite assistance he could render me, I could not refrain from speaking to him. He also had recognized me, and when I came near him, ran up to me bathed in tears, and, clasping my knees, he entreated me a thousand times to pardon his ingratitude and his perfidy. He added that he wished with all his soul to expiate his crime to be my slave for life, and that if I would receive him I might rely on his oath that he would be the most faithful servant in the world. After I had reflected on this proposal, I thought I had better accept it.

Do you not blame me, friendly reader, for encumbering myself with an attendant whose character I was aware of, and who had already robbed me, and would not fail to give me another specimen of his skill the first opportunity? I know by my own experience that evil propensities are not so soon got rid of; but now that from my own poverty I had nothing to lose, honesty did not appear to me to be an indispensable requisite in a servant. In the profession that I foresaw I should soon be obliged to follow, I should, I knew, have occasion for a virtuoso, and Sayavedra was one exactly for my purpose.

I took him therefore into my service, and I had as good reason afterwards to congratulate myself on having renewed my acquaintance with him, as I had before to regret that I had ever known him. He soon convinced me, when we arrived at the inn where we intended to sleep, that I had acted most wisely in attaching him to me. He was always on the alert to contribute in every way to my convenience, and I could not sufficiently admire the attention with which he endeavored to anticipate my every desire. In short, his extreme zeal, good understanding, and spirits conspired to console me considerably for the loss of my goods. Very early the next morning we set out again, one on horseback and the other on foot, and proceeded to Florence, which I had heard so highly spoken of. Praised, however, as it had been to me, the magnificence of its buildings amazed me exceedingly. Sayavedra, who observed my astonishment, said to me with a smile—

"It appears to me that you are somewhat agreeably surprised at the sight of this city."

"In truth, you have guessed rightly," replied I; "I am completely charmed with it; I did not think there was another Rome in the world."

"And yet," replied he, "you see nothing of its beauties to what may be seen. Some of the houses here, which might pass for as many palaces, are ornamented within with some of the most beautiful works of architecture. Florence may with great truth be called the eighth wonder of the world; since it is the flower of flowers and the flower of all Italy."

Sayavedra then related to me the history of Florence from the time of the civil wars of Catiline.

My squire Sayavedra, who was well acquainted with the town from having lived there some time, conducted me to one of the best inns, where he was pleased to make me pass for a Spanish gentleman, named Don Guzman, and nephew to the ambassador from Spain to Rome. With the greatest effrontery he communicated my quality to the landlord in confidence. Being without baggage, and having only one horse between us, seemed to belie his assertions; but, to throw something like the appearance of probability on his story, he said that we had been obliged to set out in great haste, and that we expected a servant to follow us instantly with our trunks. Although the inn was full of gentlemen of the first importance, I was shown into one of the best rooms, the landlord having been given to understand that I had come to Florence on an affair of consequence, and that I should probably make a long stay; this caused him to behave in the most respectful manner to me.

The next day the prudent Sayavedra was of opinion that we ought to buy a large chest, and give out that it contained our most valuable property, though intending to fill it at our leisure with whatever fortune might be pleased to send us. I approved of his idea, and charged him to make the purchase immediately.

CHAPTER IV

GUZMAN APPEARS AT THE GRAND DUKE'S COURT, WHERE A LADY FALLS IN LOVE WITH HIM

THE grand duchess had lately been brought to bed of a prince, or, rather, she was just recovering from her accouchement; and there was an entertainment every day at the palace, where all persons of distinction of both sexes did not fail to resort. The cavaliers who lodged in the same hotel with me, and who were of the first class of nobility of the country, being only come to Florence to join in those diversions, were so much the more assiduous in their attendance, as by these means they made their court to their prince. My host inquired of me, the first evening of my stay, whether I would eat by myself or with those gentlemen. I replied that I would do myself the honor of supping with them, and, when the time came, I entered the room just as they were seating themselves at table. I assumed an easy carriage and affected the man of consequence, of which I was quite capable, and after I had saluted them politely, I seated myself at the upper end of the room in a chair which was handed me by Sayavedra, who performed his part of the ceremony to admiration.

This bold step attracted the attention of all the company present, who, wishing to know who I was, were uselessly employed in inquiring that information of each other in a whisper. They were most impatient to hear me speak, hoping to discover my nation by accent. I was malicious enough to keep them in doubt even on this point. In vain did they endeavor to provoke me to speak by little attentions at table; I answered all their civilities either by most gracious looks or by an inclination of the head. Being obliged, however, to utter a few words, I passed in their opinion for a Roman; but afterwards giving orders to Sayavedra in Spanish, puzzled them as much as before.

One of these gentlemen, more curious than the rest, rose from table in order that he might go and interrogate the host as to who I was. In a few moments he returned to his seat with a satisfied air, and whispered something to those next him, and they to the others; and I was in a short time recognized by the whole party as the nephew of the Spanish ambassador.

As soon as supper was over all the company, looking upon me as a young nobleman, crowded round me, and one of them, addressing me, said—

"Perhaps I was not aware that there was almost every day a ball at Court, on account of the birth of the young prince; that there would be one held that very evening, and that if I had the least wish to go, they would have the pleasure of conducting me to the palace."

I replied that it would be most ungracious in me to reject so polite an offer, though, indeed, my traveling clothes formed some obstacle to the gratification of my curiosity; but that, nevertheless, as I was not known at Florence, I would have the honor of accompanying the party to partake of an amusement of which I was exceedingly fond.

All the party, except myself, were very elegantly dressed; as to me, I did nothing but change my shirt and adjust myself a little. Ill-dressed as I was, however, in comparison with the others; you will hear what happened to me at the ball.

When we entered the saloon, the duke and a large party were already assembled there. His highness fixed his eyes on me immediately, and this somewhat disconcerted me. I thought that he was either displeased at the plainness of my dress, or found something ridiculous in my person; and what convinced me the more was, that he pointed me out to a courtier who stood by him, and, as I imagined, desired him to ascertain who I was. I was not wrong in my conjecture; the courtier, whom I did not lose sight of, made his way through the crowd and accosted one of the gentlemen whom I had accompanied, whispered something to him, received an answer in the same manner, and then returned to the grand duke, to whom I saw him give an account of his commission. All this appeared to me equivocal enough, and I did not know what to think of it, when the same gentleman who had been addressed by the courtier approached, and said to me—

"You are known, Signor Cavalier; the grand duke knows that you are a relation of the ambassador from Spain to Rome. I should advise you to go immediately and salute the prince; he looks at you continually, and seems to wish that you should take that liberty."

I followed the gentleman's advice, thinking that I could not do less; and accordingly advanced towards the grand duke, who, perceiving my design, was so condescending as to advance halfway to meet me. I commenced with a most profound bow, and, addressing his highness, told him in Italian, in an easy but respectful manner, that I had but just arrived at Florence, and I trusted he would pardon my presumption for having ventured, even in a ball-room, to offer him the most humble respects; but having been informed that it was his desire to know my name, I had come to announce it to him myself.

"I know it already," answered the prince, "and I am not a little surprised to hear a Spaniard speak Italian as well as a native of Rome."

To this remark I answered in Spanish, that I had long resided in that city. He replied, in the Castilian language, that he never heard any one of my countrymen pronounce Italian so perfectly.

Then, turning the conversation on my uncle the ambassador, he told me he was well acquainted with him from

having had many affairs of consequence between them, and
that he should be most proud to testify his respect for him
in my person. He then invited me to frequent the court,
with a thousand other compliments, to which I could make
no other answer than bowing almost down to the ground.
This was not all; the grand duchess came up at that moment, and I had the honor of being presented to her by
the prince her husband, who told her at the same time who
I was; and I verily flatter myself that I got out of this
dilemma in better style than, perhaps, the real nephew of
the Spanish ambassador would have done in my place.

The ball then commenced, and I retired from where I
stood for fear of incommoding the dancers. After three
or four dances, a lady came up and was introduced to me
by the duke's desire. I affected to wish to decline dancing,
though in fact I was particularly desirous, and pleaded in
excuse, that I had not long alighted from horseback, as
might be seen by my frightful *dishabille*. The prince, who
heard me, put an end to the contest by crying out that he
was sure I could not refuse so lovely a lady, even were I
to dance in boots. At this desire I instantly obeyed, and
my dancing attracted the attention of the whole company.
The grand duchess especially, who preferred Terpsichore
to all the other muses, was so much pleased that she requested me to dance some of the newest figures, in which I
acquitted myself equally well. This exhilarated my spirits
to such a degree that I made love to all the ladies in company. I would tell you, moreover, friendly reader, were I
not fearful of being deemed conceited, that of all the
women in Italy the Florentines understand genteel behavior the best, and I was by no means badly received
among them.

Among the rest there were three young ladies present,
who were decidedly the ornaments of the ball. I never
saw more perfect beauties. It would have puzzled any
honest man to have made his choice of one of them. I
soon decided, however, in favor of a brunette, who attracted me by a certain *je ne scai quoi* which the others did

not possess. I attached myself to that lady only during the whole ball.

One of the gentlemen who had brought me to the palace, perceiving my *penchant* for this brunette, approached me.

"Signor Don Guzman," said he with a smile, "how many lovers will you distract with jealousy this night, if you continue your attentions to that lady, who is a rich widow, and has a great number of admirers."

My vanity was flattered by this information, which inspired me with the design of attempting the conquest of a heart which was disputed by so many rivals. I hazarded some soft speeches which were not ill received, but while my favorable progress inclined me to push my success, the grand duchess, who had not danced since her confinement, took a fancy to do me the honor of choosing me for her partner. In fact, foreseeing the consequences, I did all in my power to avoid it; but she would take no denial. The grand duke, though he approved of the great respect I paid the princess by my diffidence, gave me to understand by a nod, that he wished I would comply with the desires of her highness; so that there were no means of escaping. I danced and performed even better than before, which pleased the duchess so much that she would not leave off dancing with me, until the prince was obliged to beg her to desist, lest so much exertion should injure her health.

Their highnesses then retired, and I accompanied them to their apartments, together with the lords of the court, and returned with an air of impatience to the ball-room, when I found the pretty brunette was also about to retire. I made love to her with so much ardor that I had the pleasure to see that she quitted me with regret. As soon as she was gone I returned to the hotel, with the beforementioned gentlemen who had joined me. I was so taken up with the honor that had been conferred on me that evening, that I said but little in answer to the compliments they paid me on my talents for dancing. On our arrival at the hotel we took leave of each other with great politeness, and retired to our chambers.

THE SPANISH ROGUE

When I was alone with Sayavedra: "My friend," said I, "my joy overpowers me, I must ease my heart." At the same time I recounted to him all that had happened at the ball, where I had been so much distinguished, the infinite praise bestowed on me by the duchess, and my flattering reception from the duke. My confidant cared for nothing but what was solidly advantageous. Praises he looked on as smoke, but the account of the widow charmed him. His eyes sparkled with joy when I mentioned her to him.

"Think nothing of the rest," said he; "this may turn out to your advantage if you know how to profit by the favorable impression you have made on that lady."

Sayavedra and I employed half the night in building castles in the air on this subject, and in deliberating what course we ought to take to bring the affair to a happy issue. It was resolved in council that on the ensuing day we should procure the large trunk we had spoken of before and that I should purchase as splendid a suit as my purse would afford, to enable me to sustain at court the character I had already assumed.

This resolution was followed by my giving strict orders to Sayavedra to be in the field early the next morning to put our plans in practice, after which I went to bed. Not that I could close my eyes during the whole night, for it was already day when, by rocking myself so incessantly with chimeras, I fell asleep for a short time. Sayavedra, who had returned from executing his commissions, came into my room and awoke me. He was followed by a tailor, at whose shop he had found a suit ready made, which had never been worn. The tailor told me that it had been ordered by a young nobleman, who had suddenly disappeared from court after having lost a large sum of money by gaming, and that he desired nothing better than to get rid of it at a fair price. I got up directly and tried it on, and most fortunately it fitted me as well as if it had been made for me. Nothing was wanting but to fix the price, which we agreed on after a dispute which would have lasted longer if the tailor had not wanted money, and if I had not had an earnest longing for the suit, to which he added some gold lace to correspond, which completed it in the fashion of dress at Rome.

I had no sooner paid and sent away the tailor, than my host came up and informed that the grand duke had sent me, while I slept, a present of wine, fruits, and sweetmeats. This was a compliment that this prince was in the habit of making to the illustrious foreigners who visited his court. The landlord added that he would not disturb my repose to acquaint me with it. I was not sorry that I had not seen the gentleman whom the duke had sent with this present, as I must have paid pretty roundly for the carriage; and I could not be too frugal, considering how much I should need money to enable me to make any appearance at court. I thought then that I should escape this expense, in which I was a little mistaken.

Scarcely had my host ordered the prince's fruit and wine to be brought into my chamber, when his highness's gentleman was announced to me. I was obliged to endure a commonplace harangue, which ended in informing me that the duchess hoped to see me in the afternoon. I made upon that an abundance of compliments to this gentleman, and Sayavedra, like a well-bred valet, attended him to the door to slip a few crowns into his hand. I amused myself then by trying on the rest of our purchases, such as silk stockings, a superfine hat, ribbons, gay shoes, linen, gloves, and every other necessary article of dress. Seeing that nothing was wanting, I began by shaving, combing, cleaning, and powdering myself; then being dressed, and looking at my self continually in a glass, I turned towards my confidant to ask him if he thought there was anything wanting. He answered that I looked so well that he was much mistaken if I did not that day distract all the men with jealousy and all the women with love. I did not fail then to put on my elegant gold chain, and fasten below it with a ribbon a miniature portrait of my dear master, which he had given me the day before my departure.

I was like another Narcissus, enchanted with myself. I wished myself already at the palace, so desirous was I of showing myself off. I think I should have gone without any refreshment, if Sayavedra had not represented to me that it was necessary to take care of the inside, on which the outside depended; and that starvation was not very likely to improve my complexion. Though I had but little appetite—for I was puffed out with my dress, and my stomach might be said to be as full of wind as my head was—I suffered myself to be prevailed upon to eat a little of what my confidant ordered into my chamber. I was so fearful of soiling myself in eating that I was quite uneasy until dinner was finished. I tasted the duke's fruit, and drank a few glasses of verdee which had accompanied the fruits. I found this wine most excellent, and I did not doubt but it would enliven my conversation if taken in moderation.

After this slight repast, I walked up and down my room strutting about; I did nothing but question my squire as to my appearance, and he assured me that I was a very mirror of cavaliers. Satisfied with this testimony, to which my self-love very readily assented, I repaired to the palace, attended by Sayavedra, who, to do me credit, had also made a few purchases for himself at the expense of my purse, which began now to look rather foolish after such copious bleeding.

I was received at the duke's palace with as many honors as could possibly have been conferred on the ambassador himself. The prince first complimented me on my good looks; he then began to speak of the ambassador, and communicated something to me in the hope that on my return to Rome I should repeat it to his excellence. He was completely a man of the world, and never spoke but with some motive. I soon observed that he was anxious to engage me to speak of the ambassador's private affairs, but I was so completely on my guard against him that, though I stayed two hours, not a single indiscreet word escaped my lips. Finding his hints and flattery of no avail, he at length desisted, for fear of exciting suspicion in my mind, and proposed that I should pay my respects to the duchess.

I was exceedingly glad to be dismissed from a conversation which began to grow tiresome, and I went immediately to wait upon the duchess, who, after receiving me with great politeness, told me that she had been much delighted with my dancing the preceding evening, and especially with the two last dances, which she should very much like to learn. I replied that my humble ability was entirely at her service, and undertook that she should be perfect in both dances before the next ball-night. She seemed to anticipate much pleasure in the general surprise she should cause in dancing these new figures, and desired that I should not speak of it to anyone.

A fine concert was to form the amusement of the court that evening, and I did not fail to appear there in all my charms, after having taken a slight repast at my inn. I need not tell you that my first care was to see if my charming widow was among the crowd. It was not long before I perceived her; her rich and superb dress, and superior charms to all around, could not long be concealed. I advanced towards her, and we continued to converse together and admire each other, reciprocally exchanging the most tender looks for some time. All this was exceedingly pleasant, but still I was uncertain of my fate, and, thinking that I had no time to lose, I determined to explain myself more clearly now that I had an opportunity of speaking to her without being overheard.

" Madam," said I, in a voice timid but impassioned, " to what punishment would you condemn an insolent who could dare to tell you that he loves you?"

The lady blushed a little at this question, but answered that it depended upon who it might be, whether she could have resolution sufficient to wish him to be punished at all.

" In what a pitiable situation, then, am I," replied I, " in being prevented by the respect I owe to their highnesses, from this moment throwing myself at your feet!"

My charming widow answered only with her eyes, and I was myself so transported with joy that, being no longer able to speak, I remained silent for some moments, leaving my sighs to do the office of my tongue.

I had scarcely regained the power of speech, which my joy had deprived me of, when the lady, touching my elbow, said, with a confused air:

"We are observed; the duchess is watching us with an attention that embarrasses me; I request that you will withdraw a little distance from me."

I retired immediately, not without complaining of the princess's cruelty in disturbing the sweetest moments of my life. I then glided behind the duchess's chair, whence, as though I had been very attentive to the concert, I cried out:

"It must certainly be confessed that nothing can be better performed."

This was really true, for the duke had some of the best players and singers in Italy; but I had not heard sufficient to be able to decide on their merits, and the duchess, who well knew it, said satirically, "You have certainly been so extremely attentive to the concert, that you may boldly decide. But there is some excuse for you," added she, smiling; "the lady's charms are much more attractive to you than those of music."

Her highness, observing that this embarrassed me, changed her tone, and asked me what I seriously thought of the voices and performers. I then took the liberty of stating my real opinion; and if I did not answer like a master of the art, I at least made it apparent that I was not altogether ignorant of music.

In about an hour the concert was interrupted by a magnificent collation by way of interlude. I took this opportunity to return to my divinity, to whom I now publicly paid the most marked attention, in preference to the other ladies present; and my rivals now no longer doubted that I was the favored lover.

Whatever malice, however, they might on this account nourish against me, they none of them dared think of being revenged on me, which they were well convinced the duke would make them repent of. For my part I cared so little for their displeasure, that I thought of nothing but of completing the conquest of my charmer. And love seemed willing to furnish me with opportunity; for just at this moment, a musician passing close by us, I called to him, and asked if he knew the two or three new airs that had lately been so popular at Rome.

"I received them only this day," answered he, "so that I have not yet had leisure to study them."

The ladies then asked me if I knew them. I replied in the affirmative; and no sooner did they signify that they should like to hear them, than, without waiting like a professional man to be further pressed, I began to hum them in a very faint voice, pretending that I did not wish all the company to hear me. No sooner had I begun, however, than I was surrounded by all the ladies and gentlemen near me. My notes were not so very inaudible but that they reached the duchess's ear, who, advancing towards me, requested particularly that I would give my voice full scope.

I must not forget one circumstance. Her highness made signs to my widow, and some other ladies of rank near her, to join the party to partake of the pleasure she anticipated. They advanced towards her directly; and the duchess, either out of malice or goodness, placed them in such a manner that my mistress stared me full in the face. After which she whispered to me with a smile:

"You see I am willing to pay you in advance for the favor you are about to grant me."

At these words I bowed most obsequiously, and lest she should continue thus to tantalize me, I hastened to begin my song.

Have a care, friend Guzman, you will here be ready to tell me, or you certainly are going to praise yourself again. I confess that I am on the point of so doing, and since I have told you all my bad qualities, it is but fair that I should be allowed to say what I can in my own praise. My voice then was so much admired, that the saloon resounded with applause. And this is not much to be wondered at. A man who at Rome had passed for a good singer was not very likely to fail at Florence. In short, I amused the assembly until the *fête* broke up, when the duke and duchess withdrew to their own apartments, and I rejoined my widow, who was evidently waiting only to take leave of me. I had just time to say a few sweet words to her, which were repaid with usury, and to request permission to pay my respects to her at her own house. This is usual at Florence, and was most gracefully granted. The lady even appointed an hour herself, than which she could not have paid me a greater compliment.

CHAPTER V

SEQUEL AND CONCLUSION OF THIS FINE INTRIGUE

WHEN I returned home, I thought myself obliged to give my counselor Sayavedra an account of my fortune that day; even to the minutest particulars. After having listened to me with the greatest attention, he said to me:

"Everyhing goes well, and I do not doubt but the lady will fall into our snares."

"Friend," said I, "a prudent man is always in doubt about the event. When I think of the excess of my good luck, when I consider all the advantages of it, and please my imagination that in the course of two days I have reached the very summit of my wishes, I fear that fortune has hitherto flattered my sanguine expectation but to spoil and confound my rash undertaking by some sad disaster."

"True it is," replied my confidant, "that the promises of hope are often fallacious, but yet sometimes they must be fulfilled."

I slept more soundly that night than the last, and as

soon as I rose the next day I sent the present of sweetmeats I had received from the grand duke, except some
fruits and a bottle of wine, to my beautiful brunette, thinking I could not make a better use of it. I added to it
gloves, and all sorts of ribbons, which I had ordered Sayavedra to choose and buy for me. My present pleased the
widow exceedingly, as well as the note I sent with it,
and to which I was told she would in the evening give
me an answer by word of mouth, at the lady's house, who
expected to see me. Unluckily the hour appointed for
that visit was nearly the same I had promised to be at
court to finish the lessons of the two dances which the
duchess had begun to learn with me. To conciliate matters, I resolved to go somewhat sooner than I was expected
to the princess's, in the hope of thus being able still to
keep my appointment with the lady also. I was mistaken
in my reckoning; her highness, who had a great desire
to make herself perfect in these two dances, made me
dance them so often with her, that it was not possible
for me to take my leave of her for that happy assignation,
the hour of which, to my great sorrow, was already passed,
and caused within me the most expressive signs of impatience.

The duchess perceived it, notwithstanding all my endeavors to dissimulate.

"What is the matter?" said she; "there is something
that makes you uneasy. I see what it is, your widow makes
you think the rehearsal rather too long; is it not so?" I
plainly confessed the truth, and owned the cause of my
uneasiness, thinking by that she would let me go sooner,
but she did not. On the contrary, she ordered me to remain
with her; but, rather than lose my company, she sent for
my lovely widow, ordering the messenger to make my
excuses, and taking all the blame upon herself. Nothing
could be more gracious; I returned her highness my thanks
in the most grateful terms, and then recovering my usual
gaiety, I repaid so much kindness by saying a thousand
pleasant sallies, which made my conversation very agreeable to the princess.

When the amiable brunette came, extremely pleased with the honor the grand duchess had done her, her highness told her she had sent for her to make amends for the pleasure she had been deprived of while she detained me; then caressing the lady on my account, she said so many obliging and tender things in my favor, that it put me in confusion. We three then began a little ball, till the hour fixed for the great one, which no sooner arrived than we entered the ballroom, and as long as it lasted my mistress and I did nothing but exert ourselves to make our court to her highness, who was fond of seeing us dance together. From that very night our mutual love became public; everyone looked upon us as a couple of happy lovers. My rivals alone thought otherwise.

The next morning I paid my widow the visit I was to have made her the day before. I found that lady in company with two of her friends, whom out of decency she had desired to be there, but who knowing well our mutual inclination, gave us opportunity to whisper our sentiments to one another; I heard from the lovely mouth of my peerless brunette, that from the very first minute she saw me she had felt for me, what in vain her other lovers had endeavored to inspire her with. In a word, I might without affectation think myself tenderly beloved. As there was no gala at the palace that day, their highnesses being gone to honor an important wedding in the city with their presence, my visit lasted the longer. How many impassioned expressions escaped me! how many tender and obliging words did she favor me with! and how happy were we in each other's company!

It was late when I returned home. I was completely in love, and my mind so enraptured with fine ideas that I could scarcely speak. Sayavedra suffered me to remain some time overcome by this charming intoxication; but, seeing that my interest required it should be removed—

"My dear master," said he, "you indulge yourself too much with the fair prospect of your amorous intrigues; you forget that we are in a town much frequented by travelers. You may chance to meet here somebody returning from Rome, and who may know you. Every minute you run the risk of being discovered. Take my advice and come to the point; know soon from your mistress how far your lucky stars will carry you, and lose no more time like a whining lover."

The prudence of my confidant restored me to my senses, and the next day I resolved to call upon my widow, fully determined to ask her consent to our marriage. I was afraid of spoiling all by being too hasty, and it was but with a trembling voice I entreated her to complete my happiness. Far, however, from opposing the impatient desire I evinced to become her husband, she confessed ingenuously that her intentions being similar to mine, she had not the least wish for delay.

" See my relations, in the first place," she continued; " ask their approbation, and after you have paid them that compliment, my consent shall not be wanting."

I threw myself at her feet in an ecstasy of love and joy, and taking her hand without any resistance on her part, I kissed it with rapture. I then entreated her to seal her promise by accepting of a small ring that I had on my finger. It was a pretty diamond, and extremely well set. She consented to it, and suffered me to put it on her finger, on condition that I should receive one from her in return. After this we talked as freely together as if we were already married. .Indeed, I believe I might have that very day attained the summit of my felicity, if I had been more bold but besides that I was extremely fearful of giving offense, by betraying any guilty desires, I was too much in love, and had too much esteem for her, to be capable of such rashness.

When I returned from the house of my enamored widow, and informed Sayavedra of the result of my last conversation with her, showing him the token of the promise she had given me, a tear of joy sparkled in his eye.

" Cheer up," cried he, " the wind bloweth fair; you sail before it; proceed and enter the port. Do not fail tomorrow to visit your dear widow's relations, for I am fully persuaded they will give their consent."

There was no need to encourage me to it. My mistress had told me their names, and described their characters, that I might the better know how to address myself to each of them in particular. Two of them I knew already, who were about the same age as myself, and I made no doubt of securing them in my interest. But there were some grave, phlegmatic graybeards among them, of whom I was afraid. However, I saw them all that very morning. The two young sparks said presently that they consented with all their hearts, if my addresses were agreeable to their cousin. The uncles were not so easily prevailed upon. They said it was a family affair; that they would have a meeting soon, and would let me know in a day or two what had been resolved. Nothing was more prudent than this proceeding, and whatever sorrow such delay occasioned me, I could find no pretense to complain.

I went after dinner to my mistress to give her an account of all these visits. She told me it was enough; she expected the answer I met with, and that we might in the meantime regulate all the marriage ceremonies and the wedding concerns, to have it performed with all the splendor suitable to persons of our quality; as there was no doubt that their highnesses would honor us with their company. After three days' waiting, two of my future spouse's relations called upon me with an answer in the name of the rest, saying they all approved of the honor I designed their family, in entering into an alliance with their kinswoman, yet they could wish of me, for the greater decency of the thing, that I would condescend to engage my uncle the ambassador to testify his consent by a line to the grand duke, and a note out of courtesy to the family to ask their approbation.

I was sadly vexed at these conditions, but collecting all my spirits to conceal the disorder I was in, I replied with unparalleled assurance, that if that was all that prevented our marriage, they should be soon satisfied. I promised to get from the ambassador not only general but particular letters to every one of the relations. As to the grand duke, I told them I expected every post a letter from my uncle to his highness, to desire his protection in the affair of my marriage, having written to the ambassador about it already. The gentlemen were mightily pleased with this answer, and took leave of me, fully relying upon the performance of my promise.

Thus had I brought a pretty load upon my shoulders with these letters, and the recommendation of the ambassador. Had I attempted by a letter to beg of him to make my fortune, in owning me for his nephew, God knows how his eminence would have caused me to be treated by the grand duke at Florence, and in what fine style he would have recommended me. Therefore I was by no means whatever inclined to adopt such a plan; I rather preferred, and indeed it was the only resource left to me, to make the last effort, by prevailing upon my mistress to marry me instantly. I flew to her house as soon as her old relations had left me; accosted her with a sad countenance, and related what had passed between us, and how I saw myself doomed to die with impatience.

"This delay," said my widow, "will not be so dreadful as you may think."

"Excuse me, madam," said I, with the greatest emotion, "I may easily obtain from the ambassador to write in my favor to the grand duke, and to your relations; I may venture to say that he will give this proof of his regard for his nephew. But allow me to tell you his temper is the cause of my fear. He has too much prudence and delicacy not to get information first about your family, and even about yourself, dear madam, if I may venture the word, for fear it might be only the *amour* of a young man. Such an inquiry will require time that will appear an eternity to me, and almost maddens me to think of."

I then expressed my sentiments on the subject, in a manner which I cannot now detail; for when a lover speaks from the dictates of his heart, he expresses himself at the time much more pathetically than he can afterwards describe to another.

All I now remember is, that my lovely widow was moved at my representation of the sufferings I should endure by so long a delay; and being perhaps no less impatient than I was to bend to the yoke of matrimony, she replied, to comfort me, that she did not depend entirely on her relations; that what she had done was for decency's sake, and out of respect to them.

" I only desire three days' respite," she continued, " to get the consent of such of my relations as are the best disposed to it, and if unluckily they all oppose my design, we may be married privately, and leave them and Monsieur Ambassador to settle their business together afterwards by themselves."

It was not possible for me to hear words more kind, and my whole frame was in a rapture. In a word, I showed myself so sensible of her goodness to me, that I threw her into great disorder, and the lady would have willingly spared me the three days to hasten my felicity.

Who would have supposed that a day so agreeable would have been followed by the most fatal of my life! The next morning I rose to go to the church called Annunciate, one of the finest in the city, to hear mass. Hither all the fashionable people of both sexes used to resort. I met there one of my mistress's young relations, who was inclined to the match. I accosted him, and we insensibly fell into a conversation upon my intended marriage with his cousin. Whilst I was talking with him, a beggar, whom I had already sent away twice without deigning to look at him, returned a third time to the charge to ask alms. Earnestly engaged as I was in conversation so interesting, I grew impatient and struck him in the face with my glove.

" You rogue of a beggar, will you not let me be in quiet for you ? "

The poor man, who expected quite a different sort of treatment from me, gave me this answer :

"O Mr. Guzman! if you had been treated thus when you were a beggar like me, you would not have set up for a great lord as you do now."

This man's voice and words, which I heard and knew distinctly, struck me to the heart; I turned my head about, and remembered he was one of my dear comrades at Rome, when I was one of their fraternity. I changed color in an instant; I blushed, and looked on him with eyes sparkling with rage and choler. But so far from being dismayed at it, he laughed and made mouths and grimaces at me, and muttered something as he retired. All the gentlemen that were round us, and especially one of my rivals who had heard in what manner the beggar had spoken to me, and observed that I was out of countenance at the sight of him, were quite surprised. My rival, who had more interest than any to know the bottom of this adventure, followed the beggar to the church door, where he stood to ask alms. He took him aside, and after having slipped a few pieces of money into his hand, asked him if he knew me, and how he dared venture to talk to me as he had done.

The poor man, resenting yet the blow I had given him, and burning with anger against me, told him the whole history of my life, from the time of my coming to Rome, to my leaving the ambassador of Spain. This gentleman, who had the greatest pretense of any of my rivals to the hand of my mistress, rejoiced to hear such a singular piece of news, and quite delighted with the information, he gave the beggar more pence, and bade him come to his house after dinner for a coat he meant to give him; he also advised him to keep out of the way for fear of me, who might perhaps revenge the affront he had offered me in the very sight of the church. As for him, he went up again to the widow's kinsman, and seeing that he was alone, for in the confusion I was in I had thought proper to leave him, he accosted him, and burning with impatience to speak of me, he could not help giving him the information the beggar had treated him with. The lady's kinsman, somewhat disconcerted, only answered that he could not believe a word of what the beggar had said, who to all appearance took me for the wrong person.

The two gentlemen then separated; the kinsman with some suspicion that I was not what I appeared to be, and my rival triumphing in having made a discovery which was likely to rid him of his most dangerous opponent. It was half-past eleven, and consequently there was a great deal of company at the palace, it being the time when his highness sat down to dinner. My rival soon appeared, and mixing among the company whom he thought most jealous of the favors I enjoyed with their highnesses, told them as a secret all he knew of me, praying them, however, not to divulge the adventure, under a strict charge of secrecy, on purpose, no doubt, that they should be the more eager to tell it, as in effect it happened; for in less than a quarter of an hour's time it came to the duke's ears.

This prince only laughed at it at first and when he heard it was reported by one of my rivals, he took it for a tale invented by a jealous lover incited to it by despair; yet with his usual prudence, and as the grand duchess had behaved so kindly towards me, he was extremely anxious to know the truth of it. He commanded the beggar to be brought secretly before him to court, in order that he might hear him himself. He was obeyed; the poor man came, and the duke from behind the hangings heard the whole history without being seen. When the prince had listened attentively to the noble recital of these rare adventures, he commanded the beggar to be put in prison, where, however, he should be well used, with an order that nobody should see or speak to him till he was entirely satisfied on the subject.

If all this while I was not quite easy, at least I had not the slightest suspicion of what was in agitation concerning me. It is true that the cruel accident of the morning had caused me considerable concern; but I expected that by giving a sum of money to the beggar, I should have induced him to leave Florence, or at least obliged him to hold his tongue. I even returned to church as soon as mass was over, in the hope of finding him, but as he was not there I put off speaking to him till the next day. As for what he had said to me, I was resolved to turn it into a joke, if anyone happened to speak about it, pretending that it was an insolent rascal that had abused me for using him a little scurvily.

At last I had almost forgotten it, and went to court as I used to do after dinner. I desired to see the duke, but I was told he was engaged on particular private business. I then went to the apartments of the duchess, who they said would see nobody, being a little indisposed, and that there would not be any assembly that night. All this appeared quite natural to me, and well enough pleased that I should have all the afternoon and evening to pass with my widow, I flew to her house. There I found the door crowded with her old relations' footmen. I concluded there was a meeting of them on occasion of our marriage, so I let them alone, imagining my presence would disturb them. I made no stay there, and not knowing what to do with myself, I went straight home, to wait till the conference broke up. There I remained two hours after which I sent my faithful confidant to my mistress, to hear from her the event of it. Sayavedra was told she was gone out. He went there again an hour after, but the answer was, she could neither see nor speak to anyone.

Now indeed a dreadful scene opened before my eyes, and my heart became a prey to sorrow and vexation. My faithful squire endeavored to comfort me, but all his reasonings and consolation could not banish from my mind the dismal thought that fear inspired me with. I went to bed without my supper, and the next morning got up, having taken no rest during the night. I was just going to send a note to my widow, to desire the favor of her to let me know when I should come and see her, when my host brought me word that two gentlemen of my acquaintance wanted to speak with me upon business of some importance. I ordered that they should be introduced. These gentlemen entered with a sedate and serious countenance, and one of them addressing me said:

"We are come out of pure friendship to inform you that there runs a very odd report of you at court and in the city. It is said that, far from being a man of quality, you have acted mean and different figures at Rome. In a word, you have been the ambassador's domestic, and not his kinsman, as you pretend to be. We know not if the grand duke has heard of it yet; however, we would advise you as friends not to go to court, but to procure the ambassador's attestations in your favor as fast as you can, and prove the falsity of reports so much to your dishonor."

When this gentleman had concluded his speech, so mortifying to me, I was thunderstruck, and ready to swoon away; my speech failed me when I began to make an apology. I answered, however, that I could not have believed my enemies could have carried their slander so far; but before the end of the day, I would take post and go to Rome myself, to obtain authentic attestations more than enough to confound the malicious plan of jealous rivals. The two gentlemen approved of my resolution, and withdrew to make their report to the grand duke, for it was by his order that they had come to me, though they had pretended it was purely of themselves, and out of kindness to me. They were no sooner gone than my trusty friend entered the chamber, and guessing by my looks the afflicting news I had to relate, felt the greatest grief when I told him what was the matter. However, far from being cast down as I was by this misfortune, he bore up against it, and with a firmness that astonished me.

"Now, master," said he, "you must show yourself a man of courage and steadfastness. Can you be surprised, after having acted so delicate a part as you have done in the eyes of all the world, that some mischance should happen that gives a sad and gloomy turn to the plot of the play? For my part, I always expected it; but after all, our fall is not so great but we may rise again; thanks to your lucky stars, the free country is left open before you; let us make use of our time, and immediately leave Florence and the duke's territories, and betake ourselves elsewhere, to comment at leisure on this change of fortune."

This prudent reasoning restored me by degrees to my senses, and upon reflection I could not help thinking that I had deserved to be treated with more rigor than I had been. I told Sayavedra that his advice was too good not to be followed, and if we could set out post within an hour, it would be most desirable.

"Nothing is so easy," answered he; "your horse is sold, we are not without cash, and have only therefore to hire post horses, and begin our journey. Depend on me for providing everything for our departure."

"Well," replied I, "my friend, do what you think proper. Alas!" I continued, with a deep sigh, "could I but once more see my beloved widow, I should part contented!"

I expected Sayavedra would have opposed my desire, but on the contrary he assured me that he would procure me that satisfaction before we were ready to mount our horses.

While I was engaged in expressing to my confidant my satisfaction in having met with a man so entirely devoted to my interest, my landlord came and told me a young woman desired to speak with me. At first I trembled for fear, for the least thing alarmed me in the situation I was in. However, I recovered myself when I found this young woman was one of my mistress's waiting maids, who brought me a note from my widow, containing these few words:

"*I expect you at my cousin's to inform you of circumstances of the utmost importance: farewell!*"

I desired the maid to tell her mistress I would call upon her immediately, and as soon as she was gone, turning to Sayavedra—

"See," cried I, "what I wished for is come to pass. I fear it will be painful to me to endure the conversation of a lady I am so much in love with, and whom I shall never see again. Be that as it may, however, I must see her, though I die for it." I charged Sayavedra accordingly, to settle everything for me.

"Make not yourself uneasy," said he, "about anything, and you may expect that in an hour and a half at the most, I shall be with the post horses near about the house you are going to."

Everything being settled with Sayavedra, I hastened to my mistress. I found her in a *dishabille,* which betrayed more of disorder than of negligence; she looked dejected and pale; her eyes were still moist with weeping; in a word, she was so altered that she was not like the same person. On my part I was no less confused than herself. As soon as her cousin perceived me enter the room, she withdrew.

Now that my mistress found herself alone with me, she raised her eyes full of tears towards me and said:

"Have you heard all the frightful scandal that is reported of you in Florence?"

"Yes," said I, "I have been informed what horrid slander my enemies have circulated against me, and in an hour's time I take horse to return to Rome, and in five or six days I shall bring back such authentic proofs of the falsehood of their calumnies as to confound them."

These words somewhat relieved her. She then told me the substance of her relations' conference held at her house; all that the beggar had said; the terrible stories he had told of me to all that asked him anything about me: and concluded by reprobating the curiosity of the grand duke, who could condescend to listen to so wretched a fellow himself.

I suffered the lady to talk as long as she chose, without interrupting her; for I was so confused, that I could not immediately make any answer to the purpose. I shrugged up my shoulders, raised my hands and eyes to Heaven, groaned, and make a thousand gestures, which persuaded her much more of the falsity of these reports, than all the powers of human eloquence.

"Do not suffer yourself to be afflicted immoderately,"

said she with tenderness; "I have loved your person though your rank was unknown to me, and were you not what I think you are, I feel that I should still love you. Perhaps I should not have taken notice of the charms that I have observed in you, had I looked upon you at first as a person of low condition: my pride and my birth would not have suffered me to cast my eyes on such a one; but having once seen those charms I can never forget them."

Her generosity and tenderness had so powerful an effect on me, that I fell down in a swoon. She thought I was dying, and it was with the greatest difficulty that she had strength enough to call her cousin, who had much ado to manage us both, and was obliged to call in the assistance of one of the waiting women. A minute after these two persons had succeeded in restoring me to my senses, I was told that my valet was in the ante-chamber and my horses ready. It was then that I found what it was to love, and felt the pangs of parting with the beloved object. Never was there a more tender and moving farewell.

I was so little myself, and so full of sorrow when I left the house of our cousin, that I did not see Sayavedra who stood directly before my eyes, but passed by without speaking to him; he followed me, and observing I was almost distracted, spoke not a word, but led me where the horses waited for us. I mounted immediately, and galloped the whole of the first stage without speaking a word: but at the second my squire asked me if I had any object in traveling the road to Rome. I answered that I wished it to appear that I was going to that city, but at the next stage we would stop, and consult what was best to be done.

When we came to the first stage, we stopped to take some refreshment and rest, which I stood very much in need of, having partaken of neither for the last twenty-four hours. . . .

BOOK THE FIFTH

CHAPTER I

OF THE DARING ENTERPRISE WHICH GUZMAN AND SAYAVEDRA
FORMED TOGETHER IN THE CITY OF MILAN

WE remounted our horses, after having made a much
better meal than we expected on entering so inconsiderable an inn; and, far from preserving the silence we
had kept up all the morning, we conversed on various subjects. . . .

His adventures formed the chief topic of our conversation on the road towards Milan, where we arrived both
fresh and merry, and similarly well-disposed to possess
ourselves of the property of others.

We passed the first three days in walking about the
streets, examining the different articles with which the
shops were decked out, without thinking as yet of turning
our genius to advantage. Happy times for the citizens of
Milan!

As we were strolling as usual one morning, a young
man, tolerably well dressed, accosted Sayavedra who was
behind me. I always walked first, and did not perceive
him until I had got about a hundred paces on. I then
looked attentively at this young man who had stopped my
confidant, and there was something meddlesome and cunning in his appearance which I did not like. Oh, oh!
thought I, who can this chap be? what business can they
have together? This is what I must know; but how can I

possibly learn? Were I to call Sayavedra, and ask him
the subject of this conversation, he would not fail to frame
a lie in an instant, and I should not be a bit the wiser. All
I can do, then, is to keep quiet, let them go on their own
way, betray no suspicion of Sayavedra, but keep a sharp
eye over him.

Their conversation lasted above a quarter of an hour,
after which the young man took his leave of my confidant,
who rejoined me with a thoughtful air, which by no means
dissipated my suspicions. I was in hopes that he would
have explained the *rencontre* to me; but he said not a word
about it, still remaining in a reverie. I kept silence also
until after dinner, when, finding myself alone with him,
and being unable longer to contain myself·—

"Mr. Sayavedra," said I, smiling, "may I presume to
ask who that young man might be with whom you had so
serious a conversation this morning? I think I have seen
him at Rome. Is not his name Mendocia?"

"No, sir," replied he, "he is named Aguilera, and I
assure you very appropriately so called; for he shows himself a true eagle whenever he has occasion to use his claws.
He is a good companion, has a tolerable share of wit, and
is very clever in many respects. We have known each
other for a long time, have traveled in company, and have
suffered a great deal together. His head is at present full
of a scheme which, if it succeeds, will make his fortune.
He proposed to me to be a party to it, offering me half
the profits. I told him that I would undertake nothing
without first apprising you of it. I even went so far as to
add that you were so extremely kind to me, that I felt
assured you would not refuse us your advice in an affair
of such consequence."

"No," said I, "undoubtedly I would not; on the contrary, my friend, I am well disposed to assist you both.
Let me know what is the subject in debate."

"Sir," replied he, "Aguilera is to call here this afternoon, when you can speak to him yourself. He will disclose his whole project to you, and if there be any altera-

tion required in his plan, you can judge it to perfection."

He had no sooner said these words, than he was informed that a young man wished to speak with him. We had no doubt but this was Aguilera, for we knew no one else at Milan. Sayavedra ran to meet him; and after having prepared him for the conversation we should have together, he introduced him to me. We saluted each other with much politeness. Aguilera was a well-looking young man, and appeared to me to possess good sense. He confirmed everything my confidant had told me, and related to me in an agreeable manner several of their exploits together. He then informed me, that having come to Milan in the hope of making some good hit, he had found means to introduce himself to the service of a rich banker, with whom he had lived about six months as his clerk; that he had by his assiduity and fidelity entirely gained the confidence of his patron, waiting patiently until he found a good opportunity of robbing him; that such a one now presented itself; but that he had occasion for a second to avail himself of it, and that in meeting Sayavedra he looked upon him as a man sent from heaven for that express purpose, being well acquainted with his abilities that way. I asked him if there would be any difficulty in the execution of his design?

"Not a great deal," replied he, "but you shall judge for yourself. The banker has within these few days deposited in his strong box a large chamois leather purse, containing one thousand good *pistoles*. It is my intention to take possession of these on Sunday morning, while my patron is at mass, and to join Sayavedra at a certain place, where he shall have two horses in waiting. We shall be off in an instant, and ride our hacks so vigorously that we shall be far enough from the city before the banker can discover the copious bleeding his strong box shall have sustained."

After having listened to Aguilera very attentively, I told him that his undertaking was of a much more delicate nature than he himself seemed to imagine; that, being known in the town as the confidential clerk of the banker, he might meet some person on the road, who, surprised to see him traveling on a post-horse, would naturally suspect him of some roguery, and immediately communicate his suspicions to his master; that the banker on his return from mass would perhaps immediately discover that he had been robbed; that this report would soon spread itself about the town, and that it would soon be ascertained that Aguilera had set off with post-horses; the consequences of which would be, that his patron would have him pursued by certain persons well mounted, whom it might be rather difficult to escape. I urged many other objections, which convinced him that his plan was but ill-conceived. He confessed this, but told me at the same time, that he should nevertheless execute it, as he saw no better way.

"I have to do," continued he, "with a man who never leaves his house except on Sundays to hear mass, and then immediately on his return shuts himself up as before in the room in which he keeps his papers and money."

"It matters nothing," replied I, "be he never so vigilant, 'twill be easy enough to get this same chamois leather purse into our hands without exposing yourself to the danger you are willing so rashly to incur. In good faith, gentlemen, if you know no better than this, you are as yet but apprentices to your trade. I will show you a genius superior to that of many besides you. I will take upon myself, if it so please you, the charge of conducting this enterprise, and without implicating you in any misfortune that may happen to me in consequence; even though fortune be adverse to me, I will answer for the thousand *pistoles*, provided they remain in the strong box eight days longer."

Sayavedra and his friend laughed heartily at this speech, at which they were almost as much delighted as if the *pistoles* were already in their hands. They thanked me for the offer, and readily left the conducting of this affair to me; well persuaded, particularly Sayavedra, that I should not talk in this strain without being well assured of the event.

"Give yourselves no further trouble about it, then, gentlemen," added I; "you shall see that one who has been a page five or six years is somewhat wiser than a Roman bandit."

This hit at Sayavedra redoubled their mirth, and we were all very merry together. I then proceeded to question this confidential clerk of the banker's more particularly.

"By what means," said I, "did you intend to get the purse out of the strong box?—you have not the key of it?"

"Certainly not," replied he, "for my patron will trust it to nobody. He occasionally gives it to me when I happen to be with him in his private room, and some person happens to come in, when he is himself engaged, for the payment of a bill. He throws me the key to take out a bag of which he tells me the number, and while I am counting the money, he keeps one eye on what he is writing and the other on me."

"This being the case," continued I, "it would be very difficult to take an impression of the key."

"Much less so, perhaps, than you imagine," answered Aguilera. "I have, God be praised, a pretty dexterous hand, and will undertake to bring you the impression of it; and also if you think proper, that of the press in which the banker locks up his account-books and his daily cash."

At these words, which delighted me, I told him that if he could procure both the impressions we should be much more sure of success.

I did not forget to ascertain the situation of the room, the manner in which the bags were tied up, their marks—in fact, every particular that I considered necessary, of which I wrote down a circumstantial account. I then sent Aguilera home to his master, telling him that I would give him timely notice of the part he would have to play. After his departure, I told my confident that I had put his friend to a difficult trial, and that I doubted much whether he would procure the impressions of the keys. But Sayavedra, who had a better opinion of his talents, thought otherwise, and he was certainly right. Within two days after, Aguilera kept his word, and informed me, also, where I might find a locksmith who would make me two false keys, provided I paid him handsomely. I had but one more question to ask him; said I—

"At what hour is your master to be seen? for bankers are generally particular."

Aguilera answered that the best time was between ten o'clock and noon.

"Good," said I, "return home then, and remember well what I now tell you: I shall not fail to be at the banker's house by ten o'clock tomorrow morning; arrange it so that you be with him at that time, and be sure you lose not a word of my conversation with him, in order that you may be brought forward as a witness, if necessary."

Everything being so far arranged, I carried the impressions to the honest locksmith I had been recommended to, and whom I found in reality the man for my business. He promised to make me two keys immediately for two *pistoles,* one of which I paid him in advance. On my return to my inn, I espied in a shop window a very neat sort of jewel-box, which after having carefully examined I bought. Sayavedra, who accompanied me, appeared somewhat surprised at this purchase. I could not resist laughing at his astonishment.

"Friend," said I, "be assured that this little casket will not be without its use."

"I do not doubt it," answered he, smiling; "you have not made a fool's bargain. You doubtless know the use you intend to put it to, and I leave that as well as everything else to your superior judgment."

I went the next morning at ten precisely to the banker's counting-house. Aguilera was there, and two or three gentlemen on business. I bowed to the master on entering the room, and addressing him in a loud voice, told him that I was come to Milan with the intention of making some purchases previously to my marriage; that I had brought a considerable sum of money which I should be glad to place in safety; and that instead of leaving it at my inn, where there were all sorts of people, I had thought it much better to trust it to a man like him, whose probity I had heard much commended. I added, that I had a short voyage to take to Venice, which would oblige me to have a credit from his house.

The banker, greedy for gain, made me a thousand offers of service, accompanied by the most profound bows, and asked me the amount of the sum I wished to deposit in his hands. I answered, about twelve thousand francs of gold, and a small bag of silver specie, which I would send him in about an hour. He replied that my time was his; then reaching down his day-book from the press, he inquired my name, which I gave him as Don Juan Osorio. This he immediately wrote down, with the date of the day and month, the better to ensure my keeping my word.

After this, having no further business with him at that time, I took my leave after a thousand mutual compliments, entreating him not to leave his house until my return. I reached home well satisfied with the happy commencement of my scheme. Sayavedra, who was waiting for me with the more impatience as he was more interested in the business than I was, was not a little astonished when I informed him what I had just done.

"But, sir," said he, "pray where do you intend to get these twelve thousand francs which you have promised to carry to the banker's? I am at a loss to know this."

"That need not give you the least uneasiness," answered I, "he has them already. I know well enough that this is Hebrew to you, but I have my reasons. Press me no more on this point at present, but tell me whether your friend Aguilera reckons among his talents that of being able to forge writing."

"Forge!" cried he with transport, "he can counterfeit anyone's hand; it is his forte. Would to heaven that I had only the money he has touched by such means! If he had not excelled in that art, he would still have been at

Rome; but he was obliged to decamp thence somewhat abruptly, for fear of falling into the hands of a brute of a merchant, who, having discovered that he had forged his signature, was in pursuit of him."

"This being the case," replied I, "our enterprise must infallibly succeed."

The reliance that Sayavedra placed in my skill prevented his doubting the success I assured him of, though he knew nothing of my plans. All that vexed him was that I had alotted no part in the performance to him, of which he complained to me, asking if he was to be dumb in the comedy.

"Never fear," said I, "I have reserved a character for you, which you will perform to admiration."

At the same time I ordered him to take under his arm the casket I had purchased and filled with lumps of lead. In addition to this I loaded him with a bag of money, bound round with red ribbon, and stained with ink in the middle, because, as well as I could remember, there was one exactly similar to it in the strong box. We left our chamber together, as if with the intention of carrying all this to the banker's.

Having got into the street, I said to my confidant: "Return for one moment into the kitchen, under pretense of asking our landlord what hour we shall dine, and what he intends for our dinner. In short, take care that his wife and he cannot fail to observe the casket with curiosity and attention. It is very esential to us that they should both take particular notice of it before you rejoin me."

No man in the world could be better adapted than Sayavedra to acquit himself well on such a commission. He went into the kitchen, where, after having asked the landlord the question I had desired him, he displayed without ceremony the casket and bag of money. The landlord and landlady immediately fixed their eyes on them; the casket, especially, was so much admired by the wife that she could not resist requesting to be allowed to examine it

more closely. Her husband did the same, and exclaimèd:
"Good God, how heavy it is!"

"It may well be so," said Sayavedra, "since it is full
of gold coin, to the amount of twelve thousand francs,
which we are now going to deposit in a banker's hands."

"At a banker's!" cried the landlord abruptly, "though
they contained above a hundred thousand francs, both that
casket and bag would be as much in safety at my house
as at the richest banker's in the town."

The landlady, as ticklish as her husband on points of
honor, added:

"Yes, we have occasionally deposits of value left with
us; and, thank God and the Virgin Mary, we have always
taken good care of them."

"I doubt it not in the least," replied Sayavedra. "Were
you not considered honest people, my master would never
have come to lodge with you with so much money. Think
not then that he has a bad opinion of your house; but, the
fact is, that he is on the point of setting out for Venice,
and having occasion for a letter of credit to that city, we
are in fairness bound to leave these twelve thousand francs
with the banker who will supply him with one."

"That alters the case," replied the host, appeased; "I
have nothing more to say to it. What is the banker's
name?"

"Plati," replied my confidant.

"Plague on him," continued the landlord, "he is as rich
as Crœsus, but a very Jew. He will make you pay handsomely for your confidence, I can tell you. If you had
only said one word to me, I could have recommended you
to a much more reasonable house."

"It is too late now," said Sayavedra; "my master has
already agreed with this banker. But think not," continued
he, "that I can gossip much longer with you, for my master
is waiting for me. I merely came into the kitchen to ascertain whether we should have time to settle our business
before dinner."

The landlord begged that we would not hurry ourselves,

and hoped that we should always find him ready to accom-
modate us in any way while in his house.

My confidant having repeated this conversation to me,
we took a walk together quite out of the town. We returned after some time to the inn, where Sayavedra, by my
desire, entered without being observed, and replaced both
the casket and bag in my chamber. The table was not yet
laid, the landlord, out of respect to me, having kept back
the dinner, which was served up immediately he was told
of my arrival. Having dined, I retired into my chamber,
and sent for the landlord, who immediately came up, begging to know in what he could serve me.

"I have a complaint to make against you," said I; "how
could you think me capable of suspecting so honorable a
man as you? To convince you of the injustice you do me,
I entreat you to take care of this purse containing a hundred *pistoles,* until my departure for Venice."

So saying, I drew from my pocket a perfumed purse containing that sum exactly. He was so sensible of this mark
of confidence, that he could scarcely restrain his joy.

In the evening the banker's clerk stole from his master
to join us.

"Well, Aguilera," said I, "your patron was doubtless
very much surprised at not having seen me again this morning."

"In truth he was," replied he; "after having waited
above an hour expecting you, he began to fear that you
would return no more. As he cannot be ignorant of his
bad repute at Milan, he thinks that some person has been
charitable enough to caution you against him, and I could
perceive that he was extremely mortified."

"Did the three gentlemen who were with him when I
called this morning, stay long after I was gone?" said I.

"No," answered Aguilera, "nor did anyone else drop in
during the whole of the morning."

I was much pleased at this circumstance, and assured my
companions, that in three or four days, at latest, we should
bring this piece to a finale. The banker's confidential gen-

tleman, overjoyed with this prospect, wished me good-night;
but before we parted, I desired that he would not call again
at the inn, representing the consequences to him, and ar-
ranging between us that every day at a certain hour he
should repair to a certain place, where Sayavedra should
meet him, and bring instructions from me.

My false keys were brought home two days after this.
Aguilera, who was soon informed of this, told his friend
he should have an opportunity of making use of them on
the following Sunday after dinner, while the banker was
amusing himself, as was his custom, at a game of chess
with one of his neighbors. I then let Sayavedra completely into the secret, in order that he might the better
give his friend his instructions; and on the Saturday evening I despatched him to the rendezvous, entrusting to his
care the two false keys and the casket, in which I put ten
quadruples, thirty Roman crowns, and some slips of manuscript, instead of the lead which it before contained. As
for the bag of money, I begged leave to keep that at home,
having besmeared it with ink, and tied it up with red ribbon, merely that it might be exhibited to our landlord and
his wife in that state, that they might testify to having seen
it; so I had only put the lead into the casket to make it heavy,
and to make these good folks believe that it was full of gold.
As soon as my confidant saw Aguilera, he said to him:

"Now, my friend, listen to me with the utmost attention,
and be particular in remembering what I tell you. Take
these keys, and tomorrow, when you open the strong
box, take out the chamois leather purse which is in it,
and empty it into this casket; but be sure you take thirty
pistoles out of the thousand you will find there, and sub-
stitute these ten quadruples in their place. You will not
fail also to put this manuscript in, which contains a specification of the sum, and declares that it is the property of
Don Juan Osorio, which is the name my master has assumed in this affair.

"This other slip of paper," continued he, "you must
thrust into the bag in which you say there are three hun-

dred and thirty crowns, and which is stained with ink, and tied up with a red ribbon. You will at the same time extract from this bag thirty of these crowns, and slip in these thirty Roman crowns in their stead. I have but one thing now to tell, and which is most important of all; that is, to open the press in which your patron keeps his account books, and write in his journal the words you will find on this third paper, taking good care to let it be under the name of Don Juan Osorio, which you will find there entered, and also to imitate with your utmost dexterity the handwriting of Signor Plati.

"Signor Don Guzman, my master," added he, "requires nothing more of you but what will be the easiest part of the performance, namely, that on Monday, at the wind-up of the scheme, you affect to be a most zealous servant, call him all the vile names you can think of, and even strike him to make the scene more natural."

Aguilera here interrupted his friend.

"Enough," said he; "I see plainly the whole of the project, and that the master you serve is indeed a thoroughbred thief. You may assure him that I shall do everything he has prescribed for me, and it shall not be my fault if his plans be defeated."

Sayavedra thereupon delivered up to him the casket with the three papers, the ten quadruples, and thirty Roman crowns, which Aguilera carried home and hid, until the time came to make use of them.

CHAPTER II

WHAT WAS THE SUCCESS OF THIS STRATAGEM

I DID not pass the Sunday without some uneasiness, fearing lest some untoward circumstance might defeat our enterprise; but my confidant having been to the usual place of rendezvous in the evening, returned full of joy to announce to me that everything had been executed as I desired, and that Aguilera was preparing himself to play his part well the next day. This news restored my spirits, and I waited patiently for the hour when I should appear before the banker.

No sooner had it arrived than I repaired to his house; he was alone in his counting-house. After saluting him very politely, I told him I had called to request that he would return me what I had brought him a few days before. He inquired with astonishment what I had brought him.

"Zounds!" said I; "why the gold and silver specie which I deposited in your hands."

"What gold and silver?" answered he.

"Oh, oh!" replied I; "what, you affect to joke? Upon my soul, this is not bad."

"Much more of a joke," rejoined he, "that you should expect me to refund what has never been given to me."

"Let us have no more jesting, however," said I, "on matters of business, which, I assure you, is by no means to my taste."

"Surely," said he, "it must be you that jest. I recollect well enough that a few days since you called upon me, and promised that within an hour you would bring me twelve thousand francs; but you forfeited your word."

"Rather," answered I, "confess that you have lost your memory. I protest that I delivered that sum into your own hands, and will not quit this house until it be refunded in the very same coins in which I paid it to you."

"Go about your business," replied he, "or I shall grow impatient with your nonsense. I neither know anything of you, nor have I ever had anything that belongs to you. Go and get your money from those to whom you entrusted it."

As the banker and I began now every moment to assume a higher tone, all the passers-by stopped to listen to our conversation, very anxious to know the subject of our dispute. That they might not be long in suspense, I cried aloud—

"O traitor and infamous thief! may the justice of God and man unite to punish you! When I entrusted you with my money, you received me most obsequiously, but now I am come to reclaim it you affect not to know who I am, and with the most barefaced effrontery deny the deposit! Cause the money to be counted out to me on this table instantly, or I will tear your soul out!"

The banker on his side called me all the names I deserved, until from abusing each other we insensibly came to action, and he endeavored to push me out of the room by his shoulders, but I repulsed him with such a blow as laid him sprawling on the floor. Aguilera then rushed upon me with a furious air, and gave me a few fisticuffs, which I returned in such sort, that several of the spectators entered to separate us. The confidential clerk, finding himself restrained from rejoining me, pretended to struggle with those who held him, like a madman; while on my side, with my eyes glittering and my mouth foaming with rage, I defied him to approach me.

The affray had already lasted an hour, when the *bargello,* by chance, or perhaps from someone's having told him what was going on, made his appearance. The first thing he did was to ask the subject of our quarrel, and the struggle now was which of us should speak first. He desired us both to hold our tongues; then, having informed himself which of us was the complainant, he desired me to speak first, after which he would hear what my adversary had to say. At these words a profound silence succeeded, and everyone present listened attentively.

"Six days since," said I, "I came into this counting-house, and requested this same Signor Plati to allow me to deposit in his hands a considerable sum of money which I had brought to Milan with me, and which I did not think sufficiently secure at the inn where I lodge. He answered with much politeness that I had only to send him the money, and he would take care of it as long as I thought proper. I accordingly returned home immediately, and returned an hour after with my servant, who carried in a gilt casket a thousand *pistoles* in gold, and in a bag stained with ink and tied with a red ribbon, three hundred and thirty crowns, thirty of which were Roman. The banker counted and weighed the coin, which he put with their specification in the casket and bag again, and then locked them all together in his strong box."

Up to this moment the banker, not having dared to interrupt me, although in the fury that possessed him he could with difficulty restrain, had contented himself by raising his hands and eyes towards heaven to witness my imposture; but his patience now entirely forsook him, and he could hold out no longer.

"You see before you," cried he, "one of the most barefaced liars on the face of the earth. Should there be found in my house a casket such as that he mentions, I shall be content to forfeit my life and everything I possess in the world."

"And if what I have told you be not true," cried I, in my turn, "I will consent that the banker enjoy my property in peace, and that my ears be cut off like a traitor and audacious thief who dares demand what does not belong to him. It is a very easy matter," continued I, "to discover the truth. Nothing remains but to open the strong box, where you will find my casket and bag, with the accounts which will inform you that the money belongs to me. Give orders, Signor Bargello, give orders immediately, I beseech you, that this old rogue show you his account books, where you will see what he himself wrote the day he received the money."

"You are right," replied the *bargello*, "and further conversation will be superfluous. Come, Signor Plati, if this gentleman gave you the specie, there will, of course, be an entry in your books."

"Undoubtedly," answered the banker, "but I have no fear of your finding it; and if there should be any mention made of twelve thousand francs which this stranger assures you he entrusted to me, I will confess that he tells the truth, and that I am the impostor."

At the same time he told his clerk to reach him down the large account book out of his press. Aguilera had no sooner handed this to him, than I cried out—

" No, no, thou knave! this is not the book that will bear witness against thee, it was a smaller but longer one."

Aguilera then said to his master—

" He must surely mean our journal."

" Let it be the journal, then," replied the banker; " bring forward all the books in the house."

Aguilera then produced the journal, and asked me if that was the one I meant. I replied that it was. The *bargello* immediately began to look it over, and finding in it what our colleague had written by my order, he read the following words in a loud voice—

" This day, the 13th of February, 1586, Don Juan Osorio remitted me nine hundred and sixty *pistoles* in gold coin, Spanish and Italian, and ten quadruples, which make together the sum of one thousand *pistoles,* and which will be found in my strong box in a gilt casket. Moreover, I received from the said Don Juan the same day a bag tied with red ribbon, in which are three hundred and thirty crowns, thirty of which are Roman."

The company had no sooner heard this entry read than they all began to murmur against Signor Plati, thus giving me a decided advantage over him. Fortunately also for me, the banker did not pass in the town for an over-scrupulous man, so that everyone readily believed the possibility of his having played me the roguish trick of which I accused him. The *bargello* made him read these words, and asked him if he had not written them. The citizen, confounded by so extraordinary a circumstance, answered in an agitation which almost deprived him of the power of speech, that he had written the first words, but not the remainder.

" How so? " replied the officer of justice, " it appears to be all in the same handwriting? "

"I cannot deny that," rejoined the banker, "but, nevertheless, it is not all my writing."

"It will avail you nothing to deny it in this manner," said the *bargello;* "you must prove its falsity."

A fresh scene now contributed to convince the standers-by that I had not complained without cause. A voice of thunder resounded through the house, and a man with his kitchen apron and a large carving knife at his side made his appearance. This was mine host, whom Sayavedra had been in search of, and who, hearing that the banker denied having received the money, was furiously exasperated against him.

"Why," cried he as he entered, "do they not hang this arch Jew? Why not fire his house, and burn him with all his race?" Then perceiving the officer of justice, "Can you allow," said he, in a respectful and more moderate tone, "that a cavalier should be robbed, ruined, and struck, with impunity for having trusted his property to a thief. This good gentleman lodges at my house, and I most solemnly assure you that I have seen and handled the casket, as well as the bag which he has unfortunately confided to this banker, who is already but too well known at Milan for what he really is."

Signor Plati, thunderstruck as he was, said what he could in his own defense; but his feeble voice, which was scarcely audible at two paces from him, stood no chance with that of my landlord, which could be distinctly heard from one end of the street to the other. The people, therefore, who generally give the palm in such cases to him who makes the most noise, no longer doubting the justice of my complaint, cried aloud that the banker should be compelled instantly to refund.

The *bargello,* addressing himself to the accused, represented to him that it was in vain to resist in retaining money which did not belong to him; that he would be compelled to make restitution, and that it was his duty to search his house for the casket and bag. "Give me," added he, "the key of your strong box; let us begin by visiting that, as your accuser affirms it is there you have deposited them."

Plati, being apprehensive of pillage during this uproar, could not make up his mind to deliver the key; upon which the general cry was to lead him to prison.

"We will do better than that," said the officer; "if he obey not this instant, I will have the strong box forced open."

The unfortunate banker, seeing that all resistance was useless, drew from his pocket the key, and delivered it into the hands of the officer, who, after having chosen four citizens out of those present, to be witness of the intended ceremony, opened the strong box before them and Plati, who almost fainted away when the gilt casket and bag were drawn forth.

The *bargello* then turning to this poor devil, "Friend," said he, "did you not say you would forfeit your life and property if this casket were found in your house? what if we take you at your word? Good Heavens! what a trust-worthy banker."

Thus saying, he shut down the strong box, and held up the casket in one hand and the bag in the other. The company present no sooner saw them, than they began, especially mine host, to load the banker with curses and revilings. The officer, in order to sift the thing to the bottom, determined to open the casket. He asked me if I had the key. I drew it from my pocket, and handed it to him. The first thing that presented itself to his view was the specifiication in these terms:

"This casket contains nine hundred and sixty *pistoles* in gold, and ten quadruples; the whole making one thousand *pistoles,* and belonging to Don Juan Osorio."

The quadruples were in a parcel by themselves. These he showed to the banker, and then proceeded to open the bag, in which were found the thirty Roman crowns and the others with a similar account.

The cries of the company redoubled at sight of the sums exactly as I had stated them, and everyone pressed the *bargello* to give me up the casket and bag; which the officer would immediately have acceded to, if I had not declared that I would not receive my money except at the hands of justice, since we were in a city where, thank God, upright judges were to be found. The banker, being once more called upon to say what he had to allege against such positive proof, answered, more dead than alive, and not knowing what to think of an adventure which appeared so natural that it was all magic to him, and that the devil must assuredly have had a hand in it.

"If you have no better argument than that to bring forward," said the officer to him, "you have every chance of losing your cause, and being punished severely to boot."

Thus saying, he left the casket and bag in the custody of a rich merchant in the neighborhood, and went to make his report to the judges, who cited Signor Plati and me to appear before them the next morning. The banker was himself so ill that he found it impossible to attend, and contented himself by sending his wife and clerk, with some of his friends. As for me, I appeared boldly, accompanied by Sayavedra, my landlord and landlady, all three of whom were interrogated alternately, and asserted a great deal, especially the two last, more than they had either seen or heard. The judges heard Aguilera and his mistress in their turns, who confessed that not having been in the counting-house the whole of the day on which I stated that I had brought the money, they could not conscientiously swear that I had not been there.

Upon all these depositions the magistrates condemned my adversary to restore my gold and silver, and pay all costs, prohibiting him from ever practicing the profession of banker again in Milan. The *bargello,* in execution of this sentence, conducted me to the merchant with whom he had left the casket and bag, and having restored them to me, I returned triumphantly to my inn. When I arrived there, I was not a little time occupied in receiving congratulations on my success. The landlord and his wife, among the rest, could not moderate their joy. To testify my gratitude I made them some trifling presents, and all their servants had reason to praise my generous disposition.

CHAPTER III

WHAT SHARE OF THE BOOTY GUZMAN GIVES TO HIS ASSO-
CIATES, AND THE RESOLUTION HE TAKES OF LEAVING
MILAN

AS soon as I was safely in possession of a sum of money so honestly acquired, I could have wished myself far enough from Milan; but as too precipitate a departure might have raised suspicion against me, I resolved to defer it for a few days. Sayavedra was so overjoyed at our good fortune, that he scarcely knew whether he was awake or dreaming. Then, thinking of the stratagem I had invented, he extolled me above all the rogues in the world.

" I did not give you credit for such a genius," said he, " though I confess I had an excellent opinion of your abilities before; but I see clearly now that I am a long way behind you."

" Friend Sayavedra," said I, " there is nothing very extraordinary in the scheme. What will be most worthy of praise is how to avoid the possibility of danger by flight; for," added I, smiling, " than to walk into a gentleman's house, the door of which stands open, steal a velvet robe from thence, and afterwards to receive a hundred lashes for one's pains, nothing can be more easy."

We passed the remainder of the day at the inn, and, when night came on, went out together to meet Aguilera at the rendezvous. As soon as he saw us approach, he began to laugh most heartily, and we followed his example. He then complimented me on my address, after which I proceeded to divide the booty. I drew from my pocket a

purse containing three hundred *pistoles,* which I gave to
him, telling him that I intended the same sum for Sayavedra, and that I should keep the remainder myself, it
being but fair that he who had done the most work should
be the best paid. My two associates assured me they were
perfectly well satisfied. This business being ended, and
having nothing else to detain us, we bade Aguilera adieu,
and returned home, where I employed myself after supper
in counting my money. How overjoyed was I at finding
myself in possession of upwards of seven thousand francs,
independent of those I had won at Bologna. I had never
been so rich before.

As I was walking out the next day, I chanced to espy in
a shop window a gilt chain so well wrought that I mistook
it for gold. I went in and asked its weight. The shopkeeper answered with a smile that all was not gold that
glittered, but that if I wished to purchase the chain, I
should have it cheap. Being tempted by this offer, I gave
him what he asked, and carried it off with me. Sayavedra,
who was with me, could not restrain his laughter at my fine
bargain, and when we had left the shop, said to me—

"Signor Don Juan Osorio, if I mistake not, means to
make this chain more expensive to some other person than
it has been to him?"

"That is by no means impossible," replied I, and with
that praiseworthy intention, I immediately carried it to a
skillful goldsmith, who in a few days made me a chain
of gold so exactly similar to mine, that it was difficult
to distinguish the one from the other.

At length I left Milan, carrying with me these two articles of jewelry, as well as all the feathers I had plucked
out of Signor Plati's wings. I gave out at the inn, previously to my departure, that I was going to Venice; but
instead of following that route, I took that to Pavia. I
stopped some time at this latter place, in order to make
preparations for my second journey to Genoa, which I
had resolved upon making if ever I found myself in a
condition to appear before my relations without making

them blush. After some consideration I determined to act the part of a Spanish abbot returning from Rome. To this effect I purchased some fine cloth, with which one of the most famous tailors in Pavia made me a cassock and long cloak. To these I added some black morocco shoes and silk stockings, and the rest of my dress to correspond with that of a prelate. I desired Sayavedra to provide himself with two large baggage trunks, and when all was ready, I set out in a litter conducted by a muleteer, with my squire on horseback, a new valet on foot, and another muleteer who led a mule laden with my goods. In this grand equipage was Genoa revisited by that same Guzman whom it had seen six or seven years before in a situation miserable enough.

CHAPTER IV

OF GUZMAN'S ARRIVAL AT GENOA, AND THE GRACIOUS RECEPTION HE MET WITH FROM HIS RELATIONS WHEN THEY LEARNT WHO HE WAS

WE went to lodge at the White Cross, which at that time was the best inn in the place. It was already night, but as my squire had gone before us to prepare the landlord to receive an abbot of the first rank, I found the house all in a bustle when I arrived. Some of the servants were at the doors with flambeaux, and after Sayavedra had assisted me in alighting from the litter, the master conducted me to the best apartment in the house, from which a gentleman much more worthy to occupy it had been turned out to make room for me.

The inn was at that time full of people of consequence, most of whom were not a little curious to know who I was, and my new valet, well instructed by Sayavedra, told all who questioned him that I was the Abbot Don Juan de Guzman, son of a noble Genoese who had married at Seville.

I did not quit my chamber the first day, thinking it better to affect the abbot of consequence fatigued with his journey from Rome, and to get everything in readiness to show myself at Genoa the next morning in the character of a prelate. While I was employed in decorating myself with this view, my faithful squire, who was assisting me, could not refrain from saying:

" I fear my dear master grows suspicious of me, since he has not yet deigned to communicate the plan he has in contemplation."

" No, my friend," replied I, " thou hast always had my confidence. If during our stay at Pavia I procured this new dress without telling you my reasons, it was merely because it was not at that time necessary that you should know them. But I will now satisfy your curiosity; for, so far from wishing to conceal my project from you, I cannot execute it without your assistance.

" I have already told you at Milan that my father, a noble Genoese, married at Seville a lady of the house of Guzman, whence I took my name. I have even related to you the history of my life at large; but I believe I never once mentioned that adventure to you which has been the cause of my forming the enterprise I am about to discover to you. You must know that about seven years since I set out from Toledo in tolerable good plight to visit my relations here in Italy; but I took so little care of my money on the road that I arrived at Genoa in a most miserable condition.

" This did not, however, deter me from presenting myself before several members of the family, and among others one of my worthy uncles, who received me so ill, or rather caused me to be treated so cruelly, that I swore to be revenged on him if fortune ever afforded me the opportunity. This oath I intend to keep now that it is in my power; but the only vengeance that I am desirous of taking on my relations is to rob them. With this view I have assumed the dress which so much surprises you. Besides that it inspires respect, it appears to me more calculated than any other to disguise my features from those who saw me be-

fore—the alteration that time has made in them not being
so great but that I should be in fear of being recognized.
Let us prepare, then, my dear Sayavedra, to play off some
of our best tricks on our family, to which I am incited not
only by a just resentment but by interest also."

My confidant made answer that I had only to give my
commands, and he would not fail to follow my instructions.
We consulted together what was best to be done and proceeded as follows.

The second morning after my arrival I dressed myself
out in my cassock and long cloak, and when I looked in
the glass I scarcely knew myself. Without any vanity I
did not look amiss. If I had not possessed the talent
which I did to imitate all sorts of persons, I had seen at
Rome so many fine models of abbots of consequence that
I could not possibly have failed. I soon made myself
master of some of their best airs. I learnt how to draw
my chin down to my neck with good effect, to assume a
grave and austere carriage; to hold up my cassock and
cloak just high enough to exhibit one leg, which was not
ill-made, with the silk stocking and handsome shoe; to
carry my hat in a manner equally genteel and modest; to
look at people with a peculiarly absent air, and to modulate
properly the tones of my voice in speaking to them. I
possessed this knowledge perfectly well in theory, and now
was the time that I should show the city that I was as able
to practice it.

My major-domo, Sayavedra, followed with my lackey,
both very appropriately equipped. I was stared at with the
curiosity that a stranger generally excites, and many made
most profound bows to me; or rather to my fine dress;
for one is treated in the world according to the appearance
one makes. Let even Cicero present himself ill-dressed,
and he would pass for a college servant at the highest.

I continued walking for above an hour, acknowledging
the respectful civilities I received like an abbot who was
accustomed to them. After which I returned to the inn,
where the landlord immediately informed me that dinner

was ready, and asked if I had any objection to some persons of quality dining at the same table. I answered that it would afford me pleasure. Having descended into the dining-room, four gentlemen arrived immediately and saluted me with respect. I returned the compliment very politely, and, dinner being served up, I took the seat of honor, and then requested the gentlemen to seat themselves at table. The conversation was at first serious on my account. I remarked this, and enlivened it myself, and to let these gentlemen see that I was not the devil, though dressed in black, I related two or three jocular stories, which soon excited the rest to follow my example.

They were usually in the habit of amusing themselves at play after dinner, and sometimes also after supper. They played high, but very honorably. I passed an hour in looking over them, after which I retired. They would have been much pleased if I had taken a fancy to play with them, thinking me a rich abbot rather than a skillful gamester, though they ought to have known that there are a good many keen hands even among the clergy. I did not choose to satisfy their desire so soon, whatever longing I had for it. On the contrary, I professed a repugnance for play, and it was not until we became more familiar together that I could be brought to join them, and then I pretended to yield to their pressing entreaties out of pure complacence. I played only a short time, and for very small stakes, without employing Sayavedra or exerting my own skill. Thus what I lost was a mere trifle, and I never pocketed what I won. Sometimes I left it to pay for the cards, and at others distributed it among the servants. This conduct acquired me the reputation of generosity, whence it happened that whatever person chanced to drop in after dinner to look at us playing, generally crowded round me in the hope of receiving some ducats.

One day, having won about forty *pistoles,* I took up five-and-twenty of them, and left the remainder for those who stood about me. Then turning towards a captain of a galley, who was among the interlopers, I said to him in a low voice, slipping the money which I held in my hand into his—

"You have been too long in Spain to be ignorant that a gentleman who has looked over the game and taken an interest in the fortune of any particular player, never refuses any little token of gratitude that may be offered him on that account."

He appeared somewhat confused by this behavior, but there are times in this life, as is said, when one *pistole* is worth a thousand. My officer's pocket was just at this time so completely drained, that the pleasure of seeing this suddent shower of gold overcame his shame. In spite of his poverty, however, I doubt whether he was more sensible of the benefit than of the manner in which it was conferred. I completely gained his heart. This he made several attempts to assure me of, but I interrupted him by engaging him to talk of his own pursuits. I even requested him to do me the honor to dine and sup with me occasionally, for he did not usually dine at our inn, and in taking leave of him I requested his friendship.

This captain was a man of merit, of good understanding and agreeable person, and as he was known to be a very honest man, he was received in the best companies, where he made as good an appearance as his limited income as a captain of a galley would permit. He was fond of gaming, and, though extremely unlucky at it, he could never restrain himself while a crown remained in his pocket. In addition to this he was much addicted to women, which alone would have been sufficient to have ruined him had he been ever so rich. He called himself Favello, a name which a lady whom he had formerly loved had bestowed on him, and which he had ever since gone by, in remembrance of her. He told me the history of his life a few days later, which I could not hear without sighing, so forcibly did it recall to my mind my amour at Florence. The good qualities of this captain, however, were not the only cause of all my politeness to him; for I knew that the galleys would soon sail for Barcelona, and intending as I

did to profit by this opportunity of returning to Spain, after
having robbed my honest relations, the friendship of Captain Favello was likely to be too useful to me to neglect
to acquire it.

No sooner was I up the next morning than he called
to tender his services and to invite me to take a sail with
him on the water, which I gladly accepted. I was conducted after dinner to his galley, where I was received
with all the honors that the Pope or the doge of Genoa
could have expected. We left the harbor to admire the
fine pleasure-houses along the seashore, which form a
most charming spectacle. Our officer, who was a Genoese
by extraction, and spoke freely whatever he thought, did
not content himself with naming the proprietors, but added
their characters also. Among those whom he spared the
least, he chanced to mention one of my relations. I began to laugh.

"Softly, Mr. Captain," said I, "I ask quarter for this
last gentleman, for you know that I am one of his family."

"Of his family?" cried he, with surprise mingled with
confusion; "how can that be?"

"I will tell you," replied I; "my father was a noble
Genoese, but having become a bankrupt to a large amount,
was obliged to pass over into Spain. He settled at Seville,
where he established his affairs by marrying a lady of the
house of Guzman, which name I bear preferably to my
own, for two reasons: first, to secure to myself a succession which might otherwise have escaped me; and, sec-
ondly, because being at least as much the son of my mother
as my father, I thought myself entitled to make choice of
whichever of their two names would confer most honor
on me."

"You perhaps imagine," said Favello, "that you are
speaking of circumstances with which I am not at all acquainted; but you are mistaken. I am particularly intimate with two of your cousins, who have more than once
conversed with me respecting your father. They have
told me that he was shrewd, intelligent man; that he was

taken prisoner by an Algerine corsair; and that, after having recovered his liberty through the love which a lady at Algiers conceived for him, he went to Seville in search of his correspondent, where he captivated a lady of quality and married her. You are, then, the son of that illustrious house?"

"At your service," replied I, smiling again.

"Know then," continued he, "that Signor Don Bertrand, your father's eldest brother, is full of years, still unmarried, and one of the richest nobles in Genoa."

"You tell me what I was ignorant of," said I; "for I have never seen him, and my mother never had any correspondence with him."

"I am surprised," said he, "that you have not already made yourself known to him. Your relations are certainly of great consequence in this country, and I know not what should prevent your seeing them."

"What would you have me do?" answered I; "would you have me announce my name before people who do not know me, and who will naturally be apt to discredit what a man says who has only his own word as a security. No, no, I stand in no need of their acquaintance, for I want nothing of them. Let us remain as we are. Though they should know that I am here, as a stranger, it is not for me to make the first advances."

"You are right," said Favello; "but allow me to call and apprise them tomorrow morning of your arrival. I am persuaded that I shall no sooner have informed them than they will behave with proper attention towards you."

"You are a man of prudence and good understanding," replied I to the captain, "and may therefore do what you think best. Only recollect to put no restraint on their inclinations, for it is by no means my wish to intrude myself on their acquaintance."

While we were conversing in this manner, Favello had a very handsome collation of the best fruits and sweetmeats served up, which he had prepared on purpose for me, and on which he must have expended the greater part of the *pistoles* I had presented him with. We still continued to talk together, and the officer, who was perfectly well acquainted with my uncle and cousins, told me so many particulars relating to them that I soon knew almost as much of their affairs as my own. Night coming on obliged us to re-enter the harbor, where we left the galley, and I took the captain home with me to my inn, where we supped with the gentlemen who lodged there. After supper these gentlemen invited me to play a game with them, saying they had not forgotten the forty *pistoles* I had won of them the preceding day, and that was but just I should give them their revenge. I consented; and, feeling myself in good cue for playing, I said to Favello:

"At least, Mr. Captain, you will recollect we go halves this time."

He replied with a smile that he thought me so lucky that he should be proud to be my partner.

Fortune favored me from the very commencement to the end of the game. I won a hundred *pistoles,* which I divided with the captain. This was the more agreeable to him as it did not hurt his pride. Thus I gained his friendship by degrees, so that he could not possibly refuse me the favor I expected of him. He did not fail to keep his promise of going the next day to my relations to announce to them the arrival of the Abbot Don Guzman at Genoa.

You will readily imagine that he gave them a fine account of my person, merit, and generosity; for in the afternoon of the same day they called at the inn, completely dressed out for the occasion. My major-domo, to whom I had given my instructions, met them at the door, and conducted them to my apartment, where I received them with a grave face, but with much civility. At first there came only two, both children of a senator who had been dead five or six years, and who was one of my father's brothers. A third next made his appearance, the son of a sister of my father's, still living. They loaded me with compliments, and made an offer of their house, credit, and purse, because Sayavedra had given them to understand that I wanted neither. If nothing else could convince them that I was a very rich abbot, what they observed in my apartment was sufficient to impress them with that opinion of me. I had taken care to spread negligently on the table my gold chain. various other jewels, and the Milan casket with the lid open, in which their sharp eyes doubtless espied part of the *pistoles* it contained.

My uncle, who was the chief of the family, came last. It was particularly to him that I owed the grudge. He supported himself on a large stick, and seemed to walk with difficulty. I could no longer discern that venerable appearance, which had pleased me so much when I first saw him; on the contrary, my blood seemed to curdle at the sight of this malicious old ape who, with his assistant sham devils, had amused himself so cruelly at my expense. In spite of these painful recollections, however, I failed not to receive him more graciously than my cousins, who, shortly after taking their leave, left us alone together.

The old gentleman began by assuring me of his extreme joy at the sight of the son of a brother who had ever been dear to him; then surveying me from head to foot, he declared that I was very like my father, and that he felt proud of a connection so likely to do honor to the family. He then complained that I had not ventured to take up my lodging with him, where I should have found apartments more suitable than any at an inn for a man of my rank and character. I thanked him very politely, and told him that my cousins also had made an offer of their house, but that I had declined such an accommodation, being very unwilling to inconvenience any of my relatives during the short stay I should make at Genoa, whither I had come merely to ascertain the condition of the family, as much for my own satisfaction, as for that of my mother, who had desire to be kindly remembered.

These last words presented an opportunity to Don Bertrand to make inquiries respecting my mother and her children. I replied that I was her only son, and it had

almost escaped me that I had two fathers; but I restrained
my tongue in time, and praised my mother up to the skies.
My uncle, impatient to relate to me what I knew quite as
well as him, interrupted my eulogium, saying—

"I must tell you, my dear nephew, an adventure which
happened to us six or seven years ago. A little rascal
made his appearance in Genoa half naked. He ran about
the streets telling all those who were fools enough to listen
to him that he was the son of your father; and this young
beggar, who could not be mistaken for anything but what
he was, flattered himself that some of our family would
be weak enough to believe him on his word, and humane
enough to have compassion on his misery. I threw myself
in his way, with the intention of being revenged on him
for the discredit he brought upon the family, and I was
fortunate enough to meet him. I allured him into my
house by soft words, and by promising that I would, the
next day, introduce him to a gentleman who would not
fail to be of service to him. When I got him home, I
put some questions to him, which soon convinced me that
he was a little scapegrace. I accordingly determined that
he should be punished for his presumption, and perceiving that he was dying with hunger, I sent him to bed
without any supper in a magnificent chamber, where I
caused him to be tormented all night long by certain devils
in masks, who tossed him in a blanket to his heart's
content."

In relating this story to me the old rascal laughed with
all his might, and it was with the greatest difficulty that I
could restrain the rage I felt. I, however, managed to
dissemble, and, forcing a sort of grin, I agreed with him
that the adventure was comical enough.

"All that I regret," continued my uncle, "is, that he disappeared the next morning and is still at large. Could I
have secured him, it was my intention to have inflicted a
much severer punishment on him for his presumption in
daring to assert that he bore any affinity to our family."

After this declaration I changed the subject, and a quarter of an hour after the old gentleman took his leave, and I accompanied him to the street door, paying him all the respect due to my father's elder brother.

CHAPTER V

GUZMAN GIVES A GRAND ENTERTAINMENT TO HIS RELATIONS, AND MAKES THEM PAY PRETTY HANDSOMELY FOR IT

AFTER dinner I desired Sayavedra to go out and purchase four good trunks of the same size. While he was gone on this commission, Favello called upon me, to give me an account of the conversation he had with my relations respecting me, and he assured me all the famliy were charmed with my person, especially Signor Don Bertrand, my uncle.

"This good old man," continued he, "says that he almost fancied that it was his dear brother he saw and heard speak, so much was he struck with your resemblance to your father; that he regretted to find that you had embraced the ecclesiastical life, and should propose to you to throw off your cassock and marry one of your nieces on the mother's side, and that though this young lady had no property of her own, it was his intention to provide well for her, she being his particular favorite."

In conclusion, the captain protested to me, that my uncle had conceived a great regard for me. All this, however, did not in the least deter me in my intentions towards him.

I went to return the visit the next morning, first to Don Bertrand, who, in the conversation which we had together, took occasion to observe that he thought that an only son, as I was, ought rather to think of keeping up the family name than to consecrate himself to a state of life which deprived the family of one of its best branches. I might have answered, that he, having always been a bachelor, had himself wronged the family quite as much as if he also had embraced the ecclesiastical life. He then named the lady whom he had selected for my wife. To amuse him, I pretended not to be much averse to his wishes, and made an end of my visit by requesting his company to dine with me the next day. He pressed hard to be excused on account of his great age; but when I represented to him that none but relations would be of the party except Captain Favello, the common friend of the family, he allowed himself to be prevailed on, and promised to come, that I might be convinced, as he was pleased to say, of the great regard he felt for a nephew whom Heaven had sent him. After this I visited my cousins, one after another and they all promised to join the party. Nothing was now necessary but to prepare a magnificent dinner for them. My landlord told me to leave this to him, and he would undertake that my guests should be handsomely provided for.

My major-domo, who returned home while I was speaking to the landlord, told me that he had purchased four trunks as I desired. I looked at them, and was well pleased. He asked me what I intended to do with them. I told him he had only to follow me, and he would soon know. I ordered him to take our casket under his arm, and conducted him to the shop of one of the richest goldsmiths in Genoa, whom I requested to lend me for about twenty-four hours a rich service of silver plate and dishes, in consideration of an honest profit, and depositing the value of the plate in his hands. The goldsmith agreed to the proposal, we agreed as to the sum I should pay him for the loan, and choosing the service I liked best, I deposited nine thousand francs with the goldsmith by way of security. After which I desired Sayavedra to fetch the two trunks, put the plate in them himself, and have them carried home, which he did accordingly.

All my relations assembled at my lodging the next day. My landlord, who piqued himself on being an excellent cook, gave us a specimen of his ability in the difficult art of making ragouts, which he served up in so delicious a style that my cousins, and even my uncle, confessed that they had never eaten better. If they had not expected such excellent fare, how much more were thy surprised when they saw the sideboard set out with elegant plate and the plates and dishes of the same metal. They could not help observing that a traveler ran great risk in carrying such a service of plate about with him, and particularly in Italy, where thieves so plentifully abound. The good Don Bertrand, who had made the same reflections at sight of the display of silver, applauded their opinion.

"It is your own fault, my nephew," cried he; "you might easily have avoided living at an inn in a city where you have so many relations. I grant you that this is the best inn in Genoa; but that signifies nothing. You are yet young, and I, having had more experience, would caution you against trusting to the goodness of the locks or padlocks on your trunks, because either the landlord, landlady, their children, or servants, always keep two or three keys to every room in their house. If you believe me in this respect," continued he, "since you refuse to take up your residence at my house, you will at least send your plate and jewels thither, where they would be in safety until your departure, were there a million of gold."

I thanked my uncle for his obliging anxiety; and pretending that I had no fear of being robbed, I told him, that when I set out for Rome I had taken the precaution of leaving my most valuable effects in the hands of my ambassador, and that in respect to the plate, although it was troublesome to a traveler, I was not sorry that I had brought it with me, as in case of necessity I could sell it much more easily than jewels. All the family seemed to acquiesce in this reason; and as I mentioned the ambassador, my cousins began to speak of that minister. They said that they had seen him as he passed through Genoa on his road to Rome. Upon which, to convince them that I stood well with his excellence, I showed them the portrait he had presented me with. This was quite sufficient to persuade them of the ambassador's great esteem and friendship for me.

Don Bertrand, still harping upon the danger of keeping my plate at an inn, returned once more to the charge, and

I was obliged to quiet his apprehensions by promising that I would have it all packed in the two trunks in which I told him I usually locked it up, and send it to his house immediately after dinner. We changed the subject, and began to converse on my intended marriage. My uncle, addressing himself to me, said, that I ought to think seriously of marrying in my youth, and not to defer it to a more advanced age, to have the agonies of leaving orphan children behind me. He then represented to me all the disagreeable features of an ecclesiastical life, and concluded his harangue by enlarging on the perfections of the young lady whom he wished me to marry.

"She is my niece by the mother's side," added he; "of noble blood, and of ample beauty to make up for the deficiency of her fortune; besides which, she has a mother who will cherish, as the apple of her eye, both you and your children."

As the old buck seemed so determined on this marriage, I thought it more prudent not to profess myself averse to his wishes.

"You are so persuasive," said I, "my dear uncle, that you have already destroyed my taste for an ecclesiastical life; and I feel convinced that I shall be perfectly happy in receiving a wife from your hands. Permit me, however, to represent to you, that I already enjoy a benefice of ten thousand crowns a year, and am in daily expectation of fifteen thousand, which some relations of my mother, who have great influence at court, have given me hopes of. It will be most gratifying for me, should I attain my wishes, to have those two handsome presentations to bestow on the children of my cousins."

They all approved highly of my resolution, and gave me a thousand thanks in anticipation of the honor I intended them.

Towards the end of the repast, Don Bertrand asked Captain Favello if he had received any orders for his departure.

"Yes," answered he, "and we must set sail in three days

for Barcelona. We are already very busy in shipping our goods."

I was overjoyed at this news, which informed me that I had no time to lose. As soon as dinner was over, I ordered my major-domo, aloud, to lock up my plate and casket, and carry them himself to my uncle's house. The room was cleared in less than an hour, and in the presence of my relations, whilst I kept up the conversation with them. I insisted on accompanying my uncle, where I had the satisfaction of seeing, not the two trunks full of my plate, but two similar ones that we had filled the evening before with bags of sand of nearly the same weight, and which Sayavedra had very dexterously exchanged.

It was not possible to have made a better beginning. I continued successfully. Captain Favello returned at night to the inn; he told me that he regretted the precipitate departure of the galleys, which would so soon deprive him of my agreeable society.

"It is by no means certain," said I, "that we shall so soon separate. We may possibly be longer together than you imagine."

He reflected a moment on what I said, and then asked me if I had really any idea of returning to Spain.

"Yes," answered I; "for know, that it was not so much the pleasure of seeing my relations that brought me to Genoa as the desire to be revenged for an affront offered me by a Genoese who was my rival at Rome. This I tell you," added I, "having found you to be a man of prudence and discretion, in whom I may confide."

Nothing further was necessary to engage Favello in my service.

"Tell me the name," said he, with enthusiasm, "of the rascal who has insulted you, and I ask but four and twenty hours to fully satisfy your vengeance."

"Captain," replied I, "I am much indebted to you for taking up my cause so warmly; and were I in want of an avenger, I could not have a better champion than yourself. But you judge ill of me if you think that I want either strength or courage to avenge myself. I know where my gentleman lodges, and my blow is sure. All that I have to request of you is to allow my baggage to be conveyed privately on board your galley, on the eve previous to her sailing. I have more reasons than one for wishing that even my relations may be ignorant of my departure, and entreat you therefore to keep it secret."

"As to that," replied the officer, "depend upon me." Then, alluding again to my affair of honor: "You cannot imagine," continued he, "how mortified I feel, that my services should be refused in the only opportunity that I may have of testifying my zeal for you!"

He said this with such apparent concern that I embraced and endeavored to console him by saying that he would have many opportunities in the course of our voyage of manifesting his friendship towards me.

With similar mutual expressions of friendship towards each other, we parted. The first thing I did the next morning was to send back all the plate to the goldsmith's by my men, who brought me in return my *pistoles* which were there in pledge. Scarcely had I deposited them in safety again when one of my cousins called upon me to say that my uncle Don Bertrand expected me to dine with him the next day. I did not fail to accept of this invitation, and found the whole family assembled when I arrived at his house. We sat down to table in good spirits, and our conversation was lively. Before dinner was over, my major-domo, as I had previously desired him, entered the parlor, and, coming up to me with a note in his hand—

"Colonel Don Antonio," said he, "has just been to inquire for you at the inn, and, not finding you there, has charged me to deliver this letter."

I opened it without ceremony, and took great pains to read it so loud that my uncle, who sat very near me, might hear every word. It ran thus:

"I am to be married the day after tomorrow, and I shall fully expect the pleasure of your company on the occasion. I shall never forgive you if you refuse to join us. In addition to this, I have another favor to beg of you. You have often shown me some excellent jewels of your mother's, I beseech you to lend them to me. My mistress has not dared to bring her own to this country with her. We request them for two days only, and promise to take great care of them. I flatter myself that you will confer this obligation on your friend,

"Don Antonio de Mendoza."

After having read this letter, I assumed a troubled and mortified air, and, having reflected for some time, I said to Sayavedra:

"You do not, of course, know the purport of this epistle. Don Antonio requests the loan of my jewels, to decorate his intended wife on the day of their marriage. You well know," continued I, "that I left all my diamonds at the ambassador's at Rome. Lose no time, then, in informing the colonel that I am much vexed that it is not in my power to oblige him."

"I fear, sir," replied the major-domo, "he will think it a mere evasion, and that you refuse him."

"He will do me great injustice by such a thought," replied I; "sooner, therefore, than risk the possibility of such an idea, I would hire some jewels. I should imagine that if I place good security in the hands of some jeweler, he would be glad for a very trifling consideration to lend me what I want for two or three days."

"Who can doubt that?" said my uncle. "But why," continued he, "need you be at the expense of hiring what you may have for nothing? Do you suppose that we have not as fine jewels as you can procure elsewhere, and are we not disposed to oblige you in any way? Your relations will take pleasure in obliging this or any friend of yours."

"Mendoza is certainly one of my best friends," cried I; "he is a man of quality, who was very serviceable to me at Rome, and to whom I am indebted for my introduction to the Spanish ambassador. The colonel, whose regiment is at Milan, has won the heart of a rich widow in that city, who, in opposition to the wishes of some of her relations, has consented to espouse him. They are come hither, therefore, to solemnize their marriage. He is a man of the nicest honor, to whom I should not be under the slightest apprehensions in lending jewels to the value of a hundred thousand francs."

"Be he what he may," interrupted Don Bertrand, "since he has expressed a wish to see his wife decorated with diamonds, he shall have that satisfaction."

Overjoyed that he bit the hook so greedily, I told him with transport:

"Really, my dear uncle, you are too generous, and I ought to be apprehensive of intruding too much upon your goodness."

"No compliments, my dear nephew," replied he with precipitation; "I will lend you my diamonds with all my heart. To convince you, I will this moment go and choose some of the finest for your use."

Thus saying, he rose from the table and went to his closet, whence he returned, and put into my hands a case containing jewels to the amount of from seven to eight thouasnd francs. My three cousins, seeing the old gentleman treat me in this kind manner, did not wish to be thought less generous than he. They all promised to lend me some, and sure enough they brought me the next morning jewels to nearly the same amount. The most avaricious of the three came last, and in the course of a very long chat contrived to turn the conversation upon my benefice. He gave me to understand that if I was so well off as to wish to dispose of it, and would be inclined to resign it in favor of one of his own children, in preference to either of his cousins, a present of a hundred *pistoles* should accompany his thanks.

I made answer that his eldest son, having the advantage over all the other children in respect to age, certainly appeared to me the most proper to succeed to my benefice; but that, having obtained it for nothing, I should resign it on the same terms, not being a man to make such sort of bargains.

I perceived plainly that this answer did not by any means displease him. Just at this moment Sayavedra entered the room, having under his arm a small casket containing my gold chain.

"Do you still wish," said he, "that I should go where you desired me?"

"You ought to have been there and back again ere this," replied I. "Recollect only, before you apply to a goldsmith, to make inquiry in the neighborhood as to his respectability. You will then get my chain weighed, and return to tell me its exact weight."

Though my cousin had already seen this chain, he requested to look at it again, and admired extremely both the workmanship and the fineness of the gold. Then turning to Sayavedra:

"My friend," said he, "tell my servant, whom you will find below, to accompany you to a goldsmith's who lives hard by, and who will tell you conscientiously the value of the chain."

My squire was soon back. I inquired how much the goldsmith valued it at.

"Six hundred and fifty-five crowns," answered Sayavedra.

"Well, then," said I, "just return and request the loan of six hundred upon it, which I will repay him in three days, with whatever he may demand for interest."

"Honest man as he is," said my cousin, "he will make no scruple of taking three per cent. for three days as well as for six months, saying that it makes no difference to him. I regret much," continued he, "that I do not happen at this moment to have sufficient ready money at hand myself; but I know a man of probity who will be satisfied with only two per cent."

This man of probity was no other than himself, who, notwithstanding that he hoped to obtain a good benefice for nothing, rejoiced at the opportunity of depriving the goldsmith of this little profit. I failed not to assure this good cousin that he would much oblige me by getting it done for me.

"Not that I am in great distress for money," said I, "as you may see."

At the same time I drew from my pocket two large purses full of *pistoles*, which I showed to him. "It is merely by way of precaution that I wish to put my chain in pledge; for as we shall play very high at the wedding of my friend the colonel, I do not like to be at all short of money."

My cousin assured me that in two hours at furthest the six hundred crowns should be at my service.

Then taking the casket out of Sayavedra's hand, I opened it for an instant, just that my cousin might see that the chain was in it, and after having shut it again, delivered it to his servant, who returned in about an hour with the six hundred crowns.

Unfortunately for my worthy cousin, my major-domo, in bringing the casket back from the goldsmith's under his cloak, had dexterously drawn out the gold chain, and substituted a brass one in its stead.

Favello came to sup with me at night. He told me it was time for me to strike my blow, for that I must sleep on board the next night, as the galleys were to sail before daybreak the following morning.

"'Tis well," answered I; "my business shall be settled in less than four-and-twenty hours' time, and I will not fail to be on board by tomorrow evening. If you will assist me by sending some of your people about midnight for my boxes, my departure will be more secret."

The captain promised this, and took his leave of me shortly after. We passed almost the whole of the next day in getting everything in readiness for our departure. We packed up our best effects in our two largest boxes, and filled with rags the counter-parts of those which my honored uncle kept in his closet for me with such pious care. A quarter of an hour before midnight, four of Captain Favello's men conveyed our two largest boxes on board, leaving our two others to satisfy my landlord, whom I desired Sayavedra to tell not to be anxious on my account, for that I was going to sup at a friend's, where I might very likely pass the whole night at play. We at length got safe on board our captain's galley. He had been rather uneasy at my being so late, and asked me the first thing, how my affair of honor had terminated.

"My revenge is satisfied to my heart's content," replied I. "I rejoice at it extremely," said he; "for I must acknowledge that I was beginning to be a little anxious for your safety, the result of such an enterprise being always uncertain."

Favello had caused a little chamber to be fitted up for me, into which he conducted me and where I found my two boxes, and a table covered with delicate meats. We sat down, and, after partaking of a good supper, lay down to take some repose. But our several cares kept us both awake. For my part I was all night terribly alarmed lest some cursed contrary wind should detain us in port, and afford my relations sufficient time to gain information of my flight, and to obtain an order from the senate to have me arrested. My fears, however, were groundless. At daybreak I heard a noise which announced to me that the galleys were on the point of departure. I looked through a hole in my chamber, and perceived with joy that the whole crew had begun to ply their oars. We were soon out of port; then taking advantage of the wind which was directly in our favor, we spread our sails and were soon out of sight.

CHAPTER VI

GUZMAN, AFTER HAVING ROBBED HIS RELATIONS, AND RE-
EMBARKED FOR SPAIN, IS IN IMMINENT DANGER OF PERISH-
ING AT SEA, AND HAS THE MISFORTUNE TO LOSE SAYA-
VEDRA

WE had already doubled Cape Noli, when the captain informed me that if the wind did not change for three days, we should have a most agreeable voyage. We watered at Monaco, and the next morning, having put to sea again with a favorable breeze, we reached the Isles of Hieres, where we passed the night. The third day we anchored at Chateau d'If, in sight of Marseilles, and the day following at Roses.

I was congratulating myself on so fortunate a voyage, when my joy was interrupted by word being brought me that Sayavedra had the sea-sickness, and felt extremely ill. I ran to see him immediately, and found that he had a very violent fever upon him. I was much afflicted at it, but consoled myself with the idea that we should soon reach Barcelona, where he should have every attention paid to him. The morning of the fifth day dawned very differently from the preceding ones; the clouds seemed lowering, and there was scarcely a breath of air stirring. We still hoped, however, by dint of hard rowing, to sleep that night at Barcelona. But we found our mistake two hours after. So furious a storm arose, that our destruction appeared inevitable. In vain did we attempt to make to land; the oar became quite useless, and we were obliged to keep out to sea the whole of that night. What a night of horror it was for us! Sometimes the sea raised its waves to the clouds, and at others, opening its bosom, presented to our eyes the awful abyss by which we were surrounded.

Who in the midst of such a scene can attempt to paint the consternation so evidently depicted on every countenance on board, and the various indications of fear by the dread of approaching death? Some invoked the saints most honored in their own country; others offered vows; some on their knees were addressing the most fervent prayers to Heaven in private, whilst others confessed their sins aloud, and implored pardon of the Deity. Some few, though death was apparently before their eyes, were still inquiring of the pilot whether all hopes were at an end. He answered, that there was nothing to fear, and they seemed as willing to trust this liar, as a father, who, seeing his only son dying, eagerly gives credit to the quack who assures him of his speedy recovery.

For my part, like another Jonas, I was buried in a profound reverie all this while, and, believing myself the cause of this dreadful storm, said within myself: Wretch, now wilt thou meet with that punishment due to thee for having robbed thy relations. Of what service will their gold be to thee? The sea will in a short time swallow up both thyself and thy ill-gotten riches. For thyself, thou hast well deserved it, and those only are to be pitied who have been so unfortunate as to embark in the company of a scoundrel who has incurred the vengeance of Heaven.

With this impression, I awaited death with resignation. It was not so near at hand, however, as we all imagined. The weather suddenly changed, hope succeeded despair, and joy desolation. That night proved fatal only to the unfortunate Sayavedra. This faithful follower, whose brain was already turned by his fever, the violence of which was increasing every moment, lost his reason entirely when he heard the cries and lamentations which the fear of shipwreck excited in the galley. My footman watched him that night, but dropping asleep from fatigue,

Sayavedra got up in one of his fits, which gave him new strength, and threw himself from the side of the poop into the sea. The soldier who was on guard heard something fall into the sea, and informed the pilot of it. This made a great noise on board, and everyone was anxious to ascertain what it could be; and after half-an-hour's search, Sayavedra was found to be missing.

No possible grief could be greater than mine when I first learned this distressing news. No one has ever wept more bitterly for a brother than I did for my dear Sayavedra. I was inconsolable at his loss, and truly I had good reason to regret him. The joy of all on board the next morning, at finding the sea as calm as it had been boisterous the preceding day, had but little effect on my spirits, now that death had deprived me of my faithful servant and companion.

We entered the port of Barcelona towards noon. I had already prepared Favello not to expect I should make a long stay in that city, having told him after the storm, that I had made a vow to visit our Lady of Montserrat the moment I landed, and that from thence I intended to proceed to my mother's at Andalusia. He could not oppose so pious an intention; and besides, not being able to leave his galley that day, he told me sadly, as I was taking leave of him, that in all probability we should never see each other again, unless I intended to stay the whole of the next day in Barcelona. He then inquired where I should take up my lodging; I named an inn which I knew, fully resolved, however, never to go near it. Sensible of the great proofs of friendship I had received at his hands, I embraced him tenderly at parting, and presenting him with a ring worth a hundred *pistoles,* requested he would wear it for my sake. He accepted it with tears in his eyes, fearing it was the last farewell, and on my side, feeling myself too much affected, I hastened away, to spare him the pain of reading in my looks the cause of our separation.

My first care when I arrived at the inn where I caused

my trunks to be carried, was to have three good mules bought for my use. You may be sure I paid dear for them; but this signified but little in my present situation. In addition to the twenty-five thousand francs which I now possessed, four thousand more had fallen to me by the death of my companion in fortune. I hired also a muleteer who was well acquainted with the roads, and we left the city the following morning as soon as the gates were open. My impatience to leave Barcelona as soon as possible may easily be conceived; a felucca might have arrived there, with orders from my relations to arrest me. It was incumbent on me, therefore, to be active. To so prudent a fear I added the precaution of avoiding all the high roads, telling my followers, that as my sole object in traveling was my own pleasure, it was my wish to reach the Ebro as fast as possible; that, as I rode along its banks, I might be gratified with a view of the charming landscapes on both sides of it.

BOOK THE SIXTH

CHAPTER I

GUZMAN DEPARTS FOR MADRID, WHERE HE MAKES ACQUAIN-
TANCE AND FALLS IN LOVE WITH A YOUNG HEIRESS—
PROGRESS OF THIS NEW PASSION

I STEERED clear of the high roads, for the reasons I
have already told you, and spurring on my mule through
all the by-ways towards the Ebro, intending to coast it from
thence to Saragossa, I traveled with as much speed as fear.
In three days we reached the banks of the river. My mind
became now more at ease, and I began to believe myself
beyond the reach of pursuit, and to congratulate myself on
my riches, without reflecting that I was traveling through
a country in which there were as many robbers as in Italy.
I had taken the precaution, however, to purchase two fire-
locks in Barcelona, with which I armed my footman and the
muleteer. In addition to this, I concealed my jewels about
me so cautiously that no one could perceive them without
stripping me.

I shall pass over in silence, friendly reader, the adventures I met with on the banks of the Ebro, which are not
worthy to be related. . . .

I took the road to Madrid, and six days after my departure I arrived at Alcala de Henares, a town the situation of which is delightful, and which the beauty of its
buildings renders comparable with the most flourishing capitals in the world. In addition to this, the *belles lettres* were

cultivated there to perfection. I should certainly have taken up my abode there, had I not been foolishly desirous to visit St. James's once more, where I had formerly acted so miserable a part.

I stopped but eight days at Alcala, and then proceeded towards Madrid. That celebrated city saw arrive, with three mules in his train, two of which were laden with valuable property, that same Guzman who had formerly carried a basket in its market-place. I hesitated for some time as to where I should take up my lodging; but recollecting that in my time the best inn was in Toledo Street, I determined to alight there. I found it strangely changed. The landlord was dead, and his widow, though a shrewd active woman, who had more than one string to her bow, could not support its reputation on the same footing. It was certainly much fallen off; but the extreme civility with which they treated me, whom they looked upon as a rich young nobleman, prevented me from leaving them.

My next care was to make special inquiries about my old friend the three-bagged apothecary; and though I did not much fear that I could be recognized, I must confess that I felt a secret joy when I learnt that he had taken his departure for that country whither his drugs had dispatched so many of his patients before him. Ten years, however, had now elapsed since I left Madrid, and, besides that, I was much altered in person; who the devil could have recognized poor Guzman in the finery with which he was now disguised? I took great pleasure in showing myself off in my best suits, particularly in the one I had purchased at Saragossa. I exhibited myself by turns, in the morning at the different churches, and in the evening at the *prado*. . . .

One morning I saw coming out of the Dominican's Church a lady of a majestic deportment and richly dressed, whom I took for a woman of quality; and as she passed near me, though I dared not bow to her, I showed her so much respect that she took notice of it, and viewed me

"A LADY OF MAJESTIC DEPORTMENT AND RICHLY DRESSED, WHOM I
TOOK FOR A WOMAN OF QUALITY"
(Original "The Duchess of Alba," the painting by Francisco Goya y Lucientes)

with so much attention that I thought myself highly honored—in Spain even the look that a lady bestows on a man being considered a favor. My curiosity induced me to inquire who she was, and I accordingly followed her. She observed me, but walked on at a slow pace. She was followed by two duennas and a valet, which confirmed me in the opinion that I had of her being a lady of quality. When she was in the middle of the broad street, she stopped before a magnificent house and went in. I had not the least doubt that she lived there, and after some inquiries I learnt that she was the daughter of Signor Don Andrea, who assumed the title of Don in quality of being the court banker, and that this young lady had the reputation of being very virtuous.

I could not get this adventure out of my head the whole of the morning; towards evening I walked up and down before the banker's window again, and my trouble was not lost. I had a full view of the banker, who was conversing with his daughter on a balcony, who appeared to be a very personable man. As for the lady I cannot say that she was a perfect beauty, but she had an agreeable air and easy manners, which pleased me extremely, and prepossessed me in favor of her mind. If I had been charmed in the morning, how much more so was I in the evening. I returned home quite in love with her, and resolved to get acquainted with her father the very next day, which I accomplished in the manner I am about to relate to you. Since my arrival at Madrid I had the precaution to have my diamonds all new set, for fear my relations should give advice to their correspondents, and cause me to be arrested. I had even run a great risk in showing them to the jeweler. I carried these to the amount of ten or twelve thousand francs to the banker, telling him at the same time, that I had others at home of more considerable value. He looked at them with an eager eye, valued them at twelve thousand francs, and offered to pay me that sum in six months, if I would allow him to sell them for me.

As I had no other intention but to begin a train of business with him, I accepted his offer, and even refused his note of hand for the value of the jewels, telling him that I knew too well what reputation he had in the world to require him any other security than his own word. We then agreed that he should pay me in three months six thousand francs, and the other six thousand in three months later. My way of dealing charmed him so much, that he thanked me for the confidence I placed in him, and made me many protestations of service. He then showed me all over his house, which was richly furnished. I observed equipages for him and his daughter, with a great number of servants. All these objects dazzled my eyes so much, that I was easily inclined to look upon him as one of the richest bankers in Spain.

If all that was offered to my sight tended to confirm me in this opinion, his discourse was still more calculated to mislead me. He told me that he transacted business to the amount of two or three millions of francs every day; that the court always made use of him and of his purse to remit considerable sums to foreign countries; that he had access to the ministers when he pleased; that the greatest lords were his friends, and that there were but few of them who had not dealings with him.

This statement was not altogether without foundation. He had formerly lived upon such a footing with the great; but by dealing with, and trusting those great men rather too extensively, he had run himself so far in debt, that he only supported himself by his wits, which were such, at any rate, that he kept up his credit. My jewels were a great help to him in his embarrassment; for he was just at this time extremely straightened for a considerable sum of money, and raised half by them—having seized the opportunity of the marriage of the Duke of Medina Sidonia's daughter to dispose of them advantageously. As I could then only judge of his circumstances by appearances, I considered myself very happy in having made an acquaintance with him, and even secretly blamed myself for having conceived so bold an idea as that of aspiring to the hand of his only daughter, who appeared to be a match worthy of a prince.

Don Andrea, on his side, was not without surprise at my mode of proceeding. He therefore sent a trusty person to inquire my character from my landlady, and in what style I was living at Madrid. From all sides, however, he obtained favorable reports of me; for though no one was acquainted with my family, I might easily pass for a man of quality, as far as my mode of living, manners, and conversation, would impress such a belief. After such good accounts of me he concluded that I was the man Heaven had intended for his son-in-law. He mentioned it to his daughter, who told him that I had followed her from the Dominican's Church to her house; that I continually passed under the windows; in a word, that by all my actions I had given her to understand that I had conceived a passion for her. The father had too much experience not to believe the same thing, and the confidence I had placed in him, by giving him my diamonds without a note, could only be the effect of my love for his daughter. They both rejoiced at it in their private conversations, and, concluding that I was richer than a Jew, they resolved to manage it so well as not to miss so fair an opportunity of advancing themselves again in the world.

Accordingly, the banker came to visit me at the hotel. I expected him, and I took care to set out in my room all my jewels, which had a great effect upon him. He was especially struck with my gold chain, the workmanship of which he praised much, and offered to sell it for me at a third more than it cost; I took him at his word, and let him have it, as I had done with the diamonds, without a note. His joy was extreme; he made me a thousand protestations of friendship, and, beginning already to act the part of a father-in-law, gave me advice how to put out my ready money to the best advantage. A few days after, he brought me the sum he had promised me for my gold chain. This increased the confidence I had placed in him, and induced me to acknowledge his trouble by a present suitable for a young lady, which I sent to his daughter, after he had granted me leave to do so. This present having been received favorably, made me bold enough to discover my passion after the custom of the country, that is to say, by signs and looks, and it seemed she did not disapprove of it.

As for the father, whom I saw every day, I talked with him of nothing else but trade and business, waiting for the first good opportunity to declare my sentiments. . . .

In my rambles about the town I had seen a house newly built. I asked Don Andrea's advice, and he approved of it, and even managed it so that I made a very good bargain. It cost me only three hundred ducats, which I paid down before him with a much *sangfroid* as if 1 had a hundred thousand crowns in my coffers. You may imagine what an effect it had on my future father-in-law, who, though a man of rather keen understanding, had not the least doubt that he had met with a good son-in-law, and that it remained only for him to allure me cunningly into the snare. I furnished my house elegantly, and prepared to occupy it. . . .

CHAPTER II

GUZMAN PAYS HIS ADDRESSES TO THE BANKER'S DAUGHTER, AND MARRIES HER—CONSEQUENCES OF THIS MARRIAGE

I WENT the very next day to the banker's house, who kept me to dinner, towards the end of which my intended bride appeared, as if by chance; I rose immediately to pay my respects to her, and express the agreeable surprise her presence excited me. She retruned my compliments with a modest air, and would have retired, but her father prevented her.

"Eugenia," said he to her, "stay with us; this gentleman is my friend, and I am happy to let him have a proof of it by giving you leave to converse with him."

I did not fail to thank him for so great a favor, with which I was quite delighted, and more so indeed than I really appeared to be.

I then entered into conversation with Eugenia, and to increase my joy, Don Andrea, under pretense of writing some letters, retired to a corner of the drawing-room, to leave us more to ourselves.

If he acted in this manner to afford me the opportunity of a delightful conversation, he did not favor a fool, for I availed myself of this interview, not knowing when I should have a more favorable one, to declare my passion. I called forth my genius, which served me well enough on the occasion, and the lady enchanted me by the delicacy of her replies. In the meantime the father, still pretending to be very busy, now and then asked pardon for being no better company; I returned him compliment for compliment, and, following my point, still courted the daughter in a low voice, as if afraid of disturbing him in his reading. We had been three hours together, when the banker, thinking proper to put an end to our conversation, came and joined us, and Eugenia, after having made a courtesy, disappeared.

I now felt so much esteem, or rather was so much in love with this lady, that I could not forbear breaking out in praise of her; and speaking from the fullness of my heart, I told Don Andrea, that no one could possibly be more sensible of his daughter's merit than I was. The old fox listened to me very attentively, and to encourage me to explain myself more clearly, he held a long discourse on the necessity of persons of my age marrying, to avoid an infinite number of precipices to which they are daily exposed, and on the importance of the choice of a wife, since it commonly decided the happiness or misery of her husband. He then proceeded to assure me of the good opinion he had conceived of me, telling me that I had won his heart by my ingenuous manners and the confidence I had placed in him; and that I might rely that there was nothing that lay in his power which he would not do to convince me of it.

I was not much behind hand with him in professions. I opened my whole heart to him, and protested that he might make me the happiest of men in giving me Eugenia. He considered for some time, or appeared to do so, to persuade me that I set his friendship at too great a trial; however, before we parted, I knew what I had to expect. He embraced me tenderly when I left him, and told me he had certain views of establishing his daughter more advantageously, but that he had given them all up to show me how dear I was to him. At these words, I took one of his hands, and kissed it with a transport that proved more fully than all I could have said the gratitude of my heart.

From this time the banker called me his son. He managed all my affairs; the six thousand francs which he had engaged to pay me in three months, he now advanced immediately, to assist me in furnishing my house, and he bought for me, at a cheap rate, several elegant pieces of furniture, which a person in want of money was obliged to sell. In a word, I dined every day with my future father-in-law. I saw his daughter every day, and enjoyed all the privileges of a son-in-law; expect that one only, which the title of a husband could give a right to. One thing alone surprised me, which was, that in all the conversations I had as yet had with Don Andrea, he had never uttered a word about my portion. I attempted to sound him on this subject, but he gave me to understand that his intention was not to part with much ready money on the wedding-day.

"You will receive only ten thousand francs down," said he, "but you may rely on the sum of fifty thousand after my death."

I thought ten thousand francs but a paltry portion for the daughter of a man whom I had thought so rich; nevertheless, considering that tradesmen do not like to lessen their capitals, I was obliged to be contented.

I now earnestly entreated Don Andrea not to let me languish in the expectation of being in reality his son-in-law. He yielded to my solicitations, and our nuptials were celebrated with great pomp. My father-in-law paid me the ten thousand francs, as had been agreed, and I soon found employment for them. I made my bride a present of all the jewels I had left, bought her most superb dresses, kept up incessant rejoicings in my new house for the first fortnight, provided women and footmen to attend her; in a word, I set up a way of living which would soon have ruined me, had I not by my own industry supplied the means to meet this increased expenditure.

The banker, it is true, promised mountains of gold, if fortune would but smile on his speculations. He was a man of vast designs and projects, and his son-in-law being something of the same turn of mind, we thought of no less than monopolizing in a very short time the whole business of the kingdom. Unluckily, however, for the success of our enterprises, his sole reliance was on my purse, and mine on his; and the illusion soon vanished, when we found ourselves obliged to communicate the state of our affairs to each other. The eyes of both of us were opened without recrimination, for, in fact, we had nothing to reproach each other with; on the contrary, our mutual confidence had the effect of making our union more close; and being now known to each other for what we really were, like robbers we swore to be faithful.

Our partnership at first made a great noise, owing to the mysterious tone with which Don Andrea told everybody that he had chosen for his son-in-law a man who was possessed of immense riches. It was soon spread about, and everyone was for dealing with us, and came to us in preference to other bankers; and we might by our credit only have increased every day the favorable opinion they had of our wealth, if we had been contented to have associated with tradesmen, and no doubt we should have made a considerable fortune; but the uncommon weak partiality that my father-in-law always had for people of the court, put a check to our success. What he received with one hand was squandered with the other. If a marquis, a count, or a knight of San Jago were civil to him, they were sure to obtain any loan of money, and, knowing his vanity, they would not fail to lavish upon him the most flattering compliments.

If a minister looked favorably on him, the very next day he would send him some rich present to no purpose whatever. He always had his head filled with chimerical projects which he would put in execution, and if I happened to show him the folly of them, he laughed at me, and treated me with contempt, as a man who had not common sense, and was quite a novice in the business of the great world.

However, with all his experience, our best substance was soon spent, our stock grew low, and we were reduced to make use of every means to renew and uphold our credit. What engines did we not set to work for that purpose? We bought and sold anything; we received pawns; we lent money at usurious interest; in short, there was no sort of commerce which we were not engaged in. Besides what I knew already, my industry, improved by exercising it, helped me to new expedients for the good of our society. However, I must own that I was but a mere beginner compared to my father-in-law. Our gains were great, and would have been sufficient to have maintained us agreeably; and if we had understood how to live with economy, we should have been obliged to make use of some sorry shifts, which in spite of all our skill we were sometimes compelled to resort to. In addition to this our domestic expenses were most profuse. If Don Andrea was fond of luxury and good living, his daughter was not behindhand with him; there was nothing too rich or too fine for her; we kept as magnificent a table as any nobleman, more servants than we conveniently wanted, and our house was constantly full of relations and friends, whom we entertained and treated with the greatest profusion.

This bustle did not less please my humor than that of my wife, and while our affairs went on well, I did not in the least oppose it. I got tired, however, in two or three years after my marriage, when I perceived that through bad management, and some unforeseen accidents, our fortune began to diminish apace. Frightened at the prospect of distress, I ventured to remonstrate gently with Eugenia; God knows how I was treated by her! I complained to Don Andrea, who reproved her; and the whole family blamed her for her behavior; but even my softest words, the reproaches of her father, and the entreaties of her friends, did but exasperate her the more against me: in a word, she declared to me that she did not mean to have the least reform in her family. After this decree, which the temper of my wife made quite absolute, I wisely resolved not to contradict her any more, but endeavor to fortify myself with more patience for the future.

It was, however, with extreme grief that I saw melting away, like snow, all the money I had brought with me from Italy; and I could not think of the consequences of my marriage without sighing bitterly for having been so deprived of sense as to marry at all. Sometimes, to excuse myself for having acted so foolishly, I recalled to mind the rich figure that Don Andrea made when I became his son-in-law; and who could have imagined that I should find my ruin in an establishment that appeared to possess the means of the most solid fortune? When I observed that there was no longer any hope of being able to live on the same footing, I applied to my father-in-law for advice in my embarrassment.

It was on this occaion that he showed me how skillful he was in all the tricks of business. "The truth is," said he, "you must do here what I have done myself in similar cases, which is, to save the little that remains to you at the cost of others:" then without the least delay he counterfeited letters of transfer, and false contracts, and I do not know how many similar deeds, all equally worthy of a public reward, if proper justice could always be administered to all honest folks that make use of them.

He did not stop here; for in order to establish my credit, which was now become necessary to him, he made me purchase an estate of five hundred ducats a year, which his brother possessed; when I say purchase, I mean only in appearance, for we were not able, both together, to muster a sufficient sum to show the notary, that he might witness the payment of the purchase money. It cost me, however, but fifty crowns to borrow this sum for one day, and thus the sale was apparently completed. At the same time I gave the seller a deed, by which I formally declared that the said estate did not belong to me, but was as much his as ever, to whom I abandoned the enjoyment of it, having no manner of claim. I was well pleased with these shuffling tricks, because they were advantageous to me. Besides, I knew that they were commonly practiced in all trading cities.

Thanks to my father-in-law, I had now secured something to myself, let fortune be as contrary as it pleased; and being able to trade again upon the faith of this new estate, I went on in my usual courses. Unfortunately this state of things could not last long. People who have been cheated are sure to be undeceived at last; besides, my wife's always spending more than I gained, was sufficient of itself to ruin me, and I could not hold out against it any longer. Don Andrea was still lucky enough to get himself out of the scrape. As for me, I could no longer keep out of the clutches of a cursed *alguazil*, who arrested me on the part of my creditors, and led me to prison; but they found themselves overreached when they set about seizing my effects, and learned that they were secretly made over. I was not so unconscionable as to wish them to lose all; so I paid each a tenth part of what was due, promising to liquidate the remainder in ten years. I was set at liberty again on these terms.

The proud Eugenia was so extremely mortified at my imprisonment and bankruptcy, the shame of which she thought would fall on her only, that she could not be consoled, and died very shortly after; and as she left no child, I found myself under the obligation of refunding her dowry, which, under my present circumstances, could not fail to destroy my every project. To tell the truth, therefore, the tears I shed at her death were not the effect of the loss of my wife, but of regret for my money which she had so foolishly squandered, and for hers, which I had to return to her father. Notwithstanding which I did not fail to act the good husband, and ordered her funeral so superb, that my creditors murmured at it. Though I had now become a widower, I did not cease to live on good terms with Don Andrea. Besides that I could not have gained anything by tricking him, he was the only man who was in possession of all my secrets, and I had still occasion for his assistance. I submitted, therefore, very patiently to all he required of me, and he was so much pleased with my conduct towards him, that he behaved in an equally handsome manner towards me.

CHAPTER III

GUZMAN AFTER THE DEATH OF HIS WIFE WISHES TO EM-
BRACE THE ECCLESIASTICAL LIFE, AND WITH THAT VIEW
REPAIRS TO ALCALA DE HENARES TO STUDY—THE FRUITS
OF HIS STUDIES

AFTER having rendered the last duties to my wife, and her dowry to her father, I still remained in my own house, which was now all that was my own; and even this was completely stripped, with the exception of one room, which Don Andrea, out of compassion, had furnished for me with a few articles of trifling value. Here I was occupied in making reflections on the past, and in devising means for my future subsistence.

What now can I possibly do? said I to myself. I fear I shall find no more apothecaries, no banker like that at Milan, no more relations to trust their jewels to my care. What then is to become of me? O Sayavedra, my dear confidant, how I do miss you! Why can you not be witness of my troubles when I stand so much in need of your address and advice? Were you now present, we could together devise some scheme for my relief; but, alas! I have lost you! I ought no longer to rely on your assistance, which, perhaps, at this moment, you repent sorely having ever offered me.

This last thought affected me exceedingly, and I felt so disgusted with the word that I resolved to quit it. I must, said I, turn my thoughts to the Church. In the asylum I may possibly find that solid happiness which I have hitherto sought for in vain. I therefore decided to go to Alcala to study philosophy and theology. . . .

Until I could receive orders, I began to avoid all sorts of company, and to live more regularly in frequenting places of worship. One day when the weather was extremely fine for walking, I quitted the town on a pilgrimage to St. Mary of the valley, an agreeable hermitage, situated about a mile distant. On my way I overtook a great concourse of people on their journey to the same spot, and the chapel of the saint was so crowded when I arrived, that there was scarcely room to kneel down in it. A lady, who sat two or three paces from me, observing my embarrassment, retired somewhat further back, as if by that action to make room for me next to her. I was extremely surprised at this polite attention from a female with whom I was not acquainted, and who, I thought, could not know me; and in spite of my affected gravity, I could not help fixing my eyes on her elegant figure, doubting not, from her dress and demeanor, that she was a lady of some consequence.

She carefully concealed her face from me, darting, however, an occasional glance at me with one eye, which pierced my very soul. I took possession of the vacant place near her, and wishing to testify my gratitude in some compliment, I said in a whisper:

" How dangerous is this politeness! "

" I can scarcely think that you can be afraid of it," said she in the same tone.

I dared not reply for fear of being overheard by the ladies who sat by her, and seemed to be of her party. I looked at them all attentively, and in one of them I recognized the widow of one Dr. Gracia, a physician, a lady already in years, and who kept a boarding-house in the town. I knew that she had three daughters who were called the three Graces, as well on account of the name of their father, as of their lovely persons. I had now no doubt that the lady whom I had just spoken to must be one of these three celebrated sisters; and as report boasted particularly of the beauty and wit of the eldest, I could not help wishing that it might be she—a wish, however, which I could not entertain without considerable alarm for my heart. With the reputation of being extremely pretty, these young ladies had not the character of being vestals.

This was not much to be wondered at, Dr. Gracia having left his affairs in such a state as obliged his widow to take in boarders for a livelihood. If slander does not even spare young ladies brought up with the utmost severity, how could it possibly respect our three Graces, who were eternally surrounded with gallants? Their father had been a man of pleasure, and had caused them to be instructed in music and other accomplishments; more intent on fitting them for society than forming their minds to virtue.

I was perfectly well acquainted with all this; and they on their side knew well who I was. They had heard that I was well versed in music, that I had plenty of money, and a peculiar talent in spending it. These excellent qualities, which they admired in a man, made them extremely desirous to scrape acquaintance with me, and to induce me to increase the number of their boarders. This proposal had before been made to me, but I had rejected it, for fear of involving myself in some fresh intrigue. I had even made oath to avoid every snare that love might lay for me, and I did not expect that, in the holy place where I now stood, I should break this oath. Nevertheless, I felt a sort of agitation which so much resembled the first emotions of a growing passion, that I was alarmed at it.

" Guzman," said I to myself, " make not a fool of yourself here. What God did you come to worship in this church? Let not your heart be taken by surprise. Can you wish to lose the fruits of so much study? "

While my reason thus contended with my weakness, the ladies, having finished their prayers, rose to leave the church. There were seven or eight of them, all of the same party. They passed by where I sat, and I rose to bow to them. The one whom I had so particularly noticed, and who was in reality the eldest of the three sisters, managed very adroitly, under pretense of adjusting her veil, to afford me a view of her beautiful face. I was so struck with it, that it was with the greatest difficulty I could restrain myself from following her. An impulse, however, which Heaven only could have bestowed upon me, held me back from so powerful and dangerous an attraction. I dropped down on my knees again, to continue, or rather to begin my prayer, for I had as yet been so absorbed in other thoughts that I had forgotten the duty which brought me to church. I could not, however, divest my mind of the image of the enchantress who occupied it; and, more agitated than a vessel without sail or compass in the middle of the ocean, I yielded to the different emotions which possessed my heart.

My extreme uneasiness not permitting me to remain any longer in the chapel, I left it, not to trace the steps of the beauty who had made so much impression on me; on the contrary, my wish was to avoid her, and fearing that I should meet her in the road that led to the city; I took another route, and turned my steps towards the river, in the hope that while I walked along its banks I should insensibly lose all recollection of this redoubtable personage, whom my philosophy had not been able to withstand. And perhaps I should have become tranquil after a little reflection, but my stars willed it otherwise. A voice which I heard at the distance of ten or twelve paces from me, caused me to turn my head towards the spot from whence it came, and the very first thing that struck my eyes was that same Doña Maria Gracia, whose charms I was so assiduously shunning. She was seated on the grass and singing, while her sisters and the other ladies in company were preparing an elegant collation.

At this sight I was no longer master of myself, but advanced and saluted them.

"You must agree, ladies," said I, "that fate is most propitious to me today, since it has been its will that I should meet you everywhere; but to complete my happiness I should be seated by your side."

Doña Maria replied with a smile, that it was my own fault only if I were not, and that it was but just that so many fair shepherdesses should have at least one shepherd to protect them from the wolves.

This answer delighted me, and I quickly joined the party, abandoning myself to all my natural gaiety. The mother and the daughters seemed to vie with each other in politeness towards me. I thought that I had never spent many such agreeable moments, and regretted exceedingly that I had declined the opportunity of associating with so charming a family. The other ladies were also very gracious, and I told them more than once that I thought all the loveliness in Alcala was in my presence. This compliment, as you may suppose, did not in the least offend them; and to show me that there was some justice in my remark, they prepared after the collation to entertain me with a concert. Two of the ladies played guitars which they had brought with them, and Doña Maria, and the others who had voices, accompanied them. A guitar was then presented to me, and I was entreated to play some airs to dance to, which I did with much less pleasure than I felt in seeing the ladies trip to it in the meadow like so many nymphs of Diana.

The eldest sister was the dancer I took most notice of. An air of peculiar nobleness and grace distinguished her from her companions. It is not surprising then that a man who took fire so easily as I did, could not resist such fine qualities. In truth, I was so enamored of Doña Maria, that I saw nobody but her. When she left off dancing, I seated myself at her feet, and presenting her with a guitar, entreated that she would play and sing to it. This request she was willing to comply with, on condition that I would accompany her. She had heard my voice praised, she said, and she longed to hear it herself. As I had no less a longing to gratify her desire, I was easily prevailed on, and acquitted myself, as I need not tell you, very much to the satisfaction of the party assembled.

In this manner we continued to amuse ourselves until night, when the widow Gracia sounded a retreat, and we began to file off towards the town, Doña Maria and I walking last. It were useless to tell you that our conversation turned upon love. We were both too intent upon it to talk upon any other subject, and accordingly made a reciprocal declaration, and from that day perceived clearly that we were made for each other. As the other ladies in company had not so agreeable a conversation together as we had, they talked rather faster, and Doña Maria wishing to overtake them, either by chance or intentionally, made a false step, and must inevitably have fallen, had I not caught her in my arms. In raising her up I was bold enough to snatch a kiss. No sooner had I taken this liberty than, fearful that I had offended, I began to make excuses to the fair one, who, so far from resenting my boldness, told me in a lively manner that I had done well in paying myself for the service I had rendered her, which she might otherwise have been ungrateful enough to have forgotten.

When we arrived at the widow's house, she gave me an invitation to walk in, which I willingly accepted. I partook of some refreshments, and prolonged my visit till decency compelled me to take my leave. Before I retired, however, I obtained the widow's permission to call occasionally to assure her of my respect. I then bade adieu to Doña Maria, and was so transported with love that, instead of returning homewards, I took the way to the University, and only recognized my error in time to prevent my knocking at the gates. You will easily conceive that I slept but little that night, after having passed the day in the manner I have related.

The following day I went as usual to the schools of the University, where my distraction was such, that when I left them I scarcely knew what subject had been treated of. After dinner I could not resist the pleasure of visiting Doña Maria, to whom I listened much more attentively than I had done to the professor in the morning, and who detached me so completely from the University, that I soon ceased to go there at all. I renounced the orders I had been so anxious to obtain, changed my ecclesiastical for a most magnificent secular habit, and after having paid my landlord, became a boarder at the widow Gracia's; or rather, to speak without disguise, I gave myself up to the demon which possessed me. Every person of sense who was acquainted with me pitied my blindness, and even the rector of the University had the kindness to remonstrate with me on my change of conduct; but these friendly endeavors were of no avail. Fate would have it that I should persevere to my own ruin; or rather, perhaps, Heaven could no longer behold such a subject a minister of the Church.

CHAPTER IV

GUZMAN MARRIES AGAIN AT ALCALA, AND SHORTLY AFTER RETURNS TO LIVE AT SEVILLE WITH HIS NEW WIFE

I LIVED most delightfully with my new landladies; they endeavored to anticipate my every desire; in short, I was the master of the house. This life lasted for about three months, at the expiration of which time I began to talk of marriage. We soon came to terms; and, by way of making a greater fool of myself, I expended a considerable sum of money in wedding-clothes. One would have thought that I had cart-loads of money; though, to say the truth, I was almost at my last shift.

My mother-in-law, who was a good sort of woman, very easily led away by finery, seeing the fine show I made, thought that I was, of course, possessed of considerable property, and that the fortune of her whole family was made by obtaining me for a son-in-law. As it was necessary that a young man should be employed, she proposed to me to apply myself to physic, telling me that it was a very lucrative profession, and that if her husband had been more assiduous in it, he might have left his widow and children much better off than they were. To induce me to follow her advice, she offered me all Dr. Gracia's books and memoranda, not doubting, as she said, that with such assistance, and my excellent understanding, I should soon become an excellent physician. To gratify her wishes, I was complacent enough to study for about six months under some of the most famous professors of medicine; but their lessons were not at all to my taste, and I soon became disgusted with a study which, at the best, could only maintain me in my old age. I pretended, therefore, that I had received letters from one of my friends, offering me a lucrative post at Madrid, in which I could not fail to grow rich in a very few years. I imparted this news to my mother-in-law, who, believing it to be true, was the first to recommend me to accept the situation, much as she really regretted the loss of my society.

The aversion I felt for the study of medicine was not the only reason for my wishing to leave Alcala. My finances were now at a very low ebb, and I did not wish to expose my poverty in a place where I had hitherto been considered in easy circumstances. . . .

We took the road to Seville to gratify my great desire to revisit my native country. We traveled very slowly for fear of fatigue; and I own that I felt a secret pleasure in surveying the country through which I had formerly passed, although it recalled to my remembrance the sad adventures of my youth. I passed 'the inn where I had been a servant; and at the sight of Cantillana I fancied I still smelt those excellent ragouts of mules with which I had formerly been regaled; and I did not forget the cudgeling which had been so liberally bestowed on me and the muleteer by the two officers of the Holy Brotherhood. I arrived and dined at that charming inn where they made omelets of pullets. I told my wife this story, and she laughed at it heartily. At last I reached the hermitage where I lay the first night after I left Seville, and, transported with the recollection, I addressed the saint in these terms:

"O great St. Lazarus!" cried I, "when I left the steps of thy chapel 'twas with tears in my eyes, on foot, alone, and poor, but innocent; and now thou seest me return, married, and in good condition, and well mounted, but how innocent, Heaven and thou know!"

It was quite night when we arrived at Seville, so that we were obliged to take up our quarters at the first inn we came to; but the next morning I rose betimes and took lodgings in St. Bartholomew Street, whither I had my baggage conveyed. The next thing I did was to ask after my mother, but I could hear no news of her until some months afterward, when Doña Maria being on a visit to a lady with whom she had made an acquaintance, heard her name mentioned by mere chance, and was much astonished to learn that she lived very near us with a young lady who passed for her daughter. No sooner had I ascertained my mother's residence than I flew to it, found her at home, and we embraced with sincere affection.

We related to each other in a few words the adventures that had happened to us both since our parting, each of us, however, concealing whatever we thought fit. She was very anxious, for example, to persuade me that she had brought up the young lady who lived with her out of pure charity, having been attached to her from her earliest infancy. I pretended to believe her word implicitly, though I entertained considerable doubt whether she had not other views which she did not choose to confess. After a long conversation, I introduced Doña Maria to her. My mother received her very kindly, and embraced her in an affectionate manner not very common in a mother-in-law.

To celebrate our reunion, my mother invited us to several entertainments, which we returned. I proposed to her to come and live with us, representing to her how much more agreeably she might pass her time. She answered that she could not make up her mind to desert her adopted daughter, and that she feared also she should not be able to agree long with my wife. I endeavored to remove the first obstacle, by consenting to receive the young lady into my family also.

"You cannot think of it, my son," said my mother. "You must know but little of women, if you think that two lively young ladies like Petronilla and Doña Maria can live even one month together, without quarreling themselves, and indeed setting the whole house in an uproar."

I succeeded, however, in conquering the repugnance that my mother felt to grant my request. It is true that she yielded at last upon my assurance that she would always find in my wife a daughter submissive to her wishes. At last she came alone to reside with us, choosing rather to leave Petronilla to herself than to be the cause of dissensions in my family. At the beginning all went on smoothly, and the only contention was, who should be the most complaisant. Each seemed to endeavor to anticipate the desire of the other. They addressed each other affectionately, and if this good understanding had but lasted, we could not have failed in making our fortune; but, unfortunately, before the expiration of three months everything changed, and these same ladies, who had hitherto agreed so well, now began to pursue a different conduct.

My mother wished to govern despotically, which my wife would not submit to. They were constantly disputing and quarreling, and peace was entirely banished the house. Sometimes I endeavored to reconcile them, and to act as umpire, but this only brought upon me the fury of her whom I decided against. What made matters worse was, that the ships which were expected from India did not come in that year. Money became scarce. Doña Maria was not one who could listen to economy, and no clothes or ornaments were good enough for her. The natural consequence of all this was, that as our funds diminished, so in proportion our vexations increased.

As good luck would have it, I happened to become acquainted with an Italian, captain of a Neapolitan galley,

who, by order of the court, had come to Malaga to carry
the bishop of that city to Naples; but that prelate not being
ready to embark, he had came to Seville in the hopes of
meeting with merchandise to freight his vessel for Italy.
I met him by chance one day at a merchant's house, and
was delighted in having found a man who spoke Italian as
well as myself. He was, on his side, equally pleased, and
we became very intimate. · I invited him to my house, and
introduced him to my wife, who did not fail to charm him.
He made me some trifling presents, which would have been
more considerable if his affairs would have permitted him
to remain any longer at Seville; but as he could not make
the bishop wait for him, and could not bear the ieda of
parting from my wife, he found means to conciliate his
love with his duty, by persuading her to desert me, and fly
with him into Italy. After all, I believe that he did not
find it a very difficult matter to prevail upon her, for she
had been long out of humor with me, and hated my mother
more and more every day; so that we had not an hour's
quiet for her. However that might be, I cared but little
about it; and, indeed, thought myself happy and rich in
having got rid of her, notwithstanding she had taken her
jewels and everything of value about the house with her;
in which the captain had very honestly assisted her, before
I had the least suspicion of their intentions.

CHAPTER V

GUZMAN, AFTER HIS WIFE'S ELOPEMENT, RESIDES FOR SOME
TIME WITH HIS MOTHER; BUT AT LENGTH ENTERS INTO
THE SERVICE OF A LADY OF QUALITY

I WAS prudent enough to keep this affair secret, knowing that all the scandal of it would be reflected upon me.
I sold what remained of my property, which consisted only
of some of the worst of the furniture and movables, which

my wife had condescended to leave behind, and employed
the money in making merry with my friends. My mother
accommodated herself as long as she could to the life I
led, but at last growing tired of it, she returned to the
house where she had left Petronilla, telling me that she
could now live more at her ease with her than she could
expect to do with me. I offered no opposition to her plans,
and we parted again in perfect good will towards each
other.

You will not be surprised that a continued train of
expenditure without any income soon reduced me to my
original condition of life; but an adventurer, in whatever
state it may please fortune to place him, should always
find resources in his wits. Mine did not now abandon
me. I learnt one day that there resided in the town a rich
widow, whose husband had been governor of a city in the
West Indies, and had died there, leaving his lady in great
affluence. This widow, who affected great devotion, had
no children, but several relations of consequence, and was
at this time in search of a man, to whom she could confide
the management of her affairs, well knowing that places
of this discription are not always filled by men of
probity.

This post was a great temptation to me, and I resolved
to spare nothing to obtain it, knowing that my fortune was
made if I could succeed. After having tormented my
brains for some time to invent some stratagem to attain my
ends, I learnt that her father confessor was a Dominican
friar, who had an absolute dominion over all her wishes,
and that he must be gained over to my interest. To this
and I bought a purse, and put eight *pistoles* and twenty
ducats of gold in it, to which I added a ring of trifling
value, and a gold seal which my mother had presented to
my wife the first day she saw her. After which I laid
by my sword, and put on a very plain suit of clothes. In
this state I repaired to the convent of the Dominicans,
where I asked leave to speak to the reverend father before
mentioned, who was a very favorite preacher, and had

converted many. I was taken for one of his penitents, and was conducted immediately to his chamber, which I entered with a hypocritical countenance, as if afraid to cast my eyes on so sacred a person, and in a low and soft voice:

"Most reverend father," said I, "I have just picked up this purse, which appears to be full of gold and silver coins, and although I am but a poor man, I know that I have no right to keep it. I have therefore taken the liberty of asking for you, that I might place it in the hands of your reverence to dispose of as you may think fit."

The good father, charmed with so heroic an action in a person whose wants might have excused his appropriating it to himself, surveyed me from head to foot, and commended my disinterested and religious behavior. He could not sufficiently extol me; and feeling at the same time a desire to render me some service, as a recompense for my virtue, he asked me a few questions as to my situation in life and talents, that he might know what I was capable of.

"Reverend Father," said I, "I have now been at Seville for some time, entirely out of employment. I was receiver of taxes at Madrid; but finding myself inclined to spend my own money to assist rather than persecute the poor, I was compelled to resign that situation; from which I became steward to a nobleman, whose affairs were in great confusion. These might soon have been settled; but in proportion as I arranged them, he involved them afresh, so that after having served him four years with the utmost zeal and fidelity, I was obliged to leave him as much a beggar as when I first entered his service, and without even having received my wages."

The confessor listened to me with great attention; and surprised at hearing a man, whose dress did not much prepossess him in favor of his education, speak in such good terms, he asked me if I had ever studied. I told him that I had studied most assiduously with the intention of entering the church; but that after having seriously reflected on a vocation which required so many virtues which I did not possess, I had given up such an idea. He was curious to ascertain how far I had gone in theology; and as all my lessons were still fresh in my memory, I answered his questions in a manner which astonished him. My interview with him lasted two hours, and he was so well pleased with me, that he assured me of his friendship, and, in taking leave, told me that on the Sunday following he would advertise the purse I had found in his church, and that if I would call upon him on the Tuesday following, he hoped he might by that time hear of some place to suit me.

After having left his reverence I repaired to my mother's.

"I have lost," said I, "the purse you gave me, in which were your ring and casket, together with eight *pistoles* and twenty crowns in gold of my own. Happily, however, it has fallen into the hands of a Dominican father, who will advertise it in his church on Sunday. You must, therefore, go there, and claim it as your property, as I do not wish to appear before his reverence, for certain reasons which I will afterwards explain."

After a little more instruction, the good woman did not fail to repair on the day fixed to the Dominican's church, where she heard the father publish the purse as he had promised, not forgetting to bestow the greatest eulogiums on the honesty of the poor man who had found it and delivered it to him. My mother, who knew as well as I did the contents of the purse, had but little difficulty in getting it restored her, after leaving two *pistoles* with his reverence as a reward for the honesty of the persons who found it.

My purse then was restored to me with the loss of two *pistoles* only. Tuesday had no sooner arrived than I waited upon the Dominican again, who received me very kindly.

"My son," said he, "a good old woman, who has claimed the purse which you found, has left two *pistoles* with me in charge for you."

I affected to be scrupulous of receiving this present, as I had only done what was my duty, for which I did not deserve or desire to be remunerated; but the good father told me that he thought I well deserved it, and obliged me to accept it; which, as you will suppose, I no longer refused, purely in obedience to his commands.

He then informed me that he had some better news to communicate, which was, that he had obtained for me the situation as steward in the family of one of the principal ladies in Seville.

"You cannot but be happy in this family," said he, "for the remainder of your days, if you perform your duty conscientiously, for which I entertain so good an opinion of you that I have passed my word."

At words like these, so flattering to such a rogue, I prostrated myself at his reverence's feet, and embraced his knees with transport. He assisted me to rise, and assured me of his protection. Then charging me with a letter to the lady, who proved to be the widow before mentioned, he told me that he had already prepared her to receive me.

I went immediately to pay my respects to my new mistress, and it was not difficult to perceive, by the reception I met with, that the friar had told wonders of me. She addressed me, not as a man who was to be her servant, but as one of whom she already entertained the highest opinion. The good father had also taken care to fix my salary and perquisites. She asked me if I was satisfied. I answered with a modest air, that it was more than I deserved, but that I would endeavor to render myself worthy of her bounty by my care and fidelity in her service. My person and conversation pleased her infinitely, and she desired me to consider myself in her service from that moment. Accordingly, I had my trunk carried in that evening, in which was all I possessed.

A very handsome room was assigned me, and I remarked with pleasure that the other servants looked upon me as their superior, and as one whom their lady would have respect paid to. All her private papers were entrusted to me, and I applied myself so assiduously in discharge of my trust, that I despatched as much business in fifteen days as my mistress expected would have taken up six months. Overjoyed at the acquisition of so expeditious an accountant, she never saw the Dominican but she praised me exceedingly, which afforded the good father great pleasure, who really thought me a young man of integrity and virtue.

I was frequently obliged to consult my lady on affairs which could not be settled without her approbation, and these interviews sometimes lasted for some hours. On these occasions I always behaved myself with so much repect, softness, and insinuation, that I perceived I was daily gaining ground in her good will. At first she had fixed certain times for me to speak with her on domestic affairs, which were in the morning at her toilet, and in the evening after supper. This did not last long, for she would come into my room after dinner, under some pretense or other, and spend hours with me in discourse which had no relation to business. Her fondness for me increased daily, and I could not but foresee the happiness she designed me.

CHAPTER VI

HOW GUZMAN SUDDENLY LOSES HIS MISTRESS'S FAVOR, AND IS CONDEMNED TO THE GALLEYS

NO sooner had I found in any part of my life that I might swim in deep water than I was drowned. Finding that I was now beloved by my mistress, and looked upon by the servants as one whose favor was of consequence, I began to act quite a different character in the family, and set myself up to be absolute lord of all. I bought the most expensive clothes, spent money like a gentleman, and, to crown all, took an under steward to look after the business of the house. Madam herself was not a whit more prudent, and, consulting her love rather than her reason, approved of everything I did.

This was by no means the case with her relations, who,

as they had an eye to the succession, observed her steps most vigilantly. They had conceived no great liking for me when I first entered the service, being rather suspicious, and not without reason, of the very devout air I assumed; but when they learnt that I carried all before me in the family, they began to reflect seriously upon it. They knew who I was, and not thinking that I was married, became very apprehensive lest the too tender widow should eventually take me into the place of the defunct governor, if she had not already done so; especially when they recollected that she had some years before contracted marriage clandestinely with one of my predecessors, who, fortunately for the lady's heirs, had thought proper to die shortly afterwards. This made them very uneasy, and they had many meetings among themselves to deliberate upon the most efficacious mode of ridding themselves of so formidable a rival in the lady's favor. All their endeavors, however, would have been ineffectual had I not ruined myself in my mistress's opinion by my imprudent conduct.

The tender connection I had formed with the love-sick lady became daily less lively on my part; for, to say the truth, she was far from possessing qualities calculated long to attach the inclinations of a gallant man. Unfortunately, also, I had cast my eyes on a young girl in the house, a pretty merry wench of about sixteen or seventeen years of age. When she heard of it, the news struck like a dagger to the lady's heart, for she had hitherto been confident of my fidelity.

She sent for her nearest relation, to tell him that I was a complete rogue; that I had not been content with robbing her and putting all her affairs into disorder; in short, that she was determined no longer to overlook my knaveries, and only wished that I might be punished according to my deserts. She could not possibly have selected a more fit person to promote her wishes in this respect than this relation of hers, who, hoping one day or other to be her heir, had more interest than anyone to remove me from the testatrix. He was, therefore, highly delighted at so favorable an opportunity, and made haste to profit by it, lest the lady should change her mind. He knew her well, and saw plainly that she only acted this part out of some jealous pique, and accordingly exerted himself with such effect that in less than two hours he obtained a warrant against me, so that before I had risen from my bed an *alguazil* entered my chamber, and led me off to prison.

I was at first inclined to consider this as a token of remembrance, either from my relations at Genoa, or my creditors at Madrid; and it was upwards of two hours before I learnt the real cause of my imprisonment. At first I did but laugh at it, flattering myself that my mistress loved me too well to leave me to the severity of the laws, and I expected every moment to receive a message that she was no longer irritated against me, and had obtained my pardon. Buoyed up with this hope, I bore without impatience or complaint those fetters which I felt convinced love would shortly break for me; and I considered myself more like a lover punished for infidelity than a steward imprisoned for robbing his mistress.

I was, however, most grievously mistaken, for I was required forthwith to render an account of my administration, which had lasted two years. I now began to grow uneasy, for the manner in which I had dissipated the widow's money to my own purposes left so large a balance between the receipts and expenditure that I would have defied any steward in the most noble family to have filled up the gap. It was in vain for me to puzzle my brain; for, to make the best of it, I was four thousand crowns short. To complete my ruin, the honest man whom I had employed as under-steward, while I thought of nothing but my pleasure, no sooner saw me thrown into jail, than, to save himself from the same fate, which he knew he equally well deserved, he made off with all the ready money he could lay his fingers on. Being answerable for this man's behavior, the whole was laid at my door. How then was it possible for me to escape with impunity? I had neither money nor credit; while, on the contrary, my prosecutors were so powerful that I could entertain no hope of leaving prison, except *to serve the King upon the seas.*

I was so convinced of this that I made an attempt to escape from prison in the disguise of a woman, and had already penetrated as far as the outer gate, when a cursed one-eyed doorkeeper recognized me. I carried a dagger in my breast, which I drew out to intimidate him; but he roared out for help, which soon arrived, and I was led back to a dark dungeon, which I was not permitted to leave until I was conducted to the galleys, to which I was condemned for the remainder of my life.

CHAPTER VII

GUZMAN IS CONVEYED TO PORT ST. MARY WITH OTHER HONEST FOLKS LIKE HIMSELF—HIS ADVENTURES ON THE WAY, AND ON BOARD THE GALLEYS

THE chain, composed of twenty-six young galley-slaves, all decorated with the collar peculiar to the order, being ready to march, we set out for Port St. Mary, where the galleys then lay. We were divided into four bands, and chained one to another, and our conductor, escorted by twenty guards, let us along by small day's journeys. We lay the first night at Cabeças, a village about nine miles from Seville. The next morning, having started again at break of day, we fell in with a lad driving pigs. This unfortunate youth, instead of driving his beasts out of our way, was imprudent enough to allow them to pass between our bands; the consequence of which was that he lost half of them. In vain did he complain to our conductor, and entreat him to interpose his authority, to obilge us to make restitution; the conductor, who hoped to eat his share, turned a deaf ear to his prayers, and we passed on

with our prize, as proud of the exploit and as joyful as
though we had recovered our liberty.

When we arrived at the inn where we stopped to dine,
I made a present of my pig to the conductor, who accepted
it willingly, and with many thanks. He then asked the
people of the house if they could dress it nicely for him,
but it was easy to perceive from their answers that they
were but little accustomed to cooking. Upon which I told
him that if he would permit my chains to be taken off for
one hour only, I would undertake to cook for him, and
doubted not that I should give him satisfaction. He did
not hesitate to grant this request, and I provided everything in such good order for him, that he afterwards used
me much more kindly than the other prisoners.

Before we left I had another opportunity of showing
my skill at the inn, where two merchants happened to
come in to dine. Finding themselves in such honest company, they became extremely uneasy for their property.
One of them seemed determined not to leave anything that
belonged to him out of his sight, and, accordingly, placed
his wallet under the table, keeping his foot upon it. I felt
a great itch to be a match for this cunning gentleman, and
accordingly slipped very gently under the table, and cutting his wallet open with a sharp knife, I drew out two
parcels, which I handed over in charge to one of my companions, named Soto, with whom I had become acquainted
in prison.

When we had left the inn, and had walked about a mile,
I requested Soto to give me the parcels, that we might see
what our booty consisted of, and divide it. Soto replied
that he did not know what I alluded to. I thought at first
that he was joking, but that was very far from his
thoughts, and he persisted with oaths that he had received
nothing of me. When I found he was in earnest, I reproached him with his ingratitude and perfidy; but he
only laughed at my reproaches and threats, and kept quiet
possession of the parcels. His behavior quite enraged me,
and I resolved to be revenged on him, by explaining the

whole affair to the conductor, choosing rather that he should profit by the theft than such an ungrateful and impudent rascal. This resolution I put into execution at night when we reached the inn where we were to sleep.

I had no sooner related the story to the conductor, than he called Soto before him, and asked him for the two parcels. The rascal answered that he had got nothing of the sort, and that I must be a great rogue to make such an accusation.

"You will not give them up with a good grace, then?" replied the conductor. "Very well, my friend, we will treat you then as you deserve."

At the same time he ordered the guards to flog him until he confessed. Soto turned pale with fear at this cruel order; and, out of regard to his skin, shortly afterwards confessed that the two parcels were concealed in the belly of the pig he had stolen. Here they were found; and when they were opened, it appeared they were full of beads and bracelets of coral adorned with gold, of excellent workmanship. Our conductor, like a man who understood his calling, thrust them all into his own pocket without ceremony, promising me a handsome reward, which, however, I have been expecting to this day; which proves clearly that this description of persons profit by the evil actions of rogues, though they do not participate in their punishment. From that day Soto and I swore eternal hatred to each other.

We pursued our route, and on our arrival at Port St. Mary we found that six galleys were careening to put to sea. We were confined a few days in prison, after which we were divided into six bands. I was so unfortunate as to be condemned to live in the same galley with Soto. We were carried aboard our galley. I was seated over against the mainmast, and Soto on the master's bench; so that we seemed doomed to be near each other. The king's coat was then given us, a red waistcoat, two pair of drawers, two shirts, a red cap, and a sea gown. After which a barber performed the operation of shaving our chins and heads. I regretted the loss of my hair exceedingly, which was long and beautiful. But it was of little consequence; I was now a complete galley-slave, which I should have been long before if I had had my deserts.

As the commissary is an officer who possesses great authority over the galley-slaves, and which he usually exercises with brutality, my first endeavor was to gain his friendship. He ate and slept very near my seat, and I was always very officious to serve him whenever an opportunity presented itself. I was always the first to anticipate his wants, and testify my extreme desire to be useful to him. All these attentions did not go long unrewarded. I soon perceived that he regarded me with a more favorable eye than the rest. This was a great consolation to me; and to render myself still more worthy of his favor, I redoubled my endeavors to please him; in which I succeeded so well that he at length never employed any other to assist him, and made me leave my seat to provide his meals for him, having been particularly well pleased with some ragouts I had already made for him. I was not a little proud of this honor, which, in fact, exempted me from my duty as galley-slave.

Our galley was ordered to Cadiz, to take aboard some masts, yards, and ship's tackling. Here a young lord, who was related to our captain, and a knight of the Order of St. James's, came with his baggage on board our galley, intending to make his first expedition. He wore, as was customary in those days, a gold chain; but he had not been a week on board before he lost this. In vain was every exertion made to discover the thief; the chain was not to be found. Upon which the captain recommended his kinsman to take one of the slaves into his service, who should have the care of his chamber, and be responsible for everything, on pain of being handsomely flogged if anything were lost. The knight approved highly of this advice, and the only question now was, which of the slaves should have the honor of serving him. He had heard a good account of my address and capacity, and wished exceedingly to have me. Accordingly the captain called the commissary before him, and asked him if he was satisfied with my behavior. The commissary, not knowing the drift of this question, enlarged upon my merit, and spoke so highly in my praise that the knight from that moment resolved to select me. I was immediately sent for; he liked my looks, and I was enrolled in his service, to the great regret of the commissary.

Behold me now become a *valet-de-chambre* to a knight of St. James's. That I might be able to serve him the more commodiously, the first favor he obtained for me was that I should only be obliged to wear a link on my foot; after which, all his clothes, linen, jewels, and other valuables were told out to me, and given in charge to me, with the recommendation that it would be to my own interest to be faithful and vigilant. I put everything in such order that I could see the whole at one view. The servants were expressly forbidden to enter the chamber without my permission, when their master was not in it. This regulation saved me a great deal of trouble in watching these sparks, who were as well versed in legerdemain tricks as any of the slaves on board the galley.

I applied myself assiduously to study the humor and disposition of the knight, and it was not long ere I was beloved by him, and even esteemed, galley-slave as I was. He felt pleasure in conversing with me, and I appeared to him to possess such good sense that he sometimes consulted me on the most important occasions. One day he entered his chamber with a thoughtful and melancholy countenance.

"My friend," said he, "one of my uncles has written me a letter which has put me exceedingly out of humor, in which he urges me, if I wish to be heir to all his property, to marry. He has himself grown idle at the court, without having dared to take that yoke upon himself which he wishes me to submit to. I know not what answer to make, for I have no inclination at present for matrimony."

"Sir," replied I, jesting, "were I in your place, I would

write word back that nothing could please me more than to comply with his wishes, provided it were with one of his daughters."

My master laughed most heartily at this advice, which was only meant by me as a joke, and declared that he would write those very words, which he doubted not would rid him of any further importunity.

CHAPTER VIII

GUZMAN FINDS HIMSELF IN THE MOST CRUEL SITUATION OF HIS LIFE; BUT IT PLEASES HEAVEN SUDDENLY TO PUT AN END TO HIS TROUBLES, AND HE RECOVERS HIS LIBERTY

I HAD every reason to be content with the life I led in the service of the young knight, who kept so good a table that I had frequent opportunities of treating my comrades; in which I should not have forgotten Soto, notwithstanding what had passed between us; but this rascal, who had never forgiven me, took great pains to nourish my hatred by constantly speaking ill of me before my master's servants as well as those of the captain. These servants, who none of them liked me, listened to him with pleasure, and did not fail to report everything to their patrons; and, among other slanders, that I was only waiting for an opportunity to make some good hit, and that, sooner or later, the knight would know me for the rogue I really was.

Although imputations coming from such a source ought not to have been looked upon without suspicion, they did not entirely fail in making some impression on my master's mind, and I soon perceived, notwithstanding the implicit confidence he pretended to place in me, that he kept a strict watch over all my actions. On my side, without taking notice of his unjust suspicions, I continued to serve him with fidelity, keeping my eyes always open to any snares my enemies might lay for me. In spite of all my vigilance, however, I fell a prey to Soto's malice, who instigated one of the knight's servants to steal a piece of plate out of his master's cabin and hide it under my bed between two boards. I soon missed it, and told my master of the loss in a manner which ought to have convinced him that I was not the thief. But I was not believed, and it was at last found where it had been concealed. The captain, thinking that I had stolen it, in spite of all I could allege in my defense, condemned me to receive fifty lashes, but my master begged me off, on condition that if anything were again lost I should have no mercy.

Finding, by this adventure, that I had secret enemies who were determined to ruin me, I humbly prayed the captain and my master to take another in my place, and permit me to return to my oar, rather than be exposed to such another misfortune. My master misinterpreted my intentions, and, thinking that I was more desirous of returning to the commissary's than of continuing in his service, he determined to keep me whether I would or no. Patience, therefore, was my only remedy, and I stood as much on my guard as I could night and day, yet, watchful as I was, I could not escape. My master having returned from the town one night, sent for me to assist in undressing him. I gave him his gown and nightcap, and while I carried his sword and gloves from one cabin to another, some rascal stole the hatband. I never could find out how this trick had been executed, but when I was brushing the hat the next morning I discovered that the band was missing. At this sight I turned as pale as death, looked for it everywhere, but all in vain; there were thieves on board that galley at least my match.

Nothing was left for me to do but to implore the knight's mercy; but when I related my new misfortune to him, as well as the malignity of my enemies, to which I attributed it, he laughed in my face.

"Mr. Guzman," said he with a sneer, "I am well persuaded that you are a person of the greatest integrity, although you have not that reputation on board this galley, and I have been told more than once of my boldness in having trusted you. Once more I think you an honest man, and am, therefore, sorry to tell you that if you do not forthwith produce my hatband you must be delivered over to the under-commissary, who will doubtless treat you according to your deserts. This you may rely upon, notwithstanding your protestation of fidelity."

This was the knight's answer, and the captain came up at that moment. As soon as he knew what was the matter, and found that I persisted in denying that I had taken the hat-band, he flew in such a passion, and beat me so cruelly, that I fell down half dead. To increase my misery, I was driven from the poop and sent to the last seat on the prow, the most uneasy seat of all, and that in which the slaves work hardest. In addition to this, the commissary had orders not to spare me, under pain of the captain's displeasure. This officer, however, really pitied me, and notwithstanding the orders he had received to treat me with rigor, allowed me to rest for a full month, seeing that I was quite incapable of hard labor.

I regained my strength by degrees, and no sooner had I recommenced my duty at the oar than Heaven, satisfied with the hardship I had already undergone, took compassion on me, and released me from my pitiable situation. Soto, who had a devilish design in his head, which he could not execute without my assistance, my seat being near the powder-room, became extremely desirous to be reconciled with me. With this view he availed himself of the mediation of a Turk, who had the liberty of going fore and aft as he pleased in the galley; not doubting that I longed in my heart to be revenged for the cruel treatment I had met with, and that I loved liberty as well as others. He entreated me, through the Turk, to forget the past, and restore him my friendship, which he confessed he had justly forfeited. I pretended to be very desirous to be reconciled to him, upon which the Turk addressed me in these terms:

"Soto has charged me to communicate to you a project which he has formed to deliver us all. It is concerted that as soon as we reach the coast of Barbary, which we are fast approaching, we are to rise, cut the throats of the officers and soldiers, beginning with the captain, proclaim liberty to the rest of the galley-slaves, who will immediately assist us, render ourselves masters of the galley, and seek an asylum amongst the Turks. This enterprise has been in contemplation," continued he, "upwards of two months. We have a sufficient quantity of arms concealed, all our measures are taken, and we have resolved to save ourselves, Turks as well as Christians, or perish in the attempt. All that is required of you is to blow up the powder-room at a signal given. This is our plot; and after the cruel treatment you have experienced from the captain, we have thought that you would not refuse to join us."

I replied to the Turk, that he might depend there was nothing I was not capable of undertaking to be revenged on the captain, and that he might assure the conspirators that I would do what was expected of me. This, however, was very far from my intention. When the day approached that the plot was to be put in execution, I requested a soldier who came near my seat to tell the captain that I had a secret of the greatest importance to reveal to him.

"But," added I, "tell him to send for me immediately; his life depends upon his compliance."

The captain considered this as a trick of mine to reconcile myself to him, and regain my post in his kinsman's service; and though he did condescend to hear what I had to say, he resolved to make me suffer for it if I was only trifling with him. He sent for me, however, and I discovered all I knew; told him where the arms lay concealed, and named the principal inventors of the plot, at the head of which I did not forget to rank my friend Soto.

The captain, perceiving now that it was no trifling matter, resolved to proceed with caution, and ordering all the soliders to their arms, commanded a search to be made, and found a vast quantity of firearms and other weapons in the place I had pointed out. He then caused the ringleaders of the conspiracy to be seized, who, being put to the torture, confessed all. Soto and one of his comrades were condemned to be drawn in quarters by four galleys, and the rest were decimated, of whom five were hung, and the others had their noses cut off. Soto, before he died, owned that it was by his contrivance the piece of plate and hat-band had been taken out of the knight's cabin, and that I was innocent of it. The captain commended me highly for my zeal and fidelity, after the unjust usage I had met with; asked my pardon publicly; ordered my irons to be struck off; gave me the liberty of the galley; and he and all the officers signed a letter setting forth the considerable service I had rendered the king in saving the galley and so many lives, which was transmitted to court to procure an order from his majesty for my enlargement. It were needless to state with what a grateful heart I returned thanks to Heaven for such a revolution in my prospects, promising to amend, and live better for the future.

Thus, friendly reader, I have given you an account of the principal adventures of my life. What followed after the king was graciously pleased to grant me my liberty, you may expect to hear, should I live long enough to tell you.

TALES FROM THE SPANISH

———

PAUL OF SEGOVIA

BY

FRANCISCO QUEVEDO Y VILLEGAS

INTRODUCTION

The best known of Quevedo's many works is undoubt-edly *Paul of Segovia,* which is, indeed, the most famous picaresque novel after *Guzman of Alfarache.* Although it was not printed until 1626, Quevedo appears to have completed it about 1608, only a few years after the true second part of *Guzman* was published. His enemies de-clared he was himself the hero of the adventures therein recounted.

His life had, to be sure, fitted him from writing the romance. Born in Madrid of a family from the mountain region of northern Spain, he, at sixteen, went to the fa-mous university of Alcalá. He pursued the regular course, but we must not imagine him forever discussing academic topics in the cloisters or ceaselessly turning the pages of books and manuscripts in the library. On the contrary, the students were noted for their talent in music, arms, dancing, racing, and even for slipping away with pastry from the table, stealing melons at night, or filching candy from shop windows. Young Francisco more than once shocked the regents of the university, disquieted the town people, and delighted the idlers by his escapades. It seems, too, that by the time he left he had few illusions about women or morality; he appears to have been rather cele-brated for his adventures and his duels. In one of the latter he so severely wounded a fellow-student that the influence of a duke was needed to hush the matter up.

On joining the court at Valladolid he even more fully devoted himself to enjoying life, but at the same time built up a reputation as a poet—he was in fact expected to become one of the future glories of Spanish literature. It was therefore nothing surprising that before he had passed the quarter century mark he was in correspondence with the greatest scholar of his age. This did not diminish his duelling either at Valladolid or later at Madrid. His pugnacious nature kept him constantly in hot water. A Captain Rodriguez whom he nearly killed because the captain wouldn't get off the sidewalk became his firm friend. But a quarrel which arose in a cathedral at vespers was concluded outdoors by the death of his antagonist. As the dead man turned out to be a person of quality, Quevedo found it advisable to leave Spain temporarily. His whole career was equally vicissitudinous, for after varying political fortunes he died of a severe imprisonment.

So *Paul of Segovia* is not a work of imagination but a record of very keen observation. Quevedo took great pleasure in mingling with common people and laborers, picking up their slang and listening to their stories. This fullness of experience, gained through conversation and his own reckless pranks, made the story one of the best picaresque novels ever written. Many of the scenes are unforgetable. For example, Paul's experience in the lone inn of Vivros is so delightfully narrated that it has reappeared in two or three other novels of the kind. The whole book is notable for its rapid narrative and vivacious satire. The swift succession of scenes, the variety of the numerous persons that appear and reappear, the movement and impetus of the events, the high spirits of the narrator keep the reader ever on the alert. Possibly more important still is the absence of the moralizings which bulked so large in the original *Guzman of Alfarache*. Quevedo, that is, was interested not nearly so much in his satire on society, sarcastic as he was at times, as he was in the hero himself. His knavish tricks, his exhaustless ingenuity, his self-possession in every predicament, his rising serenely after every defeat,—these qualities keep the reader on the lookout for further escapades of the unabashed Paul. On this account his manifold adventures are held by Spaniards to furnish a model of picaresque fiction.

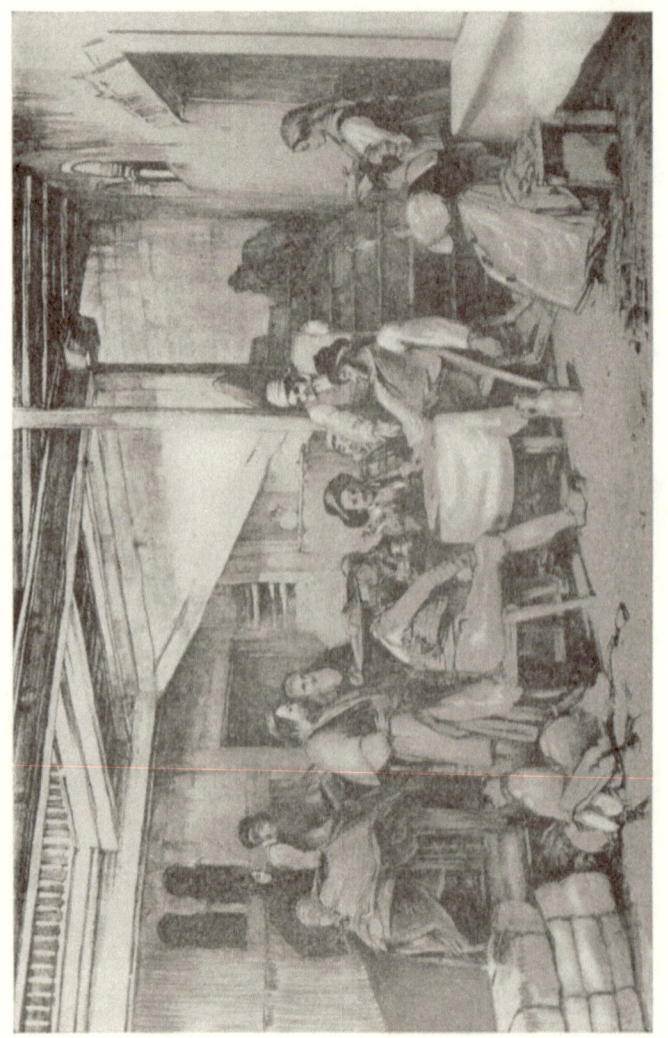

HAPPY HOURS IN A PASADA AT SEGOVIA—WHERE THE NOTORIOUS PAUL WAS BORN

(From a sketch by John Lewis)

Paul of Segovia

BOOK THE FIRST

CHAPTER I

CONTAINING AN ACCOUNT OF HIS BIRTH AND COUNTRY

I WAS born at Segovia; my father's name was Clement
Paul, a native of the same town; I hope his soul is in
heaven. I need not speak of his virtues, for those are
unknown, but by trade he was a barber, though so high-
minded that he took it for an affront to be called by any
name but that of a tonsor of beards, or the gentleman's
hair-dresser. They say he came of a good stock—and it
must have been a vine-stock—as all his actions showed a
remarkable affection for the refined blood of that glorious
genealogical tree.

He was married to Aldonza Saturna de Revollo, daughter of Octavio de Revollo Codillo, and grandchild to Lepido
Zuraconte. The town basely suspected that she was of
Jewish extraction, but she urged the names of her pro-
genitors to prove herself descended from those great men
who formed the triumvirate at Rome. She was very handsome; and so famous, that all the ballad rhymers of her
day made verses on her, which were sung about the streets.
She went through many troubles when first married, and
long after, for there were scandalous tongues in the neighborhood.

It was often proved, that whilst my father was lathering

the beards of his acquaintance, a little brother of mine, about seven years old, was as busily rifling their pockets. The poor child died of a whipping he had in the jail; and my father was much concerned at the loss, because he was such a promising, acute boy. He was himself, indeed, in prison for little matters of the same kind; yet he mostly came off so honorably, that cardinals are known to have followed in his train, and to have stuck close to him in all his misfortunes. When he left the place of his captivity half the town went behind him, huzzaing, and saluting him with turnip-tops and rotten oranges, and the ladies stood at the windows to see him pass; for he always made a good figure, whether on foot or horseback;—I do not say it out of vanity, for everybody knows I am not guilty of it.

My mother, good woman, had her share of troubles. An old nurse that brought me up, one day said in her commendation, she was of such a taking behavior that she bewitched all she had to do with; but they say that by that she meant something concerning her being rather too familiar with the devil. Her reputation here had like to have brought her to the stake, to try if she had really anything of the nature of the salamander or no, and could play tricks in the fire. It was reported, too, she was an excellent hand at renewing maiden charms, and disguising gray hairs. Some gave her the name of a pleasure-broker, others of a reconciler; but the ruder sort, by way of a joke, called her an universal money-catcher. It would have made anybody love her to see with what a pleasant countenance she heard all this, from whatever quarter it came. I need not take much time in showing what a truly penitential life she led; she had a room, into which nobody was admitted besides herself, and sometimes the writer of these memoirs, on account of his tender years. It was surrounded on all sides with dead men's bones; for the skulls, she said, helped to put her in mind of our mortality, though others, out of spite, pretended that she kept them in order to put spells upon the living. Her bed was corded with

halters, which she had borrowed from the public executioner; and she used to say to me:

"Do you see these things, child? I show them as me-
mentoes to those I have a kindness for, that they may take
heed how they live, and avoid coming to such an end."

My parents had much bickering about me, each of them
resolving to have me brought up to their trade; but I,
from my cradle, had more gentlemanly thoughts, and
would apply myself to neither. My father used to say,
"Remember, child, this trade of appropriating other's
property is no base mechanic trade, but rather a liberal
art." Then, pausing and fetching a sigh, he added, "there
is no living in this world without stealing. Why do you
think the constables and other officers hate us as they do?
Why do they sometimes banish, whip us at the cart's-tail,
and at last hang us up like so many flitches of bacon? (I
cannot refrain from tears when I think of the numerous
floggings he had received.) The reason is, they would
have no other thieves among them but themselves and their
gang; but a sharp wit brings us out of all dangers. In my
younger days I plied mostly in the churches, not out of any
religious zeal, and had been long ago carted, only I would
never tell tales, though they put me to the rack, for I never
confess but when our holy mother the church commands
us. With this business I have made shift to maintain your
mother as decently as I could."

"You maintain me!" answered his spouse in a great
rage—for she was vexed I could not learn to be a wizard—
"it was I who maintained you, sir. I brought you out of
prison by my art, and kept you there by my money. You
may thank the potions I gave you for not confessing, and
not your own courage. Were it not for fear I should be
heard in the streets, I would tell all the story—how I got
in at the chimney, and brought you out at the top of the
house."

Her passion was so high that she would have never
done, had not the strings of her beads broke, consisting
of dead men's teeth, which she preserved for particular

uses. For my own part, I declared boldly that I would apply only to virtue, and persevere in the good path I had prepared for myself. I therefore desired they would put me to school; for nothing was to be done without reading and writing. They approved of my intention, though they both muttered for a time between their teeth. One fell to stringing her dead men's bones, and the other took himself away, as he said, to fleece someone—I know not whether he meant his beard or his purse. They left me alone, praising God that he had given me such ingenious parents, and so zealous for my advancement.

CHAPTER II

HOW I WENT TO SCHOOL AND WHAT HAPPENED TO ME THERE

THE next day my primer was brought, and my schoolmaster bespoke; I went to school, and he received me with a pleasant countenance, telling me I had the looks of a sharp lad, and witty. That he might not be mistaken in his judgment, I took care to learn my lesson well that morning. He made me sit down beside him; appointed me a monitor, because I came first and went away last; for I stayed to run some errands for my mistress, and stood well in the good graces of both of them. The favor they showed me made all the other boys jealous. It was my object to keep company with gentlemen's sons, and particularly with the son of Don Alonzo Coronel de Zuñiga. I used to eat my afternoon's luncheon with him; went to his house every holiday, and waited upon him on the other days.

The other boys, either because I took no notice of them, or they thought me too high-minded, were extremely fond of calling me nicknames relating to my father's trade. Some called me Mr. Scrape; others, Mr. Tickle-beard.

One declared that he hated me because my mother had suckled two little sisters of his in the night; another said my father had been sent to his house to frighten away the vermin. Some, as I passed by, cried out " Cat "; others, "Puss, puss "; to signify my clawing descent. Another would say, " I threw rotten oranges at his mother when she was carted."

Yet for all their back-biting, I praise God my shoulders were broad enough to bear it; and though I was out of countenance, I took no notice, putting up with all, till one day a boy had the impudence to call me a son of a witch, alluding to the reports of her dealing in magic; and as it was spoken plainly, I took up a stone, and as plainly broke his head with it. I then ran for it, as fast as I could, to my mother's, and told her all the story. She said it was very well done, but that I ought to have asked who told him so? On hearing this, I observed, that some of the by-standers had told me that I need not concern myself at what he said, and laughed; which I said vexed me, and I begged to know of my mother whether it was true or not.

" Could I have given him the lie with a safe conscience, or am I the son of my own father? " I inquired. She smiled as she answered.

" God-a-mercy, lad! art thou so cunning already; you'll be no fool; you did very right to break his head, for such things are not to be said, true or not true."

This admission smote me sorely, and I resolved to pack up all I could lay my hands on, and quit my parental abode. However, I dissembled; my father went and cured the boy; all was made up, and I went to school as usual. My master received me in an angry mood, till, on learning the occasion of the quarrel and the strong provocation, he acquitted me.

The son of Don Alonzo and I continued great friends; he seemed to have imbibed a natural affection for me; I would exchange tops or toys with him, if mine were of a better quality; I gave him nice things to eat, and never asked for what he had; I bought him caricatures, I taught him to wrestle, play at leap-frog, and was altogether so obliging, that the young gentleman's parents, seeing how fond he was of my company, sent for me almost daily to dine or sup, sometimes to stay the night with him. It so happened, that about Christmas as we were going to school, a certain counsellor, called Pontio de Auguirre, passed by; little Don Diego bid me call him Pontius Pilate and run away. To please him, I did it; which so incensed the man, that he set after me at full speed, with a knife in his hand; and I was only just in time to take sanctuary in my master's house, crying out for help most lustily. My master only saved me by promising the man to give me a severe flogging; and he was as good as his word, till my mistress at last, moved to compassion, interceded for me. Every lash he gave me, he accompanied with—"Will you ever call Pontius Pilate again?"—"No Sir, never;" was my reply.

And such was the effect of the warning, that the next day, on being ordered to say our *crede* according to custom, so great was my horror of the sound, that on being asked under whom did the Saviour suffer, I instantly made answer, "And he suffered under Pontio de Auguirre!"— On this my master burst into a loud laugh, to think how well I remembered the castigation; indeed, so much was he amused at my simplicity, that he promised to forgive me the two next whippings I was to have received, for which I thanked him in the most eloquent terms.

Twelfth tide now approached, and our master, to divert the boys and make sport, ordered that there should be a king among us, and we cast lots for that honor, among twelve he had appointed for it. I was the lucky person it fell upon, and spoke to my father and mother to provide me fine clothes. When the day came I was mounted and went abroad upon a starved poor jade of a hack, that fell down upon his knees at every step; his back looked like a saw, his neck like a camel's, but somewhat longer; his head like a pig, only it had but one eye, and that moon-blind,—all which showed the knavery of his keeper, who made him do penance and fast, cheating him of his provender. Thus I went swinging from side to side like a jointed baby, with all the rest of the boys after me, tricked up as fine as so many puppets, till we came into the market-place, the very name of which scares me. Coming to a herb-woman's stall,—the Lord deliver us from all stalls,—my horse, being half starved, snapped up a small cabbage, which no sooner touched his teeth than it was down his throat, though, from the length of his neck, it reached not his belly for some time afterwards. The herb-woman, like the rest of them, was an impudent jade, and set up a cry which brought the others round her, and among them abundance of the scoundrels of the market.

Considering that the enemy's forces were all on foot, I saw it was unfair to charge them on horseback, and would have alighted, but both king and steed found themselves so terribly annoyed by showers of missiles, rotten carrots, turnips, and oranges, that we wished to sound a retreat. Before this could be effected a shot took my noble charger in the head; he reared desperately, and his strength failing him in the act, down we both came into the kennel. Imagine the condition I was in; my subjects by this time had armed themselves with stones, and attacking the herb-women in turn, soon broke two of their heads.

For my own part, after the fall, I was of little use in the action, unless it were by driving all before me by the strong weapon of gutter perfume. The officers coming up seized two of the herb-women and some of the boys, searching them for their weapons, which they took, for some had drawn their short swords and daggers. They came to me, and seeing no arms, for I had sent them to be cleaned with my hat and cloak, they begged to have them. I declared that I certainly bore offensive weapons, but such as applied only to the nose, as they might see from my filthy condition.

The officer would readily have carried me to prison,

but fortunately could not find a clean place where to lay hold of me; so some went one way and some another, while I went directly home, saluting all I met with a most infernal perfume. I told my father and mother all my adventures; but they were in such a passion at the sight and smell of me, that they would have chastised, had they dared to touch me. I made the best apology I could, laying the blame on my charger which they had provided for me; but finding nothing would appease them, I left the house and went to see my friend Don Diego, whom I found laid up with a broken head, and his parents fully resolved that he should go to school no more. He told me of the fate of my steed; finding himself hard pressed, he had saluted his enemies with his heels, but was so weak, that he put out his hip-joints with the effort, and lay in the mire expiring.

Reflecting that all the sport was now spoiled, the mob alarmed, my parents in a rage, my friend's head broken, and my charger dead, I too was resolved to go no more to school, but to stay and wait upon Don Diego, or at least to bear him company, to which his parents consented, on account of the friendship he bore me. I wrote to my father and mother, stating that I had no need to go to school any longer, for though I could not write a good hand, it was more becoming of me, because I intended to be a gentleman; so that from that hour I should renounce all schools, to save them any further charges on that head. I then informed them where, and what I was, and that they would see no more of me till they gave me special permission for that purpose.

THE SPANISH ROGUE

CHAPTER III

HOW I WENT TO A BOARDING SCHOOL TO WAIT ON DON DIEGO CORONEL

DON ALONZO determined to send his son to a boarding school, both to wean him from his tender treatment at home, and also to ease himself of that care. He was informed there was a master of arts in Segovia, whose name was Cabra, and who made it his business to educate *gentlemen's* sons; thither accordingly he sent his, and me to wait upon him. It was the first Sunday after Lent we were brought into the house of famine, for it is impossible to convey a just idea of the penury of such a place.

The master was himself a skeleton, a mere shotten herring, or like a long cane with a little head upon it. He was red haired, and no more need be said to those who know the proverb, "that neither cat nor dog of that color are good;" his eyes almost sunk into his head, as if he had looked through a perspective glass, or the deep windows in a linen-draper's shop; his nose turned up and was somewhat flat, the bridge being almost carried away by an inundation of cold rheum, for he never incurred any worse disorder because it would cost money. His beard had lost its color from fear of his mouth, which being so near, seemed to threaten to eat it out of mere hunger; his teeth had many of them deserted him from want of employment; his neck was as long as a crane's, with the gullet sticking out so far that it seemed as if compelled by necessity to start out for sustenance; his arms withered; his hands like a bundle of twigs, each of them, hanging downwards, looking like a pair of compasses, with long slender legs. His voice was weak and hollow; his beard shaggy, for he never shaved in order to save soap and razor; besides, it was odious, he said, to feel the barber's hands all over his face, and he would rather die than endure it; but he let one of the boys cut his hair.

On the night we came he showed us our room, and made us a short speech,—not longer out of sheer love of economy of words. He told us how we were to behave. The next morning we were engaged till dinner time; we went to it; the masters dined first and the servants waited. The dining-room was as big as a half-peck; five gentlemen ate in it at one table; I looked about for the cat, and seeing none, asked a servant, an old stager, who in his leanness bore the mark of a boarding-school, how it came they had none? The tears stood in his eyes, and he said:

"Why do you talk of cats? Pray who told you that cats loved penance and mortification? Ah, your fat sides show you are a new comer."

This to me was the augury of sorrow, but I was worse scared when I observed that all those who were before us in the house looked like so many pictures of death on the white horse. Master Cabra said grace, then sat down, and they ate a meal which had neither beginning nor end. They brought the broth in wooden dishes, but it was so clear that a man might have seen to the bottom had it been ten fathoms deep. I observed how eagerly they all dived down after a single pea that was in every dish. Every sip he gave, Cabra cried:

"By my troth, there is no dainty like the *olla*, or boiled meat and broth. Let the world say what it will, all the rest is mere gluttony and extravagancy; this is good for the health, while it sharpens the wits."

"A curse on thee and thy wit," thought I, and at the same time I saw a servant, like a walking ghost, bring in a dish of meat, which looked as if he had picked it off his own bones. Among it was one poor stray turnip, at sight of which the master exclaimed:

"What, have we turnips today; no partridge is in my opinion to compare to them. Eat heartily, for I love to see you eat."

He gave every one such a wretched bit of mutton that it stuck to their nails and in their teeth so that not a shred of it could reach their stomach. Cabra looked on, and repeated:

"Eat heartily, for it is a pleasure to me to see what good stomachs you have."

Now just think what a comfort this was for them that were pining with hunger. When dinner was over, there remained some scraps of bread on the table, and a few bits of skin and bones, and the master said:

"Let this be left for the servants; they must dine as well as we."

"Predition seize thee, ruthless wretch," thought I, "and may what thou hast eaten stick in thy gizzard for evermore! what a consternation you have thrown my stomach into!"

He next returned thanks, saying, "Come, let us make way for the servants, and you go and exercise until two o'clock, lest your dinner should be too heavy for you."

I could no longer forbear laughing aloud for my life, on which he grew very angry, and bade me conduct myself like a modest youth, quoting two or three mouldy old proverbs, and then took himself off. We sat down to this mournful spectacle, and hearing my great guns roar for provender, and as a new comer having more strength than the rest, I seized by force upon two scraps of bread, and bolted them down along with one piece of skin. The others began to mutter, for they were too weak to speak aloud; on which in came Cabra once more, observing:

"Come, come, eat quietly together, since God provides for you, be thankful; there is enough for all."

Now, I declare it solemnly, there was one of these servants, a Biscayan, named Surre, who had so completely forgotten the way to his mouth, that he put a small bit of crust that was given him into his eye, as if happy that he was thus saved the trouble of swallowing. I asked for drink; the rest who had hardly broken fast never thought of it, and they gave me a dish with some water, which I no sooner put to my lips, before the sharp-set lad I spoke of snatched it away, as if I had been Tantalus, and that the flitting river he stands in up to the chin. I got up from table with a sigh, perceiving for truth that I was in a house where they drank to a good appetite, but would not permit it to pledge. It is impossible to express my trouble and concern; and considering how little was likely to go into my belly, I was actually afraid, though hard pressed, of feeling the process of digestion going on.

Thus we passed on till night. Don Diego asked me how he should do to persuade himself that he had dined, for his stomach could not be made to submit, and only grumbled when he alluded to the subject. The house, in short, was a hospital of dizzy heads, proceeding from empty insides, —a different kind of dizziness to that incurred by surfeits.

Supper time came, for afternoon meals were never dreamed of. It was still shorter than the dinner, and consisted of a little roasted goat instead of mutton. Surely the devil could never have contrived a worse little beast. Our starving master Cabra said: "It is very wholesome and beneficial to eat light suppers, that the stomach may not be overwhelmed;" and then he quoted some cursed physician who has been long in Hades. He extolled spare diet, alleging that it prevented uneasy dreams, though he knew that in his house it was impossible to dream of anything but eating. Our master and we supped, but in reality we had none of us supped. On going to bed, neither Diego nor I could sleep a wink, for he lay contriving how to complain to his father, that he might remove him, and I advising him so to do; and at last I said to him:

"Pray, sir, are you sure we are alive; for to tell you the truth, I have a strong fancy we were slain in the battle with the herb-women, and are now souls suffering in purgatory, in which case it will be to no purpose to talk of your father's fetching us away, without he has our souls prayed out of this state of punishment."

Having spent the whole night in this discourse, we got a little nap towards morning, till it was time to rise; six o'clock struck, Cabra called, and we all went to school, but when I went to dress me, my doublet was two handfuls too big, and my breeches, which before were close, now hung as loose as if they had been none of my own. In fact, when I was ordered to decline some nouns, such was my hunger that I ate half of my words, for want of more substantial diet. . . .

In this misery we continued till the next Lent, at the beginning of which one of our companions fell sick; Cabra, to save charges, delayed sending for a physician till the patient was just giving up the ghost, and desired to prepare for another world; then he called a young quack, who felt his pulse, and said hunger had been beforehand with him, and prevented his killing that man. These were his last words; the poor lad died, and was buried meanly, because he was a stranger. This struck a terror into all that lived in the house; the dismal story flew all about the town, and came at last to Don Alonzo Coronel's ears, who having no other son, began to be convinced of Cabra's inhumanity, and to give credit to the words of two mere shadows, for we were no better at that time. He came to take us from the boarding-school, and asked for us, though we stood before him; till at length, seeing us with some difficulty, and in so deplorable a condition, he gave our master some hard words. We were carried away in two chairs, taking leave of our famished companions, who followed us with their eyes and wishes, lamenting like those who remain slaves at Algiers, when their other associates are ransomed.

CHAPTER IV

DON DIEGO AND HIS MAN, RESCUED FROM THE JAWS OF
FAMINE, AND RECOVERED, ARE SENT TO THE UNIVERSITY
OF ALCALA—THEIR PLEASANT ADVENTURE BY THE WAY

WHEN we came to Don Alonzo's house, they laid us very gently upon two beds, for fear of rattling our bones, because they were so bare: then with magnifying glasses they began to search all about our faces for our eyes, and were a long time before they could find out mine, from the excess of privation and suffering. Physicians were called in, who ordered the dust to be wiped off our mouths with fox-tails, as if we had been paintings; and indeed we looked like the picture of death; and that we should be nourished with good broths and light meats, for fear of overloading our weak stomachs. How can we express the rejoicing we felt inwardly when we tasted the first good soup, and afterwards when we came to eat some fowl? All these things were to us unknown novelties. The doctor gave order that for nine days nobody should talk in our chamber, because our stomachs were so empty, that the least word returned an echo in them. These precautions tended in some measure to restore us; but our jaws were so shattered and shrivelled up, that there was no stretching them; and care was taken that they should every day be gently forced out, and, as it were, set upon a last, with the bottom of a pestle.

In a few days we got up to try our limbs; but we still looked like the shadows of other men, and so lean and pale that we might be taken for the lineal descendants from the fathers in the desert. We spent the whole day in praising God for having delivered us out of the clutches of the most inhuman Cabra, and offered up our earnest prayers that no Christian might ever fall into that miserable thraldom. If we ever happened to think of our wretched fare at school, the idea alone would make us devour double the quantity at table; and we used to tell Don Alonzo how Cabra would inveigh against gluttony on saying grace, though he never felt the most remote approach to it in his life. He laughed heartily at our informing him, that, when speaking of the commandment, " Thou shalt do no murder," he made it extend to partridges and capons; indeed, to everything of which he wished to deprive us, even hunger itself, which he accounted a deadly sin. It took us three months to recover our strength, at the end of which Don Alonzo began to think of sending his son to Alcala to finish his studies. He asked me if I would go; and I, who longed to quit the neighborhood of so inhuman a monster, a friend only to misery and famine, promised to serve his son most faithfully. He then appointed a sort of steward to regulate his son's accounts, who let him know his expenses by drawing bills upon one Julian Merluzza.

We now despatched our effects in a cart belonging to one Diego Monze; there was a small bed for our master, and a truckle bed to run under it for me and the steward, whose name was Aranda; five quilts, four pair of sheets, eight pillows, four hangings, a trunk of linen, and other furniture for a house. We ourselves took a coach in the evening, and towards midnight came to the ever accursed lone inn of Viveros. The inn-keeper was of Moorish race, and an arrant thief; in all my life I never saw cat and dog so peaceable as on that day. He received us very courteously, because he and the carter went snacks, for we traveled so slowly that they were there before us. He hastened to the coach door, and assisted me to alight, asking, " Was I going to the university?" I told him I was. He put me into the house, where two sharpers were with some keeper trying to save his supper, and two scoundrel shabby girls, a curate playing by them, an old covetous shop-scholars contriving how to fill their bellies free of cost. My master, as being the last comer, and but a boy, said:

"Landlord, get what you have in the house for me and two servants."

"We are all your servants, sir, and will wait on you," said the sharpers.

"Here, landlord, take notice, this gentleman will satisfy you, so bring out all you have in the larder."

Another stepped up to Don Diego, and taking off his cloak, laid it by, saying:

"Pray sit down and rest you."

All this puffed me up so full of vanity, that the inn was too little to hold me. One of the damsels said:

"What a curious-looking gentleman it is; is he going to his studies? are you his servant, sir?"

Fancying that every word was sincere, I answered that I and the others were both his servants. They asked me his name, and it was scarce out of my mouth before one of the scholars went up to him with tears in his eyes, and embracing him as if he had been his brother:

"Oh, my dear Don Diego, who would have thought, ten years ago, to have seen you thus! Alas, I am in such a condition that you will not know me."

My master and I, both amazed, swore we had never seen him in our lives before; but the scholar's companion stared Don Diego in the face, and said to his friend:

"Is this the gentleman of whose father you told me so many stories? It is very fortunate we have met him; he is grown very tall—God bless him."

Saying this, he appeared quite overjoyed, and a stranger would have believed that we had actually been brought up together.

Don Diego paid him many compliments; and as he was asking him his name, out came the inn-keeper, and laid the cloth. Hearing what was going on, he said:

"Let that alone, and talk of it after supper, for the meat will be cold."

On this one of the sharpers placed an arm-chair for Don Diego, and another brought in a dish. The scholars inquired if he supped? and said they would wait on him, while they were preparing what the house would afford.

"God forbid, sir," replied Don Diego, "you will sit down, if you please."

The sharpers, though he did not speak to them, readily answered, "Presently, my good sir; but all is not ready yet."

On seeing this extreme readiness on all sides, my heart was in my mouth, and I foresaw what came to pass. The scholars instantly laid hold of the salad, a good dishful, and looking at my master, said:

"It would be very wrong that these ladies should be left supperless, when a gentleman of such quality is present; pray, sir, give them leave to eat a bit."

My master, like a true novice, invited them all to partake. They sat down, and between them and the scholars, there was only one end of a lettuce left from the whole salad, and this Don Diego himself ate. As the detested student handed it to him, he observed:

"Sir, you had a grandfather, who was my father's uncle, who would swoon at the sight of a lettuce, he was a man of such an odd disposition."

This said, he bolted down a great roll of bread, and his companion followed his example. The damsels were not slow to avail themselves of their good fortune; while the poor curate devoured the whole with his eyes, and the sharper was busily bringing in an entire side of a roasted kid. On this they took their places, saying to the priest:

"Well, father, what makes you stand there? draw nigh and help yourself, for this excellent Don Diego treats us all."

With these words, he too sat down, and my master, finding he had got such a party, began to betray some concern.

The marauders divided the spoil, giving my poor master only a few bones to pick, the sharpers observing:

"Pray, senor, do not eat too much supper, lest it should disagree with you;" and the cursed scholar added; "besides, sir, you must begin to be abstemious, considering the life you are about to lead at Alcala."

All this time, I and the other servant were offering hearty prayers that heaven would put it into their hearts to leave something; but alas, when they had devoured every bit, and the curate was picking the bones over again, one of the sharpers turned about and said:

"God bless us! we have left nothing for the servants; come hither, my good fellows; and you, landlord, give them all the house affords: here is a *pistole* to pay for it."

Up started, then, my master's pretended kinsman—I mean the scholar—saying:

"With your leave, sir, I must observe, this is not quite decorous; it is a sign you are not acquainted with my cousin; he will provide for his own servants, and for ours too, if we had any."

When I heard this piece of dissimulation, I cursed the vile scholar in my heart; but the evil was done; the cloth was removed; the man of charity pocketed his *pistole;* and they all advised Don Diego to go to bed. He would have paid for the supper, but they assured him it would be time enough in the morning. They stayed awhile chatting together; my master asked the scholar his name, and he answered Don something Coronel. The devil confound the deceitful dog wheresoever he is. Then perceiving that the griping shopkeeper was asleep, he said:

"Will you have a little sport, sir, to make you laugh? Let us put some trick upon this fellow, who has eaten but one pear upon the road, and is as rich as a Jew."

The sharpers cried, "God-a-mercy, master licentiate, do so; it is but right."

Thus encouraged, he drew near the sleeping old fellow, and slipped a wallet from under his feet, untied it, and took out a box, all the company flocking around, as if it had been lawful prize taken in war. He opened it, and found it full of lozenges; all which he took out, and supplied their places with stones, chips, and any rubbish that came next to hand.

This done, he shut up the box, and said, "I have not done yet; for he has a leathern bottle;" out of which he poured all the wine, and then stuffed it up with tow and wool, and stopped it. The scholar put all again into the wallet, and a great stone into the hood of his traveling coat, and then he and all the rest went to bed.

When it was time to set out, all the company awoke, and got up, and still the old man slept; they at last called him, but he could not rise, for the weight of the stone that was in his hood. He looked to see what it was, and the inn-keeper pretended to get into a passion, exclaiming:

"God-a-mercy, man, could you pick up nothing else to carry away but this stone? A fine affair, sirs, if I had not discovered it; I value it above a hundred crowns; it is a perfect charm for a pain in the stomach."

The old man, on this, vowed and swore that he had put none of it into his hood; while the sharpers reckoned up the bill, which came to six crowns, though the best arithmetician in Christiandom could not have made it up to that sum. The scholars asked what service they could do us at Alcala; the bill was paid, we breakfasted, and the old man took up his wallet; but for fear we should see what he had in it, and so have to distribute some, he untied it in the dark, under his great coat, and laid hold of a bit of lime well daubed, which he clapped into his mouth, and attempting to chew, very nearly broke his teeth with it. What with the pain, and the loathsome taste, he began to spit and make faces in a terrible way. The curate went up, and asked what ailed him? He only cursed and swore, throwing down the wallet; on which the scholar cried out:

"Get behind me, Satan; here is the cross."

The other opened a breviary, and would persuade him he was possessed; till, quite sick and exhausted, the poor fellow begged to have a little wine to rinse his mouth. We handed him his bottle, and pouring it into a small dish, out came only a few drops of wine, and so dirty as to defy the power of swallowing it. It was then he indeed fell a raving beyond measure; till seeing all the company convulsed with laughter, he was fain to grow cool, and take up a place in the wagon with the gipsy girls and sharpers. The curate and the scholars mounted their asses, and we went into the coach. We were scarcely gone, before one and all set us a laugh at our expense, declaring the wicked trick they had played upon us. The landlord too joined them, saying—"Good master Newcome, give me a scholar for a gull; he will grow wiser after a few specimens like this." The cursed scholar said—"Pray, cousin, next time scratch when it itches, and not afterwards." In short, everyone had his say; but we thought it best to take no notice, though heaven knows we were completely chop-fallen.

At length we got to Alcala, and alighted at an inn, where we spent all that day, for we came in at nine in the morning. But in reckoning up the particulars of our last supper, we could never exactly make out the account; enough, that we had come off with the worst, and smarted for it.

CHAPTER V

ENTRANCE INTO ALCALA; THE RECEPTION WE MET WITH; PAYING FOR OUR FREEDOM; AND WHAT TRICKS WERE PUT UPON ME AS A NEW COMER

TOWARDS the cool of the evening we left the inn for the place that had been hired for us without St. James's Gate, in a court full of rascally scholars. There were only three families, however, in our new house. The owner was one of those lukewarm men who keep up a good outside show, but have no religion in their hearts; they are called Moriscoes from being descended from

Moors. They quite abound here, along with your great-nosed Jews, that cannot endure the sight of bacon. Not that I mean to reflect on the people of quality, who are numerous and unspotted in blood.

The landlord received me with a worse grace than if I had been an inquisitor; but it was doubtless the nature of the beast, and quite in keeping with his usual principles and demeanor. However, we made good our entrance, and disposed our effects in the best order we could. On getting up next morning, all the scholars came running to us in their shirts, to demand entrance-money of my master. He inquired what it meant, but instead of answering him, I only hid myself under the clothes, with as little body to be seen as that of a tortoise. The wretches required a couple of crowns, and they got them; they then set up an infernal cry of:

" Long live our new fellow! let him be a member of the friendly society; he shall have all the privileges of a free-man; let him have the itch, and be as greasy and hungry as we are."

They then all tumbled down stairs together, and we hastened to dress ourselves, and set out for the schools. My master, conducted by some collegians, his father's friends, took his place; but I being assigned another place, went all alone, and began to quake for fear. Hardly had I set foot in the great court, before they all faced me, and began to cry, " A novice." The better to get out of the matter, I fell to laughing, as if I did not regard it, but it would not do; they grinned and mowed in my face, ridiculing me by every means in their power. I blushed, and one of the lads coming close to me, put his hand to his nose, then saying:

" This is no Lazarus raised from the dead, he smells too strong."

Upon this they all joined in stopping their noses, while I declared that they were quite in the right, as there was something peculiar. They afterwards assembled in a body of about one hundred strong, from which there issued out a great brawny bumpkin of a boy, who, approaching me, said, " I have got a cold," and instantly with most contemptuous gestures he spit in my face. He was followed by all the rest, each of whom exclaimed, " Thus I begin, thus I begin ! " Finding myself beyond all hope of redress, I cried out, " Oh, Lord ! I vow to God you shall pay."

I went home, though I scarce knew the way, with only a few clouts from a few more boys I met on the way. My master coming in and finding me asleep, fell into a passion, and seizing me by the hair of the head, he would soon have left me bald before my time. I made a dismal outcry, but he went on :

" Is this the service I am to expect from you, Paul ! I must turn over a new leaf, I see."

This went to my heart, and I answered : " Sir, you are a great—a very great comfort to me ; I have been made the victim of the whole school." I then began to weep, while he took pity upon me, and said :

" Look out sharply for yourself, Paul, and remember you have no father and mother to care for you here."

In short, he behaved so encouragingly, that it revived me, and I soon felt as well as if nothing had happened to me. But when misfortunes once begin, there seems to be no end to them. The rest of the sizars coming to bed, inquired with much apparent concern what was the matter with me, and when I told them the story, they expressed their wonder how people could be so wicked, and that it would not be tolerated among heathens. Others cried that the proctors were to blame for not taking means to prevent it.

" Pray should you know them again ? "

I told them I should not, but was obliged by the sympathy they expressed for me. After this they put out their light, and went to bed ; but about twelve, I was waked by one of them roaring out in a most terrific manner :

" Lord, Lord, they are killing me ! thieves ! murder ! "

At the same time I heard a noise of lashing and flogging. I jumped up, and inquired what was the matter, and in the same moment felt myself seized, and a huge cat and nine tails applied to my skin. I called out on heaven and all the saints for vengeance, and they assisted me, I suppose, to creep under the bed.

Three more now began to give mouth, and hearing the lashes, I concluded that the same strange fiend was employed in scourging us all. While lying shivering under it, some other imp leaped into my bed; and this done, the lashes ceased, while those flagellated leaped up, exclaiming:

"It is a great villainy, and not to be endured."

All this time I lay whining like a dog, cold and cramped; till at last gaining courage, I crept into bed, inquiring whether my companions in misfortune were much hurt; they said they were horribly hurt; but, in fact, they were only parties to the infernal trick played upon me; and which they followed up by others still more villainous and cruel, as if the incarnal fiend himself had instigated them.

I was so ill I could not move; and in the morning my master came up, and with an angry voice inquired, "Shall I never be able to do any good with you? Why, Paul, it is past eight o'clock; rise, you impudent rascal! your master, Don Diego, shall be informed of this."

Instead of answering, I pretended to be in a swoon (and I nearly was), when one of the rascally lads cried out: "Poor boy, he faints; pull him hard by the middle finger, it will recover him." And they pulled me till my joints cracked, and I thought I should have died. They then proposed to cramp my legs, and had already got cords to put me to the torture; I thought it wiser to come to myself, though not in time to prevent the villains pulling so hard as to gripe my flesh, and almost to dislocate my joints. They then left me, observing, "Bless us, what a poor puny creature you are;" and when I wept for anguish and vexation, they only added, "Come, come, it is all done for the good of your health, compose yourself to rest." Left to my reflections, I felt that what I had endured in one day at Alcala was worse than all I had undergone under Cabra at the boarding-school. In vain I tried to sleep.

325

About noon I dressed myself, cleaned my cloak and cassock, and waited for my master; who asked me, as he came in, "How I did?" All the family dined, and so did I, though with a poor stomach enough. After dinner we all met to chat in an open gallery. The other servants, when they had sufficiently bantered me, discovered the trick they had put upon me, and laughed heartily at my expense. I was sadly out of countenance, and mentally exclaimed, "Look better to yourself, Paul, and stand upon your guard." I resolved to begin a new course of life; we all made friends, and from that day lived as peaceably in the house together as if we had been all one mother's children; not a single soul disturbed me any more, either at school or in public places.

CHAPTER VI

OF THE WICKED OLD HOUSEKEEPER, AND THE FIRST KNAVISH PRANKS I PLAYED AT ALCALA

WHEN you are at Rome, do as they do at Rome, says the old proverb; and it is well said. I took it so seriously into consideration that I fully resolved to play the knave among knaves, and to excel them all if possible. I know not whether I succeeded to my wish, but I am sure I used all my endeavors. In the first place, I made a law that it should be no less than death for any pigs to cross the threshold of our house, or for any of the old housekeeper's chickens to run out of the yard into our room. It happened that one day two of the cleverest porkers that ever my eyes beheld slipped into our dominions; I was then at play with the other servants, and hearing them grunt, said to one of my companions, "Go see who it is that grunts in our house." He went, and brought word they were actually two swine.

No sooner did I hear, than off I set in a passion, exclaiming: "It was a great deal of impudence in them to

grunt in other people's houses." Then slamming to the
door, in sudden heat of blood, I ran my sword into the
throats of them both, and we afterwards cut off their
heads. To prevent their cries for rescue, we all set up
our voices to the highest pitch during the operation, and
between us they soon gave up the ghost. We next
paunched them, saved the blood, and by the help of our
straw bed half roasted them in the yard, so that all was
over before our masters came home, except the mere
making of the black puddings. Don Diego and our steward were informed of the exploit, and flew into such a
passion that the other lodgers, highly amused, were fain
to take my part.

The don asked me what I should say for myself when
the affair should be found out. I replied that I would plead
hunger, the common sanctuary of all scholars; and if that
was not enough, I would urge that, seeing them come into
the house without knocking, just as if they had been at
home, I really thought that they were ours. They all
laughed, and Don Diego said:

"By my faith, Paul, you begin to understand the trade."

It was well worth observing the difference between my
master and me; he so sober and religious, I so arch and
roguish, so that the one was a foil to the other, and served
to set off either his virtue or his vice. Our old housekeeper
was pleased to the very heart, for we both played our parts
and conspired against the larder. I was caterer, and a
mere Judas in my employment, ever since retaining an
inclination for cribbing and stealing. The meat always
wasted in the old woman's keeping, and she never dressed
wedder mutton when she could get ewe or goat. Besides,
she picked the flesh off the bones before she boiled them,
so that the dishes she served up looked as if the cattle
had all died of a consumption. The broth was so clear
that had it been as hard as the bones, it might have passed
for crystal; but when she wanted to make it seem a little
fat, she clapped in a few candles' ends. When I was by,
she would say to my master:

"In truth, sir, Paul is the best servant in Spain, bating

his unluckiness, but that may well enough be borne with, because he is so honest."

I gave her the same character, and so we put upon the whole house between us. If there was a store of coals, bacon, or oil laid in, we stole half of it, and soon after would say:

"Pray, gentlemen, retrench your expenses a little, for if you go on at this rate you need have a mint of money; the coals or the oil is done, but no wonder, at the rate you live; you had better order in some more. Give Paul the money, he will keep a better account of it."

It was given, and we then sold them the other half we had stolen, and half of what we brought; and that was in full.

When I bought anything at market for the real value, the old body would pretend to fall out and quarrel; and she, seeming to be in a passion, would say:

"Do not tell me, Paul, that this is a pennyworth of salad."

At this I pretended to cry and make a great noise, beseeching my master that he would please to send the steward, that he might prove the base calumny of the scolding old woman. By such simple means did we both retain our character for honesty; she appearing to look sharp after me, and I always being found out to be trustworthy. Don Diego, highly pleased, would often say:

"Would to God, Paul were as virtuous in other ways as he is honest; I see, my good woman, he is even better than you represent him."

It was thus we had leisure and opportunity to feast on them like horse-leeches. . . .

I became a great authority in all that the scholars called snatching and shoplifting, at which I had many pleasant adventures.

One evening, about nine o'clock, as I was passing through the great street, I spied a confectioner's shop open, and in it a frail of raisins upon the counter. I whipped in, took hold of it, and set a running; the confectioner scoured after me, and so did several neighbors and servants. Being loaded, I perceived, that though I had the start, they would overtake me, and so, turning the corner of a street, I clapped the frail upon the ground, and sat down upon it, and wrapping my cloak about my leg, began to cry out:

"God forgive him, he has trod upon me, and crippled me."

When they came up I began to cry, "For God's sake, pity the lame; I pray God you may never be lame!"

"Friend!" they exclaimed, "did you see a man run this way?"

"He is before you," was my answer, "for he trod upon me."

I boasted of this exploit, and with some reason: I even invited them to come and see me steal a box of sweetmeats another night. They came, and observing that all the boxes were so far within the shop that there was no reaching them, they concluded the thing was impracticable. Drawing my sword, however, about a dozen paces from the shop, I ran on, and crying out at the door, "You are a dead man!" I made a strong pass just before the confectioner's breast, who dropped down, calling for help; and my sword running clean through a box of sweetmeats, I drew it, box and all, and took to my heels. They were all amazed at the contrivance, and ready to burst with laughing on hearing him bid the people search him, for that he was badly wounded: even when he found out the cheat he continued to bless himself, while I was employed in eating the fruits of my exploit. My comrades used to say that I could easily maintain my family upon nothing; as much as to say, by my wits and sleight-of-hand. This had the effect of encouraging me to commit more. I used to bring home my girdle, hung all round with little pitchers, which I stole from nuns, begging some water to drink of them; and when they turned it out in their wheel, I went off with the mugs, they being shut up, and not able to help themselves.

After this, I promised Don Diego and his companions

that I would one night disarm the round. The time was fixed, and we set out. I went foremost with another servant of our family; and as soon as I discovered the watch, went up, as if I had been in a great fright, saying, "Is it the round?" They answered, "It was." "Then," said I, "is the governor here?" They replied he was; I then knelt down, and said, "Sir, it is in your power to do me right, and to do the public a great piece of service; please to hear me in private, if you wish to catch some notorious criminals."

He stepped aside, and some of his officers were laying hands on their swords, and others taking out their rods of authority, whilst I said:

"Sir, I am come from Seville, in pursuit of six of the most notorious malefactors; they are all thieves and murderers, and among them is one that killed my mother, and a brother of mine, without any provocation, but to exercise his barbarity. This is proved upon him, and they all came, as I heard them say, with a French spy; and by what I can farther guess from their words, he is sent" (then I lowered my voice) "by Antony Perez."

At these words the governor gave a skip, and cried: "Where are they?"

"They are in a bad house, sir," said I; "do not stay, good sir; the souls of my mother and brother will requite you with their prayers, and the king will reward you."

He then said: "Good God, let us lose no time, then; follow me, all of you, and give me a target."

I took him aside again, and added: "Sir, the whole business will be spoiled if you do so; the only way to do it is for them all to go in without swords, and one by one, for they are above in the rooms, and have pistols, and as soon as they see any come with swords, they will be sure to fire. It is better to go in with your daggers, and then you may secure them behind, for we are enough of us."

The governor, being eager to secure them at any rate, approved of my contrivance. By this time we were come near the place, and the governor, thus instructed by me, ordered them all to hide their swords in a field there is just before the house, under the grass. They did so, and went on. I had already instructed my companion that as ever they should lay them down, he should seize them, and make the best of his way home. He did so, and when they were all going into the house, I stayed out the last, and as soon as they were entered, being followed by several people they picked up in the way, I gave them the slip, and turned short into a narrow lane, that comes out near La Victoria, running all the way as swift as a greyhound. When the round was all in the house, and found none there but scholars and scoundrels—all one—they began to look about for me, and not finding me, suspected it was some trick put upon them. Being thus disappointed, they went to take their swords, but there was no sign of them.

It is impossible to express what pains the governor, attended by the vice-chancellor of the university, took that night. They searched all the town to the very beds, and when they came to ours, I was in bed with a night-cap on, and close covered for fear of being known, a candle lighted in one hand, and a crucifix in the other, with a sham priest praying by me, and all the rest of my companions on their knees about the bed. The vice-chancellor, with all his officers, came in, and seeing that spectacle went out again, supposing no such prank could be played by any there. They made no search, but the vice-chancellor prayed by me, and asked whether I was speechless; they answered I was, and so away they went, in despair of making any discovery.

The vice-chancellor swore he would deliver up the offender if he could find him, and the governor vowed he would hang him though he were the son of a grandee of Spain. I got up; and this prank makes sport at Alcala to this day. To avoid being tedious, I omit giving an account of my robbing in the open market, as if it had been on a mountain; not a box or case escaped me, but I had it home, and kept the house in fuel all the year; and as for the apple women, nothing was ever safe in their standings, for I had declared perpetual war against them, on account of the affront put upon me when I was king at Segovia. I pass by the contributions I raised on the fields of beans, vineyards, and orchards, all about that part of the country. These, and the like practices, gained me the reputation of a sharp and lucky fellow among all people. The young gentlemen were so fond of me that I had scarce leisure to wait upon Don Diego, whom I honored as he deserved, for the great kindness he bore me.

CHAPTER VII

HOW I RECEIVED NEWS OF MY FATHER'S DEATH, AND WHAT COURSE OF LIFE I RESOLVED ON FOR THE FUTURE

AT length Don Diego received a letter from his father, and with it one for me, from an uncle of mine, whose name was Alonso Romplon, a man of a virtuous disposition, and very well known at Segovia, as being the finisher of the law; and, for the last four years, the execution of all its determinations went through his hands. In short, he was hangman; but such a clever fellow at his business, it would hardly vex a man to be hanged by him, he did it so neatly. This worthy person wrote to me from Segovia to Alcala, as follows:

" MY DEAR PAUL,
" The responsible office, and pressing affairs, in which it has pleased his majesty to place me, have been the occasion of my not writing to you before; for if there be anything to find fault with in the king's service, it is the great trouble and attendance it requires; which, however, is in measure requited by the honor of being his servant. It troubles me to be forced to send you disagreeable news; but your father died eight days ago, with as much bravery

and resolution as ever man did; I speak of my own knowledge as having trussed him up myself. The cart became him as well as if it had been a chariot, and all that saw the rope round his neck concluded he was as clever a fellow as ever was hanged. He looked up all the way he went at the windows very much unconcerned, bowing to all the tradesmen who had left their shops, and turning up his whiskers several times. He desired the priest that went to prepare him for death, not to be too eager; but to rest and take a breathing, extolling any fine expressions that he used. Being come to the triple tree, he presently set his foot on the ladder, and went up it nimbly, not creeping on all fours, as others do; and perceiving that one of the rounds of it was cracked through, he turned to the officers attending, and bade them get it mended for the next that came, because all men had not his spirit. I cannot express how much his person and carriage was applauded.

"At the top of the ladder he sat down, set his clothes handsomely about him, took the rope, and clapped the noose to his ear, and then perceiving the Jesuit was going to preach to him, he turned to him and said, 'Father, I accept the will for the deed; let us have a few staves of a psalm, and have done quickly, for I hate to be tedious.' He charged me to put on his cap a little to one side; and then he swung, without shrinking up his legs, or making ugly faces, but preserved such a gravity that it was a pleasure to behold him. I next quartered him, and fixed the several parts on the highways. God knows what a trouble it is to me, to see him there daily treating the crows and ravens; but I suppose the pastry cooks hereabouts will soon ease us of that sad spectacle, burying him in their minced pies. I cannot give you a much better account of your mother, for though still living, she is a prisoner in the Inquisition at Toledo, because she would not let the dead rest in their graves. In her house were found as many arms, legs, and skulls, as would have stocked a charnel-house; they say she would fly up a chimney, and ride faster upon a broom-staff than another can upon the best Andalusian horse. I am sorry she disgraces us all, and me more particularly as being the king's officer, which kindred does not become my post. Dear child, here are some goods of your father's that have been concealed, to the value of four hundred ducats; I am your uncle, and all that I have is yours. Upon sight hereof, you may come away hither, for your knowledge in Latin and rhetoric will qualify you to make you an excellent hangman. Let me have your answer speedily, and till then God keep you, etc."

I must confess I was much troubled at this fresh disgrace, and yet in some measure I was glad of it, for the scandalous lives of parents make their greatest misfortunes a comfort to their children. I went to Don Diego, who was then reading his father's letter, in which he ordered him to leave the university and return home, but not to take me with him, because of the account he had received ·of my unluckiness. He told me he must be gone, and how his father commanded him to part with me, which he was sorry for; and I was so much more.

He added, he would recommend me to another gentleman, his friend, to serve him. I smiled, and answered:

" Sir, the case is altered; I have other designs in my head, and aim at greater matters, so that I must take another course; for though hitherto I was at the foot of the ladder, in order to mount, you must understand that my father has got up to the top of it."

With this I told how bravely he had died, at his full stretch; how he was carved out, and served up as a feast to the birds of the air. That my good uncle, the executioner, had sent me the whole account, and acquainted him with everything, because he knew all my pedigree. He seemed to be much concerned, and asked me how I intended to bestow myself. I informed him of all my resolutions; and so the very next day he went away to Segovia, very melancholy, and I stayed in the house, without taking the least notice of my misfortune. I burned the letter, for fear it might be dropped, and somebody should read it, and began to provide for my journey to Segovia, designing to take possession of what was my due, and know my kindred, that I might shun them. . . .

BOOK THE SECOND

CHAPTER I

I TOLD them I would have them order my dress, for I designed to lay out the hundred royals I had on a suit of clothes, and leave off my cassock.

"That must not be," said they, "let the money be put into the common stock, we will clothe him immediately out of our wardrobe, and appoint him his walk in the town, where he alone shall range and seek out."

I consented, deposited the money, and, in a trice, they made me a mourning cloth coat out of my cassock, cut my long cloak into a short one, and trucked the remains of it for an old hat new dressed, making a hat-band, very neatly, of some cotton picked out of inkhorns. They took off my band and wide-kneed breeches, and, instead of these, put me on a pair of close hose, slashed only before, for the sides and the back part were nothing but sheepskins. The silk stockings they gave me were not half stockings, for they reached but four fingers below the knees, the rest being covered with a tight pair of boots over my own red hose. The band they gave me was all in rags, and when they had put it on they said:

"The band is somewhat decayed on the sides and behind;

336

if anybody looks at you, sir, you must be sure to turn about as they do, like the sunflower which still moves as he does. If there happen to be two at once observing you on both sides, fall back; and to prevent being observed behind, let your hat hang down on your neck, so that the brim may cover the band, leaving all your forehead bare, and if anybody asks why you wear it so, tell him it is because you dare show your face in any part of the world."

Next they gave me a box, containing black and white thread, sewing silk, packthread, a needle, a thimble, bits of cloth, linen and silk, with other shreds and snaps, and a knife. To my girdle they fastened a tinder box, with a steel and flint in a little pouch, saying:

"This box will carry you through the world, without the help of friends or relations; this contains all we stand in need of; take and keep it."

They appointed the ward of St. Louis for my walk, and so I entered upon my emyployment. We all went out together, but because I was a novice, they ordered him that brought and converted me, to be my instructor in the trade of sharping.

We set out very gravely, walking in state with our heads in our hands, and made towards my precinct. We paid respect to all we met, taking off our hats to the men, though we had rather have taken their cloaks; to the women we bowed low, because they are fond of respect, and proud of being honored. My worthy governor, as he went along, would say to one creditor, "I shall receive money to-morrow:" to another, "Have patience for a day or two, the bankers put me off." One asked him for his cloak, another for his girdle, by which I perceived he was such a true friend to his friend, that he had nothing which was his own. We went in and out one side of the street to another, like drunken men, that find it too narrow for them, to avoid duns. Here one whipped out to demand his house rent, there another the hire of his sword, presently a third the rent of his sheets and shirts, so that it appeared he was a hireling gentleman, like a hired horse.

We went on, and at the corner of a street took two slices of ginger-bread, and as many drams of brandy, of a wench who gave it us for nothing, after wishing my director welcome to town, who said:

"This puts a man in a condition to make shift without a dinner for this day, for at worst he is sure of so much."

It went to my very heart to think it was dubious whether we should have any dinner, and I answered him very disconsolately in behalf of my stomach, to which he replied:

"You are a man of a small faith, and repose little confidence in our mumping profession. God Almighty provides for the crows and jackdaws, and even for sciveners, and should he fail poor pinch-guts? You have but a poor soul."

"You are in right," quoth I; "but still I fear I shall make it poorer; for the belly is the life of the soul."

As we were talking after this manner a clock struck twelve, and being yet a stranger to that profession, my stomach took no notice of the gingerbread, but I was as if I had eaten no such thing. Being thus put in mind again of that want, I turned to my conductor and said:

"My friend, this business of starving is very hard to be learned at first; I was used to feed like a farmer, and am now brought to fast like an anchorite. It is no wonder you are not hungry, who have been bred to it from your infancy, like King Mithridates with poison, so that it is now familiar and habitual to you. I do not perceive that you take any diligent care to provide, and therefore I am resolved to shift as well as I can."

"God is my life," quoth he, "what a pleasant spark you are; it is but just now struck twelve, and are you in such a mighty haste already? Your stomach is very exact to its hours, and immediately cries out cupboard; but it must practice patience, and learn to be in arrears at times. What, would you be cramming all day? the very beasts can do no more. I told you already that God provides for all men, yet if you are in such haste, I am going to receive the alms at the monastery of St. Jerome, where there are most delicious friars; if you will go along with me, well and good, if not, everyone take his own course."

"Farewell," said I, "my wants are not so small to be satisfied with the leaving of others; every man shift for himself."

My friend walked very upright, now and then looking upon his feet, and took out a few crumbs of bread, which he carried for that purpose in a little box; these he strewed about his beard and clothes, so that he looked as if he had dined. I coughed and hawked to conceal my weakness. wiping my whiskers, muffled up with my cloak upon the left shoulder, playing with my tens, for I had but ten beads upon my string. All that saw me believed that I had dined. All my confidence was in the crowns I had sunk, though I had a scruple of conscience that it was against the rules of our profession to pay for a dinner, being obliged to feed upon the public; but I was resolved to break the fast, and transgress the ordinances.

By this time I was come to the corner of St. Lewis's Street, where a pastry-cook lived. On the bulk lay a curious mutton pie, delicately baked, and piping hot out of the oven; my nose stumbled at it, and I made a full set like a dog at a partridge, fixing my eyes and gazing so steadfastly, that it shrunk up as if it had been blasted. It had been pleasant enough to know how many ways I cast about to steal it, and then again resolved to buy it. By this time it struck one, which put such a damp upon me, that I resolved to launch into the next cook's shop. As I was steering towards one, it pleased God that I met with a friend of mine, called the Licentiate Flechilla, who came swinging his cassock down the street, his face all dusty, and his long robes full of doglocks. As soon as he spied me, he ran to embrace me, and yet I wonder he should know me in that condition. I returned his embrace; he asked how I did? and I answered:

"I have abundance of stories to tell you, Mr. Licentiate; all that troubles me is, that I must be gone tonight."

"I am sorry for that," quoth he, "and were it not late, and that I am going in haste to dinner, I would stay with you; but I have a sister that is married, and her husband expects me."

"Is Mrs. Anne here?" said I; "whatever becomes of my business, I'll go and wait upon her; that is a duty I cannot dispense with."

Hearing him say he had not dined, made me sharp; away I went with him, and, by the way, told him, that a wench he had been very fond of at Alcala was then in town, and I could get him admittance into her house. He was mightily pleased at this notion, for I purposely contrived to talk of such things as might be pleasing to him. This discourse held us till we came to his sister's house; in we went; I made very great tenders of service to both husband and wife, and they believing all I said to be true, and that I might be out of countenance for coming at that time of day, began to excuse themselves, saying, that they would have made some provision, had they thought of such a guest. I laid hold of the opportunity, and invited myself, telling them I was no stranger, but an old friend; and should take it unkindly to be treated with ceremony.

They sat down, I did so too; and the better to stop the other's mouth, who had not invited me, nor ever thought of any such thing, every now and then I gave him a remembrance of the wench, saying she had asked for, and was infinitely fond of him, with many more lies to that purpose; which made him bear the more patiently with my cramming, for such havoc as I made in the first course was never seen. The boiled meat was served up, and I tumbled the best part of it down my throat in a moment, without nicety, but in such a hurry, as if I had not thought it safe enough betwixt my teeth. As I hope for mercy, I laid about me at such a rate, as if my life had depended on it, and was so expeditious that everything seemed to vanish in my presence. No doubt but they observed how I poured down the soup, how soon I drained the dish, how clean I picked the bones, and how cleverly I despatched the meat; and, to say the truth, at every turn I clapped a good hunch of bread into my pocket, till it could hold no more.

When the table was taken away, the licentiate and I stepped aside, to talk about our going to the aforesaid wench's house, which I represented to him as a very easy matter; but as we were talking at the window, I pretended somebody had called to me from the street, and answering, "sir, I come this moment," asked leave of my friend, promising to return immediately. I left him waiting for me, and so he might have done to this day, for I slipped away, and my belly being full, I had no more occasion for him. I met him several times after, and excused myself, telling a thousand lies, which are not to our purpose. Rambling thence about the streets at random, I came to the Guadelajara gate, and sat down on one of the benches that are at the mercer's door.

As God would have it, there came two of those creatures that borrow money upon their handsome faces to the shop; they were both closely veiled, with only one eye bare to see their way, and attended by an old woman, and a boy, half footman, half page. They asked for some very rich, new fashion, wrought velvet. To commence a discourse, I began to play and pun upon the velvet, turning and winding, till I brought it to all the waggish meanings I had a mind to. I perceived my freedom had put them in hopes they might carry off some present from the shop, and knowing I could be no loser, I offered them whatsoever they pleased. They stood out a little, pretending they did not use to accept of any from persons they were not acquainted with.

I laid hold of that opportunity, telling them, I owned it was a presumption in me to offer them anything there; but that I desired them to accept of a parcel of rich silks sent me from Milan, which that page of mine should carry them at night; pointing to one that stood over the way bareheaded, waiting for his master, who was in a shop. And that they might take me for some man of quality, and well-known, I pulled off my hat to all the judges, privy-counsellors, and peers that went by, bowing as if we had been very well acquainted, though I knew none of them. These outward shows, and my taking out a piece or two of gold of my hidden treasure, on pretense of giving an alms to a poor body that begged of me, made them conclude I was some gentleman of note. They thought fit to go home because it grew late, and took their leave, charging me to be sure the page should go as privately as might be. I begged of them only as a favor and token of their good will, a pair of beads, all set and linked in gold, which the handsomest of them had in her hand, as a pledge for me to visit them the next day without fail. They made some difficulty to part with it, till I offered them a hundred crowns in pawn for it, which they refused, hoping by that means to draw me in for a better penny; asked where I lodged, and told me their quarters, desiring me to observe, that they could not receive messages at all times, because they were persons of quality.

I led them through the high street, and before we turned out of it, made choice of the largest and fairest house I could find, which had a coach without horses standing at the door, telling them it was mine, and at their service, as were the horses and master of them. My name I told them was Don Alvaro de Cordova, and in I went before their faces. At our coming out of the shop, I remember I called over one of the pages from the other side of the way, beckoning to him very statelily with my hand, and pretending to order him and the rest of them to wait there till I came; but in reality only asked whether he did not belong to my uncle the privy-counsellor; he answered me he did not, and so I dismissed him, setting myself off with borrowed feathers.

When it was dark at night, we all went home, and coming in, I showed them the beads, and told them the story; they applauded my ingenuity, and the old woman took them into her custody to sell them, and went about saying they belonged to a poor maiden gentlewoman, who was fain to sell them for bread, having her story ready for every occasion. The old jade wept whenever she pleased, wrung her hands, and sighed most bitterly; she called all people children; and over a good smock, jerkin, gown, and petticoats, wore a tattered long robe of sackcloth, given her by an anchorite, her friend, who lived on the mountains by Alcala. Her business was to manage all the goods, to direct and conceal; but the devil, who is always kind to his servants, so ordered it, that going one day to a house to sell some clothes and other things, somebody there knew their own goods, sent for an officer, secured the old hag, whom we called Mother Lebrusca, and she presently discovered all the plot, told how we all lived, and that we were gentlemen of prey. The officer left her in the gaol, and come to our house, where he found me and all my companions. He had half-a-dozen under-catchpoles along with him, and removed the whole of our sharping congregation to the prison, where our gentility availed us very little.

CHAPTER II

THE PRISON DESCRIBED; WITH AN ACCOUNT OF WHAT HAP-
PENED TO US IN IT; TILL THE OLD WOMAN WAS WHIPPED,
MY COMPANIONS EXPOSED TO PUBLIC SHAME, AND I
CAME OUT UPON BAIL

A S soon as we came into the gaol, we were loaded with irons, and going altogether to be clapped into the dungeon; but I made use of the money I had to prevent falling into that hell, pulling out a *pistole* and making it glitter in the gaoler's eyes, saying:

"Pray, sir, be pleased to hear me a word in private."

He having seen a glimpse of the gold, took me aside, and I went on:

"I beseech you, sir, pray take pity on an unfortunate man."

Then I took him lovingly by the hand, and clapped in the piece, which he greedily grasped, being used to such ceremonies, and answered:

"I will examine into your distemper, and if it is dangerous, you shall not go down into the hole."

I understood, and submitted myself peaceably, so that he left me out, and turned down my companions. I will not take up time in relating what sport we made in the prison, and as we went along the streets; for being hunched along, it was comical to see such a parcel of raga-muffins, all patches, and parti-colored black and white, like magpies.

The officers knew not how to take fast hold of them, they were all in such tatters; some they thought to grasp by the flesh, and finding none, for it was starved all away, they feared to be answerable for disjointing the bones. Others lost their coats and breeches, by the rough hand-ling of those unmerciful fellows. When they unbound the rope they led them all in, the rags and clouts dropped off with it. At night I was carried to the common side, where I had a little bed allotted me. It was odd to see some lie down in their whole case, without taking off the least rag they wore in the day. Others, at one mo-tion, put off all the clothes they had; others played, but at last we were all made fast, and the light put out. We all forgot our irons, and took our rest very favorably.

When it was day, we all came out of the dungeon, saw one another's faces, and presently our companions de-manded the usual garnish money, on pain of a good liquor-ing. I presently disbursed six royals, but my companions having nothing to give, their cause was referred till night. . . .

I slipped out of the dungeon, desiring them to excuse me for not bearing them company, because it was not conve-nient. I greased the gaoler over again with three pieces of eight, and being informed who the clerk was that had charge of prosecuting us, sent for him by a young running thief. He came; I got into a room with him, and after some discourse concerning our business in general, I told him I had some little money, which I desired him to keep for me; and that as far as might be done with safety, he would favor an unfortunate young gentleman, who had been unadvisably drawn into that offense.

"Believe me, sir," said he, when he had grasped the ready, "the whole matter depends upon us; and he that has a mind to be a knave may do a great deal of mischief; I have sent more men to the gallows without any cause but for my pleasure, than there are words in an indictment. Leave it to me, and do not question but I'll bring you off safe and sound."

This said, he made as if he was going away, but came back again from the door, to ask something for honest James Garzia, the constable, for it was convenient to stop his mouth with a silver gag; something more he hinted at concerning the clerk of the court, saying:

"It is in this clerk's power, sir, to undo a man by turning up the white of his eyes, raising his voice, making a noise to rouse a lord mayor or recorder when they are asleep, as it often happens, and many other such dangerous actions."

I apprehended him, and lugged out fifty royals more, in return for which he bid me set my cloak right, taught me two cures for a cold I had got in the prison; and to conclude, said:

"Make yourself easy, the gaoler will be kind to you if you give him but a piece of eight, for these sort of people do nothing out of good nature, but all for interest."

I could not but smile at his observation; he went his way, and I gave the gaoler a crown; he knocked off my irons, and gave me leave to go to his house.

In short, I managed this tack so well, that he kept me at bed and board in his house, and then the honest clerk, what at the gaoler's request, and what for the bribe I gave him, ordered the business so well, that the old woman went out foremost upon a dapple grey ass, instead of the cart used in England, with a crier before her, making proclamation that she was a thief, and close at her heels the hangman, laying on her as he had been directed by the gentlemen of the long robe. Then followed all my companions upon braying palfries, bare-headed and faced, thus to be exposed to public shame, like standing on the pillory, and so ragged that they could not hide their nakedness. After this solemnity they were banished for six years. For my part I was bailed out with the assistance of the clerk; and the other at the court played his part, for he changed his tone, spoke low, skipped over his words, and swallowed whole sentences.

CHAPTER III

HOW I TOOK A LODGING, AND OTHER ADVENTURES

BEING out of prison, I went away to a lodging, where I contrived to alter my dress into the genteel fashion, to put on small breeches and a great band, and got a scoundrel by the name of a page, and two rakes as footmen, as the mode then was. One Licentiate Brandalogas, of the town of Hornillos, and two friends of his, encouraged me to do so, showing how I might make myself at once by that means, getting a wife with a great fortune, by making such a figure, which frequently happened at Madrid, adding that they would put me in the way, finding out one for my turn, and contriving how I might gain admittance.

Covetousness prevailing, and the desire of a wife, I consented; searched all the broker's shops, bought my wedding clothes, hired a horse, and mounted in great state that very day, but could not light on a footman. Away I made to the high street, and stopped at a saddler's shop, as if I were buying some furniture. Two gentlemen on horseback accosted me, "Whether I was about buying a rich embroidered saddle and housing I had in my hand?" I laid it down immediately, saying, "It was at their service, if they liked it;" and kept them awhile with a thousand compliments. At length they said they would go and divert themselves in the *prado*, where the ladies go in their carriages, and the gentlemen on horseback, to take the air. I told them I would wait on them, if they would give me leave; and left word with the saddler that in case my pages and footmen came thither, he should send them after me, describing the livery to him, which said, I clapped in between the two gentlemen, and away we went. By the way I considered with myself that none who saw us could possibly guess or decide to which of us the pages and footmen belonged, or which of us had none. I began to talk very loud of the tilting and other sports on horseback at Talavera, and of a piebald horse I had, highly commending a lusty stallion I expected from Cordova.

When we came to the *prado*, I took my feet out of the stirrups, turning my heels out, and walked easily, with my cloak hanging upon one shoulder, and my hat in my hand. Everybody gazed at me; one said, "I have seen that spark walk on foot;" another, "The scoundrel makes a pretty figure." I made as if I did not hear them, and walked on. The two gentlemen went up to a coach full of ladies, and desired me to banter awhile. I left the side where the young ones were, and went to the other, where there was a mother and an aunt, two pleasant old jades, the one about fifty years of age, the other a little less. I told them a thousand amorous lies, and they listened to them; for there is no woman, though never so old, but has a good conceit of herself; offered to treat them, and asked whether the other ladies were married? They replied, they were maids; and it was easy enough to guess at it by their talk. Then I made the usual compliment, wishing they might see them well preferred to their mind, and they were much taken with it. Next they asked how I spent my time at court? To which I answered that I kept out of the way from a father and mother, who would fain marry me against my will to a woman that was ugly, foolish, and of a mean family, only because she had a vast

347

portion; "and for my part, ladies, I would rather have a wife well born, in her smock, than the wealthiest Jew that is; for, God be praised, my patrimony is worth about forty thousand ducats a year; and if I succeed in a law-suit, which goes hitherto well on my side, I shall want no more."

The aunt, hearing this account, very hastily cried, "Lord sir, I admire you for that humor; do not marry without you like, and with a woman of good family; for I do assure you, that though I am not very rich, I have refused to marry off my niece, who has had very rich pretenders, because they were not of quality. She is poor, it is true, for her portion is but six thousand ducats, but as for birth, she is inferior to none."

"I do not question that, madam," said I.

By this time the damsels had ended their discourse with the gentlemen, asking a collation. The two gazed upon one another, and began to shrink for fear; but I, laying hold of the opportunity, told them I was sorry my pages were out of the way, because I had nobody to send home for some boxes of sweetmeats. They returned thanks, and I desired them to be the next day at the summer-house in the *prado*, and I would send them a cold treat. They accepted of the invitation, told me where they lived, and inquired after my quarters; so the coach went off, and my companions and I made towards our homes. They observing that I was so generous in offering the treat, began to take a fancy to me; and the more to oblige me, desired I would sup with them that night. I stood off a little, but not too long, and supped with them, sending out several times to seek my servants, and swearing I would turn them away.

When it struck ten, I told them that was the appointed time for an intrigue, and therefore begged they would excuse me for that time; and so went away, first engaging them to meet the next day at the summer-house. From them I went to deliver the hired horse to the owner, and thence home, where I found my companions playing at

all fours; told them what had happened, the engagement
I had made; we resolved to send the collation without
fail, and to lay out two hundred royals on it. Having thus
ordered affairs, we went to bed, where I own I could not
sleep all night for thinking how I should bestow the portion; for I could not resolve whether it were better with
it to build a good house, or to put it out to interest, not
knowing which would be most advantageous.

CHAPTER IV

HOW THE COLLATION WAS MANAGED, WITH OTHER ACCI-DENTS AND NOTABLE MISFORTUNES

IN the morning we got up to provide the plate, servants,
and collation; and there being nothing in this world but
money can command, as being a thing worshipped by all
men, I found a nobleman's butler that furnished plate,
and undertook to wait himself, with three of his fellow-
servants. The forenoon was spent in disposing affairs;
and after dinner I hired a nag, and at the appointed time
set out for the summer-house. I had abundance of papers
sticking out of my pockets; besides that, my coat being
unbuttoned, some peeped out of my bosom, as if I had been
a man of mighty business. When I came to the place, the
ladies and gentlemen were there. The former received
me with much show of love, and the latter talked to me
by plain *thee* and *thou,* in token of familiarity. I had
told them my name was Don Philip Tristian, and nothing
was to be heard in all their mouths but Don Philip and
Don Philip; but I told them I had been so entirely taken
up with some business of the king's, and the accounts of
my estate, that I had much ado to be as good as my word;
and therefore they must expect a collation provided in a
hurry.

By this time the butler came with all his tackle, plate,

and servants; the gentlemen and ladies looked at me and held their peace. I ordered him to go into the eating-room and lay the cloth, whilst we went to divert ourselves at the fish-ponds. The old women drew near to fawn and flatter, and I was glad to see the young girls barefaced; for since I was born, I never saw so delicate a creature as that was I designed for my wife. A skin as white as alabaster, delicate fair hair, a curious fresh color in her cheeks, a little mouth, fine small teeth standing close together, a well-shaped nose, large black eyes, tall of stature, charming hands, and she lisped a little. The other was not amiss, but more wanton. We went to the fish-ponds, saw all that could be seen, and by her talk I found that my intended bride would have been in danger, in Herod's days, of being taken in among the innocents. In short, she had not a grain of sense.

We went towards the banqueting-house, and as I passed along, some twig of the hedge got hold of the lace of my band, and tore it a little; the young lady stopped and pinned it with a silver pin, and her mother bid me send it to her house the next day, and Doña Anna, so was the maiden called, would mend it. All the treat was in excellent order, hot and cold, fruit and sweetmeats. When the cloth was taken away, I spied a gentleman coming along the garden with two servants after him; and who should this be but my old master, Don Diego Coronel. He drew near, and seeing me in this habit, could not take his eyes off me; talked to the women, calling them cousins, and all the time turned to look again and again. I kept talking to the butler, and the other two gentlemen, being my master's friends, were in deep discourse with him. He asked them, as afterwards appeared, my name, and they answered it was Don Philip Tristian, a very honest gentleman, of a great estate. I saw him bless himself, and at length he came up to me before them all, and said:

"Sir, will you pardon me? for by the Lord, till I heard your name, I took you for a different person than you are; in my life I never saw anything so like a servant I had at Segovia, called Paul, son of a barber in that town."

They all laughed heartily, and I used all the art I could to forbear betraying myself by blushing, and said:

"I long mightily to see that man, because abundance of people had told me I was extremely like him."

"Good God!" cried Don Diego, "like him! I never saw such resemblance; his very shape, voice, and mien. I declare to you, sir, it is prodigious, and I never beheld anything so exactly alike."

The old women, mother and aunt, asked how it was possible that a gentleman of such quality should be so like that mean scoundrel? and that I might conceive no jealousy of them, one said:

"I know Don Philip very well, it was he that entertained us at Ocanna, by my husband's order."

I took the cue, and answered. "I should always be ready to do them all the service I could, in all parts."

Don Diego offered his service, and begged pardon for the affront of taking me for the barber's son, adding:

"Sir, you will scarce believe it, but his mother was a witch, his father a thief, his uncle the hangman, and he himself the wickedest base fellow in the world."

It is easy to guess what I felt, hearing such scandalous things said of me to my face; I sat upon thorns, though I did all I could to dissemble my uneasiness. My two new acquaintance and I took our leaves, and Don Diego went into the coach with the ladies. Then he asked them what was the meaning of the treat, and their being with me? The mother and aunt told him I was heir to so many thousand ducats a year, and had a mind to marry Nancy; that he might inquire into the matter, and he would see how convenient it was, and how advantageous to their family. This discourse held them home, which was near the church of St. Philip. My comrades and I went together to their house, as we had done the night before, and they having a mind to fleece me, asked me whether I would play. I guessed at their meaning, and set to it; the cards were brought, I let them win at first, but soon fetched it about, won about three hundred royals, took my leave and went home.

There I found my two companions, the Licentiate Brandalagas, and Peter Lopez, who were practicing new cheats upon the dice. As soon as they saw me, they left off to inquire how I sped. I only told them that I had been in great danger; how I had met with Don Diego, and how I came off. They comforted and encouraged me to proceed, and not to desist from the enterprise by any means. We had now notice given us that they used to play at lanskenet at an apothecary's house close by. I understood the game at that time tolerably well; had cards made for the purpose, and knew all sorts of cheats; so we resolved to go and put in for the plate among them. I sent my friends before me, who coming, asked them whether they would please to play with a monk of the order of St. Benedict, who was just come to town to be cured of a tedious distemper among his relations and friends, and was well stocked with crowns and ducats? This set them all agog, and they cried:

"Let the friar come, in God's name."

"He is a man of note in the order," added Peter Lopez, "and being of the monastery, has a mind to divert a few hours, and does it only for company's sake."

"Let him come," quoth they, "we do not care what his motive is.'

"We tell you so much in regard to the privacy it requires,' answered Brandalagas.

"Enough," said the man of the house," you need say no more."

This satisfied them that the thing was so, and the lie went down glib. My two supporters came for me, and I was dressed with my night-cap on, in a Benedictine habit, which I had got by the wheel of fortune in my rambles, a pair of spectales on my nose, and short brushy beard, to show as if it were grown since my sickness. I walked in very demurely, sat down, and we began to play; they all combined to put upon me, but I swept all before me, being

much sharper at it than they; so that in about three hours'
time I won upwards of a thousand three hundred royals.
I scattered some small bounty, and took my leave with the
usual compliment of "The Lord be praised," charging
them not to be scandalized to see me play, for it was mere
diversion and nothing else. They who had lost their
money, cursed themselves to the pit of ——. I took my
leave again, away we went, got to our lodging, about an
hour after one, parted our booty, and so to bed.

This was some satisfaction to me for the unlucky accident before it. I got up in the morning to hire a horse,
but they were all let, by which I perceived there were
more in my circumstances besides myself. To walk the
streets afoot did not look well, especially at that time.
Not knowing how to mend myself, I went towards St.
Philip's church, where I found a lawyer's footman with a
horse in his hand, waiting for his master, who had just
alighted to hear mass in that church. I clapped four royals
in his hand to let me ride two or three turns along the
next street, where my mistress lived. He consented; I
mounted, rode twice up and down the street without seeing
anybody, but the third turn Doña Anna looked out. When
I saw her, thinking to gallant her, showing my horseman-
ship, and being but an indifferent jockey and unacquainted
with the horse's qualities, I gave him two lashes, reining
him at the same time; he reared first, then struck out behind, set a running full speed, so that I came clear over
his head into a puddle. I had no other recourse in this
pitiful plight, all beset with boys and in the presence of my
mistress, but to cry out:

"A cursed dog, my sorrel would never have done so;
I shall pay for these mad pranks one time or other. They
told me he was unlucky, and yet I would needs be trying
tricks with him."

By this time the footman brought me the horse again,
for he stopped as soon as he had thrown me; I mounted
again, and Don Diego Coronel, who lived in the same house
with his kinswoman, hearing the noise, looked out. The

sight of me startled him very much; he asked whether I had any hurt? I answered, no, though at the same time one of my legs was almost crippled. The footman pressed me hard to give him his horse, for fear his master should come out of the church and see me, for he was going to court. It was my misfortune, that as he was calling me to be gone, the lawyer came behind us, and knowing his steed, ran at the footman, laying him about the head and face with his fist, and asking him, as loud as he could cry, how he durst have the impudence to let anybody ride his horse? and what was worst of all, he turned to me, and in a very angry manner bid me get down, in the name of God.

All this was in full view of my mistress and Don Diego Coronel, which put me as much out of countenance as if I had been whipped at the cart's tail. I was wonderfully cast down and melancholy, and with good cause, to have two such misfortunes befall me upon so small a spot of ground. In fine, I was fain to alight, the lawyer mounted and went his way; and I, the better to palliate the business, stayed in the street, talking to Don Diego, and said:

"I never mounted such an unlucky jade in all my days. My cream-colored horse is yonder by St. Philip's church, and is very hard-mouthed when he sets a running. I was telling some there how I used to ride him at full speed, and take him off at one check. They told me I could not do it with a horse that stood there, which was the lawyer's you saw; I resolved to try; you cannot imagine what a restive jade it is, and has such a base saddle, that it was a wonder he did not kill me."

"It was so," answered Don Diego; "and yet, sir, you seem to feel some hurt in that leg."

"I do so," replied I, "and therefore I'll go take my own horse, and get home."

The young lady was fully satisfied that all I said was true, for I could perceive she was much concerned at my fall; but Don Diego, who saw farther, grew mistrustful upon what had happened with the lawyer in the street.

This proved the cause of my ruin, besides many other unlucky accidents that befell me; and the greatest of all, that when I went home, and came to a chest, where in a portmanteau I had left all the remains of my inheritance, and what I won at play, except only an hundred royals I had about me, I found my good friends, the Licentiate Brandalagas and Peter Lopez, had seized it, and were fled. This was a mortal stroke, and I stood amazed, not knowing which way to turn myself. At last, for fear of spoiling my marriage, which I looked upon as secure, and that it would make amends for all losses, I resolved to stay and push it on vigorously. I dined, after dinner hired a horse, went away towards my mistress's street, and having no footman, because it was not decent to be seen without one, I waited at the corner of the street until some man passed by that looked like one, and away I went after him, making him a footman though he was none. At the other end of the street I did the like, standing out of sight, until another went by like the former, and then rode down again.

I know not whether it was the certainty of the truth that I was the very scoundrel Don Diego suspected, or the fresh cause of jealousy on account of the lawyer's horse and footman, or what else that did it, but Don Diego took care to inquire who I was, what I lived on, and observed all my actions. At last he took so much pains, he discovered the whole intrigue the strangest way that could be imagined, for I pressed on the business of matrimony very hotly, plying the ladies continually with letters; and Don Diego being as eagerly importuned by them; who were in haste to conclude it, as he was upon the scent after me, met the Licentiate Flechilla, the man I invited myself to dine with when first I entered myself among the sharping gang at Madrid, before my imprisonment.

This man, taking it ill that I had not gone to see him again according to promise, happening to talk with Don Diego, and knowing I had been his servant, told him how I met him when I went to dine with him; and that but two days ago he had met me on horseback, and that I informed him I was going to be married to a great fortune. This was enough for Don Diego, who, returning home immediately, met with the two knights I had made myself so familiar with, gave an account of the whole affair, and desired them to be ready at night to give me a good thrashing in his street, where he would contrive I should be, and they might know me by his cloak, which he would take care I should have on. They agreed, met me immediately in the street, and all of them carried it so fair at that time, that I never thought myself so secure of their friendship as then. We continued talking together how to divert ourselves at night, till towards the close of the evening the two knights took their leave, and went down the street. Don Diego and I being left to ourselves, turned towards the church of St. Philip. When we came to the next turning, Don Diego said to me:

"Let me beg the favor of you, Don Philip, to change cloaks with me, for I have occasion to go this way, and would not be known."

"With all my heart," answered I; took his coat very innocently, and gave him mine in an unhappy hour, offering to go along, and stand by him if need were; but he having projected to stand by me to break my bones, replied he was obliged to go alone, and therefore desired me to leave him.

No sooner had I parted from him, but the devil contrived, that two who waited to thrash him on account of a wench, thinking by the cloak that I was Don Diego, fell on a cudgeling me as thick as hail; I cried out, and by my voice and face they discovered I was the wrong man at which they ran away, and I was left with my beating, put up three or four good bumps they had raised, and made a halt, not daring to go into my mistress's street for fear. At last, about twelve, which was the time when I talked with her, I came up to the door, where one of Don Diego's friends that waited for me, being ready with a good cudgel, gave me two blows across the shins which laid me flat on

356

the ground; as soon as I was down the other played his part, giving me a slash across the face from ear to ear. They then took away my cloak, and left me on the ground, saying: "This is the reward of false, deceitful, base scoundrels."

I cried out for help, not knowing to whom I was beholden for that usage, for to say the truth, I expected that cut from so many places that I could not be positive from whom it might come. Don Diego was the person I least suspected, and I was farthest from the mark; but still cried out, "Thieves! thieves!" which at length brought the watch, who took me up, and spying a gash a quarter long on my face, and that I had no cloak, nor could tell how that misfortune came, they carried me away to a surgeon's house, where I was dressed; then they asked me where I lived, and thither they conducted me. I went to bed, and lay all night awake, full of remorse and confusion, my face being cut in two, my body bruised, and my legs so crippled with the cudgeling that I could not stand, nor had scarce any feeling in them. In fine, I was wounded, robbed, and in such a condition, that I could neither follow my friends, nor proceed towards matrimony, nor stay in Madrid, nor get away. . . .

CHAPTER V

MY TEDIOUS CURE; HOW I TURNED BEGGAR, AND WENT TO TOLEDO, WHERE I TURNED POET

I LAY eight days in the house under the surgeon's hands, and was scarce able to go ahead at the end of them, for they were fain to stitch up my face, and I could not go without crutches. By this time my money was spent, for the hundred royals all went in lodging, diet, and cure; so that to avoid further expenses, when my treasure was gone I resolved to go abroad on crutches, and sell my linen and clothes, which were very good. I did so, and with part of the money bought an old leather jerkin, a canvas waistcoat, a patched beggar's great coat down to my ankles, gamashes on my legs, and great clouted shoes, the hood of the great coat on my head, a large brass crucifix about my neck, and a pair of beads in my hand. A mumper, who was a master at his trade, taught me the doleful tone and proper phrases for begging, so I began immediately to practice it about the streets. Sixty royals I had left I sewed up in my doublet, and so set up for a beggar, much confiding in my cant. I went about the streets for a whole week, howling in a dismal tone, and repeating my lesson after this manner:

" Merciful Christians of the Lord, take pity on a poor, distressed, miserable, wounded, and maimed creature, that has no comfort of his life."

This was my working day note; but on Sundays and holidays I altered my voice, and said:

" Good, charitable people, for Christ Jesus's sake, give one farthing or a halfpenny to the poor cripple whom the Lord has visited."

Then I stood a little, which does good service, and went on again, " See my poor limbs were blasted, unhappy wretch that I am, as I was working in a vineyard; I lost the use of all my precious limbs, for I was as strong and as sound as any of you are, the Lord be for ever praised, and preserve your health and limbs."

Thus the farthings came dropping in by shoals; I got abundance of money, and was in a way of getting much more, had I not been thwarted by an ill-looking lusty young fellow, lame of both arms, and with but one leg, who plied my very walks in a wheelbarrow, and picked up more pence than I did, though he begged not half so genteelly; for he had a hoarse voice which ended in a squeak, and said, " Faithful servants of Jesus Christ, behold how the Lord hath afflicted me for my sins; give one farthing to the poor, and God will reward you:" and then he added, " For the sweet Jesu's sake." This brought him a mighty revenue, and I observed, and for the future

I cut off the *s*, and said only *Jesu*, because I perceived that it took with the simple people.

In short, I altered my phrases as occasion served, and there was no end of my gettings; I had both my legs bound up in a leather bag, and lay in a surgeon's porch, with a beggar that plied at the corner of a street, one of the arrantest knaves that ever God put life into, and who was, as it were, our superior, and earned as much as all of us.

I contracted such intimacy with him that he acquainted me with a secret, which in a few days made us rich; which was that he kept three little boys who begged about the streets, stole everything that came in their way, brought it to him, and he was the receiver; besides, he had two small children that learned to pick pockets, and he went halves with them. Being so well instructed by such an able master, I took to the same course, and he provided me with fit instruments for my purpose. In less than a month's time I had got above forty crowns clear, besides all extravagant expenses; and at last designing that we should go away together, he disclosed to me the greatest secret and cunningest design that ever beggar had in his head, which we both joined in; and was, that between us we every day stole four or five children, which being cried, we presently appeared, inquired what marks they had to be known by, and said:

"Good God, sir, I found this child at such a time, and had I not come as I did, a cart had run over it, but I have taken care of it."

They readily paid us the reward, and it throve so well that I got above fifty crowns more, and by this time my legs were well, though I still wore them wrapped in clouts. I resolved to leave Madrid and go away to Toledo, where I knew nobody, and nobody knew me. Having made this resolution, I bought an old suit of gray clothes, a sword and bands, took leave of Valcazar, the beggar I last mentioned, and went about the inns to find some conveniency to go to Toledo.

At an inn, I met with a company of strolling players,

who were going to Toledo, and had three carts. It pleased God that, among the gang, I found one who had been my companion at Alcala, left the school, and was turned actor. I told him what a mind I had to go to Toledo, and he had much ado to know me, the scar across my face had so altered me, and he could not forbear blessing himself, standing in admiration. In conclusion, for a small spill of money, he was so much my friend as to prevail with the rest to let me go with them. We were all higgledy-piggledy, men and women together; and I was mightily taken with one of the crew, who was the chief dancer, and acted the queens and other great parts in plays, for she was a notable jilt. She asked me whither I was going, and some questions concerning my life and circumstances; and in conclusion, after much talk, referred it to Toledo to act there.

We diverted ourselves by the way the best we could; and I happened to act a piece of a play that I had borne a part in when I was a boy; which I did so well that they took a liking to me; and being informed by my friend who was in the company, of all my misfortunes and hard circumstances, which I had made him acquainted with, she asked me whether I would make one among them? They so highly extolled their strolling course of life, and I was then in such want of some support, and so fond of the wench, that I agreed with the head of them for two years. Writings were signed between us, to oblige me to stay with them; so they gave me my allowance and allotted my parts, and thus we came to Toledo. They gave me two or three prologues to get by heart, and some other grave parts, which suited well with my voice. I applied myself to it, and spoke the first prologue in the town, where we had a simile of a ship in distress and wanting provisions, which put into that port: I called them noble audience, begging their attention, pardon for all faults, and so went off. There was great clapping of hands, and I was liked on the stage.

We acted a play, written by one of our actors,

and I admired how they should come to be poets, for I thought it belonged only to very learned and ingenious men, and not to persons so extremely ignorant. But it is now come to such a pass that every head of them writes plays, and every actor makes drolls and farces; though formerly I remember no plays would go down but what were written by the greatest wits in Spain. In short, the play was acted the first day, and no soul could make anything of it. The second day we began it again, and, as God would have it, there was some warlike exploit to begin with; and I came on the stage in armor, and with a target on my arm, which was a great mercy, or else I had infallibly been pelted to death with oranges, quinces, and all things that came next to hand. Such a storm of hail was never seen, and the play deserved it, for it represented a king of Normandy in a hermit's habit, without any sense or reason; had two scoundrel footmen to make sport, and when they came to unravel the plot, there was nothing but marrying of all the company, and there was an end; so that to say the truth, we had but what we deserved.

By that time we had been a month at Toledo, acting several new plays, and endeavoring to retrieve our first fault; I was grown famous, and had given out that my name was Alonzo, to which the generality added the title of the Cruel, because I had acted a part of that nature, to the great liking of the mob and upper galleries. I had now got several new suits of clothes, and some heads of other strollers endeavored to enveigle me away from my company; but I pretended to criticise upon plays, and railed at the most celebrated actors; finding fault with one man's gestures, censuring another's gravity, and allowing another to be a tolerable actor. My advice was always taken in contriving the scenes and adorning the stage; and if any play came to be offered, it was left to me to examine.

Being encouraged by this applause, I launched out as a poet in a song, and then wrote a small farce, which was well approved of. Next I ventured at

361

a play; and that it might gain respect, made it all of devotion, and full of the blessed Virgin. It began with music, had fine shows of souls departed, and devils appearing, as was the fashion then, with old gibberish when they appeared, and strange shrieks when they vanished. The mob was mightily pleased with my rhyming to Satan, and my long discourses about his falling or not falling from heaven. In short, the play was acted and well liked. I had more business than I could turn my hands to, for all sorts of lovers flocked to me; some would have songs on their mistresses' eyes; others on their foreheads; others on their white hands; others on their golden locks. There were set rates of all sorts; but I sold cheap to draw the more custom, because there were other shops besides mine. As for godly ballads, I supplied all the country clerks and runners of monasteries; and the blind men were my best friends, for they never allowed less than eighty royals; and I always took care that they should be bombastic, and stuffed with cramp words, which neither they nor I understood. I brought up many new fashions in verse, as tailors do in clothes, and was the first that concluded my songs like sermons, praying for grace in this world and glory in the next.

It happened, as it frequently does to that sort of people, that the chief of our company being known to have got considerably in debt at Toledo, was arrested for some old debts and thrown into jail, which broke up our gang, and everyone went a several way. As for my part, though my comrades would have introduced me into other companies, having no great inclination to that calling, for I had followed it out of mere necessity, I thought of nothing but taking my pleasure, being then well dressed, and in no want of money. I took my leave of them all; they went their ways; and I . . . set out for Seville, to try my fortune there, as the greater city.

CHAPTER VI

WHAT HAPPENED TO ME AT SEVILLE, TILL I TOOK SHIPPING TO THE WEST INDIES

I HAD a good journey from Toledo to Seville, for I was sharp at play, had loaded dice both high and low, and could palm a dice, hold four, and throw out three; besides, I had false cards, and knew how to pack any, and turn up what I pleased, and abundance of other fine arts and sleights of hand, which I pass by as tedious, and for fear they might rather serve to teach others evil practices than for warnings of what they are to shun; but perhaps some few words of advice may be of use to such as are not skilled in those practices; and they who read my book, if they are cheated, may thank themselves. Never think yourself safe because you find the cards, for they will change them upon you whilst the candle is snuffing. Take care they make no scratches or other impressions on the cards; and if my reader is a poor scoundrel, he must observe that among that gang of rake-hells, they prick the cards they would know with a pin, or fold them to leave a crease. If you happen to play among a better sort of people, take heed of cards which are originally falsified, and have private marks on the pasteboard. Never trust to a clean card, nor think yourself safe with a foul one, for the cheat is equal in both. I will not let you further into this secret; this is enough to make you always stand upon your guard; for you may be assured that I do not tell the hundredth part of the cheats.

363

Being master of these arts, I go to Seville, at my fellow travelers' expense, winning all the hire of the mules, my other charges and money to boot, of them and my landlords at the inns. I alighted at what they call the Moor's Inn, where I was found out by one of my schoolfellows at Alcala, whose name was Mata, but he thinking it did not make noise enough, changed it to Matorral. He dealt in men's lives, and sold cuts and slashes, which throve well with him; he carried the sign of his trade on his face, where he had received his share. He always made his bargain to a nicety for length and depth, when he was to bestow any, and said:

"No man is so absolute a master as he who has been well hacked and hewed himself."

And he was in the right, for his face was all over seams, and he was a downright drunken bully. He told me I must go sup with him and his comrades, and they would bring me back to the inn. I went with him, and when we were in his lodging, he said:

"Come, spark, lay by your cloak, and look like a man, for this night you shall see all the brave fellows in Seville; and that they may not look upon you as a cully, tumble your band, thrust out your back, and let your cloak hang loose, as if it were dropping off, for we hate to see any man's cloak set fast upon his back. Wind about your chops, and make faces with both sides of your mouth, then talk big, swear, and be very rude."

I learned his lesson, and he lent me a dagger, broad enough to have been a scimitar, and for length it wanted nothing of a sword but the name.

"Now drink off this quart of wine," said he, "for without you blunder you will never in the world look like a true bully."

We had gone so far in my instructions, and I was half seas over with what I had drunk, when in came four of the gang, with four vizards instead of faces, bound about the middle like monkeys, with their cloaks instead of ropes, their hats standing a tiptoe on their heads, and cocked up, as if the brims were nailed to the crowns; a whole smith's shop about their swords and daggers, and the points of them beating against their right heels. Their eyes stared, their whiskers turned up, and their beards like brushes. They made their compliment with their mouths, and then, in a hoarse tone, and clipping their words, saluted my companion, who returned in like manner. They sat down, and spoke not one word to ask who I was; but one of them, looking at Matorral, and opening his mouth, thrust out his under lip, by way of pointing at me. My introducer answered in the same language, laying hold of his beard and looking down, after which they all got up, embraced, and expressed a great deal of kindness for me. I returned the same compliments, which were like smelling to so many hogsheads of wine.

When it was supper time, in came a parcel of strapping scoundrels, to wait at table, whom the topping bullies called under-spur-leathers. We all sat down together at table, and the first they served up was a dish of pickles, which, as soon as they had tasted, they all fell a-drinking to my honor, by way of welcome; and till I saw them drink it, I must confess I never knew I had any. Next came fish and flesh, all of it high seasoned, to promote drinking. There was a great bowl full of wine, like a half tub, on the ground, and he that was to pledge lay all along to drink by wholesale. I was taken with the contrivance; but by that time a few healths had gone about, we none of us knew one another.

They fell to talk of warlike affairs; oaths flew as thick as hail, a matter of twenty or thirty persons were cut out for destruction; amidst their cups, the mayor of the city was adjudged to be cut in pieces; then they reaped up the heroic actions of several famous cut-throats and murderers, and drank to the souls of some that were hanged. Some that were maudlin wept bitterly, calling to mind the untimely end of Alonzo Alvarez, one of their brethren, whose body was exposed on a gibbet for the crows to feast on. By this time my companion's brains were turned

365

topsy-turvy, and laying hold of a loaf, and looking earnestly on the candle, he said with a hoarse voice:

"By this, which is the face of God, and by that light, which came out of the angel's mouth, if you think fit, gentlemen, we will this very night maul the sergeant's man that pursued our poor one-eyed friend."

They all set up a dismal cry, ratifying the proposal made by an oath after this manner. They drew their daggers, laid their hands on the edge of the bowl, and lying along with their chops to it, said:

"As we drink this wine, so will we suck the blood of every informing catchpole."

"Who was this Alonzo Alvarez," said I, "whose death is so much regretted?"

"He was," answered one of them, "a brave fighting lad, a man of spirit, full of mettle, and a good companion. Let us go, for the devil begins to be strong in me."

This said, we all went out a catchpole hunting. Being quite overcome with wine, and all my reason drowned, I never reflected on the danger I was running myself into. We came to the strand, where we met the round, which no sooner appeared, but our swords were drawn and we attacked them. I did like the rest, and at the first charge we made way for the filthy souls of two catchpoles to fly out of their bodies. The constable took to his heels, and ran up the street crying out for help. We could not pursue because he had too much the start, but took sanctuary in the cathedral, where we were sheltered against justice, and slept as much as was requisite to discharge the fumes of the wine we had drunk. When we came to our senses I could not but admire that two catchpoles should be killed by, and a constable fly from, a parcel of mere hogsheads of wine, for we were no better at that time.

We fared well in our sanctuary, for the termagant damsels of the town flocked to, and spent all they had upon us. A strapping jade called Grajales took a fancy to, and clothed me from head to foot after her own humor. I liked this sort of living better than any I had yet tried, and therefore resolved to stick to my trusty Grajales till death. I learnt all the cant, and in a short time was absolute master among the ruffians. The officers of justice took all possible care to observe us, and kept rounds about the sanctuary; yet for all that we took our rambles after midnight in disguise. Perceiving this was like to be a tedious business, and that ill fate pursued me everywhere, though it made me never the wiser to take warning for the future, yet it tired me out like a true obstinate sinner; and therefore, with the advice of Grajales, I resolved to go to the West Indies, taking her along with me, to try whether I could meet with better fortune in another country; but it proved worse, for they never mend their condition who only change places without mending their life and manners.